THE LIVING

THE IMMUNE - BOOK 5

DAVID KAZZIE

GRUB CLUB PUBLISHING

THE LIVING

A NOVEL

By David Kazzie

ISBN-13: 978-1-7331341-0-1

ISBN-10: 1-7331341-0-7

❀ Created with Vellum

For my kids
Food on the table
All the stars in the sky

ACKNOWLEDGMENTS

To Dave Buckley, Mindy Heaton, Scott Weinstein, Wes Walker, and Rima Wiggin for their thoughtful notes and advice on early drafts of the manuscript.

To Steven Novak for his wonderful cover design.

PROLOGUE

FOUR YEARS BEFORE THE PLAGUE

Nina Kershaw nibbled on a thumbnail while they waited, pulling and tugging at the sliver of keratin, anxious to be rid of it. Then she yanked a bit too hard, and she winced as the ragged nail came off with a tiny ribbon of skin. A bead of blood formed at the nail bed, which began throbbing like it had its own little heartbeat. Penance for flying too close to the nail-biting sun, she supposed, rather than leaving well enough alone until she could get her hands on some clippers. She sighed, tamping the blood with her index finger.

Just one more thing.

Her iPhone buzzed sharply. Another sigh, as the phone would undoubtedly be bearing bad news.

A text message from her boss Eduardo. Eduardo, who had told her during the interview not to worry, he understood that family came first, but who gave her grief every time she had to take time off to deal with her daughter or with the car breaking down or even the time the dishwasher in her little house had blown a hose and flooded the kitchen.

Where are you? Call me ASAP.

She glanced at the clock on her phone. Nine-thirty. All her efforts this morning, setting two alarms, leaving the house by six to get ahead of San Diego's morning rush, eating half-frozen waffles in the car, to make it here thirty minutes before they even unlocked the doors had been for naught.

No, having things go her way would be simple, and simple was not part of Nina Kershaw's life calculus. It was going to piss off Eduardo something fierce, but what could she do? Such was the life of a single mother. Although wouldn't you know it, she wasn't going to be a single mother much longer. After four years, Jerry had finally proposed. The wedding would take place the following spring. Okay, so maybe he didn't knock her socks off, not like Adam Fisher, her daughter's father, once had, but she was getting too old for that kind of nonsense. She needed some stability in her life, a little bit of goddamn peace. Besides, Jerry was ten times the father Adam was. Jerry treated her only child like she was his own, not an afterthought to be mollified by hundred-dollar checks tucked inside fancy Hallmark cards a few times per year.

Nina and said child were sitting on an uncomfortable sofa in the pediatrician's office, waiting outside the lab for yet another round of immunizations after a quickie visit with Dr. Whatever-Her-Name-Was or maybe it had been a nurse practitioner this time. She couldn't keep up with the carousel of medical professionals spinning around each visit here. Then there was the prickle of Internet-fueled anxiety about all these vaccines, fears she often kept at bay with thoughts of Adam, even all these years later. Adam, a doctor himself, loved studying the history of vaccines and immunity, and few things drove him battier than the anti-vaccine loons on the Internet. Whenever she gave him an update on their daughter's well-being, he always asked if she was all up on her shots.

The faint lemony smell of hand sanitizer hung in the air. Around her, nurses flitted to and fro like bees, escorting patients here, carrying medical charts there. The movie *Toy Story* played on a flat-screen television above her head. Across from her, twin boys, about three years old, sat with their mother and watched the movie enraptured. They were fidgety but quiet, their faces flush with fever, their noses runny. She peeked up at the TV, smiling as Buzz and Woody argued at the gas station.

Nina glanced over at her own daughter, Rachel, fourteen years old now, getting ready to start high school. The bespectacled girl was engrossed in a book, as she often was. Her dark hair was pulled back in a ponytail, her one concession in their ongoing grooming battle. Hard to believe, and yeah, it was a thing people said too often, but it really was hard to believe that her sweet little thing was a ninth grader now. It was a cliché, no doubt about that, but where DID the time go? She had just been born, like yesterday, right? Just yesterday, the sun had risen and set on Mommy, but it wasn't quite like that anymore. From the day her daughter had set foot in middle school, something had changed.

"Mom?" the girl asked, breaking Nina out of her daydream.

"What?" Nina said, her finger throbbing.

"How much longer?"

"I don't know."

"Can you find out?" the girl asked, never looking up from her book. "I'm late for school."

Nina bristled with annoyance.

"You're not the only one who's late."

Her daughter rolled her eyes so hard they nearly popped out of the side of her head.

A few minutes later, a nurse popped up behind the counter separating the lab and the waiting area. She was young and pretty and wore her blond hair short. Nina was not surprised to see the ID badge clipped to her breast pocket identified her as Katie. Of course it was Katie.

"Rachel Fisher?" she called out.

"Here."

"Follow me, sweetie."

Nina and Rachel followed Katie to a corner of the lab, where the nurse directed Rachel to a stool. There were three needles lying on the nearby counter, accompanied by three cotton balls and three bandages bearing little dinosaurs.

"Three shots today," Katie said.

"Three?" Nina said. "I thought it was two."

"Oh?"

Katie glanced at her iPad.

"Oh, I see what happened," Katie said. "There's been an update. This third one was added last week."

"What are they for?"

"Let's see. Meningitis and Hep A."

"Yeah, I knew about those. The other one?"

Katie's lips pursed in puzzlement.

"It's only identified by the code," she replied. "If you want, I can look it up."

Nina looked at the time again. Nine forty.

"No," she said. "Let's get it over with. I'm really late for work."

Rachel sat quietly, lost in her book while Katie cleaned her arm with an alcohol wipe. The nurse, who four days earlier had been paid ten thousand dollars in unmarked bills by a man she had never met to not only administer this third injection but to make Nina wait long enough that she wouldn't ask too many questions, then vaccinated Rachel Fisher against meningitis, hepatitis A, and a third disease that a few years down the road would kill Nina, Katie the nurse, and nearly everyone else on Earth.

1

The boy studied the Monopoly board carefully, the tip of his index finger jammed between his teeth even though his mother had told him a thousand times to keep his hands out of his mouth. Germs, she'd say, and then she'd laugh about it a little because they had washed their hands and lacquered themselves with hand sanitizer, and in the end, it hadn't made a lick of difference. Besides, Will had been chewing that fingertip for his entire life, and he wasn't any worse for it. She didn't bother telling him anymore because he wasn't doing it on purpose; she'd check on him while he slept and there it would be, wedged right at the corner of his mouth.

"I'm gonna put hotels on it," he said, looking up at her with those eyes, wide and blue and endless like the ocean.

Rachel Fisher sighed softly. Either her son didn't know, or he had conveniently forgotten he needed to build four houses on each property first. Or maybe he knew all too well, and he was trying to pull one over on his mother, who was too tired and knew too much about how things were, how they really were, to say anything. She didn't always let him win, and he was probably too old for his mother to be letting him win in the first place, but sometimes she did because so many things had not gone the boy's way in his eleven years on Earth.

"OK."

He thumbed the stacks of ragged bills, tucked under the edge of the board, the purple and red and gold slips of paper that were worth about as much as the real currency that had once powered the engines of the world's economy. She didn't see paper money often anymore, but every now and again, a greenback would rear up in a house they'd scavenged or flutter along a desolate street, and she'd instinctively grab it even though it had been thirteen years since Medusa had rendered all of that quite pointless, thank you very much, forever and ever, Amen.

Will plucked eight hundred dollars from his stash and placed them in the bank. Then he carefully planted a hotel, the red fading with each passing year, on each stripe of blue, equally faded, there on Boardwalk and Park Place, turning both plots into very pricey real estate, yet another anachronism of the world gone by. All the real estate anyone could ever want, almost anywhere on God's not-so-green-anymore Earth, all you had to do was move in.

As her son lined up the hotels, Rachel pulled her blanket tightly around her and glanced out the window of the trailer they shared with Eddie Callahan, Will's father. The woodstove at the center of the trailer bled its heat into the room as best it could, but even still, she always felt chilly. That was the thing about the cold; once it got in you, it was damn hard to shake, no matter how many layers of long johns or blankets or cups of hot water flavored with anise seed. It set in your bones, became part of you until you couldn't remember not feeling cold anymore.

They were deep into autumn now, the trees bare, the few remaining grasses dormant. It was late in the year, probably early December, but they weren't exactly sure because somewhere along the line they had lost the thread of the calendar and once it had been lost, there had been no way to pick it up again. Another thing lost among so many things lost. Instead, they marked the time by the seasons and the phases of the moon and the movement of the stars and that would have to be good enough.

"Mommy!"

She started at the sweet, tinny sound of his voice. He pointed at the board.

"Sorry," she said. "Just daydreaming."

She rolled the dice and it came up double sixes, boxcars, and wasn't that just her luck because that dropped her right on Boardwalk and its unwarranted hotel.

Will clapped and threw his head back with glee.

"Yes, yes, yes!"

Sportsmanship was something else they needed to work on. Maybe that was a good reason to let him win, so she could teach him to be graceful in both victory and defeat. Theirs was a world long short on grace.

Wasn't rationalization the best?

She counted out her remaining funds and saw she wouldn't have enough to cover her debt to him.

"Looks like I'm out," she said.

"I win!"

He leapt to his feet and did a funny little dance in their tiny living room.

"I win, I win," he repeated in a sing-songy voice, and there she saw in full the little boy he still was.

She climbed to her feet, pins and needles, and shook out the sandy tingling in her right foot. Then it looked like they were both dancing and what she wouldn't have given for a camera to capture this moment so she could have it forever.

The screen door screeched open behind her, cutting their dance party short.

Super.

The man of the house had returned. Eddie came in and staggered toward the bedroom, swatting her on the bottom as he passed by, leaving a moonshine-drenched vapor trail in his wake.

"Hey, Dad," Will said, his sweet little voice spiced with hope.

Eddie treated his son to an imperceptible nod of the head and continued toward the bedroom.

"Can you come to dinner with us?" Will asked.

"Not tonight, pal," he said, not breaking stride.

"Eddie," she said firmly.

He paused and turned to face his family.

"What?"

Rage bubbled up inside her; it didn't take much to set her off anymore, a constant simmer ready to boil over.

"Will, go wait outside," she said, keeping her gaze fixed on this man she had once loved so fiercely.

Will was familiar with this tone of his mother's voice; he wordlessly slipped outside, closing the door behind him. She waited until the screen door clattered shut again, ensuring Will was out of earshot before speaking.

"Jesus, Eddie, he's your son," Rachel said, her cheeks hot. "You get that, right? The only one we're gonna have, I might add."

"Don't remind me," he said.

Rachel massaged her temples. It was important for Will to have his father in his life, right? He didn't run around with other women. He didn't beat them. He just wasn't around a lot. It wasn't all that different from the way her father had been. And her dad was a hero around here!

But standing here now, it all seemed utterly ridiculous. No woman in her right mind would put up with this nonsense. She had to be the stupidest woman alive. And you didn't have to hit someone to hurt them. What Eddie did was hit them on the inside, where no one could see. It didn't leave bruises or cuts or physical scars. But it hurt all the same.

Eddie Callahan was thirty-four years old, give or take, about three years older than Rachel. He'd been with the group almost since the beginning, hooking up with them a few months after they'd taken the compound, which they called Evergreen, an homage to the former home of roughly half of their community, a little town in Oklahoma that had burned to the ground years earlier. That was when the group was still blissfully unaware how much trouble they were all in.

A spotter had seen him staggering toward the outer perimeter, where he collapsed. At first, they thought it was Medusa, back to finish them off, which had set off a tremendous panic. He was feverish, barely coherent. But then they saw the jagged shard of bone poking out of his forearm, up near the elbow. Said he'd been living alone on a farm about thirty miles west of Evergreen, out on a supply run on his bicycle when he'd gotten hurt. Hit a pothole, went headfirst over the handlebars.

It would have been easy to turn their backs on someone who wasn't injured. But Edie had been delirious, his skin a ghastly grayish color. Turning him out would've been cruel, worse than killing him straight out. They took him to Adam Fisher, who got to work immediately. It had been one of Adam's proudest moments, yanking Eddie back from the precipice of death. He'd carefully reset the arm, closed the wound, flooded Eddie with antibiotics. It had been touch and go for a few days, but eventually, Eddie had turned the corner. His arm was never quite the same after that, sporting a permanent crook, but the fact he still had a pulse let alone his arm was nothing short of a miracle.

After he recovered, no one could bear to put him out. He kept to himself, pitched in, never complained. Hard work was valuable currency in their world, and after a while he was one of them. Their relationship blossomed slowly, over the course of a few months. Working the same shift at the warehouse, thinking nothing of it at first and then finding herself looking forward to the days they were on together, slightly annoyed when they weren't. Then one night at dinner, it had been the three of them, she and Erin Thompson and Eddie, and when he'd made a joke and Erin had laughed, she had laughed and placed her hand on his arm all familiar, and the jealousy stabbed her like a knife. Right then and there, her goose had been cooked. Was it love? Who knew? What did that even mean? Rachel didn't even know if Erin was interested in Eddie, but she wasn't going to wait to find out.

She kissed him first, one morning not long after the moment with Erin, after they'd come off duty and they had walked home in the dawn. They were tired and sweaty and she pulled him inside the front door and a few weeks later, she was pregnant with Will.

"This whole thing doesn't make any sense," Eddie said.

"What's that supposed to mean?" she snapped.

Girl, you're brewing for a fight, aintcha?

"I don't know what happened to you," she said. "I mean, it's fine. We'll be fine without you. I don't know why you checked out the way you did. Remember what it was like when he was first born?"

He stood at the window with his back to her, scraping the windowsill with a thumbnail. She looked at the outline of his back, his thick arms straining against his work shirt, the pieces of him she'd once loved with all her heart.

"I remember," he said. "It's just that..."

A long pause.

"I thought there would be others."

Her head dropped.

"Well, that is just great."

He turned back toward her, his face silhouetted in the dark.

"I don't understand how this is even possible," he said. "How he is even possible."

"And that's why he needs more of you, not less," she said. "He's starting to ask questions."

Eddie's eyes were fixed on the floor.

"What do you tell him?"

"That there are other kids."

"You lie."

"I lie."

Silence again.

"It's scary, you know," he said.

"What is?"

"You. Your dad. Will."

She stood there, not knowing what to say, not sure there was anything to say.

Eddie followed Will outside, headed for wherever it was he went when he wanted to pout.

It was all clear now. All this time, stupidly thinking that Eddie was simply a shitty father like all the other shitty fathers that had preceded him. Producing shitty fathers, that had sort of been mankind's thing. And it had been easy to lump Eddie in with all the others, her father too. It had even been understandable on a Psychology 101 level. Adam had been an absentee father when she was growing up, before the plague, so it made sense she had ended up with an absentee father for her own son. But now she saw that it something else entirely.

Scary, he'd said.

As if Rachel didn't know how scary it was. As if it were somehow lost on her that Will had been the last baby born in their community to live to his first birthday. As though it had slipped her mind that for all anyone knew to the contrary, William Fisher Callahan had been the last person to live to his first birthday anywhere.

2

Rachel tended to the low fire in the woodstove and then went outside, locking the door behind her as she went. Will waited at the fence behind their trailer, gazing west, his little fingers curled around the chain links. They had a clear view of the western horizon, of the sunsets that helped them bid farewell to another day on their lonely planet. A sharp tang in the air burned her nostrils, a swirl of woodsmoke and cold reminding you winter was on its way. The air stank of rain yet to fall. The sun, veiled by vaporous clouds, was setting like a balloon drifting to earth, looking for its nest beyond the Rockies a thousand miles to the west. It was a weak sun, barely breaking through the cloud cover perpetually blanketing the Midwest sky.

They walked north toward the employee cafeteria, past the main complex housing their food supply, a two-million-square-foot monolith, roughly the size of two city blocks. Will kicked a faded Pepsi can as they strolled across the dusty roadway, his path meandering as he followed the can's unpredictable bounces and skips. The Warehouse, as it was known, was made up of three interconnected buildings forming an S shape, and seemed to go on forever. It took a full thirty minutes to walk its perimeter. Inside was the community's lifeblood, the canned goods and non-perishable packaged foods that had sustained them through the years. It still amazed her that the food had remained viable for this long, so many years since the end. But as her father reminded her, if the cans remained intact, the cold, tasteless food inside could last indefinitely.

The cafeteria was housed in a low-slung rectangular building west of the Warehouse. Linoleum floors, the blue-and-white checkerboard tiles cracked and peeling. Years of water damage had stained the ceiling with yellowish-brown blooms that looked like dying flowers. Inside, away from the chill, the smell of cooking vegetables wafting from the kitchen made Rachel's mouth water. These were canned veggies, the kind she'd turned her nose up to before Medusa but that now literally kept them alive.

The crowd thickened as they neared the cafeteria. Familiar faces, the same people day in and day out, like waves on a beach. Never the same face, not exactly, as the days, the months, the years did their work, hardening and etching the faces with wear. The faces were changing, growing longer, bearing new wrinkles, the eyes a bit dimmer. Muted chit-chat after a day's hard labor, patrolling the grounds, shoring up the perimeter, doing inventory, disposing of garbage and waste. Later, those who were off duty would gather at the bar and drink their rotgut booze until the memory of another day was wiped away.

They were always supposed to eat together, here, in this place. That was one of their unspoken rules, breaking bread together so the bonds of brotherhood and fellowship might remain strong in a world noticeably absent of both. That was the theory at least. Pleasantries were exchanged, heads nodded. And yet, it felt like another day of them becoming strangers to one another.

They were drifting apart, the bonds that had once connected them dissolving slowly. The graveyard shift, someone had called it. All of them, on the graveyard shift. Literally. One day, they would all punch out, and that would be it. A new day would dawn on planet Earth: Population, Zero. Maybe it was better this way. Maybe it was better to adapt to this kind of isolation now because things were only going to get worse. Not in a get-worse-before-they-get-better kind of way. No, in a get-worse-before-they-get-even-worse-and-then-worse-still kind of way.

Will grabbed their trays as they approached the buffet line. A handwritten sign taped to the sneeze guard announced tonight's offering. Vienna sausages, canned broccoli, and some flatbread they had learned to make over the years. It was a bit dry, but if you soaked it in the runoff from the meal, it was tolerable. A protein, a vegetable and a starch. There were no other options, unless you counted going hungry an option.

She and Will went down the line, collecting their dinner, waiting as their names were checked off the list because there was always a list. Food was distributed based on a formula Adam had developed many years earlier. Rachel rated eleven hundred calories per day; Will got more to meet the needs of his growing body. Even so, it wasn't enough. Sometimes at night while they sat and read or played with toys, the rumble of his stomach would tell her it wasn't enough, or when they were at the cafeteria and he would vacuum his dinner and then look longingly at his mother's plate and think she hadn't seen him look. And then she would pretend she hadn't seen him look because after all, she was hungry too, there was always room for a little more, always a little deficit that made things a bit uncomfortable. She was down a good thirty pounds from her pre-plague weight, the terrible irony that she finally fit in the clothes she never really cared about, except for the tiniest sliver.

Around them, the dining room bubbled to life with the sounds of clanking silverware and chit-chat. Despite all the problems they faced, she still liked seeing the group together, even if it was no longer the slightly optimistic bunch they'd been a decade ago. It made her feel like there was still a little hope left, that things would work out somehow. She didn't know how they would work out exactly, but that was hope for you. Blind and dumb and hopped up mainlining optimism. A chewy bit of faith at the center of it.

No one joined them at their table, but that was par for the course, and she had gotten used to it. She understood. Besides, this gave her the opportunity to talk with him, about things he'd seen, things he'd learned, things he'd read.

"How come Dad didn't come?" he said, his eyes flitting around the cafeteria for his father. She watched him do it, she watched those blue eyes scan the room, a constantly shifting brew of hope and wariness.

"He had some things to do, sweetie. He's a busy guy, your old man," she said, the lie eating at her like corrosive acid.

Always making excuses for him.

Will pushed his plate away.

"I'm not hungry," he said, his voice cracking. He stared down at the worn tabletop.

"You know the rules, mister."

It was one of Rachel Fisher's non-negotiable edicts. You cleaned the plate in front of you, no matter what (and truth be told, Vienna sausage tasted a little like a melted meat Popsicle). There was too much uncertainty, too many unknown variables at play to be skipping a meal simply because you were pouting, no matter how justified the pouting was. Every meal, every bite of food was sacred now, never to be taken for granted. Ever. The next meal was never guaranteed, and that was why you always ate *this* meal.

"But I'm not-"

"Eat your dinner," she snapped, a bit louder than she had intended, and suddenly it was quiet in the dining room and she could feel the others staring, watching her and judging. A stab of heat coursed up her back, and she felt guilty and angry and alone all at once. The moment passed, and the chit-chat resumed. But Rachel felt the prickly heat of being watched; she glanced up and saw her friend Erin Thompson, the next table over, still watching her. Erin was a few years older than Rachel, a petite but hard woman with hair that had gone gray before she turned thirty. They'd met about a month after the pandemic, while they were held captive by a man named Miles Chadwick. Once she'd been Rachel's closest friend, now rapidly becoming another stranger. Twelve years earlier, her infant son, the first born in their community, had died of Medusa.

"What?" Rachel asked Erin.

"I guess everyone has their own parenting style," Erin said, her fingers tented in front of her face.

Across from her, Will looked down at his plate and began eating, painfully aware of his place in the community.

"Why don't you mind your own goddamn business?" Rachel said.

The dining room went quiet again as the others' ears perked up, ready for a little dinner theater. Erin stood up and collected her plate. Rachel's skin flushed with anger, the red splotch creeping up her chest. Her cheeks felt hot.

"I guess some people don't know how good they have it."

She stormed away to dispose of her dinnerware, leaving Rachel seething. The crowd resumed its chatter a second time, and Rachel watched Will eat, turning over the events of the last few minutes in her head.

Will picked at his food, each bite swallowed under protest, and now he was mad at her to boot, like she had committed some terrible crime in making sure he had food in his belly. Because that was parenting. Snipping the correct wire and the bomb blowing up anyway. Eventually, the plate was empty, because he was a growing boy, after all, and he'd been hungry.

They got up wordlessly and left.

The trailer was empty when they made it back. Behind them, the last bit of daylight had evaporated and darkness sank across the land, as though some bored deity had tired of his game and extinguished the light in his room. Will flopped down on the ratty old sofa and reached for a Spider-Man comic book.

"Not so fast, buddy," she said. "Time for bed."

"When's Dad coming back?" he asked.

Again, the question twisted in her gut like a knife.

"I don't know, sweetie," she answered. "After you're asleep probably."

He moped through his bedtime ritual, the brushing of his teeth, the changing into his pajamas. It probably took him thirty minutes to accomplish the task that should have taken three. Finally, he was done, and she tucked him into his bed, a twin mattress lying on the floor, and kissed his forehead.

The room was small, a typical boy's room, peppered with toys and gadgets he'd accumulated over the years. Transition, there was always a transition in progress, from these toys to those, from these clothes to those, from this book to that. His current favorite was his G.I. Joe collection, requisitioned from a Toys R Us up in Omaha. He had dozens of the action figures, all the vehicles and playsets, because, after all, there had to be perks that came along with being born after the apocalypse.

"Good night, Spoon."

"Night."

After Will was in bed, Rachel sat on the couch in the small pool of light spilling from the lantern with an old Stephen King novel, *Under the Dome*, in her lap. Tonight, the book held little interest for her. She went out to the front stoop for a cigarette. It tasted old and hot and dry. The glowing orange tip bobbed in the darkness, a lonely craft in an ocean of blackness. Eddie hated it when she smoked, which made her enjoy it even more. The next morning, he'd make some comment about it, about how it made her smell like an ashtray in a New York City cab, and it would give her a secret little thrill.

Around her the complex was dark. Good metaphor for her life. For all their lives. You could only see what was right there in front of you, no more. The years since the plague had shrunk the world down, leaving her in this small cocoon.

She pitched the half-smoked butt and went back inside.

3

Rachel sat on the edge of the sofa, lacing up her heavy work boots, shaking the thin sleep out of her eyes. It was a little past six and the trailer was quiet. Will was asleep, having stayed up late the night before reading the first *Harry Potter* novel. She had picked it up at a library in an unincorporated community a mile outside the town limits. He had never heard of the boy wizard, of course, his world devoid of even the slightest glimmer of pop culture. Wizards and Quidditch and butterbeer and dragons. All good things for a boy of eleven.

Eddie snored in their bedroom; at least the son of a bitch was here, hadn't left her deciding whether she should leave Will sleeping alone. She had done it, God forgive her, she had left him alone and asleep on the nights Eddie hadn't made it home on time and there had been no one else to ask.

She carried the lantern to the kitchen, where she opened an energy gel pack and sucked out the viscous concoction. She winced at the chemical flavor that had been injected into the package more than a decade ago. *Blueberry, my ass.* Probably tasted the same the day it had been sealed shut, unaware of its fate as one of the last of its kind. Because there were no more blueberry-flavored energy gels rolling off assembly lines in Milwaukee or Joliet or Texarkana or wherever this packet had been born.

One day, someone would eat the very last one, and that would be it. Extinct. She was lucky they had food at all, but that old sensation of not wanting anything here, atavistic, ancient, welled up inside her. What she wouldn't have given for some orange chicken from China Dragon right then and there, what she wouldn't have given. Even now, barely six in the morning, her mouth watered at the thought of the crisp battered chicken, its tanginess filling her mouth and look at her daydream take over there and run away like the dish with the spoon.

Rachel grabbed her gun, the M4 rifle her dad had given to her many years ago. It had once belonged to Sarah Wells, the late love of her father's life, brought together by chance or fate or karma in the unhinged days immediately after the plague. Using a book she found in an Omaha library, she taught herself how to care for it, maintain it, clean it, so it would always be that loyal friend she needed in this brave not-so-new-anymore world. She practiced with it religiously, and it had saved her life on more than one occasion. They all did. Weapons training was gospel around here.

After loading her pack and pulling on her coat and gloves, she locked the door and headed out into the morning mist. She hadn't always locked the door when she left, and she didn't quite remember when she had started doing it again, but it put her mind at ease. It couldn't have been a good sign that she was reverting to the old ways of distrust and suspicion. Walls were going up among them. Perhaps the others had started locking their doors and had been locking them all along and she hadn't known it, any more than the others would know she was locking hers now.

It was chilly outside, her exhalations drifting away in vaporous clouds in the pre-dawn gloom. She followed the familiar path to the warehouse. How many times had she made this trip? God might know; she did not. She liked leaving early for the morning shift - it gave her time to think, to clear her head, before embarking on the important but dull work of defending and maintaining the warehouse.

Her father lived alone in the next trailer over. Next to him lived Erin and her common-law husband Harry Maynard, a refugee from the original town of Evergreen and their community's constable. A little bit farther up, light glowed softly in Max Gilmartin's trailer as she drifted by, and she could see his silhouette moving to and fro inside. Max. It was weird to think of him as an adult now, as she still remembered the gangly, pimple-pocked teenager she'd met long ago. Her father had found him in a grocery store in the aftermath of the plague, a terrified teenager, and he had been with him as Adam crossed America looking for Rachel. He was huge now, well over six feet tall and two-hundred and forty pounds. TWO-FORTY! as he enjoyed yelling when he'd had a bit too much to drink. Now that was a guy they had a hard time feeding.

Their trailer sat in the northwest corner of this distribution warehouse complex, a few miles southwest of Omaha, Nebraska. The trailer wasn't much, a corrugated aluminum singlewide, once an office for some long-dead middle manager, now split into three rooms, one for Will, one for her and Eddie, and the tiny sitting room where they had played their game. They'd lived here for more than ten years now, ever since they had abandoned the Caballero Ranch after the crop failures and migrated north to Omaha. Making the best of a bad situation, that's what Adam had called it. They'd been unbelievably lucky to find this place, luckier still to have taken it with minimal losses. Three of them had died in the battle to take it, and tragic as those losses had been, they had not been in vain.

Now had it been three or four?

She couldn't remember exactly, but that's the way it was. People died all the time now. Death was part of life, really part of it, not like in the old days when people said it but really they meant, *oh, did you hear about Bob in Finance, he had a heart attack or a guy blowing through a stop sign and hitting a minivan carrying Andrea and three kids, you know, the one from the PTA*. Sure those things had happened, but not that often, which was what had made them so remarkable, their relative rarity. Nowadays, people died young and violently and that's just the way it was.

Her row with Erin was still chewing on her a bit; they hadn't spoken since. It was tough to let it go, no matter how much she empathized with the woman, no matter how often she told herself it was Erin's misery talking. Grief knew no timetable. She missed her son. Didn't matter that he had perished like countless billions. He was still dead, and she was still his mother. But sometimes Rachel wanted to snap back, yell it from the rooftops that it wasn't exactly sunshine and puppy breath, this thing she was going through. Mothering the only child known to have survived infancy since the plague was not an easy crown to wear. But she could never say a thing like that because it would sound ungrateful. It would sound like she didn't know how good she had it.

Beyond the fence was the inner perimeter, a long row of sandbags roughly twelve feet distant. Each corner of the compound was protected by a pair of .50-caliber machine guns, spoils of a long-ago raid on a National Guard armory north of Omaha. Beyond that, another wall of stone and brick, patched together over the years. Razor wire lined the tops like a deadly Mohawk.

Dozens of dead tractor-trailers jutted out from the loading docks on the east side; they looked like extinct parasites that fed on the retail blood of this giant host before detaching and carrying newly acquired loads to faraway destinations. They were ghosts now, relics of what had once been. Sometimes Rachel would climb up into a cab and sit behind the wheel; she would think about where these trucks had been scheduled to go all those years ago before Medusa had cast her terrible judgment on the world. Cleveland or Des Moines or Detroit. She would think about those other cities, empty and decaying, and it would make her sad all over again, but it was important she become sad sometimes because otherwise it would mean forgetting about the old world. That didn't seem right.

Several loose shipping containers had been converted to living quarters. Lined with thick insulation and supplemented by heated rocks, these containers fought off the winter chill as good as anything else. Some of their occupants had been rather creative in decorating them; Romaine had turned hers into a shrine to Hello Kitty. It was a bit weird, but, hey, whatever floated your boat.

There were thirty-six of them living here now, getting down to the bare minimum they needed to run the operation and protect the facility from the next attack. Because there would always be another attack. They were the housefly, and out there many flyswatters. One day, one of those flyswatters would come down hard on them. One day, they'd lose the warehouse. Tomorrow. Next month. Next year. It was going to happen. But what else could they do but plan and prepare and when the time came, fight. Fight as long as they could, as hard as they could until they could fight no longer.

Rachel couldn't believe they'd managed to hold the warehouse as long as they had. Six times they'd come under attack, and six times, they had been able to repel the threat. Under Harry Maynard's eye, the Defense Committee worked nonstop shoring up the perimeter, fortifying their defenses, training, and stockpiling weapons and ammunition.

A gust of wind blew across the campus, whistling in the corridors between the shipping containers, a ghostly howl that made everything seem quieter than it really was. A lone sentry patrolled the outer perimeter; maybe Oscar, but he was shrouded in the morning gloom. In the distance, beyond the perimeter fencing, she could just make out Interstate 80, still pocked with the dilapidated hulls of long-abandoned Corollas and Explorers and F-150 pickups. She took one last deep breath before the twelve-hour shift ahead, filling her lungs with fresh clean air, and then went inside.

It was blessedly warmer inside, the building still holding the heat of an unexpected Indian summer the previous week, now largely faded. Sounds of a shift ending echoed through the warehouse's cavernous corridors - a loud yawn, a violent stitch of laughter, folks happy to be headed home after a hard night's work. Rachel was scheduled for perimeter duty today, so she would spend most of her time outside, alone, and that was fine with her. She'd largely kept to herself lately, the thing with Eddie draining her reserves of patience with people generally. Simply being was physically exhausting. Being Will's mom. Being Adam's daughter. Being with Eddie. Even when they weren't fighting, weren't arguing, his presence in her life was the hill at the end of the daily marathon.

Despite the warmth, she kept her coat on as she made her way to the large office in the northeast corner of the warehouse. It was a long walk, taking her past the veggie aisle, the canned meats, past the access panel that led to the network of tunnels under the warehouse. Through the window, she could see Adam Fisher at the desk, working on something or another. He waved her in, his eyes down on his paperwork. As it always did, her heart twisted when she saw him. He was the great optical illusion in her life, looking like one thing while being something very different.

"Come in if you're coming," he said.

"Good morning," she said, taking a seat in the threadbare modular chair across from Adam. He looked tired. A few lines in his face she hadn't noticed before. A bit more gray in his hair. They were all getting older, fast. He'd be fifty-one now. Maybe fifty-two.

He continued with the paperwork as she sat there, content with letting her direct the conversation. She wondered if he found their interactions as awkward as she did. All these years living side by side had pushed them farther apart like two magnetic filings.

"How was the night shift?"

"Uneventful," he said. "That's my favorite word, you know. Uneventful."

"Good, good."

They sat in silence a bit longer, long enough for it to become awkward. All at once, she became aware how superficial their relationship was. Talk about the warehouse, about the night shift, about the day shift, about inventory and supply runs. Talk about anything but their relationship.

"Can I ask you something?"

"Shoot," he said, exhaling with what sounded like relief she had broken the silence.

"You ever wonder about it?"

"About what?"

"You. Me. Will."

She held her breath. It was a question she had never asked before, but Erin's comment, a week old now, had eaten at her. She did have it good; what she didn't understand was *why* she had it good. In all the years since the plague, no one in their community had ever met two surviving generations from a single family, let alone three. It nagged at them, gnawed at them, the itch eternally out of reach. It was discussed late at night, over drinks, in bed after sex, whispered at the cafeteria. The answer was right there and not, like they were chasing nothing but shadows.

They all wondered about the Fisher family tree's resistance to the Medusa virus, they wondered if the key to the lock was right here, walking among them buried somewhere deep in their DNA. If they could just figure it out. It drove them all a bit batty, of that much she was aware. It was an extra burden to bear, the very act of knowing Will was possible in a world where it otherwise seemed impossible, where Medusa continued to be the horrible gift that kept on giving.

Erin's baby had been the first one born in Evergreen, about five months after Rachel, Erin and some of the other women had had escaped from Miles Chadwick, the man who had started the plague. The future, wide open. Nothing settled. She remembered sitting with her dad, sipping whiskey with him in the hours after the baby's birth, and it was the last time she had been truly happy. It was the last time any of them had been, she supposed.

Cole Thompson began showing symptoms of Medusa thirty-six hours after he was born. The fever came first, followed by the coughing and the internal hemorrhaging, and topped off with a symphony of the telltale seizures that accompanied end-stage Medusa infection. Little Cole died fifty-two hours after he was born, and the impact of his death on their infant society had been nothing short of cataclysmic. Then Max Gilmartin told the others about Caroline, another survivor, whose baby had perished shortly after his birth and who had taken her own life in the wake of losing her baby.

It proved to be a very dark chapter in their lives. The next three babies born in the community succumbed to Medusa as well, and just like that, any hope of a bright future had gone up in smoke. Then a year later, she'd become pregnant, the result of a drunken dalliance with Eddie Callahan, that snake charmer. She couldn't really write it off to a simple dalliance, though, much as she would have liked to. She had loved him, he revved her engine in ways she hadn't thought possible, and she kept it secret as long as she could, hell-bent on seeing it through, unwilling to accept that it would be for nothing. Four babies weren't a big enough sample size to reach any conclusions, right? But her pregnancy turned into a deathwatch all the same.

People avoided her because they didn't want to get too close, get their hopes up. How many times do you try for the cheese on the electrified plate before you finally learn your lesson? They weren't going through it again with Rachel and her baby. She'd gone into labor virtually alone on a raw, rainy October morning. With Max helping, Adam had delivered the baby, and they began to wait. She held him nonstop, waiting for him to develop the fever, the terrible cough, waiting for Medusa to make its appearance. As she held him and fed him in those terrible minutes and hours, she fell for him in a way that didn't seem humanly possible, a flash burn of endless love scarring her forever, and she waited for him to die.

But he didn't.

A week went by.

No Medusa.

A month.

No Medusa.

A year.

No Medusa.

And how they rejoiced.

The curse was broken. Bad luck, that's all it had been.

On Will's first birthday, they threw him a party. Harry drove to a party supply store in Omaha and got paper plates and napkins and cups with little airplanes and trains and cars. Charlotte made him a cake that actually tasted pretty good. They built a big bonfire and stayed up all night drinking warm beer and eating stale potato chips. They sang a simple song Sophie had written, a tune that sounded great in front of three chords.

It had been a long time since they had sung the song, and most of the lyrics had faded from Rachel's memory. All she could remember was a swatch of it, a little piece of a picture that had once been beautiful.

Slide away darkness,
Slide away now...

Three more women were pregnant by the turn of the year, the third New Year's Day since the plague, and they faced the year with new hope, new dreams. Little Ella was born in June, Victoria in July and Lenore came in October. Ella died a few minutes after birth. Victoria and Lenore, both born in the morning, were gone before the sun set on their first day of life.

And that had been that.

There would be a pregnancy every year or so, because people still did the thing they were biologically programmed to do. Human DNA didn't know or care what would become of those babies. Life, eventually, would find a way. Right? It had to.

But it didn't.

In all the years since his birth, William Fisher Callahan was the only post-plague baby to see his first birthday, to see any birthdays. And instead of becoming a symbol of the future and the promise it held, Will had become nothing but a cruel taunt.

Adam leaned back in his chair and blew out a noisy sigh.

"Sometimes," he said. "Not as much as I used to, to be perfectly honest."

She didn't think he was being perfectly honest with her, but at least she'd gotten him talking. Will's survival had perplexed him as much as the deaths of the other children. He had drawn blood from Rachel, from Will, even from himself, comparing it to the samples he'd drawn from the other women who'd lost their post-plague babies to Medusa. But with no electricity, with no viable gasoline to power the generators, the technology hadn't been there to help him identify the anomaly that had protected three generations of his family from the greatest killer the world had ever known.

"I wish I knew why," she said.

"Luck," he snapped, smacking the desk with the flat of his hand. "Genetic chance. Believe me, Will is not the only child to have survived since the plague. Where there is one, there are others. It's how life works."

"I don't know," she said. She wondered if he believed what he was saying or if he was trying to maintain a positive outlook for all their sakes. "No one else has seen-"

"Have you ever heard of the Toba super-eruption?" he asked, interrupting her.

"No."

"No? The original apocalypse?"

She shook her head.

Adam put his reading glasses back on, which added significantly to his professorial air.

"About seventy thousand years ago, the Toba volcano in Indonesia erupted and plunged Earth into a volcanic winter. You think we've had it tough? Our little plague was nothing compared to that. Anyway, years of nuclear winter, blah, blah, blah. Way worse than what we've had to deal with."

Rachel glanced out the window behind Adam's head, more reflexively than intentionally, at the gloomy skies and shivered, thinking they'd had it pretty damn bad, when you got right down to it. Some said it was because of the nukes that had been launched during civilization's death throes. In those terrible final days, China had vaporized Moscow and much of Eastern Europe, Israel had hit Iran, and those were only the ones she had heard about before the news reports stopped. Others claimed it was due to the environment having to process seven billion human corpses in the span of a few weeks.

The cause was irrelevant. The real problem was the effect. In the years since Medusa, the global climate had undergone a massive paradigm shift. The winters were longer and harsher. The summers, shorter and cooler. It was cloudy more often than sunny and it rained constantly. And the effect on agriculture had been catastrophic.

The crop failures started that first spring at the ranch, around the time Cole Thompson had died. The early vegetables, the lettuces and green onions and early peas did well, but the summer harvest was terrible. Rachel walked the growing fields in July, bucket in hand, and studied with alarm the anemic plants that should've been bursting with tomatoes and squash and cucumbers and eggplant and peppers but were thin and pale like terminally ill patients. Above her, the weak sun had shimmered upon their little corner of the world, just enough to pump the summertime temperatures into the mid-sixties. And those were the good days. Even in the dead of summer, they were occasionally greeted with chilly days better suited for jackets and visits to a pumpkin patch.

The next year was worse. One crop failure after another, so complete and total they hadn't even bothered with the fall planting. The time, it was decided, would be better spent scavenging for the food supplies that were out there. They couldn't wait, because the other survivors would soon be doing the same if they weren't already. That fall, the group abandoned the farm and moved north toward Omaha, where they found the warehouse that would become their home.

"Some scholars," Adam went on, "believed the total human population dropped to a few thousand people. At most. That there were only a few dozen women of childbearing age left on the planet. We got through that. We'll get through this."

He was wide-eyed, a bit manic; it seemed very important to him that she agree with him, that she see things his way. But she couldn't share his optimism, dim as it already was. For years, they had been on alert, looking and listening for news of another child somewhere. But there hadn't been. Not once. Not one time.

She looked up at the clock over his head. It was the silhouette of a black cat, the timepiece set in the center of its stomach, its oversized eyes shifting from side to side with each tick, its tail oscillating in time with the beat. It was one minute to seven.

"But you haven't seen any little ones," she said. "Even when you went back to Richmond."

Several years earlier, Adam had made a long trip back to Richmond, Virginia, where he had lived before the pandemic. The purpose of the journey had been to get the lay of the land, find out how the world was faring a decade after the plague, figure out what people were doing to survive. Find out if there were other children.

"That doesn't mean they weren't there," Adam said. "We don't advertise Will's presence either. They may not hide the women anymore, but I bet they hide the children."

"Maybe," Rachel said, but not really believing it.

"I'd better get on it, then," she said, wiping her hands on her pants.

"I'll swing by and see Will later-"

A sound caught her ear, the staccato burst of small-arms fire in the distance.

She froze. Her father's face turned to stone a second later, the slight delay owing possibly to ears two decades older than hers.

"What was that?" she whispered rhetorically, even while knowing damn well what it was.

Then an enormous blast rocked the building, shaking to her very core, and bits of plaster and dust rained down upon them like snowflakes. She heard a grunt (maybe from herself, who knew). It was the loudest sound she had heard since the bomb that had destroyed the Citadel, the place Adam had rescued her from years earlier, the place where the plague had been born. That had been different though, watching from a distance, waiting for it, hoping for it and dreading it, the conflagration that would be their absolution.

Today, the calculus was much simpler.

They were under attack.

4

Rachel unslung the M4 rifle as Adam drew his Glock 19 pistol from his shoulder holster and grabbed a set of binoculars from the desk drawer. In tandem, they moved toward the door of the office, Rachel checking the pockets of her barn jacket for spare magazines. Her fingers ticked off four, two in each pocket. Her hands were steady, but it was difficult to breathe. It never got easier. Never.

Her thoughts zeroed in on Will and Eddie, hoping beyond hope they would stick to their emergency plan, the one they had drilled over and over. The tunnels. They would hide him in the tunnels, under the kitchen, until it was over. Right now, they should be on their way, covering the fifty meters to the cafeteria, around the back to the kitchen, down through the hatch that led to the tunnels.

Would he know what was happening? Would he be afraid? Would he die today?

She and Adam moved down the dark aisle, making their way to the closest exit, about fifty yards away, on the east side in this section of the warehouse. The shelves were barren here now, the canned goods moved, rotated, and consolidated as the years had drifted by. Eventually, all the shelves would be empty, she knew that, they all did, and they would have to deal with that. They had even identified their last meal, cans of chili and beef barley soup, southwestern corn, delicacies in a universe of blandness. But right here and now, they had a couple years' worth of food left, and that was worth fighting for, worth dying for.

In the gloom, shouts and orders barked. There would be eight of them inside right now, another eight on the perimeter. The others, those not on duty, would respond to the klaxon alarm sounding. Her body buzzed with fear, but her training would see her through. Once a month, they walked through a simulated attack on the warehouse, using paintball guns. They ran every permutation they could think of - a single attacker, a pair, a dozen. Everyone had a job, everyone had a position to hold. The drills were useful, if only to remind them of the danger surrounding them.

Outside, small-arms fire peppered the complex. Over that, she could hear the booming staccato of their .50-cals, raking the barren grasslands any would-be attackers would have to traverse. The complex was well fortified, difficult to approach. They were well armed, well stocked. She told herself these things so she wouldn't wet herself. Fear wrapped its hands around the deepest part of her soul, her innermost thoughts, choking them with dread.

Another boom shook the warehouse, knocking Rachel off her axis. Adam grabbed her waist and pulled her to the ground; her knees banged hard against the floor, sending shock waves of pain reverberating through her legs. To the west, a terrific rumble and clatter as part of the roof caved in. Bits of concrete and sheetrock rained down on the warehouse floor.

"RPGs," he said. "Missiles." His voice was calm and steady. She hoped his steely resolve bubbled from a deep reservoir of strength; she worried it came from somewhere else entirely. That he was resigned to their fate, that sooner or later it would all go bad, so there was no point in worrying about it.

They climbed back to their feet and sprinted the last fifty feet to the exit doors. Rachel got there first, panting, sweating yet cold at the same time. Her hair fell into her eyes; she took a second to tie it off into a ponytail with a hairband she found in her pocket. Stupid hairband might save her life.

"Ready?" she asked her father.

He nodded.

A large shipping container sat nestled in the tall weeds about twenty yards from the door; it would give them some cover as they approached the maelstrom. Still, she was cautious as she pressed the door's release bar, opening it slowly, an inch at a time, staying low. She wriggled her way through the narrowest of openings and made a beeline for cover. It took no more than ten seconds, but it felt like an eternity, like she would never get there, like she would be cut to ribbons right there, and she would die without having done a thing to protect their home, to protect Will.

She made it unscathed, gasping, her back pressed against the container's cold metal skin. Adam scooted in behind her and took up a position at the other end of the container. Crouching low, she risked a peek around the side, looking toward the perimeter fence. The staccato susurration of gunfire was inside her head, inside her skin.

The land here sloped downward slightly, just enough to give them a tactical advantage over any assailants. Through the M4's scope, Rachel saw a flurry of activity in the distance, about a quarter mile off. Clouds of dust swirling into the morning sky. A lot of activity. The biggest attack they'd faced in years. This day had always been coming, no doubt about that. Did it matter whether it was today or six months or a year from now?

"See anything?" she asked her father.

"Here," he said, tossing the field glasses toward her.

A scan of the scene turned her stomach to liquid. A dozen vehicles, Hummers and pickups mostly, skittering across the barren landscape. Where were they getting the fuel for such an assault? The gasoline and diesel pooled under the nation's countless gas stations had long since gone stale. Some enterprising survivors had fashioned a biofuel that was not nearly as efficient as standard gasoline, but it worked, and it was more valuable than virtually anything on the market. That told Rachel this was a very serious threat.

"It's a big one," she said.

"Let's not panic," he said. "They want the warehouse intact. They have to be careful with how strong a move they make."

Always clinical, always thinking, her old man. She'd been like that once, back before Will. Motherhood had injected an X factor into the equation, the variable you could always predict and never predict at the same time. Now she raced to the worst-case scenario, *Do Not Pass Go, Do Not Collect $200*. They were outnumbered, outgunned, they would all be marched out into the plains and executed one at a time. They would burn the warehouse to the ground. They would roast Will on a spit and eat him for dinner because meat was hard to come by these days. An itch to sprint for the trailer and run for the hills with her son crawled up her back like a bug.

She looked east and west, the land clear to each horizon. The vanguard appeared to be concentrating its forces to the north. This had its pros and cons. They needed to check their rear, make sure they weren't trying to run a bait and switch, a smaller contingent sneaking up their ass. A frontal assault could mean the attackers didn't know what they were doing tactically. And it would be easier to defend. Just hold them off. Eventually, they could wear them out.

Her ears perked up at a new sound in the distance. A grinding groan. She peered around the corner of the container again, staying low. The advance team had stopped firing; in fact, they had retreated a little. But the groan grew louder. She scanned the horizon beyond the trucks and picked up a cloud of dust on the horizon.

She spun the small focus wheel, bringing the cloud into sharp relief. It looked more and more like a living, breathing thing as it drew closer. Her skin tightened and gooseflesh popped up along her arms. A tempest, a dark menacing thing here to swallow them whole. Then the grinding stopped, and the cloud dissipated, revealing the threat in all its steel horror.

"Oh my God," she whispered, lowering the binoculars from her face.

"What do you see?"

"It's a tank."

One at a time, the others retreated, joining them behind the relative safety of the container. Out on the plains, the attackers remained still and silent, perhaps reveling in this sudden shift in the balance of power. The tank was about two hundred yards away.

"We need the other .50-cals," Adam said. "And the RPGs, where are the goddamn RPGs?"

"Over there," a voice called out.

Rachel glanced to her left and saw two men kneeling near the fence, the missile launchers propped up against their legs. They looked so pathetic, like oversized dart guns.

"Dad, it's over," Rachel said. "We have no chance against that thing."

"The tank is a bluff," Harry said. "They can't use it if they want to take the warehouse."

"He's right, honey," Adam said, and immediately her jaw clenched with annoyance.

Harry dispatched three teams to retrieve their heaviest weapons, her warnings falling on deaf ears. They would make their stand here whether she liked it or not.

"Listen to me," Rachel snapped. "That tank will cut through us like we're not even here. It's not worth it."

"Not now, sweetie," Harry replied.

Her body bristled with rage. They were talking to her like she didn't have a brain. Like she was a child. Talking down to her, in that way men talked to women when they didn't want their input. Because she wasn't a man, she couldn't assess the situation and see they were one hundred percent screwed? One thing the apocalypse hadn't changed, blatant sexism for sure.

"We'll set them up behind the sandbags," Adam said.

"Let's stack them higher," Harry replied. "Build a blind for each gun."

"Good idea," Adam said. "Ready?"

She watched them discuss it like they were out duck hunting. It was madness, pure madness. Their guns, their precious rocket launchers would be worthless against the tank. If they wanted to go down this rabbit hole, they could do it without her.

"This is suicide," Rachel said. "I'm going to get Will."

"The hell you are," Harry said in a low but firm voice.

She turned back toward him and found his pistol in her face.

"No deserters today," Harry said.

"Put that thing down," Adam said.

"Shut the hell up, Fisher. You know the rules."

Adam looked at his daughter.

"He'll be fine," Adam said.

She stared down the barrel of Harry's gun, wondering if he would do it. And then she saw Erin's face there, floating in the black *O* of the muzzle, and she could hear the thousand conversations she'd never heard, poison in Harry's ear about how terrible a mother Rachel was, and how she could do a better job raising that boy. She squeezed the barrel of her M4, its muzzle pointed toward the ground. She'd never get it up in time and there was no doubt he would shoot her, cut her down where she stood. She glanced around at the others; no one made eye contact.

"Put it away," she said finally, her shoulders sagging. "I'm not going anywhere."

"I won't hesitate," Harry said.

"Enough," Adam said. "We've got work to do."

Rachel steeled herself and ran on Harry's signal, not really giving it any thought, following orders now. They would die today, she was sure of it, and maybe it wouldn't have mattered whether she stayed here or went after Will. As she sprinted for the perimeter fence, she waited for that sound, the throaty boom signifying another launch of the tank's hellish spawn that would bring this all to an end.

"There, there, and there," Harry said, pointing, directing traffic.

They shifted sandbags, passing them from one set of hands to another, as they modified the wall to accommodate the guns. As they worked, the first two teams returned, straining under the weight of the guns.

A burst of static interrupted the discussion.

"Good morning," a woman's voice said, her voice booming across the flatlands. "My name is Nora. We want the boy."

Rachel's stomach flipped. She took to the binoculars again. Poking out of the tank's hatch was a middle-aged woman, probably in her mid-forties, holding up a megaphone. She had a lean build, and her hair was cropped close, sprinkled with a little gray. A pair of tortoise-shell glasses framed her narrow face, making her look more like an accountant than a post-apocalyptic bandit.

They wanted Will.

They knew about Will.

But how? And what did this woman want with him?

"What boy?"

"The child," she said. "The one born after the plague."

"There are no children here."

"You're lying."

"Hey, how about you kiss my ass," Harry called out, his deep, booming voice holding its own against Nora's, even without a megaphone.

"You have three minutes to surrender," Nora said, ignoring him. "If you give him up, walk away, no one has to get hurt. If you don't, we will kill every last one of you."

She said it matter-of-factly, without a trace of emotion, as though it were a speech she had given a dozen times before. Perhaps she had. As she spoke, her confederates took up positions around her, using their trucks as cover.

"Maybe you didn't hear me," Harry shouted. "I believe I said, 'kiss my ass.'"

Three minutes. Time enough to make a break for it, save her son, get the hell out of here. Take her chances. Another minute or two, Harry wouldn't have time to deal with her desertion. She could feel that ancient maternal pull drawing her toward her son.

"We're not surrendering," Adam said.

"Amen to that," Harry added.

She exhaled a sigh of relief. At least they weren't so far gone they'd sacrifice one of their own.

The six guns arrived, and they began setting them up outside the perimeter, three across. They adjusted the sandbag walls, leaving gaps through which they could open fire. As she watched them position the guns, a profound understanding washed over her. There could be no surrender. This warehouse was everything to them, even with its dwindling food supply. It had sustained them for nearly a decade, with its mushy vegetables and bland beans and energy drinks, its paper plates and toilet paper. They would die to defend it because without it, they were as good as dead anyway. Where would they even go, she and Will, if Harry had let her go?

The seconds ticked away, her mind filling the empty moments with flashes of the past, the years they'd spent here, from the brutal battle to take it through all the work to protect the warehouse. The long hours walking the perimeter, the sandbags, the razor wire, the weapons training. The total abandonment of any other pursuit in this post-Medusa world. Maybe that had been a mistake, looking back, but again, it was hard to second-guess defending the warehouse above all else.

"One minute," called out Nora.

"You. My ass," replied Harry.

They would be in the tunnels by now. She wondered if she would see him again. Probably not. Dammit, Eddie, you've got to step up and take care of him now. You don't have to be the goddamn father of the year. Just be there more than not.

"Time's up," Nora said.

The tank roared back to life, hitching once and belching a plume of bluish exhaust from its innards before beginning its slow roll. Then the M256 120mm gun fired once, sending its sabot round screaming across the empty plains. A second later, the projectile slammed into the north wall of the building, which exploded in a cloud of dust and smoke and rubble. Three pickups followed in the tank's wake, using the steel beast for cover. Each was equipped with a machine gun mounted in its bed, the gunners at work.

"Kill the trucks," Harry barked, the panic in his voice evident. "Kill them now. Then we focus on the tank."

"No," Adam interrupted. "If we don't kill the tank now, the trucks won't matter. Concentrate all your fire on the tank."

The whistle of a rocket-propelled grenade filled the air. It hit the face of the tank and exploded, but the tank burst through the resulting curtain of smoke and kept rolling. Another RPG let loose, this one missing the tank but obliterating one of the pickups. Joe, Rob, and Hung were at the guns, trading uncertain looks as the ammunition boxes ran dangerously low.

"That's an order!" Harry yelled. "Fire!"

The air swelled with the clipped sound of the guns unleashing their ordnance. But the third gun, manned by Joe, remained silent. He looked to Adam and then to Harry and then back again.

"What do I do, what do I do?"

Rachel shoved Joe aside and took control of the gun.

"Ready?" she yelled over the din.

Hung nodded, threading a belt of ammunition into the heavy gun. As she waited, she sighted their targets, focusing on the front windshield of the tank.

"Now!"

She pulled the trigger, eyeing her target through the rifle's scope. She'd never fired the .50-cal before; the powerful recoil ripped through her like an earthquake. Her teeth tingled, her bones vibrated, her eardrums trembled as the gun chewed through its ammunition belt.

She tensed every muscle of her body as she readied to fire the fully automatic gun again. On either side of her, the guns blazed away, the rounds ticking away like a meth-fueled metronome. The bigger men were having a bit of an easier time with the M2's recoil. But still the tank came, mercilessly chewing up the distance between them, the guns having had no effect.

"Aim for the treads," Adam called out.

She re-sighted the weapon and fired again, over and over until she couldn't feel it anymore, until her muscles burned, until her fingers were numb. Sweat flowed down her forehead, stinging her eyes, but there was nothing she could do about it. The gun required every ounce of strength, every little bit of fight in her.

But still the tank came.

The surviving pickups had spread wide, leaving behind the cover of the tank. Their flanks were terribly exposed now. Behind her, a flurry of activity, orders shouted, chess pieces moved into position.

One truck moved in close, no more than twenty yards from the fence, turning at a ninety-degree angle before coming to a stop. Harry and Adam emerged from the cover of the shipping container, laying down cover for the big gunners. But the pickup had come in close, too close for comfort. A burst from the pickup's gun caught Joe in the legs, dropping him to the ground. Screams of agony filled the air as blood pooled underneath him.

They were at a tipping point now, Rachel could sense it. A charge in the air, everything going sideways all at once. She pushed Joe's cries out of her head and zeroed in on the tank, which was now no more than fifty yards away. Another few shots. The satisfying twang of several rounds hitting the chassis of the tank, for all the good it did. She might as well have been shooting it with a water gun.

The tank fired again, a bloom of flame erupting from its huge muzzle, and its round opened another gaping wound in the building's façade. They had to fall back. Staying here was suicide.

"Fall back!" she called out. "Fall back!"

She tried taking the gun with her, but the weapon was too much for her wasted arms, rendered into jelly. Leaving the gun behind her, she risked a peek over her shoulder as they scampered toward the building. The tank rolled through the outer perimeter like it was tissue paper, turning sandbags into dust, the metal fencing folding in over itself. Then it rolled over Joe, still lying there; she looked away before the inevitable horror that followed.

Like ants fleeing an angry boot, the group of about twenty streamed back through the door. Inside, the group scattered, taking up defensive positions behind shelving deep in the building. Pulses of fear ripped through her. Her breath came in ragged, labored gasps. Breathing had become a chore, how had she ever breathed without reminding herself to do it every two seconds?

It had all come down to this. Here. Here they would make their stand. They would fight here in the aisles of this oversized Costco, fight to the death, and to the victor would go the creamed corn.

Despite everything, she liked their chances. These dark corridors were old friends, from the drafty vents to the squeaky shelves to the spot in the roof that leaked no matter how many times they patched it up. Hours and hours she had spent patrolling them, counting individual cans of food until her brain was mush. And now they would use that knowledge, hard-earned, to protect their home, to protect her son, to make sure he was safe. Their attackers would have to get out of their precious tank and come in here, come into this foreign land, in the dark, and here they would die. They would die, and word would get out that the people here in this place called Evergreen would give no quarter, never, so you bring your tanks and your rocket-propelled grenades and you'll go back in pieces.

Then the tank crashed through the wall.

5

The wall crumbled like a cookie, the sunshine streaming in, tiny particulates of concrete dust hanging in the beams of daylight. The tank paused, there in the terrible gash it had left in the warehouse wall, reminding Rachel of a creature resting in the sun. Then it roared back to life and continued burrowing inside, a tick that had found a good place to feed.

God help them.

The others stood frozen as the tank pushed deeper into the warehouse.

"Fall back!" someone finally yelled.

Rachel backpedaled from her position, never taking her eyes off the steel monster. The driver tilted to his left, taking aim at a well-stocked line of shelves. The scaffolding tipped over, and hundreds of cans of food fell under the tank's treads as it pushed deeper inside. A deep thumping sound echoed through the warehouse.

The cans were popping open like overripe fruit, pumping a strangely sweet aroma of vacuum-sealed vegetables into the air. The rich earthy smell of asparagus and cannellini beans mixed with the stink of her sweat and the industrial smokiness of the building coming down around them.

The tank continued rolling south, toppling fifty-foot-high shelving that crashed to the floor with a deafening clatter. There was nothing they could do to stop it, this mechanical bull in their china shop. The noise was deafening, the groan of the tank, the shelves collapsing, the ineffective small-arms fire her comrades began unleashing at it. The gunfire started slowly, a pop here and there before blooming into a steady chatter. At that moment, it reminded Rachel of microwave popcorn, of her mom, of watching movies on the couch on a Saturday night. She wished she and Will lived in a world with televisions and DVD players and Chinese food. How cruel it had been to be born when Will had been born.

The warehouse was lost.

They had to get out of here.

She moved toward the hole in the wall, her focus now shifting toward her son. The battle here had been lost, as she had long feared. It was time to abandon ship. She had go-bags packed for each of them, a secret stash she had told no one about. Medicine, a week's worth of food, bottled water.

Paul ran ahead of her, apparently reaching the same conclusion. As he ducked through the jagged opening in the wall, he was immediately cut down by a curtain of gunfire. His body spun around like a centrifuge as a heavy fusillade turned him into human rubble. Sheep to the slaughter. The bastards would exterminate them as they tried to escape.

Then she felt a hand grip her shoulder; a scream raced up from the depths of her soul, but it was blocked by a hand on her mouth.

"Shh, it's Dad," Adam whispered into her ear.

Relief washed through her.

"Follow me," he said. "Basement."

Her father took the point and she followed, away from the tank, which had now obliterated the south wing of the compound. Along the way, they collected a handful of their fellow citizens, pinned down, unsure of where to go.

Again the hero, the sentiment flashed in her mind, and she hated herself for it. Even now, their lives all but forfeit, and these were the thoughts percolating in Rachel Fisher's mind. A twang of metal near her head shook her back to reality and she refocused on the task at hand.

They reached the access panel a few moments later, as the tank turned and began heading their way. Harry and Adam pulled up the heavy plate and threw it clear. Beneath them beckoned the dark maw of the metal staircase, down into the bowels of the tunnels.

She turned and took stock of their motley crew of refugees. A quick count revealed ten of them here; if there were others still in the warehouse, they would have to find their own way. One by one, they disappeared into the darkness, the metal steps clanging under their desperate feet.

Rachel was sixth into the stairwell, the darkness taking hold within a few feet of the last step. The light from above faded, plunging them into total blackness. No one spoke; it was silent but for the ragged gasps of fear. It was tight down here. She could touch both walls of the corridor at the same time. The walls were cool and damp with moisture. It was humid and chilly at the same time.

"Everybody stop," a voice hissed. Sounded like her father, but she couldn't be sure. The acoustics were hell.

The human caravan paused. Rachel bumped squarely into a man's back, her mouth and nose pressing up against his sweat-soaked shirt. The sour stink of fear and exertion filled her nostrils.

"It's about two hundred yards to the farthest stairwell," Adam said. "That's the one we should go for. It'll take us to the cafeteria."

"What about the warehouse?" someone, someone very stupid, Rachel decided, asked.

"We'll deal with that later."

They began their march through the tunnel's inky void. Above her head, the tank continued along its path of destruction, and Rachel hoped the floor could support its gargantuan weight. With every step, she braced herself for the shudder and collapse of the floor above her. Would she feel anything, in that last terrible moment as the tank fell on her, crushing her like an egg? She hoped it would be instantaneous.

She wasn't afraid of dying, not anymore. What she was afraid of was suffering, of being trapped in a netherworld of pain and misery, death on a distant shore, where she would be forced to swim to it, denied the release of her suffering for as long as possible. Death was coming for all of them, never had that been more apparent than in this plague-blasted world of theirs. It might come slowly or it might come quickly, but invariably, it came.

In the tunnels, she felt like she was dead already. Only the sounds of the others shuffling through this black coil with her reminded her she was still alive. It was impossible to tell how long they had been down here. She kept a hand pressed to the tunnel wall, which gave her some reassurance she wasn't lost in time and space, that she really was still here.

She stifled a scream as she passed through a large cobweb, its silky strands twirled around her arm, gluing themselves to her face. She didn't want to be the one to cause a ruckus down here. Spiders, man, spiders, those were bad enough when she saw one in broad daylight, peacefully spinning their webs like Charlotte from the children's book. But she could picture it now, trapped in her hair, burrowing deeper until it found her neck. She slapped at her neck as a shiver rippled through her.

That part of her brain storing the most terrifying images she'd ever seen in movies got to work, the giant spider from the *Harry Potter* movie, the one from *It*, the one that cocooned Frodo in the third *Lord of the Rings* book. Movies she hadn't thought about in a decade or more, and here they were flickering through her mind like she'd seen all three at the San Diego drive-in she had gone to with her mom and stepdad. Around her, the chitter of rodents surprised by the influx of visitors peppered the air.

"How much longer?" a voice thick with fear asked.

"Shut up," another responded. "We'll get there when we get there."

"I gotta get out of here." The first voice again, so choked with fear and terror and tears she couldn't tell if it was female or male. "I gotta get out of here. I can't be down here anymore."

There was a sudden ruckus ahead, a wave of elbows and flailing. Rachel pressed her body to the wall as she felt the quick and sharp breeze of someone running past her, back toward the stairs.

"Let him go!"

Then whoever it was had disappeared, like a bubble that had floated up from the depths of a lake and then vanished once again. They kept moving as the sounds of the footfalls receded behind them. A second later, perhaps ten minutes later, there was no way to know down here where time and space had stopped and mated and birthed this anti-creation of nothingness, she became aware of a faint glow. Her heart soared; they were close now, it had been longer than she had guessed. They were near the exit. They were almost there. Will. She had to get to Will. He was all that mattered now. She pushed herself up off the ground and backed away from the din.

The others kept pace behind her. The darkness had stopped being an issue, something she'd become used to. If anything, it might have been helping keep them alive. Bring on the cobwebs, the rats, the bats, anything down here if it kept their attackers at bay.

A few minutes later, they reached a T-junction. She looked left and then right, but she might as well have been looking with her eyes closed. Each branch was as dark and inscrutable as the other. She had no idea which way to go. A damp hand clamped down on her shoulder, and she gasped.

"Which way is the kitchen?"

"Go. Right." The voice was pained, soft, a throaty whisper, but she recognized it all the same. It was her father.

"Dad? Are you hurt?"

"It's not much farther," he replied, not answering her question.

She draped her right arm around his waist and they staggered toward the exit like drunken revelers headed home after a long night of partying. As they shuffled down the corridor, Rachel became aware of a wetness on her right hand. It was slippery and warm.

"Dad, stop."

He paused, leaned against the wall, grunted. The others continued, streaming around them like fish swimming upstream. Above them, the tank continued to ravage the warehouse, but the sounds had abated some.

She held the hand to her nose and sniffed; the scent was unmistakable. The metallic stink of blood. He was most certainly not fine. He must have taken a round before they made it to the tunnels.

"Let's keep moving."

She pushed everything out of her mind, focusing instead on the task at hand. Her mind was blank, empty. If they couldn't get out of here, then everything else would be rendered irrelevant. Time dissolved into nothingness, an empty void swirling around them. They were here. They were nowhere. Dead, about to be reborn. The life they had known was behind them, a dying mother pushing them through this terrible birth canal into a world whose contours were not yet known. Every step brought them closer to the end, she told herself, each step a vital subset of the set of all the steps they would need to take to escape this dead place.

And with each step, her father weakened, the strain on her shoulder growing as his body listed toward her. Her neck and arm burned, but she pulled him tighter toward her, fully aware of the blood now seeping from his wounded abdomen. His arms were slick with perspiration, and his breath came in short ragged gasps.

"Ow!" a voice ahead called out.

"What?"

"Banged my shin on something," came the reply.

"Steps," her father whispered. "Out."

"It's the staircase," she called out. "The exit."

She gently lowered Adam to the ground.

"Sit here a second," she said. "Eddie and Will should be here."

"OK."

Adam leaned back against the wall and let out a long breath. His quick agreement to her request was what scared her the most. He hated sitting it out, always wanted to be at the forefront of the activity. Bravery, many would say, and that was part of it. He was brave. But he was also stubborn, and he didn't trust many people. If you wanted something done correctly, you did it yourself, that was one of his mantras.

Please, God, please. Rachel Fisher had never been a religious woman, much to her mother Nina's disappointment, but she found herself praying to Him all the same, because she didn't think she could handle getting here and finding out Will and Eddie hadn't made it here.

"Will!" she called out, her voice hitching.

"We're here," Eddie replied, and she clutched her chest in relief.

She ran to her son and hugged him tightly, rubbing her hands over his arms, his face, his head, unconsciously looking for any sign of injury.

"You OK?"

He nodded.

"Everyone wait here," Harry said as he made his way up the steps.

She hustled up the steps behind Harry, not bothering to ask for his permission. He was already at the top, fumbling with the latch. A moment later, he had it free, and they gently pushed it open. The pair climbed out of the tunnels while the others waited in relative safety from the tank's rampage, quiet and shell-shocked. It was quiet and dark in the commercial kitchen, the faintest of shimmer on the stainless appliances.

"I'm going to take a peek."

She wound her way through the dining room to the cafeteria's main entrance. She pushed the door open slightly and poked her head out for a view. A steady rain was falling and a thin fog had blanketed the area. The immediate vicinity was quiet.

She swung her head to the east, toward the main warehouse. A curl of smoke billowed into the sky, the byproduct of a small fire burning somewhere. But that was the least of their problems. Two of the outer walls were gone.

The interior of the warehouse was a picture of devastation. Tears streamed down her cheeks as she absorbed the scope of their loss. It was like some deity had thrown everything into a giant blender and forgotten to replace the lid. Ruined food had spattered everywhere, covering the ground and decorating the broken bits and pieces of concrete and drywall. The bandits had spread through the warehouse, collecting what remained of the canned goods. They were taking the cans now, tossing them by the armload into the bed of their pickups, working until the bed of each truck was sagging under the weight of the food. Others searched the trailers, looking for survivors, but the place was deserted. All the survivors had made it inside the tunnels.

And still the tank was working, now laying waste to the far corner of the building. It barreled along, razing the exterior walls as it went. Then it paused, a fearsome creature holding its breath. A moment later, the sonic boom of its gun firing again; the round slammed into one of the two remaining walls, the sound huge and terrifying. The gun rotated about thirty degrees and fired again, obliterating yet another wall into a cloud of dust and smoke and debris.

On cue, her stomach rumbled. She recalled Will giving her a hard time the other week about eating his dinner and if she could have right then, she would have grabbed him by the shoulders and shaken some sense into him.

You see? This. This is why I always made you eat your dinner. This. All this.

Her stomach rumbled again and she chuckled softly in disbelief.

The destruction was complete a few minutes later. The building had been completely razed, the walls a memory. Once the bandits had finished scrubbing them of their food supply, the tank made another run through the debris field, a good little worker ensuring he had done a good job. It reminded her of her stepdad after he'd cut the grass, taking in his work, returning to that little shaggy patch that had escaped his noisy lawnmower's terrible blade.

Then the tank turned west, motoring directly toward them. After clearing past the rubble, it accelerated. Onward it came, rumbling and belching exhaust as it rolled toward them. The surviving trucks followed, the bandits hooting and hollering, firing off their guns into the air. They were just going to leave them here among the ruins of their home, leaving them to suffer, not even giving them the courtesy of killing them. No, these monsters wanted them to starve to death. They wanted Rachel and the others to suffer. The convoy continued west, leaving a cloud of dust and crushed gravel in its wake.

Will was standing at the window to her left, his little nose pressed up against it. She hadn't heard him come up behind her. With each exhalation and inhalation from his little lungs, the panes fogged and cleared. She stood there, watching him, her shoulders heaving from the exertion, from the adrenaline, from the fear, from the hopelessness that swirled around her like a cloud.

"You OK?"

He nodded. He didn't turn his head to look at her; he knew the score, the mountain of shit upon which they all now stood. As she stood there, one thought kept bouncing around her mind, a lone sock left in the dryer. She couldn't bring herself to return to the kitchen to check on Adam.

Stalling. She was stalling.

If Adam died, then she would never get to call him out for the terrible job he had done as her father for the first eighteen years of her life. She could never yell at him, scream at him, ask him why he'd been clear across the country when she'd said her first word, when she'd taken her first steps, when she'd gone on her first date, when she'd done all the things a father was supposed to be around for but in Adam's case was not. If he lived, she would keep on not asking those questions, she would always be almost about to ask them, but she never would.

"I'm gonna check on Pop-pop."

He nodded again.

She kept her head down as she walked slowly back to the kitchen, trying to push away the worst-case scenario in her mind. He would be okay, her dad. Had a hard shell on him. She'd learned a fair amount of frontier medicine over the years, and she'd fix him up.

The crowd in the kitchen had formed a bubble around Adam, deep enough that she couldn't put eyes on her father. When they noticed her, they began giving way, moving gingerly, as though this kick to their collective midsection had been literal and not figurative.

Someone shifted, opening a clear line of sight for her to see Harry crouched down over Adam, who was now lying prone on the ground. She drew closer, her heart in her throat, placed a hand on Harry's shoulder. He was a big man; even with him in a crouch, she was only a bit taller than him. She didn't know why she did that.

"I'm sorry, honey," Harry said, rocking gently on his heels. It must be bad, she thought. It wasn't in Harry's nature to be magnanimous.

Adam was motionless, his shirt thick with blood. More blood had pooled underneath him, as though his body had been anxious to expel it. His face was gray, lifeless.

She didn't need a doctor to tell her which way the wind was blowing.

Adam Fisher was dead.

6

They wandered toward the ruins of the warehouse, in no rush. Here and there, a body would come into view. After taking Will home to their trailer, Rachel circled what was left of the buildings, following the zig-zag of rubble that had replaced it. Her muscles were heavy with fatigue, every step a struggle. A check of her watch told her it was eight-thirty-four in the morning. Less than two hours ago, it had been the start of just another day, another piece of the great puzzle of their lives.

But that was all over now.

There was nothing to protect here anymore.

She paused at the southwest corner of the Building 1, near a sloppy pile of ruined asparagus or maybe it was spinach. The air smelled ripe and wet. She touched a toe to the compost, calculating how many people this pile would have fed, and for how long. It made her head spin.

By the time she had completed her circuit, Rachel counted twelve dead, including her father and Max Gilmartin. It was a staggering loss for their already small community, which, no one would admit publicly, was only slightly worse than the loss of the warehouse itself.

A gust of wind whistled across the compound, chilling Rachel to her core. Debris from the ruined warehouse swirled in the air.

A group had begun collecting the dead. For an hour they worked, discharging this terrible duty, moving the bodies like sacks of flour and lining them up on an open patch of ground. Twelve in total when all was said and done. Twelve lost. A third of the people who had woken up here this morning were now dead.

(Fewer mouths to feed)

She dismissed that terrible sentiment as quickly as she could, as though someone might be able to read her mind. But she couldn't help it. Fewer mouths to feed meant more for Will to eat.

You're dead, you foolish little woman, you're all dead now.

Her father was dead. Adam Fisher was dead. This was now a statement of fact, whereas an hour ago it had not been. Strange, how flimsy, how malleable reality was. All Adam Fisher had been or would ever be was an account now settled.

A steady wind out of the west blew away much of the cloud cover, and the morning sky brightened around them. Yet it seemed ominous, invasive, violative. A spotlight on all that had gone wrong in their world. An investigator's flashlight inspecting a terrible scene. Jagged shards of concrete resembling broken teeth had replaced the once mighty exterior walls. She crossed the threshold, stepping gingerly around the rubble. The ruined innards of untold foodstuffs were thicker here. The saccharine smell of overripe fruit filled the air. Wet vegetables squished under her boots.

A machine had done this. A single solitary machine had left them with nothing.

Adam had died for nothing. The others had died for nothing.

A few other survivors sifted through the mess, picking at the debris like vultures. Eventually, an assembly line formed, and they piled up what they could save. No one spoke. When they were done, they had salvaged about two hundred cans of food. Enough for about a week, maybe two, and a belt-tightening one at that. The end had come.

"Not much," Romaine said.

"No shit," Rachel replied, shaking her head.

"What are we going to eat?" Erin asked, her voice high and reedy. Her eyes were red and puffy and she made no attempt to hide her tears. She was walking around, beating her head with her hands over and over.

"Not now," Harry said harshly, harsher than he needed to.

"But-"

"But what, Erin?" Harry snapped. "I don't fucking know what we're going to do. Stop asking."

Erin sobbed.

That was how thin the line between calm and chaos had been. And Erin's reaction would not be unique among the survivors. It wasn't too far from her own. Already in her mind's eye, she could see those blue eyes looking at her.

I'm hungry, Mommy.

At least she had the go-bags tucked away in her trailer. That would buy them another week. She didn't feel bad about it, skimming off the top, an MRE here and there. The others had done the same, she was sure of it. In their trailers, in closets and under floorboards, tucked away. And if they hadn't, that was their problem. They should have known this day was coming, and if they hadn't prepared accordingly, then they were lucky to have made it this far. All this, this had been prologue to the way the world really was.

As the morning wound on, the entire community drew in on the ruins like moths to flame. They looked so small, so weak, so vulnerable, just a couple dozen of them wandering around lost. A few arguments bubbled up, but those quickly fizzled out.

This day had always been coming, ever since they had taken control of the warehouse. The thousand-piece puzzle was already complete. It was a matter of organizing the pieces, snapping this one into that one and so on until it was finished. Like the Toba super-eruption her dad had mentioned. The pressure inside that volcano had been building slowly for eons, pointing toward that day. It had always been fated to blow on that day and there was nothing the poor people living on the planet back then could have done about it.

The feeling of helplessness threatened to overwhelm her. She was bobbing along the river of time like an empty bottle, tossed to and fro by the currents, events bigger than her, events that shaped her into whom she was, and not the other way around.

Stop stalling, Fisher.

Behind her, the recovery crew was lining up the bodies. Without sheets, the dead lay exposed for the world to see. Many of the bodies had sustained terrible damage, gunshot wounds and crush injuries and head trauma. Her chest tightened as she watched them clean the bodies, clearing off the blood and the viscera accompanying violent death.

It never got easier. Thirteen years and so many dead, not even counting all those lost in the epidemic. Eventually, you got numb to it. Someone died, you mourned them briefly, and you got on with whatever life you had. That's how it was. That's how it was because it could be you the next day. And today it was her father. Today it was Adam Fisher.

She walked gingerly down the line, down the row of the dead, and knelt by Adam's body. His work shirt was thick and cold with blood. His face was flat, unlined, almost at peace. She leaned in and kissed his forehead.

"Rest, Daddy," she whispered, stroking the back of his hand with her thumb. "You rest now."

The tears began to flow. Her shoulders heaved, and she sobbed ugly, a big nasty cry, her nose filling with congestion, her eyes cloudy with tears as she contemplated a world she had never known, a world without her father in it.

She had no use for notions of heaven or hell, believing instead that whatever bits of matter had once made up Adam Fisher would now go on to make up something else. His work on Earth was done, this burden he had carried for nearly a decade had finally been relieved. The years had been hard on him, as the finality of their situation had become more apparent.

"I'm sorry, Rachel," Harry said, kneeling next to her.

She said nothing, her eyes fixed on her dead father.

"What do we do now?" she asked, the harsh moment between them long since dissolved.

"We bury them."

"Then what?" she asked, her voice becoming a bit more manic.

"We keep going," Harry replied loudly. "We were living on borrowed time anyway. All this does is change the timeline."

Harry pointed at Adam's body.

"He died for us," he continued, making Rachel think of her days in Sunday school and Mrs. White, her young and beautiful and stern teacher. The guilt trip to end all guilt trips. Jesus died for you, you know, He hung from that cross, ribbons of blood flowing from His crucified hands and feet, suffering terrible, agonizing pain while His father, the Big Guy Himself, up there in heaven had looked on and done nothing, until Jesus' lungs had quit, all for your sorry unsaved ass.

"They all died for us. The least we can do is to keep going. It's what I would've wanted if I was lying here instead of Adam. And believe me, I'd trade places with him in a second if I could."

"Don't say that," Rachel said.

She didn't know why she said that other than it seemed like the right thing to say. She would absolutely have traded Harry's life for Adam's. She didn't like Harry, he didn't like her, and if the tables had been turned and he'd been the one lying dead here, she didn't think she'd be all that torn up about it when you got right down to it.

"I would," he said. "I sure as hell would."

And yet his words stabbed at her like tiny knives. Her father lay dead before her, and it bothered her to hear Harry express his loyalty to him? What the hell was the matter with her? He had meant a great deal to the community over the years and in many ways had been its glue. The doctor, their liberator from the Citadel, the peacemaker, the counselor, the explorer. Even his trek east a few years earlier, a journey that had taken him away from them for eight months had not diminished his standing among them. If anything, it had added to his mythos. He had been the one to go out into the empty world, to check the pulse of whatever remained of humanity.

Their fight about it had been terribly bitter. She remembered her surprise at the vehemence of her objection to him going. By then, they had welcomed another physician to their ranks, and so she couldn't make him feel guilty about leaving them high and dry. She didn't think he would ever make it back; it was too dangerous, too unpredictable to assume the journey would end in any manner but with his death. If he died, she would never get to tell him the things she needed to tell him. And when he'd left, it was like he had died.

"We have to know what's going on out there," he'd said.

One spring morning, he and a man named Dan Davies had set out from the compound on horseback, leaving the medical clinic in the hands of the new doctor, Leila Gaskin, or her friend Charlotte Spencer, who had taken to the study of medicine quickly. And that had been that for eight months. After a torturous trip to Richmond, Virginia, where he had lived before the plague, Adam had returned shortly after the first snowfall that November, emaciated, gaunt, near dead, his horse not in much better shape. And alone. Dan had elected to stay back east, deciding to make a go of it near the ocean. Adam slept for days. He kept to himself for weeks afterward, talking little of his eastward journey. That was what had scared Rachel more than anything. The whole point of the trip had been to study the world, to make observations and to report to the community what they had found. But he hadn't said much about it at all.

"Not much out there," he would say, only when pressed. "About what you'd expect."

He'd brought back mementos, photo albums, medical textbooks, his old notes, most of which remained tucked away in his trailer. A trailer that would be dark tonight. A lot of darkened windows in their little community. Not much of a community left, when you got right down to it.

Back home, she found Will waiting at the screen door, his face long and drawn. Above his head, a planter swung in the light breeze, the remnants of a long-dead house plant still hanging lifelessly over the rim. He was looking down, focused on a piece of dry skin in the palm of his hand.

"Is it true?" he asked.

She took a deep breath and let it out.

"I'm sorry, Spoon."

He looked up, his eyes glassing over before the tears spilled over and ran down his cheeks.

"It's not fair," he said. "It's not fair!"

He stormed back inside, leaving her alone outside.

7

Rachel woke up early on the morning of the funerals, two days after the attack on the warehouse. She brushed her teeth and took a bucket bath, her first in a week. Pre-plague Omaha had been serviced by a lineup of 150,000-gallon water towers, many of which had been nearly full when they had moved in. Although electricity had drawn water into the tower, power was not required to push the water through the pipes; gravity took care of that. A team drew water daily from the nearby Platte River, which they deposited into the reservoir feeding their community. It had required a bit of trial and error, but in the end, water had become something they didn't have to worry about.

If there had been one silver lining in all the dark clouds of their lives, it had been this one. They were careful to filter and disinfect all their drinking water, and to date, no one had become sick from drinking it. They also limited baths to two per week. It was the same way all over; water had never been a problem anywhere. She couldn't imagine the hellscape their world would have been if they'd had to fight over water. It was bad enough as it was.

When she was done, she felt almost human again.

She dressed Will in a nice shirt and pants. The clothes smelled a bit musty and had yellowed a bit with age, but she didn't think anyone would mind. While he waited in the living room, she settled on a plain black dress that hung loosely on her thin frame. After dressing, she went out to the living room, where a subdued Will fiddled with a comic book.

"How do I look?" she asked.

He shrugged his shoulders, not looking up.

His grief radiated from him like a fever. A terrible thing, a boy losing his grandfather. Not just a grandfather. Adam had been the primary father figure in Will's life, given Eddie's failure to step up to the plate.

"I miss him too," Rachel said.

He shrugged his shoulders again.

She sat next to him on the sofa, silent. Out of the corner of her eye, she could see him fighting back tears.

"Do you want to talk about it?"

He shook his head.

He hadn't said two words since she'd told him about Adam's passing. The first night, she could hear him crying softly for hours before she'd finally drifted off to sleep. He'd been a wreck the following day, ornery, angry. He refused to eat his breakfast, and when she had forced the issue, he had slid his plate onto the floor. She'd screamed at him for that, wasting food when there was so little to be had.

She took a deep breath and considered the day ahead. All twelve victims of the warehouse attack would be laid to rest today. Harry and Max had recovered the other victims from the ruins of the warehouse, which stopped smoldering when a rainstorm moved in later that evening.

It was hard to look at the ruins.

If they had planned better. If they had heavier weaponry. If they'd had their own tank.

If this.

If that.

You could *if* your way to the nuthouse in this world.

Rachel ignored the pang of hunger in her belly. She could make do with less, at least until they found a new source of food. Like a squirrel stashing away nuts for the winter. It would be okay. Even if she and Will had to strike out on their own, it would be okay. Two mouths weren't that many to feed, right?

It was the first time she had envisioned a life out there, beyond, her and Will, eking out an existence. It was her first conscious acknowledgment of their new reality - Evergreen was dying. She wondered if the others shared her sentiment or whether they would want to press onward together in the face of this new challenge. She wondered what Eddie would want. Would he want to come with them? Or would he be glad to be rid of them?

They bided their time until it was time to go. Will puttered around the trailer listlessly. She wanted to reach him in some way, crack through that shell he'd constructed. He and Adam had been close, very close; it seemed Adam had made a vow to redeem his absent parentage of Rachel via his grandson. Adam gave the boy what little free time he had, yet another player in the card game known as *Rachel's Feelings Toward Her Father*.

Eddie arrived a few minutes later. He hadn't shaved and his eyes were bloodshot. He appeared to be too hungover to engage in any argument. At a quarter to eleven, the trio left the trailer and made the walk to the makeshift cemetery where they had buried their dead over the years. About a dozen people had perished in their time here, forever interred in this lonely corner of the campus. Each grave was marked with a wooden cross, two thick sticks lashed together to form a T. She didn't know why they used crosses, she didn't know if the dead had been Christian or if they were even religious at all, but it felt weird not placing a marker, no better than leaving the bodies in a ditch. The markers classed it up a bit.

The sky was gray but bright, the overcast shimmer making her eyes ache. It was still the same distance to the cemetery it had always been, but the walk seemed much longer this morning. Her feet hurt, her legs felt heavy. Around her, other survivors were making their way as well, coming in dribs and drabs, their gaits, slow methodical, no one really wanting to do this. Will walked like he'd been kicked in a very sensitive spot. There was no malfeasance from him today. Just a boy who missed his grandfather.

Twelve open graves awaited them when they arrived at the cemetery. Harry had once again taken the lead in getting things organized. He had worked nonstop yesterday digging the graves, late into the night, and his face showed it.

She, Eddie and Will stood at the front, their son in between them. As she waited for things to get underway, the wooden fencing surrounding the physical plant building caught her eye. It was warped, rotting, the boards pulling away from the support posts. And then she was thinking about all the other things that were rotting around them. You could feel the world winding down around you, you could almost hear it, like an old watch, its batteries finally giving up the ghost.

"Good morning," Harry said, his booming voice jostling her out of her daydream.

She glanced around the crowd; everyone was here. The faces were familiar, the same faces she'd been seeing month after month, year after year. Her gaze settled on Erin and Charlotte, the two people she'd probably been closest to in the community. They stood side by side, together, whispering. As Rachel watched them, she couldn't remember when she'd last spent any real time with either of them. They'd been through a lot together, especially her and Erin, and here they were, not necessarily strangers, but not the family they had once been. She caught a glance from Charlotte, who gave her the pressed-lip head nod. Rachel returned the nod, and Charlotte dipped back into her conversation with Erin. If anything, she had grown closer to Charlotte over the years; Charlotte had never become pregnant, had never wanted to have kids, and remained one of the few women to not look at Rachel with envy or judgment or contempt.

Another thing winding down.

"We've suffered a terrible loss," Harry said. He went on, and Rachel drifted into another daydream as he eulogized Paul, the one who'd been cut down trying to escape the warehouse. A little story about Paul. He'd been a regional manager for Best Buy before the epidemic and he had loved the Boston Bruins. He liked the Pats, Sox, and Celtics well enough, but the Bruins had been his first love. He'd been divorced when the plague hit. Had a son in the Army, assigned to a quarantine zone in San Antonio when everything had gone to hell. She tried to listen, she should listen, but these sad, beautiful stories of those they had lost simply did not hold her attention.

Soon it was her turn.

She squeezed Will's hand and made her way to the front. Her head hurt and she could feel a twitch forming over her left eye. In her pocket, some notes she had sketched out, things she could say to celebrate the life of the man who had done so much for her, for all of them.

There was no podium, no dais, no slideshow of Adam's life whirring behind her. Just Rachel standing there, looking out over those long, drawn faces, faces she might be saying goodbye to very soon. Things were ending here, she knew it the way you knew a relationship was over, even when it was still running on autopilot. She took in a deep breath of the chilly air and let it out, the cloud of breath transfixing her. The cold air brisk and refreshing on her cheeks.

"My father was a great man," she said, reading from her note, her weight shifting from one foot to the other.

She had never given a eulogy before.

Was it supposed to be happy? Sad?

Was it for her? Was it for them?

Was it for him?

"Many years ago, he did a great thing," she said. "For me. For some of you."

It all came back to her in a rush, her time as a prisoner at a place called the Citadel. She'd been strapped to that hospital bed as those men had begun the procedure, looking up and seeing her father, positive she was hallucinating because how could he have found her out there, in the dark, in the cold, in the great nothing of the world after the outbreak. But there he'd been, against all odds, somehow, he had found her and saved so many.

Her hand absently stroked the inside of her wrist, home to the tattoo they had given her at the Citadel. A phoenix rising from the ashes. One by one, she made eye contact with the women who had been held captive at the Citadel with her, women who had identical tattoos, and each of whom nodded. The ones who would have died if not for Adam's ridiculous rescue attempt. It had been something out of a movie. A regular old Rambo.

Her hands slipped behind her back, and she laced her fingers together, crumpling the note. Her feet were crossed now. She couldn't get comfortable. She didn't know what to do with her hands. A podium would have been nice. Something to hold on to. To give her purchase, here in the roiling waters of this terrible day.

She glanced at the note again. A few sentences she had jotted down last night as sleep had eluded her. Looking at them now, in the light of day, they looked naked, exposed, the emperor with no clothes. Letters making up words which made up sentences. Squiggly lines. Sharp lines. Jagged slashes. They looked dead on the page. Broken pieces of glass.

Lifeless.

What was wrong with her?

She tucked the note back into her pocket and ran her fingers through thick, perpetually messy brown hair. Bile crept into her throat. She looked at the women Adam had saved, at the others to whom he had meant so much. Her heart swelled, but not from joy, not from pride. It felt like someone was pushing down on her chest, the way it felt when someone had wronged you, when someone had gotten the better end of the deal, when someone had gotten away with it, whatever *it* was. When there wasn't a goddamn thing you could do about it.

Like now.

The way they all looked at her with their sad faces, their tears running down their cheeks. They had that luxury, to see Adam as this post-apocalyptic savior, a martyr, might as well start calling him St. Adam, they could do that now here in the First Church of Omaha, Nebraska, in the People's Free Republic of Whatever the Hell This

Was. They did not have to know what she had known about him her whole life before the plague.

Anger.

"He was a smart man, my father," she said. "He knew how to fix things, how to fix people. And I get why you all looked up to him. I do."

She paused, conscious of what she was doing, giving herself one last chance to pull the emergency brake, bring this whole goddamn thing to a screeching halt before she passed the point of no return. But she couldn't.

"I didn't know my father well before Medusa," she said. "I grew up in California, and he stayed back in Virginia. I kept thinking he would move out to be near me, but he never did. I never understood that. He was a doctor. People in California needed doctors. Wouldn't he want to be near his only daughter?"

The words came easily now, spraying out of her like water from a hydrant.

"Let me tell you guys a story," she said. People shifted from one foot to another, exchanged nervous glances with one another. She watched the scene shift from mournful to awkward, but she didn't care. They needed to hear this about their superhero.

"He planned to fly out to San Diego for my high school graduation," she said, thinking about all the good he had done in this new world but continuing with her story anyway. "This was about a year before the outbreak. The day before he's supposed to fly out, he calls me and says that one of his patients needs him, she's had a difficult pregnancy, he's really sorry but he won't be able to make it."

Warm tears streamed down her icy cheeks, and she wiped them away with the backs of her wrists. The yard was silent now; no one spoke, no one moved a muscle. She turned toward the graves, where she could see her father's body lined up with the others. Her wise, brave, selfish, shitty father. It came at her all at once, her emotions waging a terrible battle inside her for control about how she really felt.

There was more to the story, she was sure of it, but she simply stood there in front of the other survivors, rubbing her hands together, shifting her weight from one foot to the other, not sure what she was supposed to do next. She had a point to make, an important point here at her father's funeral, but it was gone.

She clapped a hand over her mouth and ran, leaving Will, leaving Eddie, leaving all of them behind. She sobbed, her mournful howls filling the morning quiet. The tears continued to fall, her body shaking, she ran for the trailer, wanting nothing more than to hide away from Will, from Eddie, from everyone, from the world she was in.

CHARLOTTE SPENCER CAME to see her the next morning.

They sat at the kitchen table, drinking strong, bitter coffee. Rachel's hands trembled from the caffeine, her stomach sour and tight. On the table was an old photograph of her father, back from his college days. She had found it in his old things as she wandered the trailer like a troubled spirit and had spent much of the night staring at it, entranced by it. The photo was old and yellowed, snapped at a semi-formal event more than three decades ago. Adam, dressed in khakis and a blazer, stood next to a pretty girl in a strapless red dress, a string of pearls encircling her slender neck. Their smiles were broad and deep, loosened perhaps by the cheap beer in the bottle each was holding, two young people with their whole lives in front of them. Rachel could just make out the time on the girl's digital watch, tilted just so toward the camera. Seven twenty-six in the evening. On the back of the photo, in faint blue ink, the numerals 4/2, the date of the event, she supposed, were etched into the upper right corner. She felt bad for them, she hated knowing the dark future that lay ahead for them both.

Rachel had never told her father about how disappointed she'd been that he'd missed her graduation. He couldn't find another doctor to cover that patient? Doctors did it all the time. They traded patients like baseball cards. Why was this one any different? Oh sure, he'd been apologetic, he'd watched a livestream of the ceremony from her mom's iPhone, but the damage had been done. Ever since the day she was born, she had been the runner-up in the priorities of Adam's life, second to all the women who came to see him.

She had never told anyone about it until the funeral. So many times, it had been right there on the tip of her tongue. If she could have told Adam this one thing, tell him how badly it had hurt her, maybe they could repair this rupture between them, the rupture that had been there all along. But she never did. And now it was too late.

The trailer was quiet. Will was in his room, the door shut tight. Rachel lit a cigarette, old and stale.

"I wanted to check on you," Charlotte said.

"I'm fine," Rachel replied, blowing a stream of blue smoke into the air.

"We need to talk," Charlotte said.

"He was my father," she said, her eyes down in her coffee. "Not theirs."

"I know," Charlotte said. "And it's easy for people to forget that. To them, he's a folk hero. To me, too, if I'm being honest."

Rachel snorted in disgust.

Charlotte held up her hands in surrender.

"It's not fair, I know that," she said. "I know no one is perfect. It was nice to have someone to believe in, someone who never let you down."

"Don't you think I know that?" Rachel snapped.

They sat quietly. Will coughed, and Charlotte's eyes cut toward the bedroom. She took a sip of the coffee and set her mug back on the table.

"I'm sorry you had to go through that," Charlotte said. "Must've been hard."

"No one's life was p[illegible]

"Cheers to that."

Charlotte took a sip of her coffee. She started to set the mug back down but paused. She lifted the mug back to her lips and took another sip.

"There's something else I wanted to talk to you about."

As Charlotte gathered her thoughts, Rachel scraped at a piece of long-dried food encrusted on the tabletop. A cylinder of ash fell from the forgotten cigarette still clamped between her two fingers and landed in a perfect little pile. She traced her finger in the ash, leaving a dark smudge on the tip of her finger.

"You know I love Will, right?"

"I guess," she said, but not really knowing. Truth be told, she didn't know how Charlotte felt about Will at all. Everyone had their own unique relationship with Will, but she wasn't sure if any of them were normal. A bitter reminder of the past. A possible savior. A target of envy. No one knew how to act around him. It was a lot for an eleven-year-old to carry. She didn't want to open another front in this discussion, so she sat quietly. Let Charlotte say her piece and move on. She traced a circle in the ash deposit on the table with a finger.

"It's just that..."

She paused.

"It's just what?" Rachel said.

"Now that your father's gone, I worry people will forget how special Will is."

"What are you talking about?" she asked, a spike of discomfort making her shiver.

"Your dad loved Will," Charlotte said. "Talked about him all the time."

Yet another twist of the knife from dear old Dad.

"I know."

Charlotte cast her eyes downward; perhaps her words were floating in the coffee mug.

"I get it," Rachel said, her argument with Eddie playing back in her mind. "Will freaks people out."

Charlotte smiled thinly.

"No, sweetie, I don't think you do."

"Enlighten me."

Charlotte glanced at the ceiling and took a deep breath.

"I mean, that's a part of it," she said. "But it goes deeper than that.

They're afraid of him. Of you. They're jealous. They're angry. They want to know why."

"I knew that," Rachel said, although she was still a bit surprised by the depth and breadth of her hostility toward her friend. She looked back across the years, understanding now her sense of connection to the group weakening as Will had grown up. Her shoulders sagged. Alone again. As it had always been.

"Don't you think I've wondered about it?" she asked. "Don't you think I've lain awake at night, wondering what was so goddamn different about me? About my family? You think it didn't crush me to see all those babies die?"

"I know," Charlotte said. "But people are scared. And now that the warehouse is gone, it's getting worse. I mean, you wouldn't believe some of the things people have said."

"Like what?"

"Crazy stuff," Charlotte said. "But your father always shut it down. He made them believe we'd had a little bad luck, that eventually, things would turn around."

Rachel laughed bitterly.

"It's been thirteen years," she said. "I think that ship has sailed."

"Whether it has or not, your father kept the ship steady, kept it afloat."

"And now he's gone."

"Right," Charlotte said. "And without your father here to cover you, I wanted to make sure you knew the score. When people get desperate, they do crazy things. Be very careful. And what happened at the funeral yesterday, it made people angry."

Still, she felt no regret. In fact, she felt better than she had in months. Maybe years. Maybe ever. Clear. Cleaned out.

"Thank you for letting me know," Rachel said.

"You're welcome," she said. "How are things with Eddie?"

She dismissed the question with a wave of her hand.

They sat in silence for a long while, the coffee cooling in their cups, the seconds ticking by, time winding toward the inevitability of it all. She looked at Charlotte, her face hardened by the passage of time but still quite lovely. She'd been on her own all this time; her sexual orientation was well known in the community, but as fate would have it, there were no other gay people living in Evergreen. Or none that had come out.

"What about you?" Rachel asked.

"What about me?"

"Do I freak you out?"

Charlotte smiled.

"No more than anything else," she said.

Rachel tried to laugh at the joke, but she couldn't.

"I never wanted kids," Charlotte said. "Even when I was a little girl, I knew in my core that it wasn't for me. So I look at this a bit more objectively than the others. I think Will is a gift. I think you're a wonderful mother. I agree with your dad. He explained it to me once. Will can't be the only one. It doesn't make any sense. It would be one thing if none of the babies had survived. That, at least, would be explainable. But Will survived."

"I don't know," Rachel said. "Sometimes I think he would say those things, but he didn't actually believe them. He wasn't the same when he got back from that trip back east. I think he got out there, in the big open, and saw what he was most afraid of."

Charlotte was shaking her head forcefully.

"No!" Charlotte snapped, slapping her hand on the table. "I refuse to believe that this is it. This isn't the end. It can't be."

"But what if it is?" Rachel said.

Charlotte opened her mouth to say something, but Rachel held up a hand to cut her off.

"Hear me out," she said. "He never would. But please hear me out. What if this is it? What do we do? Live out our days, knowing this is really the end?"

"I don't know."

"I think about him growing up in this, and it rips me to pieces," Rachel said. "Sometimes I'll lie awake all night thinking about what his life will be like. Who's the next youngest person here?"

Charlotte scrunched up her face and gazed at the ceiling.

"I think Emily, maybe? She's twenty or so."

"And that's assuming he lives that long."

"Don't say that."

"I'm trying to be realistic," Rachel said. She pushed the coffee mug to the center of the table.

"We'll figure something out."

Charlotte took Rachel's hand between her own.

"We'll do the best we can," Charlotte said. "We fight like hell to make it. We enjoy this life as best as we can. Did you know I've started praying?"

"Oh?"

"Every night. I know you're a science geek," Charlotte said, her cheeks flushing with embarrassment. "And I never had much use for organized religion. But in the past few years, I've started to see God everywhere. It makes me feel a little better. I don't know if there's a heaven. If there's a hell, I'm pretty sure we've lived through it."

"You think all this was God's judgment?"

"Maybe," she said. "Maybe it wasn't. Maybe it wasn't a judgment any more than my shaking an Etch-a-Sketch is a judgment on all those little bits of aluminum powder. Maybe we don't even understand what judgment means."

Charlotte laughed out loud.

"I sound like a lunatic."

Rachel did not reply.

"Besides, we have far more immediate concerns," Charlotte said. "How are you on food?"

Rachel glanced toward Will's bedroom.

"Few days," she said, suddenly feeling like they'd been dropped back on the shore of their current mess. "Maybe a week."

"A lot of arguing after the funerals last night," Charlotte said. "I hung in there until dark, and then I couldn't take it anymore."

"What's the consensus?"

"There isn't one," she said. "Some folks want to hit the road and see what's out there. Others don't want to abandon the water supply. Eddie's headed up to Market to see what he can find out."

"And the others?"

"I wouldn't worry too much about them," Charlotte said, nodding toward the door, to the community beyond.

"Why do you say that?"

"Another week, and this place will be empty."

8

They set the trap before dawn, under a spray of stars stretching away to infinity. They were about four miles west of the compound, along Interstate 80, one of the few still serviceable freeways approaching the city. Still road mostly, but shaggy with moss and weeds. She and Eddie worked in silence, Rachel knowing the best way to avoid yet another go-nowhere argument would be to keep her mouth shut.

It was a chilly night, cloudy and damp. There would be rain by midday. On the trek out here, they passed by the familiar buildings in this industrial section of southwest Omaha. She knew every nook and cranny of every one of them. Metalworks here. Equipment rental over there. Inside and out, every one of them, every structure in a ten-mile radius of Evergreen, explored, dug through and spelunked.

The intricate network of roads crisscrossing America had fallen into disrepair over the years, more evidence of a world winding down. Most resembled the surface of some dead planet, pockmarked with large potholes resembling craters, the pavement buckled from endless cycles of freezing, thawing, expanding and then cracking again. Cars abandoned on the highways at the height of the plague sat where they'd last hitched to a stop, rusting, cracking, peeling, disintegrating. Many still contained the skeletal remains of plague victims who had died during their futile attempt to outrun their invisible slayer.

The steady traffic along the busier thoroughfares kept the weeds at bay a little, but it too was a losing battle. Each day, little by little, they retreated a bit more as these titanic forces of life, of nature, gained more ground. Within weeks of the plague ending, a generation of weeds and grasses had risen through the tiniest cracks and died, succeeded by their descendants, which rose before dying as well, decomposing, ashes to ashes, dust to dust, until a carpet of humus blanketed the asphalt and it disappeared forever. You could feel it all slipping away now, their grim fate set in concrete that was almost finished curing.

It had been two weeks since the attack on the compound. Even limiting rations, they were burning through food faster than they had anticipated. A day of reckoning was approaching rapidly; each night she had lain awake and decided as to whether to stay or go, whether the time had come to pull the ripcord and flee with Will. If there was food, they would stay.

But now this.

Highway robbery. Literally.

Every day for the past week, Harry had been sending two-person teams out here with orders to rob any travelers they encountered. To date, the results had been mixed. Five teams had come home empty-handed, but one pair – Dave Thompson and Brigid Correll – had returned with a few grocery bags of canned goods, some medicine, and a small cache of ammunition. They had taken the beat-up old pickup without firing a shot, sending their victims away on foot. Rumors were flying that some of the unsuccessful sorties had been because they didn't want to rob innocent people.

The trap was simple enough. Eddie used a pair of binoculars to scout for any approaching traffic. If the target was promising, he and Rachel pushed the rusting chassis of an old Honda Civic into the middle of the roadway, in the blind curve, right at the point it would be too late to turn back. Then they'd circle in behind the prey and take them before they could put up a fight.

When the preparations were finished, Eddie napped, but Rachel lay on her back and looked at the stars while waiting for sunrise. Sometimes she would start counting them, never quite sure why, knowing she would lose count after twenty or thirty. But she did it anyway. The stars were her favorite thing about their world, on the rare occasion the skies cleared long enough to give them a view of the heavens. So many stars scraping the roof of the world that it looked like the sky was bleeding starlight. Without electricity, you could see entire galaxies, you could see the constellations the way their ancestors had and you understood why they named them the way they did, glorious names like Orion and Cassiopeia and Aquarius and Aries.

Dawn approached and she willed it to stay dark a little bit longer. She liked the darkness, she liked the night; it let them hide from the world for a little while. Because when the sun came up, there the world was, in all its dying and barren grotesqueness.

Eddie was still asleep, and that was fine with her. She took the first shift watching the road. It was boring and tedious but at least it kept her mind off the cold temperatures. By mid-morning, Eddie was awake and a light drizzle had begun to fall. The air was dank and Rachel was shivering. Beside her, Eddie lay prone under a giant billboard for a McDonald's, the Egg McMuffin and cup of gourmet coffee long since faded. He was propped up on his elbows, the field glasses pressed to his eyes. She sat with her knees drawn into her chest, rocking back and forth to stay warm. The M4 lay next to her like an obedient dog.

"You really made a mess of your dad's funeral," he said, startling her. It was the first time either had spoken since they trekked out here.

She glanced at him. With all the problems they were facing, her eulogy was about the last thing on her mind. That said, she felt a tightness in her chest. She shouldn't say anything, she should just let it go and eventually Eddie would let it go too. But she couldn't resist.

"He was my dad. Not yours," Rachel said, her nostrils venting vapor like smoke in the morning chill.

"Not sure where you get off."

"I'm not going to even dignify that with a response."

"I can't have you flying off the handle about every goddamn thing," Eddie said. "Makes us look bad."

"Makes you look bad is what you mean."

Instead of replying, he pressed a finger to his lips and gestured toward the highway. He handed her the binoculars and she focused on the flutter of movement in the distance. She adjusted the lenses until the scene came into view. They were still a ways off, maybe a mile away. Three of them, sitting abreast in a horse-pulled wagon under that brooding sky. In the middle, holding the reins, was an older man, probably in his late fifties. He wore a thick beard heavily dusted with gray. His dirty barn jacket hung loosely over a thin frame. A young woman sat on his left, her cheek bearing a nasty scar. Her hair was tied off in a messy ponytail, and her eyes puffed with exhaustion. A shotgun lay on her lap. On the old man's right was a boy of about fifteen or sixteen, his face pockmarked with acne. He wore a gray sweatshirt emblazoned with the five Olympic rings and the words *Rio 2016* printed underneath.

Their faces were narrow and gaunt, the angular visages of those who had not had a warehouse full of food at their disposal for the past decade. They stared straight ahead, their heads bobbing as the wagon jostled down the road. The look in their eyes spoke of people who did not seem to care all that much whether they made it to their destination. Even the horse looked uninterested. His ribs jutted from his dull coat, a living fossil.

A black tarp covered the wagon's cargo area, but the corner flap had folded back over itself, revealing part of its load. Rachel caught a glimpse of a case of baby formula and several boxes of dry soup. A sharp ache spiked up Rachel's midsection, part hunger, part guilt.

She tapped Eddie on the shoulder; when she caught his eye, she shook her head slowly and deliberately and made a cutting motion at her throat, the signal to abort the mission. Eddie rolled his eyes and slapped her hand away.

"We are not doing this," she said sharply under her breath.

"That's meat for the pot. For Will."

"Look at these people," she said, tipping her head toward the wagon. "We'd be killing them."

"You'd rather our son starve?"

Oh, he was "our" son now. And he was right, of course, the little shit.

But there had to be a line somewhere. Every day they drew ever closer to it, assuming they hadn't already crossed it and they were too far gone to realize it. Was survival worth the price of her humanity? Did she want to cross that line? How far was too far?

She looked through the binoculars again. Quarter of a mile away now. Three minutes, maybe five. The road behind them was empty. Was she serious about trying to stop Eddie? She could scare him with the gun. She could do that. She could press the barrel of this steel serpent against his temple and whisper into his ear that they were not going to do a goddamn thing to these people, that they were going to let that scrawny horse clomp on by.

But she didn't. A grainy movie of a possible future played out in her mind, the story of Will starving to death because they were out of food and she'd think back to the time they had let this wagon go because she'd wanted to do the right thing.

They kept coming, the horse's hooves clocking loudly on the weed-choked pavement, the wagon's occupants blissfully blind to the threat that lay ahead. Guilt coursed through her veins; it wasn't fair that these people had no chance, that nothing more than dumb luck had brought them to this point. Rachel pressed low to the ground as the wagon curled south, the road funneling them into the trap.

The woman was the first to perk up as the wreck came into view, her hands going straight for the shotgun. She stood up as the wagon slowed, placing a hand on the old man's shoulder for balance. Her head swiveled from side to side.

"Aw, what the hell is this," the old man muttered as he pulled on the reins, bringing the horse to a stop.

"Quiet," the woman said.

Rachel locked eyes with Eddie, who nodded. They bounced from their hiding spot and drew up behind the wagon before the woman could turn to face them.

"Nobody fucking move," Eddie barked.

They froze, their bodies locking up as the paradigm shift was driven home for them. A few moments ago, it had been just another day, but now everything had changed. The woman's shoulders sagged.

Eddie kept his gun trained on the trio as he eased around the side of the wagon to the front. Rachel drifted to the left, keeping the woman squarely in her sights.

"Where you folks headed?" Eddie asked.

No one answered.

He stepped forward and aimed the gun at the woman's head. His nostrils flared and his brow was furrowed, which made Rachel nervous. He was in a bad mood, worse than usual.

"I'll ask again."

"Market," the old man said, his voice gravelly.

"Well, we're going to save you the trip," Eddie said.

The old man scratched his face, the sound of his fingernails against his rough beard huge in the morning quiet.

"Leave us half," the man said. "This here's all we got in the world."

"I'm not negotiating," Eddie replied. "You folks kindly step down from the wagon, and we'll be on our way."

There was an ease about Eddie that Rachel found disconcerting. It was a big deal what they were doing. Just because something was necessary didn't mean it should be easy or enjoyable. It mattered. Robbing these people was akin to signing their death warrants. Maybe they'd find another week's worth of supplies somewhere, maybe not. That's what she told herself. Out there, that big empty world was getting emptier by the day. People, innocent people, died for no good reason every single day.

It would bother her tonight and tomorrow and next month, as it always did. Theirs was a world of takers and victims and today they would be the takers. Tomorrow, perhaps, they would play a different role.

"What's your name, old timer?"

Old timer?

Did he think they were in a Western?

"Austin," the man said. "Adam Austin."

"Mr. Austin, nobody has to get hurt here today. Toss the gun into the grass."

Austin nodded toward the woman. As she picked it up from her lap, the boy lunged for it and wrenched it from her; she struggled with him, that instinct to resist kicking in hard. It happened so quickly Rachel barely had time to react. The boy got off one shot at Eddie, but it flew wide. The horse reared back and neighed in terror before slipping its reins and bolting up the road.

Eddie returned fire, the report of his gun roaring across the plains. His first shot struck the woman in the forehead, caving it in. Blood splattered across the sleeve of Austin's jacket. The boy fired another shot, again missing badly. Eddie returned fire again, catching the boy in the stomach. The kid dropped the gun and staggered to the edge of the wagon before tumbling out like a sack of potatoes.

The guns fell silent, the sulfuric smell of discharged weapons hanging thickly in the air. Rachel stood frozen to her spot, her gun still trained on the wagon. It was over. Two more dead in the ledger of the plague. The older man slowly raised his arms high over his head. From here, she could see his thick wrinkled hands were gnarled with arthritis, the fingers drawn tight like leathery claws.

"Dammit!" Eddie bellowed. "This didn't have to happen. This is on you."

Rachel drew up next to Eddie, her jaw clenched tight. It had happened again. Another thing gone straight to hell. More bodies, more death, more unhappy endings, and here was Eddie acting like the man had tapped his bumper in a Walmart parking lot.

She cut her eyes toward Eddie; his face was beet-red and he was chewing on his lower lip. The gun in his hand dipped and dove, almost like it had a mind of its own, anxious in Eddie's sweaty palm. You could almost feel the gun wanting to go off, to do the thing it was designed to do.

"What am I supposed to do with you?"

He looked at Rachel.

"What am I supposed to do with him?"

The rush of adrenaline faded, and she shivered in the cold damp air.

"Let him go," Rachel said. "Let's take a look at their stash."

She walked gingerly to the back of the wagon, her stomach clenched, her leg muscles tight and stiff. Using both hands, she peeled back the tarp, which made a strange zipping noise as it folded back over itself before sliding to the ground in a heap.

"What do we got?" Eddie called out.

Her heart soared when she saw the full scope of their score. Baby formula, canned goods, medicine, guns, ammunition, soap. A jackpot, one that bought them a little more time. One unusual item caught her eye. It was a large metal briefcase. She fiddled with the latch, but it was locked.

"A lot," she said, feeling guilty and relieved at the same time. These would fetch a hefty price at Market and, she briefly forgot about the blood that had been spilled in the acquisition of this bounty.

Eddie laughed, a high-pitched cackle that was equal parts victory and desperation.

"Fuck you," the old man said.

Eddie clocked the man on his forehead, opening a wide gash above his eyebrow. Blood leaked from the laceration, which resembled a small mouth, its thin lips parted just so. Austin made no move to address the wound, letting the blood trickle down his cheek before rolling off his chin in fat crimson drops. Even when the trail of blood changed course, curling in toward the corner of Austin's mouth, he sat stoically, unmoving.

"Shut up," Eddie said. "Nobody's talking to you."

Rachel rejoined Eddie, uncomfortable with the tension still lingering. It should have been over, the spasm of violence defusing the situation. But things were still buzzing. Eddie was obviously still charged up, the adrenaline still flowing. This had to be fear driving him, controlling his strings like a puppeteer.

"Folks is waiting for me over at Market," he said. "I don't show up, there's gonna be questions."

Eddie pressed the gun to the man's head.

"Could've been anyone," Eddie said. "Highways are dangerous."

"Why don't you hit the road, my friend," Rachel said. "I'm sorry it turned out this way."

"He's not going anywhere."

A burst of frustration then, that feeling of skin tightening and stomach turning to stone when someone simply would listen to reason.

No more. They were going to let this man go.

"Make you a deal," the man said.

"You're not in any position to be making deals."

The man continued, ignoring him. "You give me the briefcase, I'll pin this on someone else."

"What briefcase?"

"There's one in the back," Rachel said, her eyes narrowing. "It's locked."

"Let's have the key," Eddie said.

Now it was the man's turn to laugh.

"I don't have the key. I'm just the messenger."

"Stand up," Eddie ordered. He patted the man down, searching every pocket, every inch of fabric in his clothing. Maybe Eddie would order the man to strip and conduct a body cavity search.

"Search the others," Eddie said to Rachel.

"Don't bother, miss."

"What's inside the case?"

He laughed again.

"I don't know, and I don't want to know." A shimmer of fear rippled across his face.

Rachel was struck by the man's sincerity.

"And what's in for you?"

"Two months' worth of supplies."

"You lie," Eddie said.

"No," Rachel said. "I don't think he is."

"Shut up, Rachel. He's lying. Now tell me what it's in the briefcase."

She stepped up to Austin and jammed the muzzle of the M4 under his chin.

"You're not lying, are you?" she snapped. "You better not be lying."

It was a gamble, a mild escalation in lieu of a far more serious one. By taking the offensive, Eddie could live vicariously through her. She wasn't going to shoot him, but Eddie didn't know that. It had a certain bravado to it, and that was the point. Launching a successful conventional attack rather than risk a catastrophic nuclear one. Eddie stepped back, lowering his weapon. She leaned in close to Austin until their faces were an inch apart, until she could smell the decay on his breath, the sour stench of days-old body odor.

"I ain't lying."

"Good."

Austin chuckled. He tilted his head to the side and looked over Rachel's shoulder.

"You always let your bitch run the show?"

She turned to wrap her arms around Eddie's waist before it was too late, but it was already too late. It unfolded in slow motion: Eddie putting the gun between the man's eyes, Eddie pulling the trigger, the small dime-sized entry hole appearing in the man's forehead. Austin's head rocking backward from the impact, his body slumping over in the wagon, coming to rest in the lap of his dead traveling companion. The echo of the gunshot reverberated across the chilly land. The single report had seemed louder to Rachel than the gunplay that preceded it. It felt more final, more definitive. Her left ear was ringing and deadened, a sonic anesthetic mainlined into her eardrum. She touched a hand to her ear and it came away bloody. Eddie had ruptured her goddamn eardrum.

"You believe this asshole?" Eddie said, his voice shaky and small.

"Was it worth it?" she yelled. "Was it?"

The world sounded muffled and far away.

She walked away, leaving Eddie with the bodies of his victims and the wagon of supplies, the smell of coppery blood and smoke hanging in their air.

9

When all was said and done at the end of that fateful and terrible summer thirteen years earlier, nearly ninety-nine percent of the world's population had perished in the viral holocaust. Of the seven billion humans alive and kicking on the day Medusa had been dispersed at Yankee Stadium, only about one hundred million were still around on Labor Day some four weeks later. In the years that followed, natural selection got in on the act, culling approximately one-third of those survivors in a variety of ways, either by accident or means most foul or, most cruelly, from random illness that would have been easily treated in the old days. Put another way, you did not want your appendix to flake out on you in this new world.

The population of the continental United States shrank to about four million, less than half the number of people living in pre-plague New York City. While Adam Fisher had trekked westward looking for Rachel in the months after the epidemic, the vast majority of the other survivors had had no such heroic quest. These survivors spent their time attending to far more mundane tasks. Staying alive. Not going completely insane. Food. Water. Shelter. Medicine. Self-defense. Survivors sheltered in place, remaining in their homes, venturing out only when necessary to obtain supplies, slowly coalescing to form small communities. PTSD was common. Many people turned to drugs and alcohol to cope with the disaster.

In Omaha, Nebraska, Medusa spared about three thousand people, nearly all of whom remained in and around the city after the epidemic ended. They were scattered from the inner city to the suburbs. When the outbreak began, the nation's cupboards had been stocked with tens of millions of canned and dry goods, enough to meet the needs of a tiny population for a good while. For the first few years after the plague, there had been little need for commerce, as the supply of virtually everything had far outstripped the demand. Few communities formed in those early days, as the survivors were too scattered to find each other in large numbers, and many were too frightened to join with people they did not know.

Even after taking the warehouse, Rachel and the others scavenged the neighborhoods in the western Omaha suburbs. It never ceased to amaze her how many homes there were, how much food the average family had stockpiled. It could take a team of four a full day to clear five houses of their various and sundry supplies. They learned to make bread and hunt, until the crop failures began wreaking havoc on the wildlife. For a while, it seemed as if the food would never run out.

But time took its toll, both through consumption and spoilage, and exacerbated by the fact that virtually nothing new was growing. Eventually, shortages began to pop up, particularly of food and medicines. Rachel began noticing how many X's they'd marked on their maps to note neighborhoods they had cleared. One day, they'd encountered another gaggle of survivors a bit farther east toward downtown, an encounter that briefly turned violent but ended with only one person wounded. Five thousand people in a city designed to hold many times that didn't seem like much on paper, but she was surprised by how crowded it felt.

The story was that a group in east Omaha needed a stockpile of antibiotics after two of their members were badly injured in an accident. What they did have was fresh milk from a cow they had nursed back to health; they traded the milk for the medicine another small community had stockpiled, and lo and behold, capitalism was reborn.

A month later, as legend had it, the two parties to the initial trade met again, this time here, at the West Omaha Farmer's Market, where a gallon of biofuel was swapped for a bottle of twenty-year-old Pappy Van Winkle bourbon whiskey. Word of the market began to spread across southern Nebraska, and each month brought a handful of new faces. A fight erupted at one Market about a year in, leaving four dead. That led to the Market Compact, which every trader was required to sign before participating. Any violation of the Compact was punished by immediate and permanent expulsion from the Market.

Every first Thursday of the month, the Market opened at dawn.

RACHEL AND EDDIE left while everyone slept, or more specifically, slept fitfully, if at all. Whatever the case, the compound would be quiet today, as there were no more shifts to cover, no watches to keep, no more defenses to fortify. They were on vacation now, a brief pause before whatever lay ahead. She tried not to think about it, but her mind was pulling on it like a tractor beam, these thoughts of a terrible future now imminent.

She and Eddie set out on foot, planning to cover the six miles to Market in about two hours. There had been a brief discussion of cycling there, but Rachel preferred to walk. A bike left her feeling naked, exposed. It was too easy to let the world slip by. But on foot, she could keep her finger on the trigger, keep her wits about her, let her surroundings in slowly.

It was going to be a dank, chilly day. They walked briskly, with purpose, heading north to I-80 and then swinging east toward the city proper. Eddie carried the silver briefcase, the mysterious valise swinging to and fro as they made their way toward the city.

They were living through the end of the world again, this time writ small. Rachel had slept little since the attack, her nights spent on the floor of Will's room, waiting for something, anything, what, she didn't know. It was all going bad, even faster than she had anticipated. The night of the funerals, fifty cans of food had disappeared. Twenty-four suspects in the theft and not a one was talking. Tina Fortune had been assigned to guard the supplies, and she claimed someone had cold-cocked her when she wasn't looking. She had the head wound to go with it, but even that hadn't been good enough to dissuade the conspiracy theorists.

She stole it!

She smacked herself in the head to make it look good!

String her up!

Someone had suggested torturing her to confess, but that discussion deteriorated into another bitter argument, and another fight broke out. Then two nights ago, a drunken Mark Covington attacked Harry Maynard with a broken bottle in the cafeteria, and Harry had taken a shard of glass in the arm. Harry had shot Covington, killing him.

It was all going south in a hurry.

She hadn't wanted to leave Will behind today, but Eddie had forced her hand. Despite her pleas, he would not stay with the boy, and she didn't trust Eddie to pull this exchange off himself. She had pleaded with Will to stay in his room, the curtains drawn, to not answer the door for anyone. She promised Will the moon if he could do this one thing for Mommy. The benefit outweighed the potential risk, she had decided. Her next step would depend on what, if anything, they'd be able to get for the case.

What if someone comes inside?

Then you hide under the bed, sweetheart.

What if? What if? What if?

He peppered her with questions until she told him to shut up, she had actually used those words, and he had cried, and then she had felt even worse. But that had taken the fight right out of him and he agreed to do what his mother asked, his big eyes wet with tears.

As they made their way along the highway, she kept seeing those eyes, the image burned on her brain. Beside her, Eddie whistled softly while they walked, a tune she found familiar but couldn't quite place. It nagged her to her core, the name of the song right there on the tip of her brain but she couldn't come up with it. She didn't want to ask Eddie what song it was because that meant interacting with him.

It was hard to believe that once upon a time, they had been a happy little family. That was the thing people didn't understand about relationships. They didn't always fall apart all at once, with an affair or a punch of the face or blowing it all on the Patriots. Sometimes they died a little bit at a time. A chip in the wall here, a crack there, wounds that were never repaired. Enough of those and even the Great Wall of China would come tumbling down.

Strange though, they had spent more time together since the attack than they probably had in the year preceding it. It didn't change things between them, not a bit; it was more of a reminder of all that had gone wrong between them over the years. Winding down.

An hour out from the warehouse and signs of urbanization greeted them under a gloomy sunrise. The sky lightened to the east as they passed an old vintage movie theater that had played second-run movies for ninety-nine cents, the marquee still announcing a Captain America movie. A hint of indigo bled on the horizon, a glimmer of the day to come. Cornfields gave way to small squat buildings in this industrial section of Omaha. Once comforting to Rachel in their familiarity, they now seemed ominous, dead, harbingers of things to come.

She lit a cigarette.

"You gotta smoke those goddamn things?" Eddie asked.

"Shut up."

As the development grew denser, they began moving with more care, keeping an eye out on the dark corners, on alleyways, up to the rooftops. They were in neutral territory, largely because there wasn't anything worth fighting over here anymore. That said, you could never be too careful. Mankind hadn't exactly been on its best behavior in the absence of civilization. After pitching the half-smoked cigarette, she curled her finger around the trigger of the M4, the strap set snugly around her neck.

In the east, the dead skyline of Nebraska's biggest city rose before them, well into its second decade of disrepair. The buildings were dirty, many of them sporting a greenish coating of mildew. Virtually all the windows were blown out, victims of vandalism and weather and time. To the north, grain silos reaching skyward like outstretched fingers broke the up the flat horizon.

"How much farther is it?"

She ignored the whininess of his query; he sounded like a child complaining to his parents on a long road trip.

"Two miles. Maybe three."

Forty minutes later, they arrived at the outskirts of the Market, which had been set up in a city park, the previous home to a farmer's market that had been popular with Omahans before the plague. Here and there, people milled about, chatting, arguing, dealing. An old FEMA banner hung limply from the outer fence. The agency had set up a processing center here during the outbreak, including a series of trailers that had been conscripted into service for the Market. The banner had faded but you could just make out the lettering that read QUARANTINE IN EFFECT.

Rachel focused on a middle-aged woman, frightfully thin, standing outside the gates. Her clothes hung loosely on her frame. Even from where she stood, Rachel could see the sunken eyes, the hollow in the woman's cheeks. She stopped each person who passed through the gates, begging for a handout, but no one paid her any mind. Eventually, a Market security guard came by to talk with her. He spoke for a few seconds, and the woman shook her head vehemently. Rachel knew what the man was telling her. The woman did have something to sell, yes, indeedy. It would be a matter of whether she had reached that line.

Rachel watched her and her heart broke, but not from any sense of empathy. She was the woman; the woman was her.

No.

That wouldn't be her. She was strong where this woman was weak. She would find a way. Today was the first step toward that.

She pulled her focus back from this a microcosm of misery and took in the forest rather than the trees. It had been a while since she had come to Market, at least four months, maybe six. The sight of so many people always shocked her a bit; you forgot how many different faces you used to see every day in the old world. Faces of people you'd see once and never see again. Faces at the gas station, at a stoplight, standing in line at the bank, sitting next to you at your favorite pizza place. And then all those faces had vanished, all at once, and you'd go weeks or months without seeing a new face, and then you would forget there were still other people in the world. Then you came to Market, and it was sensory overload, even though when you got right down to it, there really weren't that many people here at all.

Rachel liked seeing new faces, it gave her a little thrill to see other people again. Young people, old people, white faces, black faces, Asian faces, Hispanic faces, faces that might look like one ethnicity or another, but you really couldn't tell at all.

She and Eddie fell into the queue, which was starting to thicken ahead of the Market's opening at dawn. As they waited, she scanned the crowd, considering how to play it. Was someone here waiting for the briefcase? Had someone already spotted it? It wasn't lost on her that they might already be in terrible danger, that the last moments of their lives might already be sluicing away, the last few grains of sands whirlpooling toward their date with gravity.

At dawn, a bell clanged, and the Market opened.

A BAND HAD STRUCK up the music as they entered the gates. The smell of meat cooking on a fire somewhere wafted through the air, the aroma making her mouth water. She pushed it out of her head, knowing the price for such a treat would be too rich for what they could afford to pay. As they wandered the grounds, the Market revved to life, people setting up tents and tables, dragging coolers and crates of goods to sell. Everything would be for sale, food, medicine, weapons, ammunition, even sex.

There would be dice and gambling and prostitution and sport, probably a fight at dusk, when someone would build a big bonfire, and two pugilists would whale away on each other to the delight of the crowd. It was loud and boisterous and sometimes a bit frightening. She found herself drifting to their usual spot, where they normally set up their table. They didn't have their table today, but she felt safer here nonetheless.

"Morning," said their neighbor, a middle-aged fireplug of a man named Andy. He was a thickly built man, balding but for two strips of bushy gray hair flanking each side of his dome. His face bore a long scar beginning above his eyebrow and curling upward to his hairline. He had an astonishing array of guns and ammunition at his disposal, which he usually traded for food. He fancied himself the pit boss of the market, in no small part due to his arsenal. He always came solo and never spoke of anyone else; his background was a bit of a mystery.

"Andy," Rachel said sweetly. Ordinarily, she detested making small talk, especially with Andy, but today she would have to, and she would have to do it well. He often doled out nuggets of gossip he picked up along the midway. People were afraid of Andy, and probably with good reason. Best to curry favor with him and stay apprised of the comings and goings of the post-apocalyptic plains states.

"The love of my life," he said. "You still with this jerkoff?" Andy asked, nodding toward Eddie. The two men did not get along, and Andy was not afraid to express his disdain toward Eddie. He had taken a shine to Rachel, though, and he had always been fair with them. He was their primary ammunition vendor.

Eddie stepped toward the man, his chest puffed out.

"What'd you say to me, asshole?"

Andy shoved him aside like a child pushing away a boring toy.

"I'll let that one go," Andy said. "My way of paying my respects."

"What are you talking about?" Eddie asked stupidly.

She nodded. Andy knew about the battle for the warehouse. She didn't reply, wondering where he would take this conversation. He liked to talk, that was for sure, hated empty silences.

"Sorry about your pop," Andy said, turning his attention back to Rachel. "Kind of a legend, that man."

Adam was well known at the Market, having run a medical clinic there for years. Few doctors had appeared at the Market, and his services were frequently in high demand. There was simply no escaping the man's shadow.

"Anyway, lotta folks talkin' about your warehouse," he went on. "Biggest one in months. Probably the way things is gonna be from now on. Y'all ain't the only ones running out. Food's getting expensive."

"Any idea who hit us?"

"No."

Rachel eyed him, trying to decide if he were telling the truth.

"There's more out there," Eddie said. "We'll find it."

"If there were more, it'd have shown up here," Andy replied. "Population around here's been getting bigger every year. People abandoning the coasts."

"Why?" Rachel asked.

"The big cities, they're death traps," Andy said. "Controlled by warlords. That's where the worst of the worst set up shop. They went in, scooped up all the food and supplies. Now the food is running low. People starting to stream to the middle. It's no secret there are tons of warehouses and distribution centers in the Midwest, near the Mississippi. Like a funnel. It's only going to get worse.

"You know what happens when there's a shortage of a vital resource?"

War.

Rachel shuddered.

On the plus side, if they all killed each other over a dwindling food supply, then their baby problem wouldn't be all that big a deal. In fact, without the lid on their population, they may have run out of food long ago. Strange that had never occurred to her before.

"If I was you," he said, "I'd start thinking real hard about what else you got to trade for food."

He winked at her, and disgust swept through her. Disgust at what he was suggesting, but an even more thorough revulsion at knowing he was right, and that she would do anything to ensure Will's well-being. God help her, she would do it.

"What's that supposed to mean?" Eddie asked, this question even dumber than the last one.

"Your missus knows what I'm talking about," he said, crossing his arms across his broad chest.

Eddie dumbly swung his head toward her.

"And she knows I'm right."

"Enough," she said sharply.

Andy quieted down and went back to the work of arranging his wares on the table. She took the briefcase from Eddie's hand and set it down. Andy looked up at her but didn't say anything. His face was blank. If he had any knowledge about this briefcase's provenance, he wasn't letting on.

"Know anything about this?"

He kept his eyes on her.

"Where'd you get that?"

"Doesn't matter how I got it. I got it."

"All right then."

"Do you know whose it is?"

"I might."

"You might."

They stood silently.

"Why do you have to be such a prick?" she asked, her shoulders slumping.

"Wasn't loved enough as a child."

She laughed, not because the joke was funny, but because of how stupid this was. How everyone was trying to out-badass everyone all the time. Deep down under the harsh exterior was the man who'd watched the world collapse a decade ago, but who worked desperately to cover it up.

"What were you like?" she asked. "Before, I mean."

"Doesn't matter anymore."

"I think it does," she said. "Let me guess. A software engineer?"

He smiled.

"Taught biology at a community college."

"From teaching to this."

"You do what you gotta do."

"OK, listen up, Professor. I'm going to find out whose briefcase this is, with or without you. And if I have to do it without you, I'll make sure the owner knows I did it without you. How do you think that's going to play?"

Her heart was pounding and her mouth was dry; she hoped she sounded more convincing than she felt. His right cheek bulged as he probed it with his tongue.

A flicker of fear in his eyes.

She held his gaze until he looked away, her breath coming in ragged gasps. He spat in the grass behind him.

"I'll find out."

"You do that."

While Andy worked on his promise, Rachel and Eddie gingerly made their way through the midway, pausing at each booth to browse. At the first, a raggedy pop-up shelter, there was an elderly man hawking salted meats for a fortune. Rachel had a sudden vision of someone trailing the man home and murdering him for his food supply. And then that was all she saw. From booth to booth, visions of brutal, violent deaths for these vendors, everyone slaughtering each other in humanity's last terrible war for a case of black beans flickered in her mind.

She glanced around for Eddie, but he was nowhere to be seen. A quick survey of the crowd, starting to thicken as the afternoon wore on, failed to reveal his whereabouts.

"Dammit."

She didn't actually care where Eddie Callahan the man was. What she did care about were the current whereabouts of her partner, her backup, the one supposed to be looking out for her as she did for him. There was some semblance of law and order at the Market, but it wasn't as safe as, say, Grandma's house. Tempers flared from time to time, and rules didn't mean a whole lot when you took a shiv in the gut for looking at someone funny.

Typical Eddie.

Probably trying to walk his way into a freebie at the Cat's Paw. He'd tell her he was scouting things out, laying low. He'd probably snuck in something of value without telling her because that would be just like him. Something he could trade for five sweaty minutes between the thighs of some woman who would look at him at nothing more than a meal ticket, something to be endured so she could stay alive a little longer.

What did she care? They were through. If he wanted to bust his nut and pick up a case of herpes for his efforts, that was his business now. There hadn't been a formal breakup, no papers signed, but they were through. They hadn't had sex in years; he was nothing more than the annoying roommate she couldn't get rid of. His parentage of Will hardly mattered to him so even that bond was shaky at best.

As she looked for him, she could feel herself running a system check, searching her hard drive for something acknowledging the death of her time with Eddie, other than the objective certainty of it. Grief, heartache, regret, a twinge of nostalgia for the good times gone by. Something. But there was nothing.

She didn't know if she should feel good or badly about that. It was probably a good thing, because theirs was a world that didn't treat kindly those who dwelled in the past. There was a lot that could crawl out of the swampy fog of the past, grab you in its clutches, pull you down, drive you mad. Much had been lost forever, things far better and more important than her relationship with Eddie and to spend too much time wandering through the muddled remnants of the past was to invite ruin. They couldn't pretend to keep living in the old world, they couldn't even keep living in the ghost of the old world.

It was like letting go of that first love, the one that had shown you the wonder and electricity possible in the universe and the one you'd held onto for too long, long after you were the only one still holding anything.

She did a quick loop of the midway, passing all manner of vendors pushing salt, medicine, ammo, biofuel, some food. There were green onions, wilted and thin, baby lettuces, even some rhubarb, heartier crops waging valiant battle against their bizarre climate. A few booths hawking canned goods, a little salted meat. Not much though. A chill ran along the nape of Rachel's neck. It was more than a bit frightening.

The brothel set up shop in a small trailer at the far end of the quad, about a hundred yards from the Market entrance. Rachel hated the place but couldn't help but respect it in some twisted way. Men were stupid, still thinking with their dicks, apocalypse or not. and the place helped level the playing field a bit. They'd all done things to survive, things they never could have imagined a decade ago, but things that had to be done. The arguments that might have had a place in pre-plague America simply did not hold water anymore.

Last time she'd been here, Rachel had chatted with the proprietor of the Cat's Paw, a smooth-talking, pale-skinned woman named Vania. She was short, her hair cut short, and she talked a million miles a minute. Each of her arms was tattooed with bullet holes, red ink spatter skirting thick black dots from elbow to wrist. She and Rachel smoked cigarettes and she explained to Rachel what was what.

"This here?" she had said, pointing between her legs. "Doesn't mean nothing. This," she went on, pointing to her stomach, "is what matters. They're stupid, morons. I own them. I lie down for thirty minutes and I eat for a week. They call me bitch and slut and whore and they think I give a shit about that. They really think that matters. They'll keep coming back until they have nothing and then they'll die, and I'll still be here. I'll tell you, I ain't in no hurry to die, I want to be an old lady. I didn't live through all this shit to starve to death now."

The self-assuredness of it all was what had stuck with Rachel. This woman would do what she had to do, same as Andy, same as her. Funny how priorities changed over time. Maybe the way they had lived in the past was the real lie; maybe tying that to emotion or self-worth had been the mistake in all this. You used what nature gave you, up to and including the thing that made men stupid.

A few minutes later, she had made her way to the Paw. There was no doubt he was here because Eddie was stupid and he would compromise his own safety and well-being and that of everyone around him for a quick squirt. Sometimes she wondered if men forgot they could take such matters into their own hand, literally. Then again, these were men she was talking about.

Idiots.

As she stood awkwardly near the entrance, in between it and the gambling tent next to it, because how else did one stand at the threshold of a whorehouse, she heard a harsh yell, male, followed by an explosion of shouts. Some kind of scuffle. The voices swirled together, making it impossible to understand what was being said.

She slipped around the corner, toward the main entrance, where she saw someone rushing into the crowd. A few seconds later, Eddie staggered behind him. He was bleeding from a deep laceration on his forehead and his lip was split open. At first, Rachel was so taken aback by his appearance she didn't notice it. Only after she had a moment did she see.

The briefcase was gone.

10

"Eddie, where's the case?"

He ignored her, pulling up the tail of his jacket and pressing it to his wound. It was bleeding heavily, flowing like a ruptured water main. Her father had taught her head wounds were the worst, home to countless capillaries buried below the thin skin; even minor cuts were messy.

She stared at him as he tended to his wound, wondering not for the first time how the man could be so stupid. She squeezed her fists tightly, hard enough that she could feel her nails digging into her palms. She wanted to scream at him, smack the ever-living piss out of him, but she couldn't because then he would clam up and they'd waste the precious time she would need to sort out the mess he'd made.

"Eddie!"

"Guy jumped me. Fucking believe that?"

"Who?"

"I don't know! He took off. Leave me alone!"

She swept the crowd, men and women coming and going, but the case was nowhere to be seen. Gooseflesh popped up across her body as panic set in. Just like that, it was gone. The one thing that might have been in the same galaxy of justifying the carnage out on I-80 that morning was that it would help save them, save Will, and Eddie had been stupid enough to let it get away.

She left Eddie to lick his wounds and bolted into the crowd. This kind of inattention could mean the difference between life and death now. Stupid, stupid.

The crowd kaleidoscoped around her as she made a loop through the midway, all at once becoming a swirl of faces and clothing and bags and guns, until she couldn't tell where one person ended and another began. Sweat slicked her body, even in the chill of the late morning. Her stomach lurched, and she began dry heaving. She hadn't eaten in more than a day, so nothing came up as her body quivered and heaved. When she was done, her stomach muscles were tight and her jaw hurt.

She began to cry, and this time she couldn't stop the tears from falling. God, she hated to cry, but the hopelessness of it all roared up and washed over her like a rogue wave. Hopelessness on top of hopelessness. Did it even matter that they'd lost the case? So they died two weeks from now instead of two months from now. What difference did it make? Dead was dead.

But it made a lot of difference. It wasn't just full bellies food provided. It bought probably the most important resource – more time. More time to get their shit together. More time not suffering. More time to find food. More time with Will.

She wandered the grounds of the Market fruitlessly, her hope of spotting the briefcase fading like a dying candle. There weren't any tears left by the time she made it back their spot. Eddie sat on the ground cross-legged, smoking a cigarette. The bleeding had slowed significantly if not stopped entirely; thick red blood had caked around his eyebrow, and his lower lip had puffed up. He looked pathetic, when you got right down to it.

"I'm sorry," he said, his eyes cutting downward, but flitting back up every second or two, in that way of his, looking for instant forgiveness from her. He wasn't really sorry. He just didn't want her to be mad at him. He wanted outside confirmation for his deeply held belief that he never did anything wrong.

She wanted to yell at him, but she didn't have the energy for it. Her shoulders ached and a headache was coming on like a hurricane nearing shore; her head was throbbing, pulsing, her brain pushing right up against her skull.

A sensation of being watched washed over her; she glanced to her left and saw Andy taking it all in. He was loving this, she bet, he loved it when others crashed and burned.

"What?" she snapped.

"Nothing," he replied sweetly.

Rachel raked her hands across her face, through her hair, before crisscrossing her arms across her chest.

"You're gonna have some explaining to do," Andy said.

"Meaning what?"

"While you were all out," he said, nodding toward Eddie, "doing whatever it was you were doing, I found who you were looking for. She wants to meet with you."

"Not much point now, is there?"

Andy's jaw went tight, and his typically dour visage grew even more so. His lips tightened and his eyes went blank. A chill ran through Rachel; she had never seen this side of him.

"I went to a lot of trouble setting this up," he said. "This is not someone I mess around with. And by the transitive property, I am not someone that you mess around with."

"What are you going to do, kill me?"

He raised his eyebrows and tilted his head to the side.

"Fine," Rachel said, sighing. "Let's get this over with."

"She'll meet you at sunset."

THE NEXT FOUR hours drew out slowly, like a slow drip. A front moved in during the afternoon, bringing wind and rain and cold temperatures. People huddled together in ponchos, under umbrellas and tents, drinking bitter coffee and smoking old cigarettes as the chilly rain pelted down.

Rachel and Eddie hovered near Andy's booth. Eddie complained about his head hurting, but there wasn't anything she could do about it, and she didn't care much anyway, so she said nothing. Part of her, and not a small one, reveled in his suffering. He deserved it. He brought it on himself.

The meeting dominated her thoughts.

They could be in a bad way here. People were killed over much less. She could make a break for it. Just up and haul ass out of here. Let Eddie meet with the woman, explain to her how he'd managed to lose the briefcase while getting his dick wet. She scanned the area, looking for a clear line of escape, but one that would give her cover in the event Andy went off and started shooting.

But could she really leave Eddie behind? They'd probably kill him, and she tried to feel guilty about it. She took a deep breath and let it out slowly. This line she feared she would someday cross, she was on its precipice every day, the front lines of a terrible civil war raging inside her soul. But could she leave him? Right now, at this moment she could.

Ask me again in thirty seconds, I might have a different answer for you.

Eddie would probably leave her, because he was that kind of person. And not because he would be thinking of Will's welfare, but because he'd be looking out for Numero Uno.

"This cat got a name?" she asked Andy, breaking a lengthy silence.

"Priya."

"Who is she?"

"Just somebody."

"She must be somebody special, put a scare like that in you."

"I've seen how she does business."

Rachel pressed the index and middle finger of each hand to her temples.

"Can you cut the cloak-and-dagger bullshit and tell me who she is."

He guffawed.

"She's a goddamned nightmare."

Rachel gave up.

Obviously, Andy stood to benefit from this somehow. Possibly paid off in food. Whoever she was, she wielded a certain level of clout, as Andy was more likely to tell you to kiss his ass than say boo. She worked it over in her mind as the hours drifted past, but she couldn't think of a happy outcome to all this.

As the sun set, a buzz began building in the crowd, people ready to blow off steam after a hard day's work. Around them, people loaded their remaining inventory into their vehicles for the night and turned their attention toward the recreational portions of the festivities. Andy sat on a chair under his tent and worked a cigar while he sipped a foul-smelling liquor. The industrial stink of the thick smoke made Rachel's eyes water. She found cigars repellent, the way they sat nestled in the V of fat sausage fingers, the sheen of saliva on filters gnawed and chewed within an inch of their lives, the crutch of insecure men who wanted to seem anything but.

As the day's last light faded away, Rachel felt that void growing in her belly; she and Eddie hadn't eaten since splitting a stale protein bar earlier that morning. They had a bit of food in their pack, but they really needed to make their meager supply last.

Tomorrow, you can wait until morning to eat, but the more she repeated this mantra, the hungrier she got. Her head began to swim and her hands trembled as her blood sugar reached critical levels. Her mouth watered, her hunger so sharp her Pavlovian reaction hadn't even needed any sort of trigger. Ten minutes, she would wait ten minutes and this wave of hunger would crest and fade. She needed to fight through it.

But ten minutes came and went and instinct kicked in, focusing on a can of black beans in her pack. All her thoughts zeroed in on quelling the beast in her belly, on shutting it right the hell up. She opened her pack, ran her fingers on the can, heavy and feeling just right. Her will broke. She pulled the pop tab, the smell of the beans tickling her nose. There was no spoon, so she ate with her hands, not caring one whit or whittle about etiquette or how she looked. Even cold, the beans were a revelation, the feeling of the beans breaking down under her teeth, the sensation of her belly filling orgasmic, better than that because sex had never felt this good.

When she was done, a small part of her regretted it because she could be dead by the end of the night and the food would have been wasted. But the rest of her made excuses, about needing to be on her game for this impending meeting, about needing strength, about playing the long game. This meeting was something new, and anything new was a risk, anything out of the ordinary was dangerous. Life was dangerous enough; these kinds of encounters distilled them into a concentrated broth of peril.

The evening progressed, but there was no sign of Priya. Rachel looked up and down the midway, looking for someone to pop out, for some sign their wait was coming to an end. She paced, she chewed her nails. Her stomach roiled; maybe the beans had been a bad idea. The meeting consumed her, the way things often did. When she became focused on something, it was at the expense of everything else. She had never understood people who could bury themselves in work or Netflix or gardening to keep their minds at ease. It didn't make your problems go away. The problem going away made it go away.

"Christ, sit down, you're making me nervous now," Andy said, his words running together a bit.

He'd been hitting the sauce pretty hard, which only served to make Rachel even more nervous. He was scared and he didn't have anything to be scared of.

"Good luck getting her to do that," Eddie called out.

"Shut up, both of you," Rachel replied, her attention zeroing in on two men approaching the tent. They wore jeans and black leather jackets. One was black, about her age, the other white and quite a bit older. Andy was out of his chair before the men reached the tent, his hands clasped together at his waist. Rachel had never seen him take such a submissive pose.

"This her?" asked the younger man.

Andy nodded.

He curled two fingers toward her.

"Let's go."

She looked at Andy, who simply shrugged his shoulders.

"Where?"

"Now."

Eddie slowly rose to his feet, sighing as he did so. Jesus, she wanted to punch him. He was going to be a pain in the ass about this, not out of any sense of rebellion, but because he was being put out. Her jaw clenched.

"Eddie, now," she hissed.

"Fine, I'm coming, I'm coming."

"Let's have the weapons," the older man said.

She looked to Andy once more, for what she didn't know, perhaps a sign of encouragement, but he gave her nothing but a blank, stony stare. She handed over the M4, and Eddie relinquished his Glock pistol.

Perhaps sensing her discomfort, the man added: "You'll probably get them back."

Rachel and Eddie followed the men down the midway to the Cat's Paw, where the bouncer admitted them without comment. She had never been inside before. The muffled sounds of whispered conversation and desperate exertion filled the air. It was dim but not dark. The interior smelled faintly of bleach and sweat, not particularly pleasant but not offensive. She followed the men to a small room in the back.

"Please sit," a pleasant female voice said as they entered the room.

The men guided Rachel and Eddie to a pair of chairs.

"Are they clean?" she asked.

The men held up their confiscated weapons.

"Good," the woman said.

They sat in silence. Rachel concentrated on her breathing, on keeping her heart rate steady. Footsteps on the tile floor. Then a woman sat down in a third chair.

"Let's have a chat, shall we?" the woman said, lighting up a lantern.

An Indian woman's face appeared in the soft glow of the lantern. She appeared to be in her thirties, thin and strikingly beautiful. She was quite tall, taller even than her two male companions. She wore jeans and a heavy coat. Rachel was struck by how put together the woman was, like she was headed out for an evening of cocktails with friends.

"My name is Priya," the woman said. "These two gentlemen that brought you here are Jesse and Phillip."

Rachel nodded.

"We're very sorry to hear about your father's death," Priya said. "My deepest condolences."

"Thank you," Rachel said slowly. She chose her words carefully, making her way through a minefield. Again, she marveled at the speed at which news traveled in this world. Forget electricity or the Internet. They didn't even have a Pony Express. And yet there didn't seem to be anyone who didn't know about their staggering defeat.

"We'll get back to the warehouse," she said. "But I'd like to begin with some good news."

"What good news?" Eddie said reflexively.

Rachel wished for a roll of duct tape so she could seal those flapping gums shut. She closed her eyes and waited for the wash of annoyance to fade.

"We've recovered the briefcase."

Rachel's stomach flipped. She didn't know whether this was good news for Priya or for her and Eddie.

"I'm sorry we lost it," Rachel said,

"Yes," Priya said. "That was careless. But all's well that ends well."

"Good," Rachel said. "Can we go now?"

The woman clicked her tongue rapidly.

"I'm afraid not, my dear. Would you like to know what was in the briefcase?"

"No," she said.

"I'd like to know," Eddie said simultaneously.

"Eddie, shut up."

"You two are lovers, no?"

Again, they spoke over each other, giving diametrically opposing answers. Rachel did not know why it was important for this woman to know she and Eddie were most definitely not lovers. A word she detested anyway. It rang of thin men with slicked back hair smoking long cigarettes.

"Anyway, the briefcase contained a stock of seeds."

"So?"

"Bred to grow in these unusual growing conditions with which we've been blessed."

"Do they work?" Rachel asked.

"Not to date," Priya replied. "But this batch is rumored to show promise."

The idea of viable crops electrified Rachel. Years earlier, they had tried breeding weather-resistant crops, but each iteration had failed to produce any significant yield.

"So, you can see why this case was important."

"Where did they come from?"

Priya smiled, revealing in the low light twin rows of radiant teeth.

"A girl has to have her secrets," she replied. "But I know you understand the importance of this project."

Rachel didn't reply.

"Which brings me to the loss of your warehouse. That's a devastating thing. I truly sympathize with your plight. In this day and age, it won't be easy for your community to survive."

"We'll make do," Rachel said. Eddie remained dead silent.

"Perhaps you will," Priya said. She crossed one leg over another and tapped a finger to her lips. "The thing is, it didn't have to go that way."

"What do you mean?"

"You know, I briefly considered having you killed," Priya said, ignoring her question.

The statement itself did not surprise Rachel; it was the cool, detached way in which Priya delivered it that blasted her soul with ice.

"But as I said, all's well that ends well. And I hate unnecessary bloodshed. It's pointless. That being said, I was quite a bit put out by your carelessness."

"You got your case back," Eddie snapped.

Priya nodded to one of her goons, who punched Eddie in the side of the head.

Rachel had to fight the urge to smile as he grunted in pain.

"What can I do to make us square?" Rachel asked.

"I have a business proposition for you," Priya said.

"What?"

"I'm talking about saving your community," she said. "About saving your group from starving to death. Or worse."

"Worse?"

"People will do anything to survive," she said. "And I do mean anything. You've heard about what goes on outside Lincoln."

Her skin crawled. Yes, she had heard about what was going on outside Lincoln. She had heard the stories of people disappearing, of the rich, gamey smell of cooking meat wafting for miles even though there was virtually no game left around here, culled by the twin specters of hunting and starvation. She had heard the stories about what people were doing when there was nothing left to eat.

She nodded.

"Tell me something," Priya said.

Rachel raised her eyebrows.

"Are you a hopeful person?"

Rachel turned the question over in her head for a minute before responding. Her belly was quiet and sated. Weird how one's outlook changed depending on which way the wind was blowing.

"I don't know."

"At least you're honest. See, people these days lie to themselves. They don't think it will happen to them. Because they've made it this far, they think they will keep on making it."

"True."

"And they let opportunities get away from them, opportunities that once gone are gone forever. In our world, opportunity rarely knocks and never more than once."

Where was she going with this?

"Is it true?"

"Is what true?"

Something began to nag at Rachel. She couldn't quite put her finger on it, but she did not like where this discussion was going.

"Your son. He was born after the plague."

Rachel's stomach flipped. Of course.

"He's not my son," she said. "He lived in my neighborhood. I heard him crying one night after it was over. I couldn't just leave him there."

It was a story she had told many times, one she had rehearsed over and over until she almost accepted as fact. She had told it so often she had begun to accept it as canon. She did her best to conceal the miracle that was Will from the world at large. That was one thing the community did support her on; they didn't want to draw any more attention to themselves than was necessary. It was a tough sell, she knew that. Without anyone to take care of them, most of the babies and toddlers who had survived the plague quickly perished from dehydration, starvation, or accidents. Other than Will, the youngest survivors were now deep into their teens. And he looked very young.

"What's his name?"

"His name is Will."

Priya leaned back in her chair, crossed one leg over the other, clasped her hands around her right knee. She tapped her lips with her finger again.

"You're not being honest with me."

"Suit yourself."

"We have very good intelligence on the issue," she said. "You'd be surprised what you can learn for the right price."

"You believe what you want. He was a few months old when the plague hit."

Priya tapped her fingers together as she considered Rachel's story. A thought took hold of Rachel, deep inside, but strong like an ocean current. She could feel it swelling up, a large wave, fear and terror, as she suddenly realized what it was Priya wanted.

"It was you," Rachel sputtered with rage. "You attacked the warehouse."

"Like I said, it didn't have to go that way."

"No," Rachel said, jumping out of her chair, flipping it over, backing away from the woman like her body was strapped with explosives.

"He was there," Priya said with a trace of annoyance in her voice.

"Wait," Eddie said. "Let's hear her out."

"Will is the most important person alive right now," Priya said. "The fate of the human race may depend on him. He'll be perfectly safe, perfectly cared for. You won't have to worry about whether he has enough to eat."

"Let's go," Rachel said, turning for the door. "We're leaving."

"Lady, what do you want?"

"You appear to be a reasonable man," Priya said. "I hope you can help Rachel understand that this is the best deal she's going to get. You get all your food back. Two years' worth, if I had to guess."

"In exchange for what?" Eddie asked.

"You goddamn idiot," Rachel said as she made her way toward the door.

"She wants Will!"

11

They took the long way home.

She had waited outside nearly ten minutes as Eddie had heard the woman out, listening to her abominable offer to take Will away in exchange for a few truckloads of canned goods. It was ludicrous. And Eddie was actually trying to convince her to go through with it.

"Listen to me," Eddie was saying as they curled around the edges of the dead city. "I don't think we can dismiss this offer-"

"I will not listen to you," she snapped. "Either you stop talking or I blow your fucking brains out."

"You didn't even wait to hear what she had to say," Eddie went on. "Don't you want the kid to be safe? To be looked after?"

The kid. The kid. Always the kid.

"Oh, I'm supposed to believe this woman has Will's best interests at heart?" she replied. "She'll turn him into a goddamn guinea pig."

"And you'd rather he starve to death with the rest of us?"

"I'm not going to let that happen," Rachel said.

"Listen to yourself," Eddie said. "You know how naïve you sound? You can't just say it and make it so. People are dying out there every day. Every day. This way he gets a chance. And if they can figure out what makes him different, all the better."

"You know how naïve you sound? You think she's going to give you a big warehouse full of food? I'll tell you what she's gonna do. She'll put a bullet in your empty head."

That he was even considering it mystified her. Did the man have no paternal instinct at all? Had he been born without it, shipped from the manufacturer missing this vital component? And God, the irony of it all. Eddie Callahan might be the last man to become a father and he wanted no part of it. It had a certain demented beauty to it.

Above them, a sliver of moon hung in the sky like a broken piece of pottery. The moon. Man had walked up there once. Had she ever told Will about how America had gone to the moon? About the space shuttles that had been lost, about the brave astronauts that had given all they had so mankind could push the boundaries of what they knew? Would he even believe there were human footprints up on the lunar surface right now? A little American flag, the symbol of these once-great United States? She'd been excited about the prospect of a manned mission to Mars, the preparations for which were well underway when the plague had hit. In fact, a year before the outbreak, NASA had successfully landed the first unmanned supply ship on the red planet. Now the vessel sat up there, alone and forgotten, perhaps forever.

And now here we are, killing each other over diced tomatoes.

Forget the moon. Will remained skeptical of the entire concept of electricity, and truly, trying to explain lights and televisions and iPhones and the Internet had been like trying to explain magic. He couldn't grasp it, any more than she'd been able to grasp its sudden disappearance. She missed technology, she missed computers, she missed trying to make them better.

Some years ago, she'd gone up into Omaha after Market and taken an iPad from an Apple Store. It sat on the desk in her bedroom collecting dust, but she liked having it there. It reminded her of what they had been capable of, once upon a time, and perhaps could be again.

Unless, of course, the human race went extinct.

"Rachel!"

Eddie was talking again. She wanted to tune him out and slip back into her singular focus on the road, on the trip home, where Will would be waiting for her, asleep, his hair matted down on his sweaty forehead.

"What?"

"If you think about it, you would see that this really could be the best option," he said.

"It's a terrible option," she said.

"I didn't say it was a good option," Eddie said. "There are no good options. We could be dead inside of a month. Will too. This way he has a chance."

"We could hit them first," Rachel said coldly.

"How?"

"We find out where they are," she said. "Kill them and take their supplies."

It sounded dumb, but she didn't want Eddie to know she knew that. She didn't know who Priya was, where she was from, how large her group was, how heavily armed they were. She could be bluffing, or she could have an army of cannibals at her disposal. You never knew anymore.

"You live in this fantasy world," he said. "Everything is black and white to you. We're the good guys, so we're going to win. Is that it?"

"I'm his mother," Rachel said. "How many times do I have to explain that to you? It's my job to keep him safe. Our job, actually."

"That attitude really worked out for all the mothers who watched their kids die in the plague, didn't it?"

"Go to hell."

Eddie dismissed her with a wave of his hand, and for that, she was thankful. She had no desire to continue this ridiculous conversation.

They made it back the outskirts of the compound a little after midnight. They walked in silence, the void between them catching bits of civilization here and there. A shout. An engine revving. The occasional gunshot. Those sounds blew in on the breezes in the preternatural quiet from miles away, like distant radio broadcasts. The cold air felt good as she walked; it re-energized her, cleaned out the bad funk that had permeated this disastrous trip to Market.

The silhouette of the perimeter fence came into view. The end was coming for their little community, for her time with these people. How long before they all went their separate ways, off to find their own destinies, off to deal with the terrible, inevitable end facing all of them? Sooner than later, she feared. Much sooner.

"You change your mind?" he asked when they were at the door.

She ignored him and went inside. Charlotte and Will were asleep on the couch, tangled in a mess of blankets. She picked up Will, groaning a bit under his weight. As she carried him to his bed and covered him with the blanket, he sighed and mumbled something under his breath. Her chest tightened and the tears fell again. He rolled over onto his side and curled up into a fetal position.

She watched him sleep, his side rising and falling rhythmically.

Why you?

What was it inside him that had gone so right when inside all the other post-epidemic babies it had gone so wrong? What gene, what cell, what bit of DNA, what antibody flowing through his veins, invisible, hidden, infinitesimally small, had risen up and kept him safe from the most terrible of invaders?

She sat with him for a very long time.

THE NEXT MORNING, she found Will in the living room, where he was messing around with one of his latest projects, a Lego Death Star he'd been working on for weeks. He loved playing with the famous toy bricks. Over the last couple years, she'd made a point to snag him a set whenever she came across one during their scouting missions. Charlotte was on the couch reading.

"Look who's up," Charlotte said, looking up from her book. "Feeling better?"

Sunlight streamed in through the window; particles of dust

danced in the curtains of light shimmering in the middle of the room, a tiny little ballet. Rachel stared at them, mesmerized by the synchronicity of the seemingly random, swirling, circling, twisting. They seemed to coalesce into something bigger and then dissemble just as quickly.

"Yes."

"You never sleep this late."

"Worn out, I guess," she said.

She could feel her old self coming to the forefront, taking over, declaring an emergency. The engineer inside her, the computer scientist who had no use for emotion, no use for anything but deductive reasoning, solving problems, testing hypotheses, discarding wrong answers, hammering away the impurities until the only thing left was the shine of truth.

"Anytime," she said, climbing out of her seat. "I'm gonna head home."

"Thanks for looking after Will."

The women hugged, Charlotte's strength taking Rachel's breath away a little bit. It reminded her how hard Charlotte worked around here, how hard she had worked to keep the warehouse safe, to keep them all safe.

Charlotte knelt and rubbed Will's head.

"See ya, shortie," she said.

"Bye," he said, never looking up.

Charlotte left, leaving mother and son alone together.

"Willy?"

"Yeah?"

"We need to talk, buddy."

He rolled his eyes as he sat up.

"Don't do that," she said firmly.

His face went blank. He hated being scolded, but there was something inside him that insisted on defying her. Just a part of growing up, she supposed. If Will was to be the last kid to grow up, then he was going to play the part perfectly.

CHILDHOOD'S FINAL RUN! WILL **NOT** *BE HELD OVER!!!!*

They sat on the couch, Will's eyes darting around the room, clearly anxious to be done with this little pow-wow so he could get back to the business of being eleven years old.

"There's no easy way to tell you this," she started, "but I think we're probably going to be moving soon."

"Why?" he asked, his eyes wide and worried.

She took a deep breath and let it out slowly. Maybe bringing this up now was a mistake, but it had to be done eventually. The sooner the better. It wasn't going to get any easier. In fact, it would get harder as the reality of their situation set in deeper. She couldn't hide her son from the way the world was.

"Because we need more food," she said. "And there isn't enough here for everyone."

"Oh," he said.

He sat quietly for a few minutes.

"Can I take my toys?" he asked.

She felt her heart shatter, splinter into a million pieces as the very little boy he was appeared before her.

"Yes," she said. "I can't promise we can take all of them, but we'll take as many as we can."

"What about Dad? He'll come too, right?"

What about Dad, indeed.

"Here's the thing, Spoon," she said. "My job is to take care of you, no matter what. It's the best job in the world. You know that, right?"

He shrugged his shoulders.

"Well, believe me. It is. Being your mom has been the greatest thing in my life. I love you more than anything. But sometimes being your mom means I have to make decisions you're not going to understand, that you're not going to like."

His face darkened.

"Dad's not coming," he said.

"I don't know if he will or not," she said.

"Well, if he's not going, I'm not either," Will said matter-of-factly.

"Sweetie," she said.

"This is bullshit!" he yelled, the intensity of it rocking Rachel backward a little. It wasn't the profanity that bothered her; she was as guilty as anyone of causing Miss Manners to spin in her grave. In that outburst, she saw a bit of his father in him, his terrible rage, rarely put on display but wise to avoid when it was.

He flung his Lego set against the wall, where it splintered into a shower of red and blue and gray bricks. Then he ran to his room and slammed the door; it was a good slamming door, heavy enough and set just so in its frame that a firm launch could shake the trailer.

Rachel kept her seat on the sofa.

She stared at the Lego pieces scattered across the table.

12

Sleep eluded her all night, her quarry remaining out of reach. Her eyes would droop, and then she would hear a noise, a raccoon outside her window or the trailer settling or one of those other mysterious things that went bump in the night, and then she'd be back up again, her heart racing. On her back, on her side, on her stomach, it made no difference because she simply kept replaying her conversation with Will.

Her window faced east, a window through which she had watched countless nights. From getting up for the first shift at the warehouse, to shepherding Will through infancy, there had been many opportunities to be up late. Will had been a terribly fussy baby, colicky in the evenings and possessed of a circadian rhythm that kept him awake all night. He didn't sleep through the night until he was a year old.

She would never forget that moment, not as long as she lived. It had been her day off, and she was ready for another sleepless night. He'd fussed a bit before bed, and so she'd lain down on the floor next to him, just for a minute. But she dropped off quickly, probably before he did, and when she woke, the room was filled with light, the sun already above her top window sash. Her mind was clear, her body rested, so much so that for the briefest of moments, she thought she was back in her bed at Caltech, the plague nothing more than a terrible and vivid dream. Then she remembered, and she peeked into his crib with dread, afraid Medusa had come for him in the night, that the virus had been extra cruel to her, to simply come and take him after letting her think he had escaped its terrible kiss. But there he had been, still asleep but stirring. His diaper was full but his pajamas were dry, and that little chubby finger was wedged in the corner of his mouth.

An eternity had passed since then.

Her eyes were thick and heavy and it felt like sludge flowed through her veins. But the die was cast; she'd soon have to face this day with no sleep. All she could hope for was clarity of mind, as there was much to think about today. Many decisions to be made.

A sharp knock on her front door broke her from her trance, setting her heart abuzz. More bad news, it was going to be more bad news. Hell, if it wasn't for bad news, they wouldn't have any news at all. She threw on her robe and hustled out of her bedroom as the knocking increased in its fervor.

"Rachel, it's Charlotte."

Charlotte rushed inside the house as soon as Rachel had opened the door wide enough to accommodate her narrow frame. Outside, it was still dark, perhaps an hour until sunrise.

"You're in trouble," Charlotte said. "You've got to get Will out of here."

Rachel's throat closed up with fear.

"What? What's happening?"

"Eddie made the deal."

"He what?"

"Willy," Charlotte called out. "Get up, we're going on a trip."

"I don't understand," Rachel said.

Charlotte made a beeline for Rachel's room. Rachel followed, her head swimming, feeling like she was moving in slow motion. It was a dream, another dream. Maybe she had simply gone insane somewhere along the line. Maybe she was still wandering around San

Diego, insane with grief, a victim of a psychotic break and unable to handle the disaster. Or maybe the plague had never happened at all, and she was in the loony bin after eating some bad mushrooms with her college buds.

"You pack," she said. "I'll talk."

Rachel stood in front of her dresser, frozen.

"He's been planning this ever since you first met that woman. He made the deal that day and has been selling it to the others. Everyone is in. They just wrapped up their meeting. They're buying her story. That she's going to give us two years' worth of food."

She paused.

"Really? People are buying it?"

"They're desperate," Charlotte said. "They want to believe it. They want to believe she can figure out why Will is different. They want to believe."

"Jesus."

"Dammit, girl, pack," Charlotte snapped. "This is it. You've got to go, and I mean now. Eddie thinks I'm on his side, thinks I'm here getting you to agree to it.

A noose of terror suddenly cinched itself around Rachel's throat.

"Is she here?

Charlotte was shaking her head.

"She'll be here at daybreak."

"Brilliant," she said. "Because Priya won't kill him and take Will anyway. How can everyone be so stupid? She's not giving us two years' worth of food."

As the reality of what Eddie had done settled in, she hustled out to the hall closet, where she'd kept the go-bags. Every few months, she updated based on the season and accounting for Will's growth. Inside them, she had packed MREs, water purification tablets, some medicine, clothes, waterproof matches, a gun, and a few other items to give them a head start in case they needed to escape quickly. The supplies would only last a few days, but they would be enough.

"He did this without asking me," she said, mostly to herself.

A knock on the door startled her. She pressed her eye to the peephole. Eddie. Alone. He looked tired, his face gaunt and unshaven.

"It's Eddie," she whispered to Charlotte.

Rachel opened the door after Charlotte had disappeared into her bedroom.

"What do you want?"

"We need to talk," Eddie said, slithering inside the narrow gap between the doorjamb and her body. Like the snake that he was.

"I didn't invite you in," she said, hoping her voice was steelier than she felt.

"Can we not do this right now?" he said. "Something's come up."

His eyes drifted toward the gun in her hand.

"What's with the piece?" he asked, nodding toward the weapon.

"I heard a noise," she said, sliding the gun into the pocket of her sweatshirt. "I didn't know it was you. What do you want?"

"I have some good news."

This was how he was playing it. Make it seem like he was doing them all a huge favor.

"Well, it's good news, but it's not easy news," he said, taking a seat on the couch. "It's about Will."

She remained silent, spooling out all the rope the man would need to hang himself with.

"I've been thinking a lot about what you said. About Will."

He tipped his chin upward and sniffed, as though he were searching the innermost depths of his soul. Then he sighed.

"You're right. I haven't been the best father. I should've done better by him."

"Thank you for saying that," she said.

"But I think I have a way to make things up to him. To you."

"You don't owe me anything."

"Your first instinct will be to hate me," he said.

She couldn't disagree with him there.

"You know what?" he said, craning his toward the bedroom. "Will should hear this too. He asleep?"

"Yes," she said as firmly as she could.

"I'll wake him up," said Eddie. He started to get up off the couch. "It really can't wait."

"Tell me first," she said, wrapping her fingers around his arm tightly. "Then I'll decide if it's something he needs to hear. That's what parents do, you know. They discuss things together and then they decide what's best for the kid."

Eddie took his seat again, rubbing his forearm where she had grabbed him. She could see red marks in his flesh where she had buried her nails.

"I made the deal with Priya," Eddie said.

"You asshole."

He chuckled softly.

"No way this is happening," she said.

"Oh, it's happening," Eddie said. "It's unanimous."

"You're right," she said. "He's not going."

"You and I don't get a vote," Eddie said "Conflict of interest. Everyone else voted in favor of the trade."

"We don't get a vote," she repeated. "We're only his fucking parents."

"These people have a say in this."

"They don't actually. These people can kiss my ass," Rachel spat. "Do you really think she's going to swoop in here with a tractor-trailer full of food? She's going to take Will and then she's going to kill you."

He smacked her, a hard slap across her cheek. It stung, rattled her marbles a little bit, but strangely, it didn't bother her too much. The man he had once been was dead to her, nothing more than a stranger on the street. The slap felt no different than catching her finger in a drawer, than stubbing her toe on a coffee table. Pain came in many forms, and although he had never hit her before, this changed nothing. Was it worse than the prospect of starvation, of growing old in an increasingly empty world? Worse than losing her son? Please. It was a bug bite. Everything she and Eddie had ever been, from the passion of those early days to the comfort they found together to the joy of bringing new life into the world, it was long gone, long dead.

"Will," he called out. "Dad's here. Come out here a second, buddy."

"He's not going," she said as he looked toward the bedroom.

"Maybe he'll want to go," Eddie said.

"He's eleven years old. He does not get a say in this. God, how do you not get this?"

He slid down to the couch, out of her reach, and stood up. She leaped across the cushions, wrapping her arms around his legs and pulled him to the ground. That had been the element of surprise; he was much bigger and heavier than her. She felt like one of those little birds that plucked insects from the hide of an elephant. He threw her aside and walloped her across the back of the head. Her teeth clicked together, catching her lower lip between them, and her eyes lost their focus for a second.

He got up and smoothed out his shirt, because he was nothing if not conscious of his appearance, and she didn't quite understand how she had let herself fall for this nimrod. She pushed that out of her mind with the typical *if-no-Eddie-then-no-Will* rationalization.

"Will," he called out again.

She pushed herself up to her hands and knees, feeling a little blood drip from her lip where she had bitten it. Her hands drifted to the pocket of her sweatshirt, her fingers dancing along the cold steel of the barrel, across its worn grip. Without thinking about it, the gun was out, the safety off, a round chambered, and it was up, and oh, Jesus, wasn't this a scene straight out of a nightmare.

"Mommy!" called out Will as he ambled out of his room.

"It's OK, sweetie," she replied, as she aimed the gun at Eddie. "Mommy's here."

Eddie quickly glanced over his shoulder, then did a double take as he saw Rachel's weapon drawn on him. A stone-cold silence fell on the room like the season's first snowfall. She was aware of everything. The weight of the gun in her hand, the sound of a moth flitting against the lantern, the sound of her dry lips separating from one another.

"What the hell are you doing?"

"Get out," she said.

He smiled, his huge high-wattage grin revealing a set of teeth that had yellowed a bit over the years. That smile had weakened her resolve, even her thighs, many times over the years, the lovable scamp caught with his hand in the cookie jar. But now it seemed wrong, out of place. A bright flower growing amid the rubble of a fallen office tower.

Her heart throbbed fiercely and she could barely breathe now. She glanced down at the gun, which felt foreign in her hands, like she was a third party watching this scene unfold. A flash of movement in the corner of her eye. When she looked up again, she saw a blur in Will's doorway. She paused, unsure of what to do next.

"Daddy, I don't want to go," she could hear Will saying, his voice tight and high-pitched, as it became when he was under stress.

"Come on, buddy," Eddie said. "It's going to be great."

"Eddie," she said. "You are not taking him anywhere."

"What do you think you're going to do with that?" Eddie asked dismissively, the tone of a husband looking curiously at a homemaker wife holding a hammer. She ignored him. His hands flashed behind his back and suddenly, he had his gun was out, aimed squarely at Rachel's chest.

"Come over here, Will. Get behind Mommy."

Will glanced up at his father.

"Don't look at him," she said. "Do what Mommy says and everything will be fine."

"Not one step," Eddie said. "Don't you move, son."

Will stood awkwardly, one foot in front of the other. His gaze bounced from parent to parent manically, as though he were watching a high-speed tennis match. Rachel kept her eyes fixed on Eddie but occasionally allowed herself a glance at Will; the look of utter confusion on his face crushed her, but there was nothing she could do about that now. Now simply surviving this was the goal. Emotional scars would have to be bandaged later. If there was a later.

"Why do you have guns, why do you have guns, no, guns are bad, you told me guns are bad," Will said. His voice quivered and cracked as the words rushed out of his mouth.

As Will reacted to the showdown, Rachel detected movement to her left. She willed Charlotte to stay out of this, tucked away, not introduce this explosive element to an already unstable chemical reaction.

But because nothing, not a goddamn thing was going to be easy about this, out came Charlotte, her own weapon drawn and aimed at Eddie.

"Shoulda figured," Eddie said, glancing at Charlotte. "You were awfully quick to go along with this."

"Don't blame her," Rachel said. "This was never going to happen, whether she told me or not."

"It's the only chance we've got," Eddie said.

"I was going ask you if you actually believed that woman, but here we are."

"I don't know why you don't believe her."

"Two years' worth of food? I just..."

She blew out a noisy sigh.

"It's over, Eddie," she said, lowering her weapon. "I'm not going to argue with you. But this isn't happening. I know you. You won't go through with it. I know you."

They stood there a moment, the three of them, and in the space of that moment, Rachel thought she had judged Eddie correctly. That when it came down to it, despite all the fear and confusion and mystery surrounding his son's very existence, he would not do it. The others, she could almost understand. They had no skin in the game. Will was a scientific anomaly and a valuable one at that. His presence among them put them all in danger. But Eddie was his father. Those were his shoulders that Will had ridden on, *go horsey go*, many years ago. He was the one who was supposed to teach Will about being a man, especially in the world they now occupied.

He would not turn over his own flesh and blood to a monster.

But then his jaw set, and his eyes widened, and she realized how very wrong she had been. She did know this part of him, this dark side of him, all too well. As Eddie's finger pulled back on the trigger, she was already diving for the ground. The gun roared, the report deafening in the small confines of the living room. Her ears rang and felt like they'd been jammed with cotton.

Dead, she was dead, her body rolling up against the side of the sofa. Returning fire was not an option because there was a chance she would hit Will, and she couldn't do that. She had made her choice and now she would have to live, scratch that, die with it, because until the bitter end, she had been unable to accept the fact Eddie had been a father in biology only.

She pushed herself to her knees, using the sofa as cover. Eddie, perhaps thinking he'd removed Rachel from the equation, had turned his attention toward Charlotte, who had retreated behind the doorjamb.

"Mommy! Mommy!" cried Will, his desperate, panicked voice like a thousand knives to her heart.

She fired.

13

The blast from Rachel's gun shook the trailer, but this one did not seem as loud, perhaps because the first shot had deafened her, or maybe because she'd been hit and couldn't feel it and her senses were starting to go, one at a time. A scream of bloody murder, Will, it was Will screaming, that crazy son of a bitch had murdered Will.

Eddie lay on the floor, writhing around, his hands clenched at his belly and slick with blood. Will's arms were wrapped around Charlotte's waist, his face buried in her hip. Charlotte still had her gun up, aimed directly at Eddie. She watched Eddie, whose gyrations weakened in intensity as blood leaked from the gaping wound in his midsection.

"You guys OK?" she croaked out.

"Mommy!"

Will ran toward her and threw his arms around his mother. His touch galvanized her, and she climbed to her feet, her son still wrapped around her like he had done when he was small. She held him tight, kissing his head and his face and never wanting to let go.

"Jesus, I thought he'd killed you," Charlotte said, her breath coming in shallow gasps, her eyes never leaving Eddie.

“Another half second,” Rachel said, “and he would have.”

Will began to cry, and she pulled his face down into her shoulder. His whole body quivered and shook as the sobs burst forth, as the reality of it all set in, as he experienced his own personal apocalypse. Rachel hugged him tightly.

“We have to go,” Rachel said. “Right now.”

Charlotte nodded.

“I can get some supplies from my place,” Charlotte said.

“No. Too risky. You can take Eddie’s bag,” she said.

Charlotte’s eyebrows rocked upward.

Rachel motioned toward her son and Charlotte nodded in understanding.

Perhaps sensing they were talking about him, Will simply latched onto her even more tightly, squeezing her chest so hard she could barely draw a breath. As he hung on her, she hurried to the bedroom to collect the go-bags. As she worked, a knock at the door, the third in the last half hour, froze her.

On her way to the door, she passed Eddie, whose body lay in an ever-widening pool of blood. He appeared to still be alive, but he wouldn’t be for much longer. His breathing was slow and shallow, and blood trickled from the corners of his mouth. His eyes were closed, and he didn’t make a sound. She found herself hoping he was unconscious, that he wasn’t in any pain. As the life drained out of his body, she wondered how it had all come to this.

No map for this.

No one to look to for help.

Making it up as they went along.

“Who is it?” Rachel whispered as Charlotte pressed her eye to the peephole.

“It’s Harry.”

She couldn’t stall, she couldn’t hesitate, or he’d know something was up. She took a deep breath. Her eyes felt a bit puffy, but there wasn’t anything she could do about that now. Maybe it would be smarter to ignore the knock, but on the other hand, that might have drawn even greater suspicion.

"Go hide," she whispered.

"Coming," she called out when Charlotte was safely hidden.

She opened the door halfway, the distance she would normally open it. Eddie's body was behind the sofa, out of view. Harry's face was set tight, his lips pressed together.

"You heard the shots, right?"

"Yes," she said in as worried a tone as she could muster. "Any idea where they came from?"

Will toddled up behind her, his face blank, his eyes wide open.

"Scared the little guy something fierce, that's for sure."

"Sounded like they came from this direction."

"They were pretty loud," she said. "Maybe from the cafeteria?"

Harry craned his head, peeking around Rachel for a look inside the house. Again, she made no move to block his view. As long as he didn't go behind the couch, he could look at anything he wanted.

"Eddie here?"

"No," she said, tossing a little contempt in for good measure. "I don't know where he is."

"He hasn't been here to talk to you?"

She shook her head.

"We've been having some problems. Taking a little break."

"Sorry to hear it," he said, continuing to scan the trailer's dim interior.

She could see him working it out in his head, trying to guess how much she knew. There was an opening here for her, so she ran with it, try and make him so uncomfortable he wouldn't want to stick around.

"You know, I don't talk about this much, but I've been keeping it to myself. I don't know why he is the way he is."

Rachel paused and placed a hand on Harry's arm.

"You've always been good to us," she said. "And he ignores us."

His eyes cut downward and his cheeks colored red.

Harry started backing away from the door, uncomfortable as he had always been with the baring of emotions. The last thing he'd want would be to become involved in a domestic situation.

"OK, honey, if you hear anything else, let me know," he said.

"Will do."

"The three of us need to have a talk anyway," Harry said.

"About what?"

He scratched his stubbly cheek.

"About the future."

Silence wedged in between them.

"I may poke around the backyard, if you don't mind."

"Of course," she said.

He reached out and tousled Will's hair.

"It'll be OK, buddy," he said. "Me and your mom will keep you safe."

He turned and lumbered back down the trailer steps. He nodded toward Charlotte, who returned the gesture. When he was gone, Charlotte held up her hand and twirled her index finger quickly.

It was time to go.

She turned and surveyed the familiar landscape of her living room one last time. She didn't know what lay ahead, but she knew one thing – this was the last time she would ever see this place. It was the only home Will had ever known, and it was about to become a memory.

Her arms ached as Will clung to her like a tick. He had stopped crying, which was good, but he had gone completely catatonic, which was bad. After grabbing the two go-bags, she hustled down the steps and started for the main gate.

They had one chance at this. She kept her head down, her body hot. She didn't know if it was guilt, shame or betrayal coursing through her. She was sorry they had run out of food, and she was sorry the world was the way it was. Then Will whimpered, the noise barely audible, and she pulled him tight against her body.

"We'll hide out somewhere today," Rachel said. "Then we'll make camp, get a good night's sleep and deal with tomorrow, well, tomorrow."

"Works for me."

Rachel watched her friend.

"Sorry you got caught up in all this," she said.

Charlotte was shaking her head before Rachel was even done speaking.

"Fuck that," she said. "That was done the second Eddie made that deal."

"Just like *Thelma & Louise*, the two of us, eh?"

"Who are Thelma and Louise?" Charlotte asked without the barest hint of sarcasm.

"Forget it."

They began walking, toward the perimeter, past the main gate, and out into the world beyond.

14

They spent that first night in a nice neighborhood in the western suburbs of Omaha, in a big brick colonial sitting at the top of a hill sloping gently toward the street. Sunset had been about an hour away when they found the place, which gave them time to run a bit of reconnaissance, make sure the neighborhood was deserted. It was cold and cloudy, and the air smelled of rain. She'd never been to this part of Omaha before, and even though it looked like any other neighborhood in any other city in America, it felt alien, unfamiliar.

The house was set back about fifty yards from the road. A jungle of waist-high grassy bushes choking what had once been a front yard swayed in the afternoon breeze. The structure appeared to be in reasonably good shape, but the exterior walls bore a greenish tint from the mildew that had had years to do its work. A few of the windows were still intact, but most had blown out, victims of rain and wind and general inattention. An old Range Rover sat in the driveway, but the weeds had grown up around it, crept through the undercarriage and into the wheel wells, into the engine block, a chlorophyll-fueled monster enveloping its victim. The exterior was badly rusted and lacquered with bird droppings.

Rachel checked on Will. He stood vacantly, his eyes were open wide, but they didn't seem particularly focused on anything. Not only had she been unable to protect him from the horrors of this world, but this time she'd brought them all the way to his bedroom door. Certainly, in the old world, seeing your father killed in front of you would be worth years of therapy. But that was in the old world; she didn't have that luxury here. She would simply have to hope she had put enough rebar in him, a steely core that would strengthen the man growing around it.

"I'll have a look around," Charlotte said, checking the clip on her gun.

Rachel nodded. She lit a cigarette, a habit Will detested, but she didn't think he would mind right now. She paced around the car, stretching out her back, the muscles tight from the time spent on the road. By now, the others would know Eddie was dead, almost certainly by her hand. They would panic at the ruin she had brought them by scuttling the deal. The cigarette was down to the nub by the time Charlotte completed her sweep of the house. Rachel dropped it to the ground and stamped it out with her boot.

"Place looks clear," she said.

"You know of anyone else with gas back home?"

Charlotte scrunched up her face as she considered the question.

"Harry, probably. He always liked to be one step ahead of everyone."

"Yeah. I agree," she said.

Charlotte tapped her lips with two fingers; Rachel handed over a cigarette.

"What now?" Charlotte asked after taking a long drag.

Rachel took a deep breath.

"Beats me."

They went inside, Charlotte first, Rachel and Will trailing behind. The house was empty, had been for some time, that much was obvious. A thick layer of dust covered the hardwood floor before them, pristine, virginal, like a fresh blanket of snow. A smell of decay hung in the house, but it was not entirely unpleasant, the smell of a used bookstore perhaps, the pages within aging and browning and exhaling their fine woody, nutty breath. The walls bore a layer of green mildew. A heavy gloom filled the house, the dying light of the day filtering in through curtains that had become brittle after years of exposure. When Charlotte went to open the curtains covering one window, they simply disintegrated in her hands. It was cold, of course, but the structure provided some relief from the chillier temperatures outside.

There was a small sitting room to the right, a couch, and a flat screen television mounted on the wall. A bookcase stood in the corner, stuffed with dozens of paperbacks, damp and swollen from years of exposure to the elements. Rachel set Will down on the couch and examined the bookcase, sliding her thumb across the books' cracked spines. Always a reader in her youth, she'd come to almost worship books in the years since the pandemic, Books held a talismanic spell over her, a doorway to other worlds where this terrible plague had never happened. She immersed herself in every kind of fiction, the classics, romance, mystery, chick lit, even a post-apocalyptic story now and again, which was a particularly weird experience, like looking at yourself in one of those haunted funhouse mirrors.

But her favorites were the mysteries, especially the ones set in the big cities, stories of Los Angeles or New York or Chicago, giant megalopolises pulsing with life, people crowded into streets and tenements and office towers slipping and sliding around each other. She liked the idea of crowded places because there were so few of them anymore. She hoped storytelling lived on, in the little pockets of humanity out there, but it made her sad to think there were no children to read bedtime stories to. It was all these books, the ones here, and the ones back at the trailer and sitting unread in all the homes and libraries and bookstores of the world, together that told their story.

A quick sweep of the first floor was uneventful.

"I'll check upstairs," Charlotte said.

"I'll come with you."

"You stay with Will."

"Be careful," Rachel said.

Charlotte patted her gun and smiled.

"Always."

She knelt next to Will, who had curled up in a ball on the couch.

"Buddy, I'm going to look for some food."

He blinked once.

Charlotte's footsteps upstairs echoed through the empty house as Rachel made her way to the big galley kitchen. It was a time capsule, a frozen moment, two glasses and a coffee mug still sitting on the counter. Next to the mug was a bottle of cough syrup, half full, but its contents long petrified into a thick purple rock. Droppings here and there, little gifts from the animals that had found this place over the years. As she surveyed the kitchen, a huge crash startled her.

"Sorry!" Charlotte called out. "Stepped on some rotted flooring."

"You OK?"

"Fine."

Rachel exhaled.

She went for the pantry first, which was mostly empty but gave up a few treasures. Two cans of tuna and one can of vegetable barley soup. After checking them for rust or bulges that might signify the presence of botulism, she tucked them into her pack. This would do quite nicely for tonight, but the mostly barren pantry served as a reminder that the bill would be coming due very soon.

She checked the freezer next, not for food, but because people often stored batteries and cigarettes in them, both of which would be useful, if not for themselves, then for barter. But this freezer contained nothing but spoiled, vacuum-sealed food. Any stench of spoilage had long since faded. As she finished the sweep of the kitchen, she heard Charlotte coming back down the steps.

"All clear," Charlotte said. "The upstairs is in bad shape, though. A lot of rot from the rain. A few holes in the roof. Another year or two, this place is going to come down."

"What else is new?" she said.

Charlotte shrugged her reluctant agreement.

"It'll work for now," Rachel said. "We'll hunker down here for a bit until we can figure out the next step. There are other communities out there, maybe we can hook on somewhere."

"What about Will?" Charlotte asked.

"One thing at a time."

THEIR SLEEPING BAGS were arranged in a triangle around the remains of the previous night's blaze they'd built in the huge fireplace. Rachel lay awake, staring at the moon through the living room window. The thick layer of grime and dust on both sides distorted her view; the moon looked bloated and dingy, a dirty lightbulb in a cold and dark dungeon. It was quiet, quieter than anything than she could remember in her life. Back at Evergreen, there had always been glimmers of life wafting across the compound, popping like popcorn kernels, people coming and going, coughs, sneezes, laughs, even the throes of passion. Here though, there was simply nothing, a photo negative of existence.

Rachel spent part of the evening tending to Will, trying to get him to choke down a little bit of dinner. After he took in a few bites, she tucked him in on the couch and waited for him to fall back asleep. Probably for the best. A bit of self-preservation. A chance to reboot the hard drive. While he slept, Rachel scoured the house for supplies. She found a map of the plains states, a .38-caliber revolver, some empty bottles and jars to store drinking water, which they set outside in the off chance it rained.

When they were done, she lay down next to Will, but she couldn't sleep. Ironic how nighttime forced you to face your issues head on. Darkness had a unique way of shining a bright light on the biggest problem you had. All around her, darkness gripped the land hard, but she felt like she was sitting in a chair, smoking a cigarette, a bright light blinding her vision.

They were in real trouble now. She and Charlotte were out in the wild for the first time in years, her son for the first time ever. Fresh water they could find in the numerous streams and rivers dotting the plains, but food was going to be a real issue. No matter which way you sliced it, *haha no pun intended*, they could be in for some rough seas ahead. They would be living a life stripped to its barest form, a life of simply surviving. The good life was over, and the idea that living on canned goods in a trailer in the middle of a post-apocalyptic Nebraska had been the good life was really saying something.

But there had to be a future somehow, somewhere. They wouldn't be able to stay in Omaha for long. Eventually, Harry and the others would find her. No, they needed to expand the map, think bigger, think wider. There wasn't much to the west until you got to Denver, more than five hundred miles across empty plains. They were better off moving south toward Kansas City or east toward the larger cities in the Midwest, Detroit, Chicago, or Indianapolis. She'd learned from her visits to Market that most of the communities had popped up around the big municipal areas, which were serviced by the big water towers. Rumor had it that some had rebooted enough electrical power to pump water out of the Great Lakes.

She got up at first light and checked on the others. Will was sleeping deeply in the small sitting room; his hair was matted down on his forehead and his cheeks had pinked up in the humidity. She let him be. Another morning. Another day closer to the end of the journey, whatever that journey was, and whatever that end would entail. She had no idea how many days stood in between her and the end of this transition period, but there was one less than there had been yesterday.

Rachel went outside to relieve herself behind a bush. Her mouth tasted like a raccoon had died in it. What she wouldn't have given for a trip to the dentist. They'd been able to maintain some minimum threshold of dental hygiene over the years, but none of them would be starring in a toothpaste commercial anytime soon.

A long, low rumble of thunder broke the morning silence. In the quiet of the western plains, it was deep and guttural, reaching inside Rachel and rattling her core. To the west, a low ridge of clouds.

Will was stirring when she got back inside; he sat up and stretched, his eyelids at half-mast.

"I'm hungry," he said.

There it was again. That swirl of helplessness and guilt rising inside her like a balloon. He didn't mean anything by it, there was nothing accusatory about it. It was a statement of fact, of instinct, from an eleven-year-old boy who wasn't getting nearly enough to eat.

"Working on it, bud."

She drifted into the kitchen, where she found Charlotte cleaning her gun. The skin under her eyes, themselves spider-webbed with red veins, was puffy and dark.

"This weather, huh?" Rachel said.

"Be nice to see some rain for once," she said. "It'll be refreshing."

"If you say so."

"I do say so."

They stood silently, the absurdity of discussing the weather embarrassing Rachel.

"I'm sorry," Charlotte said.

"For what?"

"That it all went down like this," she said. "I know it's not your fault."

Rachel didn't reply.

"I ever tell you about my brother?"

She had told her several times, but Rachel shook her head and let her tell the story again. They needed to tell their stories, sometimes more than once, to flush the lines. It was one way of treating the post-traumatic stress disorder that had haunted all of them over the years. That was something you never saw in the movies or TV shows about the end of the world. It twisted your noodle something fierce, going through what they'd gone through. Even hearing someone cough was enough to set her off, make her feel panicky, sweaty, dizzy.

Rachel frequently had bad dreams. A recurring one left her in the bowels of Scripps Mercy Hospital in San Diego, wandering corridors lined with plague victims. She could never find her way out, no matter how far she walked. Hallway after hallway, the bodies stacked floor to ceiling, leaving barely enough room to negotiate. The bodies were fresh and she could smell the rich, sweet scent of decay, she could feel the heat generated by the exothermic reaction of steady decomposition. She would begin to tremble and panic chewed away at her insides like termites until she snapped awake, her breaths coming in big gasps.

"His name was Joey," Charlotte said. "Ten years younger than me. He was the sweetest little boy. When he got sick, he was so scared. He kept saying, 'Charlie, Charlie' – that was his nickname for me – 'I don't wanna die, I don't wanna die.'

Her eyes shone with wetness.

"On the nights I'm not dreaming about the Citadel, guess what's behind Door Number Two?"

"I'm sorry," Rachel said.

Charlotte laughed a sad laugh, wiped away tears that had spilled silently down her cheeks.

"Oh, I know we all have sad stories," she said.

"Do you want to stay here for a couple days?"

Rachel scrunched up her face in thought.

"Much as I'd like to, we probably need to leave Omaha," she said. "They'll be looking for us."

"Yeah. Too bad, though. It's quiet here, and we may not find much better out there."

"Let me get Will up," Rachel said, her mind focused on the long to-do list facing them. "We've got a lot of work to do."

She drifted back toward the sitting room to check on Will. When she got there, the room was empty, the sleeping bag crumpled up in a heap on the floor. A shimmer of worry, but she didn't panic. His habit upon waking in the morning was to head outside to take a leak. Back at the compound, she had potty-trained him by teaching him to pee through the chain-link perimeter fencing. They made a game of it. But she felt uneasy. She pressed a hand to the cushions; they were still warm from his body heat. He hadn't been up long.

She went outside, priming her ears for the sound of a boy's powerful urine stream. Eddie once told her nothing made him feel older than the sound of his son taking a whizz. When Will had to go, it sounded like someone spraying a firehose. But outside, the morning air was quiet, almost preternaturally so.

"Will!" she called out, the worry swelling inside.

No answer.

Will was gone.

15

She began a loop of the property, picking her way along the creek bordering one side, then keeping close to the line of ash and birch trees that guarded the back side of the yard. In the absence of humanity, nature had been encroaching upon what had been a well-defined yard, thick grasses and small bushes laying the groundwork for the trees that would one day grow here. She didn't think Will would have gone into the woods; it was dark and claustrophobic and he hadn't been on his own enough to have the cojones for such an adventure. This wasn't an indictment of her son; it was the reality. She had raised him close to the vest, for better or worse.

"Will!"

Now she was jogging, cupping her hands around her mouth and screaming at the top of her lungs. A flicker of movement out of the corner of her eye drew her attention, her heart swelling with anticipation, thinking she'd found him. But when she turned her head, she saw it was Charlotte out on the deck.

"What's wrong?" she called out across the expanse of yard.

Rachel stopped and turned toward the deck.

"You seen Will?"

She shook her head.

"I'll look inside," she said, turning and slipping back through the sliding glass door.

Rachel felt lightheaded, this yard, this house, this neighborhood suddenly feeling very far away. She drew in a deep breath and let it out slowly, trying to throw a little drag on the terror accelerating within her. She hadn't had time to think about the impact Eddie's death had had on Will. Would he ever understand what she had done? Would he play that game people often did and blame himself for Eddie's death? She was an adult, and she was not dealing with her father's death well. Now her young son had lost both his father and grandfather days apart. What a fucking nightmare.

God, the abject unfairness of it all. It was enough to break you.

Charlotte was back, alone. She shook her head.

Jesus no.

"Will!" she shrieked, drawing out his name until her vocal cords began to fray.

"Let's go," Charlotte called out. "He couldn't have gotten far."

Charlotte's words galvanized her. They collected their guns and quickly loaded their packs with a day's worth of supplies. As they headed out, she conjured up her last memory of him. He was wearing dirty blue jeans and a dark-blue hooded University of Virginia sweatshirt. He was probably wearing his hat, a red Washington Nationals baseball cap his grandfather had procured for him several years earlier. It was not among his things. With each passing minute, her panic grew exponentially and she wanted to yell at him, ask him if he knew what he was doing to his mother. But then all she could think of was what she had done to him.

They made their way down the brick walkway, Rachel keeping her eyes open for any sign of him. At the sidewalk's end, she noticed a tread print in the dirt, pointing away from the house.

"C, look."

Charlotte paused and studied the shoeprint.

"His?"

"Has to be," she said. "Doesn't look like anyone's been around here in a while."

"You think he ran off?"

She chortled as Charlotte examined the clue.

"Wouldn't you? I killed his father."

"You can't beat yourself up about that," Charlotte said.

"I've ruined his life. I've been ruining it since the day he was born. He's helpless without me."

"What are you, a shrink?"

"Gotta be," she said. "I don't have health insurance."

Charlotte smiled, and it made Rachel feel good for a moment. Somewhere deep down, her sense of humor was hanging on, maybe in critical condition, but still breathing. She smiled as well, not at her own joke, but at Charlotte's sudden flare of good cheer, and it helped calm her nerves.

Rachel crouched and studied the thin layer of dust and dirt blanketing the wide street carving through the neighborhood. There. Another print. And another, all running at an angle away from the house. She motioned toward them, and Charlotte nodded.

They crossed the street, curling around the side of another house, a big brick colonial. The long driveway sloped gently toward a big backyard, looping past the home's side entrance. A big blue trashcan and a green recycling bin sat wedged against the house atop a concrete pad, giving Rachel a strange sense of déjà vu. Every now and again she'd see something like this, something frozen in time and it would rock her. One day many years ago, someone had dragged these cans back from the street for the last time and that had been it. Maybe they'd started feeling a bit under the weather or maybe they'd caught wind of this serious epidemic that was starting to worry people.

Here the trail was harder to follow, but she found half a shoeprint at the edge of the driveway that terminated at the edge of the big open yard. A thick line of trees, about fifty yards wide, ringed the perimeter of the cul de sac. A few pines here and there, but most were bare, giving them a skeletal appearance, the bony branches twisted and wrapped around each other. She could make out the neighborhood on the far side. Even absent its foliage, the little forest was dark and shadowy.

Then: a high-pitched shriek.

She crashed through the brush, the branches and brambles tearing at her face and arms. Ahead, she could hear someone running, heavy footfalls crunching dead leaves and sticks. In a clearing, she paused to catch her breath and find her bearings. A flicker of movement to her right; Charlotte was on her flank, scanning to the north.

"Will!"

She waited a moment, her heart beating so hard it felt like it was choking her.

"Mommy, help!" he called back, his voice scratchy and broken.

His voice came from everywhere and nowhere, bouncing across tree trunks and rocks. That was followed by a low guttural growl that loosened her bowels.

Charlotte bolted ahead, continuing north. Rachel followed, hoping Charlotte had been able to triangulate his location. They ran hard for a minute, slaloming around a thick copse of pines, the air thick with their clean scent. A flash of movement in the corner of Rachel's eye stopped her dead.

"Wait," she hissed at Charlotte, turning her head toward the movement.

They were in a clearing now, the space enclosed in shadow under a sky thick with clouds. Will was about thirty feet distant, lying on his side. His eyes were red from crying and his face was drained of color, pale with terror. There was a hole in his pants and his knee was stained with blood.

On the opposite side of the clearing was a large cat, probably a mountain lion. It was large, full grown, but frightfully skinny. Rachel could count his ribs from where she stood. He looked mangy, his skin bare in multiple spots. She didn't have to think hard about how hungry it probably was. The animal paced back and forth but its eyes never left Will. Charlotte was closer to both Will and the cat than Rachel was, about equidistant from the pair.

"Will," she whispered. "Don't move."

She didn't know why she was whispering.

Rachel readied her weapon; she had a clear shot at the animal.

"You got it?" Charlotte asked.

Her hands were sweaty but steady.

"Got it."

She nestled the stock of the weapon into her shoulder, tilting her head to sight the target through the scope. The mountain lion had stopped pacing, perhaps aware of the dynamic changing around him. His big head twitched once, and then he licked his chops, a string of drool dripping from his mouth. Now his attention was focused squarely on Will, sizing him up, ensuring he wasn't underestimating his prey.

It was the biggest animal Rachel had ever seen in the wild; it was quite magnificent, a symphony of power and beauty and terror. Just being near it was disorienting and made it hard to breathe. People weren't supposed to get this close to nature. As she eyed it, she considered her options. Ideally, she would take it down with a burst to the head, but that was a high-risk shot. Her best bet was to aim for the large center mass, for the cat's torso.

The cat was weak, Rachel could tell. Weak and probably crazed with hunger. She'd have to drop him with this burst, she had to empty the clip into him before it got within biting distance. Even wounded, he could finish Will off in short order. She took one step toward it. Then another. Then a third. Each step brought her a bit closer to putting her body between the cat and Will. But there was still a relatively clear line between predator and prey.

As Rachel prepared to fire, Charlotte circled behind the wildcat, far enough off his haunches that he paid her little attention. She didn't know what Charlotte was doing, but she pushed it out of her mind. She was no more than twenty feet away from it now, well within her firing range. Charlotte swooped in opposite her, leaving the animal pinned in between them.

"Hey!" Charlotte called out, swinging her arms over her head.

The cat ignored her.

Rachel inhaled deeply and let it out slowly, the breath coming out in herky-jerky fits and starts. She pulled her finger taut against the trigger. A little more pressure and the gun would fire. She tensed her body in advance of the imminent recoil.

A twig snapped underfoot.

The cat charged.

She fired.

It all happened at once.

The cat was little more than a flash in her field of vision. She held the trigger tight until the clip was empty, a span of no more than a few seconds. The gunfire was deafening but she could hear muted screams and grunts in the ether.

The clip was dry, she was on the run, her feet working independently of any conscious thought. She had to get there, make herself the last line of defense between the cat's jaws and Will's flesh. The scene was still unfolding in blurry, jagged pieces, and she couldn't process what was happening – she'd had a goddamn machine gun and she had missed and now they would all probably die out there.

She heard a scream, a terrible, terrible howl of pain as she drew closer to Will, jumping across the last few yards and shielding Will's body with her own. It had descended into total chaos now, a tangle of teeth and arms and legs and blood and hot saliva. She wrapped her left arm around Will's torso while pushing back against the mountain lion using her legs and free arm, waiting for the inevitable clamp of jaws around their legs.

Then Charlotte was on the cat's back, her left arm coiled around its throat, and she rode it like a rodeo bull, pulling back on its windpipe, using her right arm for leverage. Its oxygen supply cut off, the animal went berserk, struggling to buck Charlotte free, but giving Rachel and Will enough margin to wriggle free to safety. When he was safe, Rachel crawled back toward them, scrambling for the weapon Charlotte had dropped in the clearing.

Charlotte struggled with the animal, which had knocked her to the ground and pinned her under his baseball-glove-sized paws. Charlotte's arm was up, pressed under his jaw, and he struggled mightily to find purchase with his teeth. Rachel wrapped her fingers around the grip of the gun and rolled onto her back, less than five feet away from the cat's head.

Charlotte lost her grip and the cat's jaws snapped down on her left arm, biting clean through the flesh and bone, taking her arm almost to the elbow. She howled in agony as blood sprayed from her ruined arm like a geyser. Rachel pressed the muzzle to the animal's temple and pulled hard on the trigger; the gun roared, the blast deafening her. The bullet pierced the cat's cheek and blew out the side of its head.

The cat slid to the ground, a strange moaning noise emanating from its throat. That brought everything to a dead stop, the cacophony of chaos around her frozen, and then she could see, she could really see what the cat had done to Charlotte. She was on her side, cradling the ruined stump of her arm close to her chest. Her jacket was soaked with blood. She was making strange noises and her eyes were rolling around in their beds, unable or uninterested in focusing on anything.

Quickly, Rachel peeled off her jacket and wrapped a sleeve tightly above Charlotte's bicep as a makeshift tourniquet. She yanked the knot tight, as tightly as she could, until the flow of blood had slowed to something resembling a trickle. This seemed to settle Charlotte down, and her flailings began to subside. She rolled onto her back and looked skyward, her eyes open but blank. Her breathing was slow but steady.

It was quiet around them, so quiet she could hear the dry ground drinking up the pools of Charlotte's blood. She glanced over at Will, who was standing over them, his eyes wide, his face pale as the reality of the situation settled over him. In those eyes, she could see the man he might one day grow into. A hard man, hardened by days like today.

"Will, don't-"

She almost told him not to look. Not to look at Charlotte, who lay dying here before them. How cruel that would be, to tell him not to look at the woman who had saved his life. Besides, what was she protecting him from? The truth? This was what happened. This was how it was.

She looked back at Charlotte.

She was still breathing, but her eyes were closed.

16

Heavy clouds blocked the sun for the balance of the day. Will gathered wood and together they built a fire. Charlotte was too weak to move, and Rachel didn't know what else to do but keep her warm and hydrated. When Charlotte bubbled up to something resembling consciousness, Rachel would tip a bottle of water to her lips. Charlotte would drink it down quickly, but then her strength would flag and the water would overflow her lips and spill down her cheeks.

The blood loss had slowed, but it had not stopped. Eventually, Charlotte would reach a point of no return, and that would be that. Will sat huddled against her, silent. He hadn't said a word since it happened. Rachel focused on the small fire before them, ripping, cracking, biting. The corona of flame, its wild hair flailing in the wind. The heat radiating from the blaze felt good, and for a moment here and there she would forget their terrible predicament.

The afternoon wound on and the daylight, weak as it was, began to fade. The fire grew brighter in the dimming light, the blues in the core of the blaze drawing Rachel's focus. She wanted to help her friend but she had no idea how. Major trauma. Life-threatening trauma. She thought about her father, about how he would handle this. He wouldn't beat around the bush, he would tell it like it was. Focus on the problem.

The bleeding.

If she couldn't stop the bleeding, then nothing else mattered.

The bleeding.

She stared at the fire.

It crackled with terrible heat.

An ember popped, landing on Will's arm before quickly dying.

"Ow!" he mumbled.

The fire.

And then it became clear to her. What she would have to do.

Her head swam and she felt faint.

No.

She couldn't do it.

She glanced back at Charlotte, whose eyelids were fluttering now. They opened again and she looked around. Then she winced heavily, a wave of pain washing over her. Rachel took her friend's remaining hand and held it as Charlotte surfed the pain curling through her body.

She held Charlotte's gaze.

"I have to close you up."

"How?" Charlotte eked out.

Rachel quickly cut her eyes to the blaze.

Charlotte moaned, a low guttural mumble from her throat, a mumble of reluctant agreement.

Rachel studied the scene carefully, trying to figure the best way to cauterize Charlotte's arm. Was she supposed to simply dip the stump into the blaze and hold it there until it sealed shut?

No.

Metal.

She needed a piece of metal.

The flat of their hunting knife.

Rachel slid in behind Charlotte until her back was pressed up against her chest. Charlotte's shirt was drenched in sweat and Rachel could feel her heart thrumming against her breastbone. She pressed her hand to Charlotte's forehead; it was cool to the touch, but she doubted it would be for much longer. Infection would set in soon.

Inch by inch, she scooted her bottom along the ground, closer and closer to the fire. Charlotte was barely conscious; her head lolled back and forth, jerking to attention for a moment before dipping to one side or another. The heat from the blaze intensified as they drew closer to it, uncomfortably warming Rachel's left flank as she jostled their bodies around toward the fire. Will paced back and forth near the fire, running his hands through his hair. His eyes were red with tears and his upper lip was shiny with the mucus running from his nose.

Oh, what a mess what a mess what a goddamn mess.

Charlotte was less than a foot from the fire now; Rachel took care to support the girl's body lest she tip forward into the blaze and make a big problem even worse. Rachel slid around so she was perpendicular to Charlotte.

"Will, come here. Sit behind her and hold her up."

"What are you going to do?"

"We're going to use the fire to seal up her arm."

His eyes boggled.

"It's her only chance. We have to stop the bleeding."

"Will it work?"

"I don't know. Just do what I ask."

The boy obeyed his mother for possibly the first time in his life and took his spot on the ground, propping their nearly unconscious patient up.

Rachel took a deep breath and let it out.

"Buddy, this is going to be awful, worse than you can probably imagine, but no matter what, you have to hold onto her. She's going to scream like hell, and it's going to hurt her worse than anything you can imagine, but she'll die if we don't try."

He nodded, his eyes big and wide.

She tilted the knife into the flames and let the heat do its work. She held it as long as she could, using a swatch of her jacket sleeve to protect her skin as the handle grew hotter. As the blade began to glow, she hugged Charlotte and kissed her gently on the cheek.

She wrapped her fingers around Charlotte's upper arm. The tourniquet had come loose and the wound was leaking again, tracing ribbons of blood around Rachel's fingers and hands. It was slippery and made it hard to keep purchase on the knife. She got her first close look at the wound; it was huge, uneven, ragged, shredded skin and muscle and fat hanging limply from the stump.

"I'm sorry."

Her hand trembling, Rachel pressed the knife blade to the wound and Charlotte's body jerked briefly as the hot metal kissed her flesh for the first time. The acidic smell of singed hair and burning meat filled the air. Rachel's stomach roiled from the odor and she began to dry heave, her stomach clenching and hitching, trying to expel food that wasn't even there. And they were just getting started. They had a long way to go, several more inches of open flesh to close. Tears triggered by the smoke streamed down Rachel's cheeks as the heat sealed off the outer edge of the wound.

Then Charlotte began to scream. It was otherworldly, blurring Rachel's vision as Charlotte's howls of agony penetrated her, violated her.

"Shh, shh," she whispered, feeling as colossally stupid as she ever had in her entire life.

She pulled the knife away from the skin, which had turned bright red and puffy. But Charlotte was still bleeding, still screaming.

"Hold her tight, buddy, wrap your arms around her waist."

Charlotte was mumbling now, the howling on hold for the moment. Rachel leaned in, pressing her ears to Charlotte's lips.

"Stop, please stop, please stop, please stop..."

Rachel leaned away from her, but Charlotte continued mumbling.

"You're doing great, sweetie, we're almost done."

She couldn't stop, she had to keep going. Charlotte would die otherwise.

The knife went back into the fire for another minute, until the steel was glowing red. Rachel began the second round of cauterization, holding the metal toward the devastated center section of the wound. The effect on Charlotte was galvanic, her scream apocalyptic, like nothing Rachel had ever heard in her life. Her hand trembled as the metal did the work, cooking away flesh and hair and skin. Her will began to fray at the edges and other thoughts began to creep in like mold.

Pointless.

No point.

She's dead anyway.

Already dead.

The howling, somehow, deepened, Rachel's entire arm shaking now. Will was crying now, burying his face in Charlotte's shoulder blade as he wept, his arms still wrapped dutifully around her waist.

She couldn't.

She lifted the knife from Charlotte's arm and immediately, the girl's body went slack, like a puppet whose strings were cut, and the screaming stopped.

It was for Charlotte. She couldn't keep inflicting that kind of torture on her friend. For what? For a negligible increase in her odds of survival? Statistically speaking, Rachel was elevating Charlotte's odds from precisely zero to about zero.

It certainly wasn't because Rachel couldn't do it, nope, heavens no.

It wasn't because Rachel didn't have the stomach for it, that she would do literally anything to keep Charlotte from screaming again. Because that would be the act of a coward, of someone who had failed a friend in her most desperate hour, someone who wasn't really cut out for these types of things, who would lead them all to their deaths.

And she wasn't a coward, right?

It wasn't that Charlotte was dead because of her and then it wasn't that Will would be dead soon and then she would be too. Or maybe she would die first because she was dumb and she would leave Will all alone out there and he would die alone and afraid and it would be because his mother was nothing more than a coward, the worst kind of coward.

But that would only be if she were a coward.

Which she most certainly was not.

She gently pulled Charlotte away from the fire, away from Will's embrace and laid her down on a soft patch of ground. Her eyes were closed, and her chest rose and fell slowly, her breathing slowing in the aftermath of the trauma she had endured.

This was it then.

Charlotte would die and there was nothing anyone could do to stop it.

"Are you done? Did it work?" Will asked, his voice spiced with a hint of hope.

"We're done, sweetie."

Rachel lifted Charlotte's head into her lap and gently stroked her hair. Her back ached and her butt was sore, almost numb from sitting on the ground, but she did not move. At dusk, Charlotte's breathing slowed. Rachel pressed a finger to Charlotte's wrist. She found a pulse, but it was faint, like the twinkle of a faraway star.

When the dusk had melted into darkness, the terrain beyond the reach of the fire black with night, Charlotte Spencer took one last breath and died.

17

They carried Charlotte's body back to the house. She was a wisp of a thing, maybe a hundred pounds, but it had been awful, excruciating work. Rachel slept fitfully, her brief stretches of sleep punctuated by dreams about the mountain lion, about Charlotte's agonizing last minutes of life. The next morning, Rachel spent an hour cleaning off her body, freshening up her face with a makeup kit she found in the master bathroom vanity. She didn't put much because Charlotte would have hated it. Only enough to make her look as beautiful in death as she had in life. Then she dressed her in a black cocktail dress from the woman's closet. It was about two sizes too big, but it would have to do.

While she tended to Charlotte's body, Will saw to the grave. There was a rectangular-shaped raised garden where the soil had been soft and made for easy work. He had dug the grave himself, simply starting without prompting, carving out the weedy patch of ground, working silently for hours until the hole was big enough.

Together they had laid her body in the shallow grave. Will backfilled the dirt, gently tamping it down with the back of the shovel, making it nice and neat. When he was done, he placed a large stone above Charlotte's head. His hands and face were black with dirt.

They spent the next two days holed up in the house, each mourning in their own way. Their minds were scattered, and she didn't want to risk any excursions when they were at less than one hundred percent. They passed the time in the sitting room, leafing through paperbacks and old photo albums belonging to the family that had lived here. Little was said, as Rachel wasn't sure how to discuss what had happened with Will. Three of the most important people in his life, snuffed out in a matter of weeks. A crash course in the real world. And it was her fault.

When she tired of reading, she wandered the rooms, looking for work that would need to be done. Some plywood to cover up the windows, keep the elements at bay. There was water damage, of course, but that was true of any uninhabited structure still standing these days. She wasn't ready to leave Omaha yet; they were too shell-shocked. They needed a few days to collect themselves.

But it was time to start scavenging, laying in supplies and hopefully finding some canned goods in the surrounding neighborhoods. She wasn't optimistic, as most places had been picked clean over the years. But what choice did they have? Winter was on its way, and the bony specter of starvation cast a long shadow, the edge of which was right at their heels. She found herself doing the math in her head constantly now. They had three days of food on hand. Three days. They had three days to find some food before the shadow would start to overtake them, before the gnawing in the belly would become the center of their worlds.

"Follow me," she said to him on the morning of that third day.

This elicited no quarrel from him, which underscored the heft in her voice.

She needed to train him how to use a gun. Something she should have done years ago, and that was something Eddie had been right about, bless his shitty soul. But she had put it off and put it off, telling herself she would get to it someday. But she hadn't because she hated guns and to teach him to use them would be admitting they lived in a terrible world, that Will would never have a happy childhood because she would have taught him to kill.

Look where that had gotten them.

A little boy wandering in the woods and Charlotte ends up dead.

There it was.

Charlotte was dead because of her.

If she had done a better job raising Will, he wouldn't have ended up cornered by that goddamn lion and Charlotte would still be alive. End of story. The simplest If-Then statement imaginable.

"What are we doing?" he asked as he followed her down the hallway to the large galley kitchen.

"Come stand next to me," she said as she set a Glock on the speckled granite counter. The heavy weapon hit the granite with a satisfying thud.

"Need to teach you about guns," she said

His eyebrows rocked upward.

"Really?"

"It's time. We might be on our own for a while. And you need to be able to protect yourself if you get into trouble."

He looked down at the floor; she hadn't meant to make him think about Charlotte, but it was inevitable, she supposed. He was old enough to understand there were consequences to actions, even if he didn't think about them before taking those actions.

"This is a Glock," she said.

After making sure it was unloaded, she walked him through each of the gun's components. They went over it until he could identify each part himself.

"I want you to remember something," she said, recalling the lesson her father had given her. "If you fire this gun, other than when we are practicing, you have made a decision to end a life. That doesn't mean you won't miss. That's not the point. The point is that the sole purpose of a gun is to terminate life, and that's the only reason it should ever be used. Understand?"

His eyes were wide and bright, and he nodded slowly.

Her heart broke.

"Sweetie, I'm sorry you have to know about these things."

"It's OK."

"When I was your age, I was in the sixth grade, watching movies and texting with my friends. My stepdad took me to baseball games. I never had to worry about my next meal."

"S'OK, Mommy."

Her will began to waver, and she debated putting the gun away for one more day, preserving his innocence and childhood for a little bit longer. But that time had come and gone. His childhood had ended long ago, if it had ever even started. He was born into a world that demanded adulthood from the get-go, and she had pretended it didn't.

She removed the Glock's magazine and racked the slide to make sure the chamber was clear. Then, following the guidance her father had passed onto her, she racked the slide multiple times before aiming the barrel away from her and Will and pulling the trigger. After hearing the satisfying click, she flipped the weapon upside down, pressed the release button and removed the slide, the spring, and the barrel, explaining each component as she went along. A score of parts made up a Glock, but she focused on the four main components – the slide, the barrel, the frame/receiver, and the guide rod/recoil spring assembly.

"How many bullets does it hold?" he asked.

"This one holds fifteen."

"Do you have to clean it?"

"Yes, every few months," she said. "But it's a very reliable gun. It was one of the most popular types in the old days. We can go through a few hundred rounds between cleanings."

She put it back together, keeping the magazine to the side, and held it out, muzzle pointed downward, for him to hold.

"Go on."

His eyes fixed on the gun, and he reached out slowly, like a frightened puppy considering an offer of a treat. He took it from her hand and wrapped his fingers around the grip.

"It's unloaded," she said, "but you still never point it at anyone unless you plan to use it."

Will nodded imperceptibly, his eyes wide open, his lips pressed tightly together. He seemed to grasp the gravity of the situation, of the lesson underway here. Simply by handing him the gun, she was telling him she wouldn't always be there to protect him, that he would have to protect himself, and that in this world, he might have to do violence. Not like the old days, when your gun was far more likely to be accidentally fired by a toddler than by you against an intruder. No, the odds were good he would have to use it for real.

They went outside to the expansive backyard, where she set up a series of targets on a folding table, using the tops of cardboard boxes she pilfered from the family's collection of board games. She folded each top in half, forming a reasonably stable triangle at which to take aim. She took a few steps back and eyed the box tops, adorned with the bright imagery of happy families playing Life and Monopoly and Trouble.

"A few rounds today," she said. "To give you the feel of it."

She spent a few minutes going over the correct firing stance, again repeating the lessons Adam had taught her, the lessons he had learned from his own father when he was a boy.

"Stand behind me now," she said. "Watch carefully."

She waited until he took a spot to her four o'clock, about ten feet off her right hip. Then she sighted the first target and squeezed the trigger at the Trouble box. The Glock was a remarkably stable weapon, hitching only slightly as it let loose the 9-mm round. Her aim was true, and the box top burst into the air before floating back to the ground.

"Good shot, Mommy," he said.

"Thanks," she said. "Your turn."

She handed the gun to him.

"Remember," she said, "there's already a bullet in the chamber."

He took the gun and mimicked her movements, assuming a decent firing stance, gripping the weapon properly.

"It's going to buck a little when you fire it, but not too badly," she said. "You might be sore tomorrow."

He nodded, took a deep breath, let it out slowly. His hand trembled, giving the barrel a slight shimmy. He took another breath, steadying the gun before nerves washed over him again and the barrel began wobbling once more.

He fired.

The report of the gun blast echoed across the yard, across the neighborhood; her thoughts flickered briefly to those unseen strangers who would have heard their gunfire and wonder what was happening.

"I missed," he said.

"It's OK," she said. "Try again."

"I don't wanna do this anymore," he said.

Irritation rippled through her and she bit down on the corner of her lip to keep herself from lashing out at him. Time. It was going to take time.

"It's OK," she said.

She gently took the gun from his hand and cleared the chamber.

"We'll try again later."

"No."

"It's important for you to learn."

"No!" he said, turning and fleeing for the house, leaving her standing alone in the yard.

THEY ATE dinner by the dim light of a candle. Will hadn't said anything about it, and she was hesitant to bring it up, lest she drive him farther away from the lessons he needed to know. The good news was that, despite the failed gun lesson, she had managed to teach him something valuable before they ate.

"I can't find the can opener," he said to her as they prepared their meal.

"It's OK," she said. "I know a trick to open cans without a can opener."

"You do?"

She nodded.

"Your grandfather showed me."

His face tightened up and he nodded.

"I'll show you," she said. "Outside."

"Put the can face down," she said when they were on the stone porch. "Then scrape it back and forth really hard."

"Really?"

"The friction and the heat will chew away the seal."

He set to work, focusing on the task at hand. The susurration of the stone biting into the metal lid filled the air. As he worked, he chewed on his lower lip, reminding her very much of her father in deep concentration.

"Is that enough?" he asked, pausing and looking up at her. His cheeks were red from exertion and a sheen of sweat slicked his forehead.

"Let's see," she said. "Hold it tight, up near the top."

"OK."

"Now give it a hard squeeze."

He did, grunting as he did so. After a few moments, the metal seal failed and the lid popped free.

"Wow!"

But the excitement had faded as their reality crashed in around them. All alone. Charlotte dead. He pushed around his food, half a can of creamed corn, before abandoning it entirely. He got up and wandered around the living room, pausing at a family portrait hanging over the fireplace.

Five of them, mom, dad, and three kids under the age of ten, including a set of twin girls. They were dressed in khaki shorts and bright white polo shirts, kneeling in the sand at the beach. A date in the corner of the photograph indicated it had been taken in July, scarcely a month before the outbreak. She wondered what had become of them. If they had died in the plague, they had done so elsewhere, as the house had been empty of bodies.

"What was it like?" Will asked.

"What was what like?" she asked, scooping up the last bit of corn in her bowl.

"The plague."

She froze, the spoon suspended halfway between her mouth and the bowl. He had never asked about the pandemic before. It occurred to her that although he had never experienced anything resembling a normal childhood, he had been spared the horror of living through those terrible death-filled days.

"It was very bad, buddy."

"Were you scared?"

"Yes," she replied. "Everyone was scared and panicked. And people do terrible things when they're scared and panicked."

"Were you afraid of dying?"

"Yes," she said. "The disease killed almost everybody. I kept waiting to get sick. Every time I sniffled or coughed, I thought I was coming down with it. Some days I still think that."

A memory spun to the forefront of her conscience. It was right about the time things were starting to collapse. The Internet had gone down, and electricity had become spotty. Her mom Nina was dead, but her stepdad Jerry was still alive, although very ill. There was a little market just outside their subdivision, one that sold fancy cheeses and wines and gourmet sandwiches but also sporting a small apothecary. She wanted to get some medicine for him, anything to slow down the infection's dizzying course. He was burning with fever by then, coughing up blood.

It was the first time she'd been out in days; Jerry wouldn't let anyone leave the house in the hopes that a self-quarantine would keep them safe. Her neighborhood was silent but for the rustle of the leaves on the trees, the flapping of wings of vultures circling overhead. She jogged the whole way, this neighborhood she'd lived in for three years now terrifyingly unfamiliar. It took her ten minutes to cover the distance.

The acrid tang of something burning tickled her nose when she made it to the little commercial strip that was home to Brigid's Market. A black column of smoke drifted sideways in the sky, but she couldn't tell where it was coming from. The market appeared intact, the Open sign still hanging in the window. It was dark inside, though, as the market was on the same electrical grid as her neighborhood, which had lost power the day before.

It was a bright beautiful San Diego morning, mid-seventies, the air still, absent even the slightest breeze. Despite that, she was shivering, her teeth chattering together. Her heart was pounding so hard that in the massive quiet she could hear it in her ears. She cupped her hands around her face and pressed up against the glass, hoping she'd be able to see if anyone was lurking about. She felt naked, exposed and she was beating herself up for not bringing Jerry's handgun, even though she had never used it.

But she had to try, goddammit, she had to try something. She pulled the handle on the door, which swung open without resistance. She took a step inside, keeping one foot in and one out. Then another step. And another until she was inside. The market appeared abandoned, and a yeasty aroma hung in the warm stuffy air. Ahead of her was a wire-rack display of wine bottles identified as STAFF RECOMMENDATIONS! A Merlot from Good Luck Cellars in Virginia (*great with Brie!*), another one from Polar Bear Vineyards (*strong start, smooth finish, hints of oak*) in Napa. Below each bottle was an index card bearing the notes of the staff member who had recommended it.

She took another step, which was as far as she got. In the first aisle, there was a little girl, maybe eight years old, sitting with her back against the cooler. She was still alive, barely, dressed in pajama bottoms and a short-sleeve t-shirt from Branson's House of Wings. Her white-blond hair was tied back in a ponytail, revealing her bright blue eyes.

Her nostrils were dripping blood like a leaky faucet. In her lap was a small dog, which began growling as soon as Rachel rounded the corner. Its fur was thick with congealed blood. The animal made no move toward her, but it was clearly warning her to stay away. The girl's head lolled gently toward Rachel; her eyes struggled to stay open but she managed to get them to half-mast.

"Hi," she said softly. Rachel barely heard her.

Rachel clapped a hand to her mouth, trying but failing to hide the shock of seeing the girl's ruined face. It looked like she had been crying blood and her skin was gray. She had no idea how the girl was still alive; she certainly wouldn't be for much longer. The dog continued to growl at Rachel. The girl looked down at her wee protector and gently stroked her fur.

"Ajax, shhh," she whispered. She closed her eyes and seemed to fall asleep.

Ajax never once took his eyes off Rachel, standing a lonely vigil over his pee-wee-sized master. Not wanting to leave the little girl alone, Rachel sat on the floor and crossed her legs. She waited silently, as her butt went numb on the hard floor. The girl did not open her eyes again, and Rachel did not try to speak to her. An hour later, maybe two, the final seizure rippled through the girl and her body went slack. She was dead.

The dog tilted its head toward the girl's face and whined softly. But it made no move to abandon its owner.

"What now, boy?" she asked. It didn't seem strange to ask the dog what she should do now because it was unlikely she had a better idea than it would.

She whistled at him and held out her hand, hoping to coax him her way. She didn't know why she did it; she supposed she couldn't stomach the idea of leaving the dog behind in this mausoleum. She did it without thinking about how she would even care for a dog that wasn't hers. She rose to a crouch, holding out her hand, pleading with the pup to come to her. But in the end, she didn't have to worry about how to take care of the dog because he refused all her invitations. After raiding the store shelves for supplies, Rachel checked on the girl one last time. The dog had burrowed up into a little ball in the dead girl's lap, casting a wary gaze at Rachel.

All these years later, she still dreamed about Ajax, standing watch over that beautiful, ruined little girl.

"Do you think this family died?" Will asked, his gaze still fixed on the portrait.

"Yes," she said. "They probably all died."

"These kids were my age," he said, his voice thick, cracking.

"It made almost everyone sick," she said. "Even kids."

"How come you and Pop-pop didn't get sick?"

"I don't know, sweetie."

THEY HAD HUNKERED down in the huge master bedroom at the back of the house. It was wide and airy, the previous owners going minimalist in here. The bed sat on a wooden platform, covered by a musty bedspread. Two lights so unpretentious that they swung back around to pretentiousness hung from the ceiling. There was a simple chest of drawers up against the wall. A flat-screen television was mounted above it.

Will fell asleep quickly, but slumber eluded Rachel. The little dog Ajax ran free in her mind. How long had he waited with the little girl, how long had he protected her? How long before his own survival instinct took over? Why torture herself with questions that could never be answered?

Her body cried for sleep, her eyes thick and gritty with fatigue. She counted sheep, she practiced some breathing exercises. Slow inhale to a count of eight, hold to a count of four, exhale to seven. It took a few iterations, but eventually, her body loosened. She began slipping over the edge of consciousness when a sharp noise yanked her back from the precipice.

Her heart racing again, she considered the possible sources of the noise. House settling. It must have been the house settling. These houses were wearing down and with the world so quiet, every pop and creak was amplified. Yeah, that had to be it. The house settling.

Cannibals, cannibals were breaking in and they would kill and eat her and Will.

She pushed that thought out of her head, that was crazy, paranoid thinking. No one knew they were here, the odds of a bandit breaking into *this* house on *this* night were astronomically small. Math didn't lie, folks.

Creak.

No, math did not lie, because math never said the odds were zero. In the pitch-black dark, her head throbbed with fear, her breath doled out in shallow spurts. It felt like the oxygen had been sucked out of the room. She turned her head gently toward Will. His deep, even breathing told her he was still asleep.

She primed her ears, her breath frozen, lying perfectly still so she could detect the slightest noise.

Creak.

A pause.

Sniff.

She froze.

There it was.

Houses didn't sniff. Joists and floorboards did not sniff.

She slipped out of bed, reaching for the M4 she'd left leaning against the nightstand. Another sniff, another creak, perhaps on the stairwell. The acoustics in the house were strange, made it difficult to triangulate the source of the noise. Death was close now, she could feel it.

She needed a plan, but it was hard to focus. Fear caromed through her, scattering her thoughts like bowling pins. One option was to blindly fire down the stairwell and ask questions later. But not knowing how many there were, if she didn't get all of them in the first burst, she could leave herself and Will open to a lethal counterattack. On the other hand, if she didn't open fire now, she might not get a chance to fire at all. She racked the M4's charging handle and tapped the forward assist before switching the safety off.

Then someone spoke, the voice flinty and high-pitched, chilling her to the marrow. Probably a man, but she wasn't certain of that. Behind her, the susurration of Will sliding out of bed, his little feet thumping the floor.

"Wakey, wakey, eggs and bakey!"

She shivered in the darkness, the knowledge that someone was in the house with them making her feel cold.

"Mommy," Will called out.

"Hush," she snapped.

"We know you're up there."

She held her tongue.

"This doesn't have to be messy," the voice continued. "We just want your food."

There was a desperation in the voice, gilding the speaker's words with truth. Behind her, Will stirred. She didn't know what he was doing, only that he was confirming for these intruders that they were here.

"Mommy," Will said.

"Quiet," she hissed.

She could make her last stand here; they weren't getting their food without coming in this room. Simply cut them down as they bottle-necked at the door.

"You have sixty seconds to come downstairs with all your goodies."

"Mommy!"

"What?"

"I know how we can get out of here."

"What are you talking about?"

He motioned under the bed, so she got down on her knees and hazarded a look. A rectangular box was wedged between the bedframe and the floor. A shine of her flashlight revealed its contents – a fire escape ladder.

"Help me get it out."

Will crawled under the bed and pushed on the box until she could get purchase on a corner. Together, they yanked it free and quickly removed the ladder from the box. Her last move was to pack up their remaining canned goods, a week's worth of victuals.

"Time's up!"

"In the bathroom," she said, hustling across the room with the ladder under her arm, the straps of her backpack digging into her shoulders. "We'll get out through the back."

While Will unrolled the flexible ladder, Rachel went to work on the window, which was badly misshapen from years of neglect and inattention. Using her legs for leverage, she pushed hard against the sash, praying for it to break free and slide upwards. Try as she might, though, the window would not give.

"Mommy?"

"Yeah bud?" she replied, straining against wood so badly warped into the frame that it might as well have been a single piece.

"Do you smell that?"

She paused and slowly drew in a deep breath. A faint yet tangy aroma hit her nostrils.

Shit.

It was smoke.

These assholes had set the house on fire.

Using the barrel of the M4, she broke out the bathroom window, sweeping around the edges to clear the leftover shards of glass. With Will's help, she hung the ladder's frame over the windowsill. The ladder swung gently in the night breeze.

"You go," she said. "I'll be right behind you."

He nodded, his eyes wide open, his gaze fixed on the open window, the reality of their situation settling in on them. Seconds ticked by, but he made no move toward the ladder. He was gnawing on his lower lip, a sure sign of indecision in the boy.

"Sweetie, we have to get out of here."

He nodded again but he remained rooted to the spot. The smell of smoke grew stronger.

"Just hold tight, and take one step at a time."

"I can't. It's too high."

Her chin dropped, and a sigh of sadness escaped from her throat. Once again, decisions she had made long ago were coming back to haunt her.

"It's OK."

"Are you sure?"

"They're hungry. We'll give them some food and they'll go away."

They went back out to the bedroom and made their way to the door. She didn't want to bring Will down with her, but the setting of the fire had left her little choice. Besides, did it even matter if people knew he'd been born after the plague?

"I'm coming out!" she announced.

"Nice and easy," the voice said. "Hands on your head. No one has to get hurt."

After draping the M4's shoulder strap around her neck, she placed her hands on her head and motioned Will to the same. They stepped gingerly into the hallway and then carefully made their way down the darkened stairwell, one step at a time. In the gloom, she could make out the outlines of several figures waiting at the bottom of the stairs. Her heart was in her throat, as there was nothing stopping these people from murdering them where they stood. That was the world now; these people could simply kill them and leave their bodies to rot here in the foyer of this half-million-dollar house.

As they reached the landing, the group retreated slightly, making room for Rachel and Will. The foyer was dark, but not completely black, illuminated by lanterns the group was carrying. She counted six of them, four men and two women, all of them frightfully thin.

They were armed with handguns, aimed directly at them. It was an unsettling situation to be in, but the presence of the women reassured her a bit. Will pressed close against her, his body trembling. One was holding a thick piece of wood that was smoking heavily. Dammit. The house wasn't on fire. It had been a ruse designed to flush them out.

"What do we have here?" the man on the far left asked. "A little family?"

He was the one who'd done all the talking earlier. He was short, only about an inch taller than Rachel, and very thin. He wore a thick beard, which covered up a face that had once been full but was now droopy with sallow skin. Several teeth were missing from his grill. The whole group bore scars of malnourishment and starvation, sharp collarbones pushing against skin and clothes that hung too loosely on underfed frames.

"How old are you, boy?" the man asked.

"Fourteen," Will said, a fiction they had agreed on.

"Kind of small for fourteen, ain't ya?"

Will shrugged his shoulders as only a real teenager could.

"Whatever. Get the bag," the man said, nudging the woman standing next to him.

The woman approached Rachel and carefully worked the backpack off, one shoulder strap at a time.

"Can you leave us something?" she asked.

The woman leaned in close.

"Sorry," she whispered. She gently squeezed Rachel's upper arm.

"Here's the deal," the man said as the woman handed him the backpack. "If there's food in here, everyone walks away happy. If there isn't, well, let's hope we don't have to cross that bridge."

He crouched and sifted through the bag, squealing a bit as he did so.

"Anything?" asked one of the others.

"Ravioli, three cans, tuna, eight cans. Energy gels."

Will's stomach growled loudly, silencing the group.

The man looked up from the bag.

"We're not bad people," the man said to Rachel. "You get that, right?"

She didn't reply.

"We ain't eaten in a week," he said. He licked his dry lips. "A week. I hate to do this to you folks, but, you know, it is what it is."

Indeed.

"Search the house," he said, directing the others.

"There's nothing else."

The man and one of the women kept watch over Rachel and Will as the others confirmed what Rachel had told them. Everything they had was in that blue LL Bean backpack. Once upon a time, she and Will had been one of the *Haves* in a world of *Have-Nots*. Not because they were good or special or heroic or brave, but only because they'd had the dumb luck to find the warehouse at precisely the right time with the right combination of people and weapons to take it and keep it. And now that was over.

"Don't try and come after us," the man warned.

The man looked at his group and nodded toward the door. One by one, they left, the house emptying out until Rachel and Will were alone in the foyer.

18

They rode.

On bikes they rode west, out of Omaha, skirting the ruins of their warehouse to the south. The decision to ride bicycles had not been made easily; she worried it could leave them exposed, run them up into a dangerous situation they hadn't had time to prepare for. But walking meant taking far more time to cover the same territory, and that was a luxury she and Will did not have. They needed to find food.

It was only about fifty miles from Omaha to Lincoln, but in their weakened condition, they had could only manage a few miles a couple times a day. The rest of the time they spent resting or foraging the plains for edible vegetation. They had taken to eating grasses and hard berries, Rachel hopefully remembering what they could safely eat. One evening, she had guessed incorrectly and they were both up half the night with diarrhea, which had probably put them farther behind on their nutritional requirements than if they had just gone without.

She had transitioned to a new stage of hunger, one she hadn't experienced before. The end of the previous stage had been a constant gnawing in her belly, the shakes that accompanied the dropping blood sugar, the inability to focus for long stretches of time, but deep down a long-ago programmed sense of knowing a balm for what ailed her was coming soon. Never in her life had she gone more than a day or two without food, not even after they'd abandoned the farm in Kansas. Back then, canned goods were readily available, as the impact of the climate change had not really hit home yet.

But now it had broken free into some other dimension of need, of desire, even of lust. It was animalistic, primal, irrational, buried down deep in her DNA, some line of code crafted long ago that worked perfectly, executing, running, warning. You need to eat, Rachel, you need to eat, or you will die. They passed by barren bushes and trees and dead grasses and her body yearned for them anyway, for the flowering plants that had once been there. She had abandoned all other thought processes in service of this one great pulsing need.

Eat.

Her worry that they would stumble across an Evergreen search party hunting for them quickly fell by the wayside. The world was too big, the land overlaid with too many roads to make crossing paths with someone anything more than the longest of longshots. In this world, once gone, it seemed, you were gone.

The road cut straight through the flat endless plains, broken up only by the tiny hamlets peppering the Nebraska landscape. The plains were flat and endless, the horizon broken up by faded billboards and utility poles, the drooping power lines an endless series of smirks against the landscape. As they continued west, Rachel couldn't help but wonder if she would ever come back this way again. Never had she felt so lost, adrift.

On their fourth day, they reached the little town of Greenwood, Nebraska, the two-lane road rolling up into the town's quaint downtown area. Mother Nature's hardiest soldiers had long been at work here, giving the once-picturesque main drag a greenish coat. Weeds and scraggly bushes grew haphazardly from cracks in the road and sidewalks, vines crawling up and around mailboxes and street signs.

As was their practice, they stopped at the edge of the town and hid the bikes. It was early afternoon, the weak sun slowly sliding toward the western horizon.

This was the fourth town they'd come across. She always felt a little better when they came to a town, if only for the hint of civilization. A strange thing, given that the greatest danger lay in places like this, where people would gather and build and defend.

What struck Rachel was the desolation of it all. It was very easy, too easy, to picture herself and Will as the last two people left on Earth. They weren't too far away from that as it was, but the emptiness of the plains, the land flash-frozen in time, made her head spin a little. Two little ships bobbing along the surface of a vast terrestrial ocean, no beginning, no middle, no end.

She didn't expect anything in a burg this small, but hope had a funny way of messing with you. The next pantry, the next cabinet or closet would be hiding a case of canned black beans or spaghetti or a two-pound bag of beef jerky.

"Remember, Spoon," Rachel whispered. "Eyes wide open."

"I'm hungry," he replied. At least he was whispering.

"I'm working on it, buddy."

Then she tapped her index finger against her lips. This time he nodded silently.

Rachel held a pair of binoculars to her eyes and scanned the landscape ahead. There were a handful of buildings fronting the main drag. A law office. A dry cleaner. The town newspaper. A diner. A drug store. Main Street, U.S.A. A handful of long-abandoned vehicles lined each side of the street, all rusted and resting on flat tires, the radials dried and cracked. The windshields were brown from years of accumulated grime. She scanned the rooftops for signs of spotters, forgotten beer cans, lawn chairs, empty cigarette packs. Nothing.

She packed away the binoculars.

Anxiety prickled her. There it was. It was part of her now, endlessly coloring their lives. It seasoned her soul, her every waking hour, her restless sleep. Post-apocalyptic road warrior that she was, she would never get entirely used to the constant threat of danger surrounding them, made worse by her constant fear for Will's safety. She remembered the parenting culture wars that had raged online before the plague, helicopter parents and a ridiculous debate about whether kids should be allowed to walk to the park by themselves. God, they had been so stupid, so naïve. Scared of their shadows. She wondered what kind of mother she would have been in a world where Medusa had never happened. She wouldn't have the perspective of having been through it, of not knowing if she would be able to find enough food to stave off starvation for yet another day.

"Stay behind me," Rachel said to Will.

They crept up Main Street, edging along the sidewalk that materialized at the border of downtown. As they moved westward, Rachel noticed a sharp contrast in the coloring of the building's exterior walls; from the ground to her knees, the walls were quite a bit darker than they were higher up, suggesting a flood had ravaged the downtown area at some point in the past. She brushed her foot along the base of one wall and found it to be soft and crumbling, like a soggy muffin.

They stopped at the town drugstore first. From there, they would fan out to the other establishments. The front door was shattered, its glassy remains puddled at their feet and glinting in the sunlight. Dried mud, residue of receded floodwater stained the flooring, which had yellowed and cracked. The air was musty, thick with invisible spores of dust and mold and decay.

It was difficult to tell how long it had been since anyone had been in here, more a guessing game than anything else. There was an old footprint in the mud a step inside the store, the outline of a shoe tread, a child's pointy mountain range, plainly visible, but it could have been a day old or a month old. She moved behind the counter, which abutted the storefront window. It gave a nice vantage point of downtown. She motioned Will to join her.

"Keep an eye outside. If you see anything or anyone, whistle. You think you can do that?"

Will took a deep breath and nodded, his chest puffing out with pride.

"Stay low, behind this counter."

He gave her two thumbs up.

"Mommy?"

"Yeah?"

"At least it's not zombies, right?"

She smiled, feeling a spark of joy inside her; her little Will, growing up in front of her, a little bit at a time but seemingly all at once. How he knew what a zombie was, she didn't know. An old comic book or novel perhaps. Didn't matter. He was right. At least it wasn't zombies.

She took a few steps backward, reluctant to turn away from him, reluctant to thrust him into this role, to force him to be a man sooner than was fair. *Fair*. A word that didn't carry a lot of weight these days. Everything was decidedly unfair these days, which meant the world *was* fair. If anything, it was fairer than it had been before Medusa, when the color of your skin or the size of your parents' bank accounts had a lot to do with where you ended up, irrespective of talent or hard work. But now everyone was on equal footing. But that meant everyone. Even innocent eleven-year-old boys.

Rachel decided to start with the last aisle and make her way back to the front, toward Will. The shelves were mostly barren, long since picked over, but she found a few items worth purloining. A few tubes of lip balm. Travel-sized shampoo bottles.

She went behind the counter next, swiping a carton of cigarettes that had been overlooked. Perhaps these she could trade for food. One last quick sweep of the little workspace revealed nothing worth taking. There was a door to a small office opposite the register. She turned the handle and gently kicked the door open, raising the muzzle of her M4 just in case. A shimmer of red in the corner caught her eye, and she smiled. It was something she hadn't seen in years.

She picked up the twelve-pack of Coca-Cola, still in its cardboard packing tray, and carried it out to the front. She snapped off two cans from the plastic rings.

"Let's have a drink, shall we?"

"Here," she said, handing Will his very first can of soda.

"What's this?" he asked, gingerly handling the can like it was a bomb.

"Open it," she said, tugging on the pull tab, priming her ears for the reassuring pop of carbonation escaping the can. It was an old can, but a faint hiss greeted her, buried deep like a distant radio signal. Will fumbled with the tab, confused by the strange mechanism before him.

"Slide a finger under the tab there," she said, demonstrating with her own, "and pull straight up."

It popped open on his second try. He held the can under his nose and sniffed.

"Smells weird," he said. "Kind of tickles."

"That's the carbonation," said Rachel. "Take a sip."

"What is it?"

"That, my son, is Coca-Cola," she said. "It's a soft drink. A soda. A pop."

"What?"

"It was a very popular drink before you were born. In the old days."

"Have I ever had it?"

"No," she said. "There was some at the warehouse when we first moved there, but someone stole it."

His eyes widened at that revelation.

"Who?"

Rachel cut her eyes toward the floor.

"We never figured that out," Rachel said.

"A mystery! Cool!"

Only it was no mystery. The morning after the few cases of soda went missing, a man named Martin had confessed to the crime. Harry had marched Martin into the center of the compound and fired a bullet into his head. He did it without hesitating. The rules had been clear from the get-go. Theft from the collective would not be tolerated. How naïve they had been. No one believed anyone would ever do it; the threat of execution had been a lark more than anything. But there they'd been, watching the public execution of a confessed thief, someone they knew, someone they'd worked alongside, drank with, broken bread with.

It had been years since she'd had a Coke. This old flat soda would be a poor facsimile of a once precious treat, but it would have to do. Maybe having one with Will would help erase the memory of that terrible long-ago morning.

"So what is it?" he asked again.

She shrugged.

How *did* you explain a soda to someone who'd never had one before?

"It's sweet. And bubbly. And cold, Spoon, there was nothing like it."

He took a sip and grimaced.

"Too sweet for me. And not very bubbly."

He set the can down on the counter, having already lost interest in this relic from her world. Rachel's shoulders sagged. A dark cloud had slid in above them. She didn't know why; it was just a stupid can of soda. But it simply highlighted the huge chasm between the world that had been ripped away from her and the world into which Will had been born. She took a sip; it was saccharine and oily and reminded her of warm spit. It tasted like the morning after the party. It tasted like the day Harry had executed that poor man. She set the can back down on the counter.

"Yeah, it's not very good now, is it?"

"It's terrible."

She nodded.

"Let's go ahead and finish them though," she said. "We need the calories."

They sat quietly and drank flat soda, working their way through two cans each. Her head buzzed from the sugar rush, and eventually, she could drink no more. When Will finished, they packed away the remaining cans for later.

They spent another hour exploring the small neighborhoods branching off the main drag but they found nothing. Like the corpse of a gazelle worked over by the vultures, the town had been picked clean. Satisfied there was nothing else to scavenge, they boarded their bicycles and began pedaling west. At the edge of town, where the downtown area began morphing back into natural plains, Will braked hard, leaving a skid mark on the moss-covered road. Something had caught his eye; she followed his gaze toward a small shop, standing alone, set back about twenty yards. An old faded sign reading *Brooke's Books'n'Things* hung in the window of the skinny little colonial, its yellow coat of paint long since faded to a sickly hue.

"That's a bookstore, right?" he asked.

She nodded.

"Can we go in?"

She glanced up at the sky and sighed softly. Daylight was running short, and she was hoping to find one more town to search today. She was hungry, so hungry, and she could only imagine what a prepubescent boy was feeling. He was in between growth spurts, but he wouldn't be for long, and God help them if they didn't have a steady supply of calories on hand when the next one hit.

Suddenly, traveling even one more inch seemed impossible. Her head swam and all she could think about was food. Any food at all. Her thoughts raced to the grilled fish tacos she had once enjoyed from a little place called Mike's Taco Club in San Diego. You could sit on the patio and take in the Ocean Beach Pier while you ate, watch the sun dip low until it kissed the horizon, until its light spilled across the edge of the world like a broken egg yolk. Her favorite had been the mahi with the shredded cabbage and she had asked for the extra hot sauce that would make her head itch and she would still smell it in her clothes the next day.

During high school, she had eaten there once or twice a week with her mom and Jerry and they would try to get her to tell them more about school or her friends. Her mom desperately wanted her to fit in. That was one thing she had liked about Jerry, he didn't get on her about being popular or making more friends.

"Let the girl be," he'd said to her mom during one particularly painful argument. "if she's happy, why can't you leave her be."

He took a long swig of his Heineken and gave her a wink.

He'd never been her favorite person, but she had to give him credit for that. In fact, he'd always treated her like his flesh and blood; had she ever thanked him? He never judged. He was never condescending. He loved her unconditionally. He was as laid back as they came, the kind of ease that accompanied successful men. And he had been successful. And he was there. From the time her mom had met him when Rachel was ten years old until the day he died, he had been there. He traveled for work but always took the earliest flight home he could get. He took Nina out on a date once a week, without fail.

He had been a good man.

And she became angry at Adam all over again.

"Mommy?"

She glanced over to see Will watching her like she was having a mental breakdown, which she may have been, when you got right down to it. Tacos, tacos, tacos. It was all she could think about. She was having a hard time focusing.

"Sure, buddy. It's getting late. We'll get some books and spend one more night here."

IT WAS a bookstore from the deepest recesses of her imagination. The building itself was in remarkably good shape. A few water stains marked the ceiling, but the windows were intact, and the bookshelves and bookcases appeared unmolested. The walls were painted a light yellow, which hadn't faded too badly over the years. Posters and artwork lined the walls, some professional, others clearly birthed from the hands of little ones. At the front of the store stood a bulletin board, pinned with flyers for upcoming literary events, poetry readings, signup sheets for writers' groups or book clubs.

Omaha Writers' Conference October 14-16!

Greenwood Writing Group, Meets Every Third Thursday of the Month

Brooke had died with her books. Will found her skeletal remains leaned up against a bookcase in the back of the store, her nametag still pinned to her blouse. A stack of books sat next to her, another one still open in the poor woman's lap. Rachel had no idea what had happened here, but she liked to think Brooke had died as she had lived.

Rachel crouched next to the desiccated corpse and flipped up the cover. She had a morbid desire to know what the woman had been reading at the end of her life. It was a hardcover copy of *A Wrinkle in Time* by Madeline L'Engle, one of Rachel's favorites when she was a kid.

"Have you read that one?" Will asked.

"I did," she replied, her mind boomeranging back to Mike's Taco Club. Sometimes she went with the brisket tacos, which came topped with this relish-slaw thing that was so good you'd eat it straight, with your hands if you had to.

"What's it about?"

"It's a science fiction story about two kids looking for their dad after he disappears."

"Is it good?"

"I loved it."

"What happened to their dad?"

"He was a scientist who disappeared while working on a secret project for the government."

"And they went looking for him?"

"Yes."

"Were they scared?"

"I'm sure they were."

He pondered this, scrunching up his face in thought. It made him seem so grownup and so small at the same time.

"Do you get scared?"

She considered her response.

"Sometimes."

"What are you scared of?"

She reached out and gently touched his face with the palm of her hand, quickly enough that he didn't have a chance to pull away from her. His face blurred before her.

"Mainly I worry about you."

He cut his eyes to the ground.

"It's OK to be scared, you know."

He continued staring at something on the ground. Had he spotted a bite to eat? Maybe a taco?

Tacos.

"Even the bravest people who ever lived were scared."

"They were?"

"Yes. Being brave doesn't mean you're not scared."

"It doesn't?"

"It means being scared and doing it anyway."

"I miss home."

"I know," she said. "We're going to find a new home though. A new place for us to be happy."

"When?"

"Bud, I'm going to be totally honest with you," she said. "I really don't know. I hope it will be soon."

He nodded.

"Can we get some books?"

She took a deep breath and let it out slowly. Something wet landed on her arm and she observed with some horror that she had been salivating.

"Yes. Grab some books," she said. "I'm going to sit down for a second."

As Will toddled off to browse, Rachel's muscles failed her. That last bit of fuel powering her engines was spent, leaving her with no more to give. Her legs gave out underneath her and she slowly sank to the floor next to the inimitable Brooke.

Sitting down felt good. She pulled her knees up to her chest, wrapped her arms around them. It did not strike her as odd that she was sidling up next to a decade-old corpse.

Will wandered the store, grabbing one book after another, stacking them by the wall. After a while, he sat down to read. As Rachel watched him, sitting side by side with the late proprietor of the store they were ransacking, she wondered when they would eat again.

19

 A house.

What day was it

Walls.

What year was it

Floors.

Where's Will?

Books.

Who's Will?

Your son you dumb bitch.

Bitch was a good word.

You didn't hear it enough.

You didn't hear anything enough.

Like the sizzle of a steak hitting the grill. Nothing then a hiss of the juice hitting the blaze and a bloom of flame leaping to kiss the inch-thick ribeye. Then the air would fill with the rich, succulent scent of cooking meat. In the corner of the grill was a big eight-ounce potato, wrapped in aluminum foil, awaiting its destiny to be split open and loaded with cheese and sour cream and butter, a thick pat of butter that slid over the firm flesh of the spud.

No, you definitely did not hear that sound often enough.

Did people still eat steak?

Were there still cows?

Rachel woke up. Her head was clear, but it wouldn't be for long. She didn't know if that's how starvation worked in other people, but that's how it had been for her. Cycling between lucidity and madness, the periods of clarity growing shorter until they would be gone, and she would drift along in madness until she died not even knowing she needed to eat.

Lincoln now. They needed to get to Lincoln.

A decent sized city. Lots of nooks and crannies.

She touched her flank, counting her very visible ribs one at a time like she was thumbing through a file cabinet. Food. They had to eat.

Captain Understatement reporting for duty!

She wasn't even hungry anymore.

But she was dying.

She and Will were dying.

A noise.

She sat up quickly and her head swam and she toppled over on her side. She primed her ears for the noise again, but it didn't repeat. The bookstore settling perhaps. Or maybe someone breaking in to kill them and eat them. Because that's what she would do.

She laughed.

Yessiree, she would gladly kill the first person she met and sauté the meat from his thigh with some onions and eat until she was good and stuffed. Or maybe she wouldn't even bother with cooking the meat, just go after it tartare.

Will was asleep next to her. He slept a great deal now, his body conserving what little energy it had left. The clinician in her awoke and gave her the bad news that she gave her every morning.

No more than a couple of days now.

He wouldn't last much longer.

It had been seventeen days since Charlotte died.

Give or take.

They should've eaten the mountain lion. Looking back now, leaving the carcass behind had been a bad choice. The odds it had been rabid were awfully low, and it could have fed them for days. Sure, it would've been a risk, but it would've been a risk worth taking. Besides, they would have cooked the meat and if it did have rabies, which it probably didn't, that probably would've killed the rabies virus it almost certainly did not have. And if it had had rabies and they died of rabies then they could have died with bellies full and even that would have been better than this.

She struggled to her feet, using the wall for leverage. It took a good minute, but eventually, she had managed to get herself upright. The nearest bookcase was about eight feet away from her; in her weakened condition, she would use the bookcases as way stations. Will would probably sleep the entire time she was gone. Even if he didn't, he would stay put, knew his mother had gone scavenging. He was too weak to disobey her. At least that was something. She threw one more glance at him. He was stretched out on the floor, a stack of books next to him.

She shoved off, her legs like overcooked spaghetti underneath her, shimmying across the threadbare carpet. She reached the bookcase and grabbed tight, leaning up against it. Then one step at a time, she edged her way down the aisle, lost in a fog of brightly colored children's books and stuffed animals standing guard atop the cases.

She became aware of a sticky, popping sound; her dried lips almost glued together from dehydration. Water. How could she forget about the water? Jesus, all the shit she had to keep straight. It wasn't fair. Was this what people thought about as they died? The inherent unfairness of it all? You're going to starve to death inside a bookstore in BFE, Nebraska. Quite the epitaph for her life.

She made it to the door. A turn of the knob and a jingle of the little bell and she stepped onto the stoop. It was chilly outside. She held the railing as she went down the steps, her legs rickety underneath her but holding on. The tiny town of Greenwood, which didn't seem like it had been much busier before the plague than after it, spread out before her. The town was an afterthought, a skin tag on the map of Nebraska.

To the west was an automobile scrapyard, crowded with hundreds of rusted-out vehicles, abandoned long enough that they were starting to disappear under the foliage growing up around them, growing up through them. In the breeze that morning, the carpet of vines pulsed.

Part of her wondered if they should have done more searching off the beaten path, away from the throughways between Omaha and Lincoln. Those would have been the most heavily trafficked and as such, the least likely to have any food. But drifting away from the main routes took them far away from population centers. She didn't even know why she was bothering conducting another search of the town.

Maybe she'd missed something.

She wandered east along Main Street. There had been a small market about a quarter mile west of the house, but it lay in ruins. The roof had collapsed at some point in the past, leaving three walls and not much else.

It reminded her of a pie crust.

Pie. Apple pie. Cherry pie. Boston cream pie.

She didn't realize she was salivating until a string of spittle struck her hand. It startled her back into reality. She continued up the road, past a line of cars parked by the curb of the erstwhile downtown area. A dry cleaner. A law firm. *Heaton & Associates*. Wills & Family Law. Talk about a dead industry.

She hit the law office first. Inside, the air was musty and old, rich with dust of decaying papers and books. It was dim, almost dark, but over the years, she'd become quite adept at scavenging in the dark. After a few moments, her eyes adjusted to the low light. There was a large appointment book at the reception desk, still open to that fateful August so many years ago. Each block on the calendar was chockfull of appointments. An old newspaper still sat folded on top of the desk, a copy of the *Lincoln Journal Star*. Above the fold, a headline screamed EPIDEMIC RAGES UNCHECKED. As she often did, she tried to picture the last day anyone had sat at this desk in the *Time Before*. The secretary, feeling sick, scouring the Internet for news about the outbreak. Her boss, telling her to go on home. As they always did, these little slices of life at the end of the world made her stiffen with sadness.

She checked the drawers, hoping beyond hope for a can of soup or spaghetti but coming up empty. There was a plastic bread bag in the bottom drawer, its contents long morphed into dust. She pressed deeper into the office, checking the small break room, the attorney's office, the conference room. Nothing. If there had been anything useful here, it had long since been scavenged.

Back outside, another layer of hope stripped away, which would undoubtedly be replaced with another bit of hope, albeit a smaller dose. She didn't know why she still had any hope left, but every building, every house, every office was steeped with potential. Like an addict, hooked on the next high, the next score, the next, the next. That's what it was.

Onto the next.

The idea of searching for food electrified her, which struck her as silly. Why couldn't she give up hope like a regular person? Just accept their fate. Let them enjoy their last few hours or days together and then die. What was she trying to keep them alive for anyway? This dead world, barren in more ways than one.

She took a step and felt her knee buckle underneath her, sending her down in a heap. Her elbow scraped against the ground and she hoped the scratch wasn't too deep. Infection was never far from her mind, because wouldn't that be something, a tiny cut metastasizing into a cesspool of necrosis and sepsis and killing her dead. She lay there, trying to summon the power to climb back to her feet, but the tanks were dry. This was it then. She would die here because she didn't have the strength to stand back up. Everyone had a breaking point. She had reached hers.

"Mommy, get up," Will whispered.

He was on his hands and knees, staring down at her with those eyes of his, the ones that reminded her of her father. How did she tell him that she couldn't get up, that this was it, that he would be on his own now? He would never make it. She had killed him. She had killed her own son, no different than drowning him in a bathtub. She had been killing him for years, hiding him away from the world instead of teaching him the things he needed to know to survive. Even she hadn't been willing to do the things she needed to do. She had given up on Charlotte. She had let the meat from the mountain lion go to waste. Hell, even Eddie had been the one to ambush the folks on the wagon.

She sobbed. Her dehydrated body heaved as she wept, but no tears fell from her barren eyes. As Will stared down at her, she looked up into his eyes, desperate to impart some wisdom upon him at the end of her life. To give him something, some snippet of advice that would help him get past this crisis and onto the rest of his life.

The rest of his life.

She laughed at the cruelty of it all.

He would be dead in a week.

Voices.

Voices around her.

Now she was hallucinating.

Will lifted his head and looked around.

Great, maybe he was hallucinating too.

It'd be easier that way. Better than being too aware of one's imminent demise. Talk to unicorns, run around in a downpour of doughnuts, play bass with ZZ Top maybe and fade away from this mortal coil.

"Mommy," he said. "Someone's here."

His voice was small, tinged with fear.

Fear blitzed through her like an electrical current. She turned her head slowly, her eyes sweeping the landscape. A woman with a graying ponytail. She wore dirty blue jeans and a camouflage vest. A University of Nebraska baseball cap sat perched atop her head. Behind her, two more people, roughly the same age as Rachel. A younger man and a woman about Rachel's age. They looked thin but healthy.

Rachel's mouth watered at the very sight of them, a primal instinct buried deep within her that nevertheless made her feel ashamed. The very thought of it made her dry heave, the throaty grunts of her retching breaking the quiet around them.

Get up.

Get up and move.

Get up and kill them.

Will.

You have to protect Will.

But her body refused its orders, a mutinous soldier betraying her commanding officer. She pawed at the ground with weak arms, her brain telling her to push herself up and do something. The scraggly weeds poking up out of the ground felt cool under fingers as she tried to regain her footing. She felt Will's hand snaking under her arm and then sliding around her back as he tried to help her up. But he was struggling, Rachel about as useful as a giant bag of rocks.

He grunted once, loudly, as she felt his arm give way. She slid back down, her chin catching the ground first, splitting the skin open. Her teeth clicked together hard, catching her tongue in between, and a burst of blood filled her mouth like warm chocolate from a truffle.

Then she passed out.

20

The sun streaming through the large plate-glass window woke her more than anything else, its warmth baking her skin. She blinked twice to clear out the sleepiness still lingering in her eyes. A thin sheen of sweat slicked her arms. As she regained her bearings, she drank in her surroundings, a sip at a time. She couldn't quite remember where she was or how she'd gotten here, but there was a strange familiarity about it, the sense she had been here before. She was indoors, lying on a twin bed.

Somewhere, perhaps the next room over, a noise.

Will.

She knew the sounds he made even when he was out of her sight. The way he shifted a chair or rustled through his belongings, even the tinny clang of his utensils against a plate while he ate, she could isolate the sounds he made from those of anyone else on earth. She didn't know what he was doing, but she could tell from the languorous movements that he was in no danger.

There was a plastic water bottle by her head. Looking at it reminded her how thirsty she was. She reached out for it, her thin arm trembling from the exertion, but she didn't have the strength to reach that far.

"Will," she called out, her throat dry, her voice small and cracked.

She waited a moment, but he did not respond.

"Will," she repeated, this one a bit louder. The effort made her feel lightheaded and the room began to dissolve around her. A wave of nausea rumbled through her like a lonely freight train. She hoped he heard her because she couldn't bear to call his name a third time.

No answer.

She slept again.

When she woke up, it was dark. The room shimmered in the light of a candle. Things would be a lot better if this were a dream and she were back in her trailer at Evergreen or even better if she was eighteen and still a freshman at Caltech. She touched her forehead again and found it cool this time. She tried getting up, but again her muscles failed her.

"Are you thirsty?" a strange voice asked.

She nodded. Her tongue felt swollen and thick, like it couldn't get out of its own way. A bottle at her lips. The cool liquid against her dry, cracked lips stung and felt exquisite at the same time. Her jaw twitched, and a bit of liquid ran down her chin and into the hollow of her neck.

"What time is it?"

"It's almost eight."

"Where are we?"

"Lincoln."

This bit of news galvanized her. That bookstore had been thirty miles away from Lincoln. She had no memory of anything since stepping outside.

"Lincoln? Where's my son?"

"He's fine," the woman said with a hint of a Southern accent. "He's sleeping in the next room. Cute as a button, that boy."

"How did we get here?"

"You've got to take it easy, honey," she said. "We'll get to all that. First, we've got to get a little food in you."

There was a tray on the nightstand next to the bed. On it was a small bowl of applesauce and some thick bread.

"It's not much, but there's more where that came from. Besides, I don't think that skinny little body of yours can take too much. Even this bread might be too much for you to handle."

"Who are you?"

"Sweetie, my name is Millicent."

Millicent. Of course. Maybe next they'd start talking about cotillion and cucumber sandwiches.

"Rachel. My son's name is Will. Did my son eat?" Rachel asked, biting off a small chunk of bread. It was lighter than she expected, still warm. She could not remember the last time she'd eaten something this delicious. Granted, at this point, she'd probably think the same thing about a moldy piece bread that was hard as diamond.

"Yes, like a horse. How old is he?"

"Fourteen."

Millicent's eyes narrowed as she considered Rachel's obvious lie.

"And he's your real son?"

"No," she said. "His family lived in my neighborhood. I found him wandering the streets after it was over. Couldn't leave him behind."

"Bless his heart."

Rachel took another bite, slightly bigger this time, and took in her surroundings. Plain bedroom, about eight by eight square. A chest of drawers opposite the bed. The bed she was convalescing in sagged in the middle but was comfortable enough. The ceiling dingy but free of water stains. The bedroom connected to an open powder room, gave her a sense of place. They were in a hotel.

"What happened?"

"You collapsed," she said. "We found you and your son on the street in that town. Just in time, from the looks of it."

"How long have we been here?"

Millicent closed an eye and tilted her head as she did the math.

"Two days."

"Two days?"

"Y'all were pretty out of it. We got some fluids in you first, kind of a sugary saline mixture we have, to bring you back from the edge. Got you cleaned up as well."

"Well, thank you," Rachel said. And she meant it. Whatever came next didn't matter. This woman had saved their lives and for that, she was owed their hearty appreciation.

"And my son is okay?"

"Yes, relax, Momma."

Rachel took in a deep breath and let it out slowly. Whether now or later, she would have to pay the piper. Nothing in this world was free. It would nag at her until she knew.

"So what now?" Rachel asked.

Millicent leaned back in her chair and crossed one leg over the other. Her face was fresh and smooth and radiant. Her skin was creamy ivory. She was thin, of course, but not distressingly so. It was hard to tell how old she was. Framing her young face was a mane of blonde hair streaked heavily with white. She pulled it back in a ponytail, tying it off with a hairband looped on her wrist.

"Well, sweetie, that's up to you."

Rachel stayed quiet.

"These last couple days of Southern hospitality, well, that's our gift to you. Things have been good for the last few months. But if you'd like to stay, and you are welcome to, you're going to have to work for it."

Still, Rachel said nothing.

"Have you ever been to Lincoln?"

Rachel shook her head.

"It's become quite a busy little town," she said. "We even have a governing body, although that's probably a bit generous of a description. We see a lot of traffic. It's the first big settlement coming out of the plains between here and Denver.

"Anyhow, I've been here since it happened. I was here on business, up from Montgomery, couldn't get home after they grounded the airplanes. Things were so crazy that it seemed smart to ride it out here. Of course, I didn't know I'd be one of the few people still alive when it was over."

"But I digress."

"The longer you take to tell me what it is I'll have to do, the more I'm guessing I won't like it."

"I won't lie to you," she said. "It's not for everyone, and it can be dangerous. But you'll be fed. You'll be safe. And that sweet little boy will be too."

"What will he do?"

"That's up to you," she said. "There are some older teenagers around town that we can introduce him to. We got books, libraries."

"And me? What, do I have to sell my body for food or something?"

Regret knifed through her before she had even finished saying the words. She could almost see them spilling out of her mouth like milk from a glass that had tipped over. Her cheeks flushed with embarrassment and she closed her eyes, waiting for a dressing down from her host. When she opened her eyes again after a few seconds, Millicent was looking at her with a bemused look.

"You seem embarrassed," Millicent said.

"I'm sorry, I just..."

Just what?

She didn't know what she was thinking.

"Sweetie, there is nothing to be embarrassed about," Millicent said. "You and I, and the other girls who live here, we have a commodity. One that is in high demand. One that men pay plenty for. And as fate would have it, we're down a girl."

Rachel's head was spinning as Millicent spoke. She recalled Vania, the hooker (*and already the word felt wrong, so wrong*) from the Market, and how she sounded like this woman Millicent. It was a product. A thing to sell.

"What happened to her?"

A sheen of gloom spread across Millicent's face.

"Oldest story in the book. Thought she'd fallen in love with a client. She went to live with him. Turned out to be a lunatic, like so many of them. One night, he had too much to drink, got rough with her, she tried to run. He didn't let her. That was that."

Millicent told the story matter-of-factly, with nary a hint of emotion. Not that Rachel could blame her. People died every day, for good reason and for bad. For reasons one could never have believed before the plague, and for reasons that were entirely pedestrian and stupid before the plague and still were long after.

Matter of fact.

She'd been offered a job as a prostitute as casually as a job serving up lattes at the long-defunct Starbucks Corporation.

"I know it's a lot to take in," Millicent said. "But it's tough out there. Tough enough for one person, let alone two."

"And what do we get in exchange for my work?"

"Safe place to live, food."

"What's the food supply situation?"

"We're part of a larger group," she said. "The people who first established the community here spent those early years assembling a food supply. One was a climate scientist who predicted the problem with the crops. Before the gas went bad, we spent eighteen, twenty hours a day collecting canned goods, packaged foods. You wouldn't believe how much we pulled together."

"And how much work do I owe you?"

"Four clients a night," she said. "Five days a week. We start when the sun goes down and work until we're done with those four."

Her head was spinning; she could not believe she was having this discussion. Sex with twenty different men a week. For how long? Forever? Until her body was old and battered and used up and she couldn't feel anything from the waist down or the neck up?

"Do you use protection?" she asked.

"Condoms ran out years ago," she said. "We've got a homemade device we use, but it's not perfect. I recommend all the girls wear it, but I can't be in the room all the time. And some of them like it when the guys finish faster. Like I said, there's a risk. We've been doing this for seven or eight years. We've had infections that antibiotics take care of. No HIV or AIDS we're aware of. We think one girl had hepatitis a few years ago, but she died of an overdose before the disease advanced too far."

"And pregnancies?"

Her face darkened.

"We've had a few. Nine."

"And?"

"After the first three, we figured out what was happening," Millicent said. "After the baby's born, we all spend time together, holding the baby. When the baby starts to show signs of Snake, we wait. We wait and hope they pull through. But they never do. And that's that."

Rachel's stomach flipped and her skin felt hot. She wanted to yell not just no, but hell no, she didn't have to subject herself to this degradation, serving herself up as a fluid depository for lonely post-apocalyptic losers; but then her hand drifted to her flank, touching ribs that were jutting out, pressing so hard against her it was a wonder her skin didn't tear. Feeling herself go mad a little bit at a time. To say nothing of watching Will starve.

"They ever get rough?"

"We have some muscle here. Big guy named Lumen, really looks after the girls. He has a little discussion with each client before they go in. That's usually enough. Every now and again, a client will forget his manners, and Lumen reminds them. We've had a few black eyes, a broken arm, but nothing too terrible. Like I said, there are risks."

"So it's about as safe as anything these days."

"Pretty much."

"How would I keep Will away from this?"

"This here is the residence. We work next door. Honey, we don't eat where we poop. There'll be someone to look after him when you're working."

"And if I say no?"

"Sweetie, it's still a free country. Tomorrow morning, we say farewell and wish you luck."

"Don't suppose there are other jobs you need filled?"

Millicent laughed.

"Sweetie, I need you filled."

Rachel winced. She walked right into that one.

"Sorry. I couldn't resist. I know it's not a glamorous life, probably not how you imagined your life playing out. You're what, thirty, thirty-five?"

Rachel nodded.

"I'm forty. You think I ever saw myself as a madam? I have a marketing degree from Missouri. I traveled for work forty weeks a year. I had Cobalt status with American Airlines. The year of the plague? I'd already taken sixty-five flights. After my trip here, I had a trip to Costa Rica planned. I still have the plane ticket in my room. And here I am."

"What are the clients like?" she asked softly.

Simply asking the question made her lightheaded.

"We get all kinds," she said. "Lumen has the right to refuse anyone. Some shy, some loud, some think their shit smells like roses. Some are lonely. Some are sweet, and some you want to hurry up and the get the hell out."

This. It had come to this.

"Sometimes it's not too bad. Some aren't bad looking, and you know, they know what they're doing."

Now Rachel did flush with embarrassment. The idea she would enjoy selling her body was too much to wrap her head around. It went against everything she'd learned during her formative years, when the thing that made Rachel Fisher who she was had been baked into her.

The words of her middle school health teacher, Ms. Burns, echoed loudly inside her head.

DON'T GIVE IT AWAY GIRLS! IF YOU DO YOU CAN'T GET IT BACK! MAKE SURE YOU LOVE HIM, MAKE SURE HE LOVES YOU. WAIT UNTIL YOU'RE MARRIED AND IT WILL BE SO MUCH BETTER.

Lordy, lordy, lordy.

But they weren't in that world anymore, the world of health classes and sex ed and girl power memes on the Internet. Or maybe they were, and she was looking at it all wrong. These men were willing to pay for a few pumps and a squirt between a pair of thighs, and all she had to do was lie there, maybe put on a little show, and she would eat. And Will would eat and grow and live. And if she got sick and died, if one of these men lost it and smacked her too hard, well, it would be worth it.

"What if something happens to me? What happens to Will?"

"Once you join us, it's for keeps. We look out for each other. Always."

Rachel looked down at her tray.

"Why don't you rest and think about it," Millicent said. "You can let me know what you decide in the morning."

"No need to wait."

"There is," Millicent said, pressing an index finger to her lips. "Don't make a rash decision. Think long and hard about it."

21

In the end, there really hadn't been much of a choice at all. She did think about it, as Millicent had suggested, all night, staring at the ceiling, considering her offer, considering the alternatives. If it had been just her, she wouldn't have done it. She would have managed on her own. But that was not the hand she had been dealt.

There had been no other options. Far to the west lay Denver, but in between was a no man's land where food would be almost impossible to find. To the south, Kansas City was the best bet. But even if they made it that far before starving to death, there was no guarantee they'd be able to survive there either. It was unlikely she'd find another offer this good. She'd probably end up dead; Will would be roasted over a spit.

There was no hope.

And the absence of hope did a funny thing to people.

When Millicent came to see her the next morning, she had cast her lot in with them. After she accepted Millicent's offer, they gave her a week to regain her strength, get her system accustomed to regular caloric intake again. She spent her days with Will, who asked few questions, apparently satisfied with her explanation that they had found a new place to live. As the days slipped by, the color returned to his cheeks and his clothes began to fill out again. They read books and played board games. This time, she didn't let him win. She swelled with happiness; she slept soundly. She had kept the Reaper at bay, perhaps for a good long while this time.

On the night she started her new job, one of the other girls, Rebekah, played cards with Will and made him a special meal. Rachel waited in her room, wearing nothing but a tattered thin robe. Shortly after dark, a knock on the door, and he came in, escorted by Lumen. He was an average looking guy. Shaved head. Thick beard. Not much taller than she was. He was thin, but he wasn't emaciated. He could spare the hefty fee of a dozen cans of food for twenty minutes with Rachel.

"My name is-" he began nervously.

"No names," she said, cutting him off. It was out of her mouth before she'd had time to consider it. She really didn't want to know his name.

"OK," he said, his voice barely above a whisper.

Her heart raced and her stomach churned. She was glad she had skipped dinner, seeing how vomiting on a client who hadn't requested such a special service would probably be frowned upon.

She had already equipped herself with the homemade birth control device, a kind of female condom that would hopefully maintain a barrier between her insides and the client's liquid gift. She motioned for him to join her on the bed.

"This your first time?" she asked, trying to hold the trembling in her voice under control.

"No," he said. "I always get nervous though."

He took a deep breath and let it out slowly. Then he sat next to her on the bed. She pulled the knot on her bathrobe free and it fell away, leaving her naked before this man that she had never laid eyes on. Her breath felt ragged and shallow and she was worried she would pass out from fear. His gaze dropped from her face to her breasts and then even lower, and it took every bit of willpower not to cover herself up because he had paid for this view and he had paid for a whole lot more than that too.

"Nothing to be nervous about," she said, a shimmer creeping into her voice. "We're just gonna have a little fun."

She lay back and stared at the ceiling and she saw Will's happy face there, and what the hell was that about? Should she really be thinking about her preteen son as she began her life as a prostitute? She pushed his face away and zeroed in on the task at hand.

The room was quiet but for the sound of the man's belt unbuckling, the susurration of his jeans sliding down his legs, the discordant jingle of the buckle hitting the floor. He leaned down against her, his body against hers, their faces inches apart. He smelled musty but not entirely unpleasant. He did not attempt to kiss her. A soft gasp broke free from her throat as his hardness slid up against the inside of her thigh, and then up against her. He started pushing inside her, but it wasn't easy because this wasn't sex for love or lust or even because she was bored and lonely. It was for her very survival, for Will's right to live another day.

She took long slow breaths and focused on relaxing her midsection, telling herself that the quicker she relaxed, the quicker this would be over. Above her, the client grunted, his eyes closed, his face contorted into a visage that appeared equally happy and sad at the same time. Then he was inside her, and he held himself up with his hands, his heavy mass pressing down on her abdomen. Her hands slid around his waist to his back, Rachel hoping this added touch, this little bit of extra intimacy would rush him along the path to completion.

His body rocked back and forth above her for a few moments and a rush of pleasant heat spread through her. It faded as quickly as it appeared; she didn't know what to make of this. It never occurred to her that she would derive any pleasure from this act, this commercial transaction that was as far removed from love and happiness and togetherness as she could imagine.

After another minute, the man's thrusting ramped up in intensity.

Then a shudder, and his body went rigid as he finished. She bit her tongue as she felt the warm spray of fluid inside her.

Great.

The homemade condom had failed.

He sighed deeply and let out a long slow exhalation, the ripples of a man whose most primal desire had been satisfied.

He withdrew from her wordlessly, pulled his pants back up, left.

A little while later, she took her second customer of the night.

DUSK FELL as she sat on the balcony outside the room she shared with Will, smoking a wretched-tasting cigarette, sipping the even-more-wretched moonshine that was popular with the girls. Her period was in full swing, so she was off this week. It had been three months since she'd started her new job; her time working for Millicent hadn't been as bad as she feared, but it hadn't been easy, either.

This week, she was nursing a black eye and a broken nose, a gift from a client who had unexpectedly turned violent in the middle of the act. The nose would forever be slightly off-kilter, and a large bruise covered the upper right quadrant of her face. The assault had earned her attacker a pair of broken arms, courtesy of Lumen when she'd managed to cry out for help. He was lucky he was still alive. Lumen had proven to be a decent man who took his job of protecting the girls seriously.

The broken nose had left her in a perpetual state of congestion, and her eye had a tough time rising above half-mast. The time off her back had given her time to rest and recuperate; it was her first long break since she started working. By her estimation, she had had sex with at least forty different men, some more than once. Most were harmless and were done quickly, but a few frightened her, although she could not articulate specifically why.

Giving birth to Will had permanently ruined her uterus, so an unexpected pregnancy was not a concern of hers. And she'd managed to dodge any infections (at least those with a shorter incubation period), but she wrote that off to dumb luck. Every other girl had picked up something along the way; it was only a matter of time before she did as well. The important thing was that Millicent had held up her end of the bargain. Two meals a day, even more food than they'd had back at Evergreen (what was left of it, she wondered, were they all dead now?). Will had put on at least ten pounds, their arrival here coinciding with and probably triggering a growth spurt. He wasn't as tall as she was yet, but he would be soon. Not that that was a very high bar to clear.

She'd become tight with the other girls. The attachment she felt to them reminded her of her nearly four months at the Citadel, a prisoner of Miles Chadwick, the man who had unleashed the apocalypse. Miles Chadwick. Leon Gruber, the man Chadwick had worked for. Names that hadn't crossed her mind in months. What would the others think, knowing she'd been face to face with the man who had ended the world? Would they even believe her?

With each passing year, the myth and legend surrounding the plague grew. About its origin, about its purpose, about their fate. The theological implications of such a catastrophic culling of humanity. The barren years since. It was terrorism, it was aliens, it was an accident, it was North Korea. It was God's judgment on man. What did it mean? Why did it happen? No, her story was just one of many, the ramblings of someone driven mad by the madness surrounding them.

But she wasn't mad.

She really had been there.

Whether by chance or by fate, she had ended up as a guinea pig in a desperate experiment to determine whether the Citadel women's infertility had been a side effect for all survivors of the plague or only the conspirators who had been vaccinated against it. And looking back, it could not have been a coincidence that her baby had been the one to survive infancy. Nearly all the Evergreen women who'd been with her at the Citadel had tried to have babies, only to see them die. And nagging at her ever since was the sense she'd never seen the complete picture. That even though they had found and killed the man who had unleashed the Medusa virus on an unsuspecting world, there was more to the story, just off stage, just out of reach, a piece of the puzzle that had disappeared from the box.

It was enough to twist her mind into a pretzel.

An endgame was always on her mind. She didn't know what that would look like, but she had to believe there was a future that didn't involve fucking four men a night for the rest of her life. She would do it, God forgive her, if that's what it took, but all things being equal she'd rather be tending bar on Maui, thank you very much.

Her stomach rumbled. That such a sensation no longer sent her into panic mode was remarkable. There was a meal waiting for her at the end of this hunger pang, waiting for Will. She got up and made her way to the hotel's dining room, which had been converted into a makeshift bar and restaurant, where the clients sized up the girls before meandering over to the other building for their festivities.

The dining room was large, eating up a good half of the first-floor reception area. The walls were wood-paneled, giving the place a ski-resort feel. The sconces had been retrofitted with candles, filling the rooms with a warm, inviting light. The room was awash in chatter as the girls cast their lines, trying to lock down a customer for the night. She took a seat at the bar, which Rebekah was manning.

"Hey girl, how's that eye?"

"Better," Rachel replied, absentmindedly placing her hand over the bruise, suddenly self-conscious about it.

"Swear to God, I'da cut his nuts off for ya,"

Rachel smiled as Rebekah poured her a tumbler of moonshine. The woman had no filter, enjoyed talking in hyperbole.

"Thank you, sweetie," Rachel said. She took a sip, winced at the burn, took another sip.

"Glad Lumen took care of him."

"How's it looking tonight?" she asked, anxious to change the subject. Getting the shit kicked out of her was not an event she wanted to relive. The man had turned on her like a cobra, first wrapping his fingers around her throat and then slamming his fist into her face. He'd been a big man, outweighing her by at least a hundred pounds.

"Big group came in earlier," she said. "Up from Kansas City. Headed to the UP."

The UP was the Upper Peninsula, on the Great Lakes. As the food supply dwindled, more and more people were making their way to the waterways, hopeful that fishing would be their salvation. It was a hard life, dangerous. The lakes had been a rough place to make a living before the plague, and you were as likely to die as you were to catch anything. Most folks didn't know what they were doing, just running out boats that had been abandoned, throwing in a line, praying. Frequently underestimated were the rough water, the violence, the piracy. Put another way, it wasn't any easier on a boat than it was on land and that was before you added the risk of drowning in the cold water.

She swept her gaze over the room, taking in the evening's clientele. It was a big crowd; it would mean a good haul for the house. Canned goods, ammo, cigarettes, whiskey, all fungible items Millicent and Lumen could barter at the weekly swap meet in downtown Lincoln. The men were ripe, the air thick with the scent of musk and body odor. All part of the game, she reminded herself.

A tall man sidled up beside her and took the seat to her right. Rachel gave him a cursory glance. He was broad through the chest, reasonably healthy, suggesting he'd spent at least some of his post-plague years with a full belly every night. He wore a faded blue shirt and blue jeans.

"What'll it be, sweetie?" Rebekah asked in her sultriest voice.

He held up two fingers on his right hand. His shirtsleeve, dirty and frayed, slid down his arm, revealing his bare wrist. A flash of red caught Rachel's attention, and her eyes zeroed in on the tattoo on the anterior side of the man's wrist.

Her breath caught in her throat as she fixated on it.

A bird of prey, its wings spread wide, rising from a bed of flames.

Exactly like the tattoo Rachel had.

22

Her heart raced like a spooked thoroughbred as she tried to eye the man's ink without drawing too much attention to herself. Casually, she leaned forward in her seat and tilted her head to the side for a better view. Now she had a clear line of sight, and now she saw there was no doubt. It was the same tattoo, inked using the same template, down to the little swirl of the phoenix's feathers. She took a deep breath and let it out slowly, trying to analyze the ramifications of what she was seeing.

Her tattoo, also adorning the underside of her right wrist, had been a gift from her captors at the Citadel. Back then, she had looked at it as a brand more than anything, an exercise of dominion and control over their female captives. She rarely looked at it, thought about it even less.

You belong to us now.

And that was all fine and good because it explained why she had the tattoo. What she didn't know was why this guy also had one.

"Cool ink," she said as nonchalantly as she could.

"What?" he said, barely acknowledging her. "Oh, thanks. Whatever."

"Can I see it?"

He turned to face her, and for a moment, terror gripped her hard, like a python. What if he was one of them? One of the men from the Citadel, one of the murderous monsters who'd held her hostage, who'd slaughtered many of the other women. But his face was unfamiliar to her, and no flash of recognition appeared to register in his face either.

"How about we go somewhere quiet and I'll show you anything you want."

Of course.

Her mind was racing now.

A plan took shape.

"Yeah," she said, nodding. "Let's go somewhere a little more private."

She glanced over at Rebekah, who watched the scene quizzically. Rachel nodded toward her, and Rebekah returned the gesture. None of the girls worked if they didn't have to. There was something special about this client, something that went beyond the ordinary course of business. This man had something Rachel wanted.

"Take 276," Rebekah said.

She took him by the hand and together they wound their way through the dining room, which was getting rowdier by the minute. The pregame activities were reaching a crescendo, the moment the girls had worked these men into such a lather they'd give up anything for a couple of minutes between their soft thighs.

They ducked out into the corridor and into the stairwell, which they ascended to the second floor. The hallway was dimly lit with lanterns, giving it a bit of a medieval look. When he tried to engage her in conversation, she turned suddenly and pressed an index finger to his lips.

"Not yet," she whispered.

He nodded excitedly.

He remained silent until they reached their destination, Room 276. The room was unlocked, as they all were, as there was no electricity to power the locks. She let herself in, the man following close behind.

"I have something special for you," she said.

"You do?" the man asked incredulously.

"I guess you caught me on a good night. I'm feeling a bit adventurous."

"All right."

She pointed at the bed.

"Strip."

He did as he was told, and it reminded her of the old movie *Heathers*, when the Veronica character had unknowingly set up two jocks for their eventual murders by ordering them to strip on the promise of a threesome in the woods. Much like Veronica, Rachel wasn't planning to kill the man, but she was planning to put a good scare into him. That was why Rebekah had sent her here, to Room 276.

It was a standard hotel room, a single queen bed, a round table, a bureau containing the useless flat-screen television. But they didn't use it for carnal activities.

They kept it for meetings of an urgent nature.

"There's something I want to do for you."

He clapped with glee. She felt a little bit bad for him, this sad little man whose wiener was powering his engines. He hadn't done anything to deserve this kind of treatment. But hey, life wasn't fair.

She turned toward the chest of drawers next to the entertainment center and pulled open the drawer. Next to the Gideon Bible sat a loaded Glock pistol. In one graceful move, she pulled the gun and spun around.

A look of confusion clouded his face as he tried to deduce how the gun fit into their imminent sexual escapade. But that didn't last long, the confusion quickly morphing into fear, the survival instinct kicking in. She had to be careful. The man hadn't made it this far by being a complete idiot (his current state of undress notwithstanding).

"Hey, what the hell is wrong with you?" he barked.

"The tattoo," she said, holding up her wrist. "Where did you get it?"

Confusion again, his face twisting up in puzzlement.

"Where did you get yours?" he asked.

"I'll ask the questions," she snapped, taking a step toward him.

"OK, OK," he said, scampering backward on the bed. He looked ridiculous in the nude. His penis, which had been at full attention, had retreated so far into his body she could barely see it.

"I'm going to ask you a very simple question," she said. "All you need to do is answer it."

"OK."

"Were you at the Citadel?"

"What's the Citadel?"

"Don't lie to me."

Her arm stiffened, the gun trained squarely on his face.

"I swear to God," he said, cowering, his hands up. "I've never heard of it."

"Then where did you get the tattoo?"

"In Colorado."

"What's in Colorado?" she snapped, her anger radiating from her in saves. "You better start giving me specifics, you son of a bitch, or I will shoot your tiny little dick off. It's not much of a target, but I won't miss from here."

"OK, OK."

"If you're not talking at the count of three, you're dead.

"One.

"Two.

She increased the pressure on the trigger.

"My name is Oliver Clarke," he said. "Before the plague, I worked for the Penumbra Corporation. Do you know it?"

"Doesn't ring a bell."

"Big multinational. Agriculture, pharmaceuticals, weapons systems, artificial intelligence, you name it they did it."

"OK. How does the tattoo fit into this?"

"I'm getting there."

"A few weeks before the outbreak, I went to a Penumbra facility outside Denver. Up in the mountains."

He scrunched his face up and looked up at the ceiling, perhaps trying to decide which part of the tale to tell next. Her arm began to tire, so she switched the gun to her left hand. As she did, he pounced like a tiger, leaping off the bed and tackling her to the ground. The gun came loose and clattered to the ground. He wasn't particularly strong, but he'd gotten the drop on her. He reared back and punched her once in the face, the blow rattling her teeth. Then he let her go, scrambling for the gun, which had come to rest under the bed. Blindly she grasped at his crotch, finding his testicles, grabbing and squeezing for all she was worth.

Clarke howled like a bear. As he rolled on the ground, tending to his wounded jewels, she leapfrogged over him and grabbed the gun. On her ass now as he struggled to his feet. She pointed the gun at his midsection, no more than eighteen inches away from him. He slapped desperately at the gun, knocking it free a second time. It somersaulted through the air, end over end, before striking the edge of the entertainment stand. The gun went off, the roar of the blast deafening in their small enclosure.

A loud *UNNNNHHHH* filled the room, and Rachel didn't know if she'd been hit. Then everything went silent. She opened her eyes and saw Oliver Clarke pawing at his throat, blood spurting through the gaps in his fingers. He managed to stay upright for a few seconds, but the rapid blood loss quickly took its toll, and his legs buckled underneath him. His mouth opened and closed, but no sound came through – only an upsetting glugging sound, like water squirting from a kinked garden hose. Slowly, his body crumpled to the floor, his legs folding awkwardly underneath him.

Just then, the door to the room blew open, and Lumen rushed in, his gun drawn.

She held up a hand and Lumen stood down. Together they watched the man twitch and writhe before the last vapors of his life slipped free into the ether. She knelt down and held up the man's lifeless arm, studying the tattoo carefully. Her brain struggled to process what she was seeing. Her world, perhaps the world of everyone around her, had changed in a fundamental way.

"You OK?" he asked.

Rachel nodded, not once taking her eye off Oliver Clarke's body.

She screamed in frustration. All she had was Penumbra.

Who was this man? Was he telling the truth?

Colorado. Penumbra.

She had to go to Colorado.

23

The meeting was not going well.

They were in the dining room, she and Millicent, in a back booth, away from prying eyes and ears. Will sat at the bar near the front door, transfixed by Rebekah, on whom he had developed the sweetest schoolboy crush.

It had been a week since the man with the tattoo had died. The left side of her face ached dully, injury heaped upon injury. Oliver's fist had connected with her already bruised cheek, turning her face into a giant hematoma. The pain had started to fade, finally, but she wasn't sure her face was ever going to look right again. Her nose hadn't finished healing from the previous beating it had taken, so one couldn't really say it had been broken again. No, it was just *brokener*, if that was even a word.

On the table between them sat a plate of hard cheese and salted beef, which they ate with flatbread. But by her third bite, when she realized Millicent was not joking, that she was not going to let Rachel and Will leave, she didn't give a good goddamn what Rachel's reason was, the food had lost much of its appeal.

"I thought I'd made it clear when you joined us," Millicent said. "This here's a permanent arrangement."

Millicent sliced off a wedge of cheese and set the knife down on the table between them. She chewed slowly, clearly enjoying her supper, and this made Rachel hate her, made it rise up in her, made her feel hot, the spark deep inside her catching a splash of accelerant.

"This is such good cheese, don't you think, sweetie?"

Rachel faked a smile, which only caused her to wince. Even fake smiling hurt.

"So that's it? We're on our backs forever?"

"No one put a gun to your head."

"But this is important. You have no idea how important."

Even as she said it, she recognized how ridiculous it sounded out loud.

I really AM the special little flower.

"You're one of my best earners," she said. "The boys pay extra for you."

Rachel rubbed her forehead in frustration

"That supposed to make me feel better?"

"I'm not terribly concerned with whether it does or not."

Millicent's tone gave her a chill. It was a side of her she'd never seen before. The meeting was barely five minutes old and it had all gone south in a hurry. It had been so unexpected, this sudden yoke she felt around her neck leaving her breathless.

"What's to stop me from walking right out the door?" she asked, placing her hands flat on the table, jutting her chest out a bit farther.

Millicent smiled demurely.

"You won't do that."

"Why?"

"Because that boy's not going anywhere."

Rachel clenched her hands into fists, let out a frustrated breath. This had been a courtesy call, nothing more. She could've disappeared into the night with Will, but she thought she owed the woman who'd saved their lives a goodbye.

"But this could change things," Rachel said, her voice taking on a pleading quality that embarrassed her a little. "For all of us."

This earned her nothing but a continued disinterested stare from her employer.

"You're being ridiculous," Rachel said.

Millicent struck like a cobra, slapping Rachel hard across the left side of her face, lighting her up with a fresh bolt of pain. Rachel shut her eyes tight as the pain radiated through her, her face feeling like it had been set ablaze. Her stomach flipped and the room snapped off-center; she set her hands flat on the table to steady herself, hopefully prevent a reappearance of her meager dinner.

"Please don't speak to me that way."

Rachel remained quiet as she regained her bearings.

"I really cannot believe we're having this conversation," Millicent said. "Do you understand anything about loyalty, about keeping a promise?"

Rachel stared at her blankly.

"You needed me a lot more than I needed you," Millicent said, tenting her fingers together. "Do you remember what you looked like when we found you? What Will looked like?"

"I'm very appreciative of what you've done for us, really, I am-"

"Then you should shut your mouth and do what I tell you."

Millicent sliced off another bite of food, the hard sausage this time, and set the knife back down on the plate. Rachel watched the woman eat without a hint of emotional distress. She didn't care. She simply did not care about Rachel or Will. She'd been a fool for letting herself think a bond had formed between her and this woman. Rachel was a hole, nothing more, nothing less, a hole to be filled for Millicent's benefit. A stitch of laughter from the other side of the dining room drew her attention. Will tossed his head back in glee at something Rebekah had said. From where she sat, she could make out Rebekah's face; a look of contentment, of something real there, something she rarely saw.

It was remarkable, the binary nature of what was happening here. Across from her sat Millicent, the poster child for the way the world was. Behind her, Will and Rebekah, the way the world was supposed to be. That was why she had to go to Colorado, to find out if there existed any hope of a possible future. Because this, the way things were now, was not going to work. They were already dead.

Already dead.

The survivors wandering the ruins of America, they were already dead, whether they knew it or not. They were machines executing a code, a prime directive, nothing more. That wasn't living. That was existing for the sake of existing, for turning oxygen into carbon dioxide, in a gray world with gray walls and gray skies and gray thoughts, where nothing mattered. Where there was no love or art or music or gentle breezes or watching the sunrise with the love of your life.

Rachel picked up the knife and sliced off a piece of sausage. She chewed it slowly, savoring the smoky, salty tang of the meat on her tongue, the way the flavor popped in her mouth.

Then she leaned across the table and jammed the knife straight into Millicent's throat.

Desperate hands grasped at the knife's handle, but it was already too late. Her eyes bulged in shock, and Millicent struggled to take a breath, her mouth snapping open and closed like a fish flopping on a boat deck. Blood cascaded down her hands, down her arms, splashing on the table, running down to the floor. As her body slumped out of the chair, Rachel was on her feet to catch her, to lower her gently to the ground. She glanced back at Will and Rebekah, who appeared oblivious to what had happened.

She tucked the remaining cheese and sausage into her pocket and made a beeline for the bar, her mind blank, focused on a singular goal of getting the hell out of here. Without stopping, she grabbed Will's hand and pulled him off his barstool.

"Mommy!"

"We need to have a talk, young man," she said as sternly as she could. He tottered unevenly behind his mother.

"Uh oh," Rebekah said, "looks like someone's in trouble." A smile still draped the lower half of her face, the woman, for the moment, falling for Rachel's ruse.

They were within ten feet of the door when she heard a shout behind her.

At the door, she paused and took Will by the shoulders long enough to utter four words to him.

"Will, run, or we die."

His head bounced up and down obediently, his eyes wide with fright. They pushed through the door and out into the hotel parking lot. It was dark, difficult to see, but it would make it easier for them to hide. She'd become familiar with its layout over the past few months. They cut across the parking lot to Main Street and turned north, not running, but not exactly out for a leisurely stroll either.

Two hours later, they made it to the city limits, where the commercial development began thinning out, the promise of the empty plains still ahead of them. Will hadn't said a word during their flight and she hoped it meant he was starting to understand how the world really worked. She had said it, that their lives were in danger, and he had fallen in line.

They would run with the clothes on their back and the little food she had squirreled away in her pockets. They had full bellies and their muscles were strong. They could make it, they would find food, they would take food. They would stop being the hunted, they would stop being the victim. In this world, you took or you got taken.

For all these months, she had been the latter. For all these years, she had been the latter. Taken by her father's abandonment, taken by Eddie's abuse, taken by Millicent's manipulation. That ended tonight, that ended right now. They would go to Colorado, and they would find Penumbra, God help her, or they would die trying.

24

It felt good, having a purpose again. A moonshot they could devote their lives to now. A goal beyond simple survival, which, standing alone, was a pointless and hollow thing. Survival. All that meant was not dying until you did. And if all you were doing was surviving, then what difference did it make whether you died today or on a Wednesday evening in September twenty years from now?

They cycled along I-80, about a hundred miles due west of Lincoln. Both rode mountain bikes, which made traversing the weedy and potholed highway much simpler. Visibility was good, giving them a clear view of all points of the compass in these flatlands. On their second day, she spotted a search party out of Lincoln, but they had easily outmaneuvered them. Far off in the distance, the ghostly outlines of the Rocky Mountain foothills beckoned them. But that was many days away.

One thing at a time.

She sipped water from the hydration pack strapped to her back. It was a bit uncomfortable, the pack having to share her back with the M4, but a full ration of water was a gift. She cut her eyes toward Will, who seemed to grow taller with each passing day.

It was a cold, cloudy day, the sky threatening rain but never following through on its promise. They'd been on the road since first light and hadn't stopped since, perhaps their longest ride without a break since fleeing Millicent. Her legs felt a bit rubbery, and she began thinking about a lunch break. The idea of having a lunch break was intoxicating. They had stumbled across a small cache of canned goods two days out of Lincoln, a supply that would last them another two days. The big score had been the HK machine pistol and a few boxes of ammunition, as she'd had to abandon her M4 back in Lincoln.

But today. Today!

Ravioli.

Ravi-fucking-oli.

She felt a thump and the bicycle shimmied underneath her. She had time for a brief yelp, enough to draw Will's attention before the bike tipped over. The bike clattered to the mossy asphalt beneath her. Her feet hit the ground running, trying to keep her upright. For a flash, she was right there, avoiding a fall, but then she hit another small pothole, her right ankle turning underneath her. White-hot pain shot up into her leg like magma from a volcano.

"Dammit!" she bellowed, crumpling to the ground as her leg gave out underneath her. She held out her arm to brace her fall, her body hitting the ground awkwardly, the asphalt peeling a layer of skin from her arm. She lay there, catching her breath, waiting for the shock to wear off, for the pain to bleed through the sudden jolt of adrenaline currently protecting her.

Rachel tested the injury, putting as much weight down as she could. Which, as it turned out, was very little. The slightest step injected her foot with liquid fire.

"Mommy, you OK?"

"I'm fine," she said. "Give me a minute."

She took a deep breath, trying to will away the pain.

It's not so bad.

A step.

Fire.

Another step.

Fire.

No more.

That was it. Two steps were all she had in her.

Down. She had to sit down.

She lowered herself to the ground, careful not to put any weight on the foot. Being down on her ass was a relief, the knowledge her foot would be spared any additional trauma for now. She untied the laces on her left boot, loosening them as much she could to grease the extraction of foot from shoe. But even with the boot wide open, the slightest movement triggered pulses of pain through her heel, into her calf, up into her kneecap.

She didn't even have to take the sock off to know how bad it was. The ankle was already swelling, pushing tightly against the thick fabric of the sock. She put the boot back on in the hope it would hold down the swelling.

"You OK?"

"Twisted my ankle," she said through gritted teeth.

Will rushed to her side and knelt by his mother.

"Is it bad?"

She let out a shaky breath.

"Yeah, I think so. I'm gonna have to stay off it for a while. Any houses or buildings nearby?"

Will stood and swung his head around, scanning the area.

"There's a farmhouse up the way a bit," he said.

"Hand me the binoculars," she said. "In my pack."

He handed them to her. The building was about a quarter mile off the main road and looked deserted. Two vehicles sat by the side of the house, a rusted pickup and a small school bus, enveloped in a tangle of weeds and vines. There was a small barn off the northwest corner of the house, its roof missing.

"OK," she said. "Doesn't look like anyone's home. Better than nothing. Help me up?"

He crouched next to her while she snaked her arm around his neck. Using her good leg for leverage, she pulled herself upright, leaning on her son for support. Only then did she realize he was nearly as tall as she was, virtually eye level with her.

"What about the bikes?"

"Pull them to the side of the road, and you can come back for them after we make sure the place is clear.

She held a flamingo pose while Will saw to the bikes, tucking them in the tall grasses at the road's edge. As she watched him, it occurred to her she would be depending on him for a while now. The tables had turned. Fear hardened in her belly, whispering to her that she hadn't done enough, that by trying to protect him from this world for all those years she had done nothing but doom them both.

"Ready?" he asked.

She nodded.

IT TOOK them thirty minutes to cover the distance, Rachel's arm slung around Will's back for support. She did her best to put as much weight down as she could because that would mean it wasn't as bad as she thought. Within fifty feet, however, she had to concede the ankle was a wrecked mishmash of torn ligaments and broken blood vessels. If anything, the pain had worsened and the slightest movement or weight was agony.

"If you can get me to the house, I can use the walls for support."

"OK."

"Give you a break." She smiled and squeezed his arm.

"Sorry about your ankle," he said.

"Nothing to be sorry for."

"I should have seen that pothole, called it out for you."

His eyes were wide and glassy, shimmering with tears. The kid was really beating himself up over this.

"It was stupid of me."

"Hey, Spoon, it was an accident. These things are gonna happen. The important thing is that we don't let it drag us down, that we figure it out and keep going."

He nodded, the tears starting to fall.

"Buddy, this a tough world we live in. A tough world. You've got to be able to roll with it."

She chuckled softly, her time at Millicent's brothel rushing back to her, all the nights she'd spent on her back to keep them alive. After all, that fell squarely within the purview of rolling with it.

"You can't get hung up on what happened before, on what's behind us. You do that, you'll miss what's coming. And, Spoon, that is not something we can afford to do."

"It's so hard," he said, his body starting to tremble. "Why's it gotta be so hard?"

"I don't know," she said.

"It's so hard."

"You know what grownups used to say to kids when I was your age?"

He shook his head.

"You kids these days, you have it so easy."

"Was it?"

"I don't know really," she said. "Some things were easier. We had technology. You could look up anything you wanted whenever you wanted. You could order any kind of food you liked and it would be delivered to your house in thirty minutes."

"Wow," he whispered.

"I know. It sounds ridiculous. Compared to what you've been through, we lived in paradise. You got a raw deal.

"But here's the thing you have to remember," she said. "It's going to be hard no matter what. Complaining about it won't make a bit of difference. All complaining does is take your eye off the ball. And out here, that could get us killed."

Then, out of the blue:

"Is that why you shot Dad?"

The question staggered her. She stood mute, unsure of how to respond. It had been there all this time now, like the way the sun got in your face no matter which way you turned, annoying you, even blinding you to the full picture. It had to be dealt with.

"I had to keep you safe," she replied. It was all she could think to say.

He considered her response for a moment, holding her gaze, perhaps trying to decide if she was putting him on or if this was the truth.

"I'm sorry I had to do it," she said.

More silence.

As she stood there, she hoped for a hug, a tearful absolution for this thing that Eddie had made her do. But there wouldn't be. Not today. Perhaps not ever. There was no way to know what effect it would have on him. Not even Will knew what effect it would have on him. It wasn't as if he was standing there hiding a prefabricated response to the death of his father at the hands of his mother.

She felt cold and hard teaching him these lessons. But they were lessons she had to teach him. It was her job, it was her duty to teach him these things. He wiped away the tears, nodding. But she saw a stiffness in his stance, an acceptance, begrudging perhaps, that his mother knew what she was talking about. She leaned in and kissed him on the cheek. Out here, all alone with no one to see, he let her. She pulled him close, hugging him tightly, inhaling his scent, the sweetness of the little boy still there, even under the accumulated sweat and grime. He did not hug her back, but he did not pull away, at least initially. She didn't know how many more discussions like this one they would have, in which he would listen to her, really listen to her.

He cried for a bit, and she held him until the tears dried up, until his breathing returned to normal, until he was calm again.

"Now we go," he said, finally pulling away from her. No resolution today.

She gave his cheek a quick rub.

They followed the long dirt road running toward the main house. It was weedy but not completely overwhelmed, suggesting that it had seen some maintenance in the not-too-distant past. Halfway down the lane, they stopped again for another peek with the binoculars. Still no sign of life around the buildings. No crushed vegetation at their feet, no markers of foot traffic. If there had been a community here, they had packed it in some time ago.

Wide tracts of empty farmland stretched away to the east and west. It still fired her up, watching the earth lay barren year after year. It had to end sometime, right? At some point, the climate would recover and they would grow crops again and they could end this interminable war. She would think about those last days of civilization, when scared men had made bad decisions to launch those nukes, to demand of those who would live on past Medusa one last crushing debt even after they had paid so much.

But that was the hand they had been dealt. All they could do was play the cards.

Another few minutes of staggering and limping brought them to the road's terminus, where it opened on a circular clearing fronting the main house. Small potholes full of the previous night's rainwater pocked the ground. The front door of the house stood ajar, and a chill frosted the back of her neck. There it stood, about a third of the way open on this cool, cloudy day, a wedge of darkness lurking beyond.

"There's no one here," she whispered to Will, as much for herself as for him. "Nothing to be scared of."

Oh yeah, if there's no one here, little missy, then why the hell are you whispering?

She stared straight at the house, not turning toward Will lest he see the terror on her face. Her gaze remained fixed on the door as she wondered whether they should make their way down the road. Certainly, they'd find another place to take shelter soon. But the idea of subjecting her ankle to any more trauma today made her sick to her stomach. All they had to do was check the place out, something they would do anyway.

"Ready?" Will asked.

She nodded.

The house had once been painted white and she could see it in her mind, a bright white gleaming under a cloudless Nebraska sky, the fields flush with corn from one edge of the horizon to the other.

She preferred that image to the current reality, a crumbling museum of a world gone by, the paint long since faded, the fields empty.

It was a big house, three stories, the main homeplace set off from the rest of the acreage by what had once been a long fence. Much of the fence had failed, the rest racing to catch up. The planks had buckled and snapped, hanging onto the support posts by a thread. It looked like the stripped skeletal remains of a great beast that had wandered these plains millennia before.

"We'll look around outside first," she said.

He nodded.

They began a clockwise loop of the house, Rachel using the wall for support. Somehow it made her feel a bit better, not leaning against her eleven-year-old son. The HK was cradled under her left arm, her finger curled gently on the trigger.

Abandoned equipment and junk and littered this side of the property. A couple of oil barrels, a bandsaw, a pair of axes, some not terribly rusted. A large tarp bearing a large dark stain. Faded soda cans. Rachel paused at the corner of the house, peering toward the large clearing that ran toward a meandering creek about fifty yards distant.

A large fire pit, about twelve feet in diameter, had been scooped out of the land. It was about twenty-four inches deep and stacked with the remains of long-burned firewood. Spanning the length of the pit was a crude spit bearing a long cut of raw meat, still dripping onto the cold kindling underneath. Ash blanketed the sooty fire-blackened edges of the pit. Scattered haphazardly about the area were several bones, the sight of which made Rachel's stomach flip. There was a haunting familiarity to the remains, a splinter in her soul.

"See anything?" Will whispered behind her.

"Shh," she replied, her response coming out choppy and breathy.

She swept her gaze wide, beyond the fire pit, down toward the creek, looking for any sign of activity, her trigger finger itchy now.

"Binoculars."

He handed them to her.

She scanned the area again, taking her time, sweeping from west to east, on high alert. The sensation that they weren't alone began niggling at her, frosting her insides, making her shiver.

Then: a cough, a quick sharp hack.

The sound was unmistakable, coming from inside the house.

Someone was in there.

25

Rachel looked over her shoulder and pressed a finger to her lips.

Will nodded, his eyes wide.

Quickly she took stock of their location. There were four windows on this side of the house, two on each level. It was difficult to tell how exposed they were here. Her brain cycled through their options, what steps they would have to take to survive the latest fastball from their terrible world. As it was, they had probably already pushed their luck to the limit by not being spotted. Unless they already had been, and they were too naïve to know it, unless they were already in a terrible trap they could not see.

Flight was out. Her ankle was simply too injured. They were here now, and she doubted the occupants of the property would be welcoming them with open arms. She glanced back at the fire pit, telling herself she wasn't seeing what she was seeing, wondering if by sunset she or Will might be roasting on that spit.

You don't know for sure.

That could be a deer or a boar, maybe one of those mountain lions like the one that killed Charlotte.

The sound of footsteps clomping on wood drew her attention

back to the front of the house. Someone was coming out, out on the porch, the metronomic thump, thump, thump of feet descending stairs. She slithered around Will, putting herself between him and the front of the house. Coin flip here. If this stranger came around this way, she would open fire without asking any questions. There was too much at stake.

Then the sound slipped away from them, the susurration of boots on gravel retreating into the silent void of the afternoon. She motioned again to Will to stay quiet, and he nodded. Her back to the wall, her arm around Will, she edged back toward the yard, her heart up in her throat. There was evil here, pure evil, something dark and ancient. You could feel it crawling on your skin, up your nostrils, down into your lungs.

A lot of variables were in play here, leaving her body tight with stress, like her skin didn't fit her frame anymore. Who lived here, what were they up to, were she and Will already trapped, were they the proverbial frog in the slowly warming pot of water. She felt naked here in the long shadow of the house, sitting isolated on this barren stretch of land.

Will's body tensed against hers and she froze. His young ears had picked up on something, and she primed her own as she tried to play catch-up. The soft crunch of gravel again as the footsteps drew closer once again. She inched her way toward the corner, risking the slightest glance toward the yard. From the other side of the house emerged a very tall, very thin man wearing a butcher's apron carrying something in his arms, covered with a blanket. A shadow of stubble graced his narrow face. His pants were filthy. His eyes were red and puffy.

He set his load down at the edge of the fire pit before taking a seat on the ground, his legs crisscrossed underneath him. He sat there for a while, staring into the center of the fire pit. As she studied the peculiar scene, she became aware of a faint sound, a whimpering or neighing sound, maybe a cat or dog. The man glanced over his shoulder at the house but did not appear particularly troubled by it.

After a very long while, he rose to his feet and peeled back the tarp from the item he'd been carrying. At first, Rachel couldn't see what it was, the man blocking her view. Then he stepped around to the side and began working the fire pit, stoking the kindling, giving her a clear line of sight. She gagged instantly, and it took every atom of willpower not to vomit.

It was a human torso.

The shock of it froze her where she stood.

The ghost stories, the rumors, the whispers in the dark she'd heard over the years, the things she knew to be true but didn't want to admit were now laid bare before her. The nadir of humanity on display now. This was where their humanity had ended, where it had morphed into something base, something twisted, something that transcended any plane of existence with which she was familiar. Heat spiked up her back as she watched the man work, lighting the blaze in the pit, the blackened chunks of wood.

As the man stoked the fire, the sound emanating from the house ramped up in intensity, from a whimper to a full-throated groan, unquestionably human. This time he paid it no mind at all, focusing his attention on the fire before him. After a few moments, perhaps a minute, the fire took hold, rippling to life in the belly of the pit, the waves of heat shimmering and dancing above its corona.

She glanced back toward the front of the house, back toward the highway. They could slip away now while this barbecue from the depths of hell unfolded, away from this living horror show, even if they carried with them an abscess of darkness on their souls. Her ankle throbbed but running for your life had a funny way of curing what ailed you.

Another moan.

Someone was in there right now, someone for whom the arrow of fate pointed at that roasting spit, and it wasn't her problem, really, now was it, it was every woman for herself out here. She had a responsibility to take care of Will and injecting herself into this equation meant abdicating that responsibility in favor of something else.

But did it?

Keeping Will alive, while the most important piece, wasn't the only piece of the puzzle of her life. What would she be telling him if they walked away and left that poor soul inside to become this thing's dinner? There had to be more.

Justice.

That was what was wrong with their world.

No one was held accountable anymore.

If she walked away now, this man would continue to snare unsuspecting travelers off the road because that was what the world had become. By simple dint of untold horrors happening over and over in every possible way, they had become used to it, and becoming used to it had facilitated a de facto acceptance of it.

No more.

There had to be justice.

As quietly as she could, she checked the HK's readiness.

"Stay right behind me," she whispered.

He nodded his understanding.

She limped around the corner, the HK's muzzle up. Will hung back off her left flank. Her eyes darted from side to side while keeping her quarry in view. A rusted tractor sat by an equally rusted propane tank on the far side of the clearing. In front of it sat a pile of bones, which caused her to shiver with rage. How many? How many, she could not help but wonder. The more she thought about it, the angrier she became.

She cleared her throat as loudly as she could.

The man froze, his spine stiffening and straightening. He turned around on his haunches. She tightened her grip on her rifle when she spotted the long, curved knife in his right hand. He was maybe fifteen feet away from her, twenty at the most.

"Who's inside?" she asked.

He didn't reply. He simply stared at them, not unlike the way the mountain lion had before attacking Will.

"Who's inside?" she asked again.

A flutter of movement to her right, drawing her eye away from the man for the splittest of seconds. He charged at them, the blade high and ready to strike. She squeezed off a burst, catching him squarely in the chest, knocking him backward a handful of steps before he fell directly into the fire.

She turned to see a large woman wearing a dirty housecoat lumbering toward her. She fired again, missing this time. The woman was deceptively quick, or maybe it was because Rachel was too slow. As the man howled while he burned alive, Rachel fired off another burst, this one catching the woman in her meaty legs. She was close enough that the blood spattered against the cuffs of Rachel's pants. She tumbled to the ground in a heap, grabbing at her mangled shins. Rachel stepped forward and fired a final burst into the woman's head.

She glanced back at the fire pit, where the man was now fully engulfed in flames. If he were not dead yet, he would be shortly. She turned back toward the house, which sat quietly now, not as haunting, like something had been exorcised from it.

It was over.

Rachel felt her bladder let go, a warmth spreading through her midsection and down her thighs. Her legs gave out under her and she sank to her knees, feeling the cold, damp earth under her. The rage drained away, a storm front losing its punch.

What had she done?

She glanced up at Will, who had wandered over toward the fire pit, watching the fire consume the cannibal's body. He stood there, watching it burn, and she was sorry, sorrier than she had ever been in her life. There was nothing left to hide from him; he now knew it all, he now had seen all there was to see. It was more than any eleven-year-old, more than any human being should ever have to see, but you couldn't fix something until you saw what was broken.

"You OK, Spoon?"

Without turning away from the fire, he gave her a shaky thumbs up.

"You know why I did this?"

An almost imperceptible nod of his head.

"There may be people trapped inside."

Another nod.

"We need to try and save them."

He nodded.

"I know."

"It could be very bad in there."

He took a deep breath and let it out slowly.

"I know."

THEY SLOWLY MADE their way toward the house, Rachel gingerly moving on her wounded ankle. The back door hung open like a broken wing. As they neared the threshold, the moaning started up again, and now she could hear someone calling for help.

"Is someone there?"

Rachel looked back at Will and pressed a finger to her lips.

They stepped inside the small country kitchen, dim in the weak light of the gray afternoon. The smell of decay and mustiness was almost overpowering. Behind her, Will retched and then threw up on the floor.

"You all right?"

"Yeah," he said, his voice shaky but firm.

A series of meathooks retrofitted into the ceiling swung gently in the breeze flowing in through the door. Mercifully, the hooks were bare. On the counter, however, was a horror to counterbalance that – a human head, desiccated. There was no point in telling Will not to look. If anything, it was counterproductive, it hurt him not to see the world for the way it was.

They moved into a small corridor, darker here away from the ambient light of the day. To the right was a small sitting room jammed full of junk and debris. Old magazines and books, knick-knacks and piles of trash stacked above her head. The walls might have been a pleasant yellow once upon a time; now the color was inscrutable.

"Please help me!" The voice echoed pitifully through the house.

"Where are you?" Will called out.

She grimaced at Will's impertinence. She didn't think there were any hostiles left but there was no way to be sure. The graveyard of history was full of men and women better than her, smarter than her, faster than her, nevertheless felled by good motivations fueling bad decisions.

"Downstairs!"

"Who else is here?"

"Please don't hurt me. Please, God, don't hurt me!"

"You're safe now."

"No," came the reply. "Noooooooooooo. No, no, no. Please hurry before they come back."

The wailing continued, filling the house with a dreary, mournful cry; her skin rippled and tightened with gooseflesh. Part of her screamed at her to turn tail and run, put as much distance between this place and Will as she could. She didn't know what he was screaming at, whether someone was down there now, carving him up or some memory that had broken free.

They came to a closed door at the end of the hallway.

"Will."

"Yeah?"

"Open the door. Slowly."

His hand trembled as his fingers curled around the knob and twisted it. The door squealed on its hinges as it swung open, revealing a dark stairwell beyond. The stairs descended to a basement, out of sight.

"Who's there? Is someone there? Please don't hurt me."

"Stay right behind me," she whispered.

She leaned up against the wall of the stairwell, mindful of her throbbing ankle, taking one step at a time. It was hot in here; sweat slicked her body and the air tasted rank and stuffy. Each step was an eternity, each one a nightmare unto itself. The only light came from the upstairs hallway, and that was weak at best.

She flicked on the flashlight in her pocket; the beam of light was dim, a reflection of the weak batteries at their disposal. Another dozen steps to the bottom. Then six. Then three. It was cooler down here, damp. The smell of metal hung thickly in the air.

"Is someone there? Who's there?"

She swept the flashlight across the cellar. It was bigger than she thought, perhaps equivalent to the entire square footage of the house. A large trough sat in the middle of the room. There was a work table built into the wall to her right, on which sat four human heads staring back at her. The beam continued its trip across the room, freezing when Rachel came across the room's sole occupant.

She stood frozen, her mouth agape. A thin man stood against the wall, his arms chained above his head. He wore dirty khaki shorts but no shirt, revealing a bare torso stained with blood and only God knew what else. His body trembled in the damp cold of the basement. Rachel couldn't tell if he was awake, as his head was drooping down toward his chest.

"Are you OK?"

He started at the sound of her voice, his head popping up, his body recoiling away from her. He began to sob as she watched him. It was an ugly cry, tears and mucus dripping from his face and nose.

"It's OK," she said.

He trembled violently as he wept.

"We're going to get you out of here."

She let him be while he cried, studying his shackles. Each of his wrists bore a cuff, connected to a short chain mounted in the drywall.

"Hey, what's your name?"

"Alec," he said in between teary gasps.

"Listen to me, Alec, I've gotta break you out of these cuffs, but I'm going to have to shoot out the anchor."

"Will, stand right behind me."

When Will was in position, she raised the muzzle to the eyebolt restraining his left hand and squeezed off a shot. The drywall crumbled, releasing the anchor from the wall. She repeated the step with his right hand, freeing him from his shackles. His arms swung down heavily, the chains scraping across the ground. He crumpled to the ground.

"We have to get out of here."

He pushed himself to his feet, but he was unsteady, like a baby giraffe taking its first steps. Together they staggered toward the stairs. Rachel's ankle throbbed as they ascended, each step pure agony as she bore not only her weight but a good bit of Alec's as well. The number of stairs seemed infinite; they would spend eternity climbing and never reach the top. She stole a glance at Will, grimacing and grunting from one step to the next, his skinny arm wrapped around Alec's waist, and this galvanized her. As the landing drew closer, she shifted the HK, sliding the stock under her arm, snaking her finger around the trigger.

"Can you hold yourself up for a second?" she asked Alec.

"Yeah," came the reply, raspy and shaky.

On the landing, he leaned back against the wall and let out a sigh. Rachel's arm burned with fatigue, which left the gun a bit wobblier than she would have liked. She hazarded a peek down the corridor, first to her left, back toward the kitchen, and then to her right. It was clear in both directions.

"Let's go."

As they lurched down the hallway, she reflected on the abject stupidity of what they were doing. So much risk, so much danger, and for what? Was it worth her life? Was it worth Will's? They'd been lucky enough to survive the encounter outside, and she'd gone on and pressed their luck even farther. Why? To feel good about herself? To show off to Will?

The door was still ajar, as it had been when they'd first laid eyes on it, what, thirty minutes ago? What horrors had swum past them in that time, evil seen and unseen, here and there and everywhere. As they stood here, saving this man, elsewhere terrible things were happening to good people and there was nothing she could do about it. And that was the answer to the question. There was something she could do here. She could help this man who could not help himself. The simple act of doing something was what mattered.

Rachel stepped through the door first, covering the area with her HK. Behind her followed Will and then Alec. He stumbled toward the railing; as he looked out across the farm, he began to cry.

"Thank you."

"We don't have any food to give you," Rachel said, reality crashing down on them. One way or another, this world was going to get you.

"It's OK. I'd rather die out here than live another second in there," he said, tilting his head back toward the house.

"Besides," he said. "I have food to give you."

26

The land stretched flatly to the horizon in every direction, eternal and unforgiving. Once the farmhouse faded from view, they saw nothing and no one.

They walked.

They walked slowly in the rain, Rachel limping, Alec on legs that had atrophied during his time in captivity. He had to rest every few hundred yards to massage his quads and his calves, as though he were trying to jump start them.

"They said it made the meat easier to chew," he said, and that had been the last he'd spoken of it.

It had been more than enough commentary on what they had been through, and it kept her up for hours, long after they'd pitched camp and packed it in for the night. She lay awake now, the faces of the people she'd killed hovering about her subconscious. Eddie and Millicent and the two people from the farm. It was the first time she'd ever taken such an inventory.

Initially, she'd been wary about sharing space with this stranger, because. But he had dropped into a deep sleep seconds after climbing inside his tent, his snoring loud and rattling her teeth. The man probably had years of PTSD-related insomnia ahead of him, but tonight, sleep would come first.

Beside her, Will snored. When she asked him how he was doing, he'd said he was fine. She didn't know whether to believe him. The idea of Will lying to her was strange to her, alien, almost impossible to comprehend. Lying. That was how you learned your kid was his own person, that he wasn't an extension of yourself, a dummy satellite floating through the ether, simply executing the same lines of code.

She crept out of the tent and sat cross-legged at its mouth, looking up at a sky pockmarked with glittering stars. She felt that old yearning again, the desire to be part of a community again. God, people. People. People had done nothing but grow worse, the masks society had forced upon them shattered like porcelain. People had been shitty, but the rules, the laws, had helped hide away what people had been really like.

Then the plague had come and wiped all that away in one fell swoop, returning the survivors to their default setting. That was the funniest part of all this. Recorded human civilization had lasted a few thousand years, and they had treated each other like shit for all but maybe six months of it. Without their gargantuan social construct, which had been nothing more than a house of cards, it had all come crashing down. Her Sunday school classes came back to her, the lesson that God had created man in His image. In His image? If God had created man in His image, then their God was a terrible one indeed. And given the events of the last thirteen years, it was difficult to conclude otherwise.

Yet here she was, longing for human contact all the same. Dangerous, unpredictable, potentially deadly human contact. She missed Charlotte. Now that had been a good woman to the end. And Charlotte was dead because of her, because she had been too weak to teach Will what this world was like, to do the job she was supposed to do. She had gambled on protecting him from the reality of the world, and it had blown up in her face.

Hell, sometimes she missed Eddie. The old Eddie, the one she'd first met. She missed how he'd felt close to her, how he'd felt inside her when sex had still been a regular thing between them, the way he smelled, how he'd slept. The Eddie before he'd taken off his mask.

The flutter of a zipper unzipping startled her; she glanced over to see Alec crawling out of his tent. Immediately, her mind went on red alert, her hand tensed on the HK. Her skin went tight, her muscles taut. What was he doing up? He was coming to rape her, to slit their throats, to cook them up himself because hell why not, it had worked for those monsters back at the farm.

"Hey," he said. "Couldn't sleep?"

She shook her head.

"Bad dream," he said, taking a breath and letting it out slowly. "Took me a minute to remember I wasn't down there anymore."

Rachel relaxed, her muscles releasing.

Another problem with their world. This man had been subject to the worst horror imaginable and her first instinct had been to distrust him. That might have been how you survived in this world, but that didn't mean it was good.

"Where are we going?"

"I live at a boarding school not far from here," he said. "We've been there since it started."

"How many of you?"

"Thirty-five, give or take."

Rachel's eyes widened in the dark.

"That many? How did you end up together?"

He laughed softly.

"I'm guessing this is going to be hard to believe."

"What?"

"We were living there before the plague."

Rachel looked for something to say, but words failed her.

"I know, it's hard to believe."

"You were all immune?"

"Oh, I doubt any of us were immune," he said. "I think we got very lucky. The school is in a very remote area. There were about sixty of us there for summer school. Normally, there were about five hundred students. Gravy – he's the headmaster – he quarantined us when the outbreak started getting bad. No one got sick, so we sheltered in place for a year. We had enough supplies, we had enough water. Eventually, our supplies started to run out, and we had to send someone on a supply run. It was either take a chance or starve to death. Gravy believed if the disease killed anyone who wasn't immune, then there wasn't anyone left who could transmit the disease."

Not entirely true, but she understood their thinking.

"Gravy was the one to go."

Alec laughed and his eyes filled with tears as he recounted the memory.

"God, he was so scared. He was supposed to be back a week later, but that came and went, no Gravy. We started to assume the worst. Then he comes back ten days later, still healthy, no symptoms. He's quarantined for a week, never gets sick. We figured we were safe."

"The babies still die from it, you know."

He glanced at her, his eyebrows raised up.

"Oh?"

"No women at your school, I'm guessing."

"No," he said, shaking his head. "All boys. Men, I guess, now. I still think of us as kids. I was seventeen when it happened."

"You have food there?"

"It's rationed," he said. "Not sure you'll be able to stay very long, but you are welcome to my rations for the coming week."

"That's very generous of you."

"Least I can do. As I said, I'd rather starve to death out here."

"We're almost there," Alec said, pointing at a small sign bearing the school's name, the arrow painted pointing east.

They picked up the pace as best they could, Rachel accelerating from a limp-walk to something resembling a slow jog. They turned right onto a narrow road that was passable but showing signs of decay. It took twenty minutes to cover the last half mile, Rachel's ankle reaching the end of its usable life for the time being. Fatigue was setting in, the adrenaline firing her engines since they had fled Millicent's clutches draining away rapidly. All she cared about was a decent meal and a good night's sleep, a place to put her foot up for a while.

She was done, worn out. She had given all she could and needed time to recharge. If this all went badly and she and Will were walking into a trap, well, there was nothing she could do about that now. She took a deep breath and let it out slowly, simply glad to be alive. That was a status increasingly difficult to maintain. Alive. Still kicking when so many others were not. If this was the end for them, then she was proud of what they had done.

They drew close to the school's outer gate, which was manned by a lone sentry. He was too far away for Rachel to get a good look at him. He noticed them about fifty yards out, drew his weapon, pointed it at them.

"Stop right there!" he called out.

"Chung, it's Alec!"

"Alec? Holy shit!"

Then he paused, the fact that Alec wasn't alone suddenly registering with Chung. He held his firing stance as they approached the gate. Chung was a small man, not much taller than Rachel, but stoutly built. The gun looked like a child's toy in his hand.

"Who are they?" he asked after Alec embraced him.

"It's fine, they rescued me."

"What the hell happened to you?"

"It's a long story. Gravy around?"

Chung unhooked a small walkie-talkie from his belt and spoke into it, quickly summarizing the situation before him.

"Wait there," came the reply. "We'll send some backup."

As they waited, she took in the campus. A cluster of dormitories to the west, a football field and other athletic fields to the east. The goalposts looked ominous in the moonlight. Three larger buildings sat in the middle of the campus.

As the minutes ticked by, panic fluttered inside her like a butterfly.

Had she really thought this through? Putting her faith in this man Alec simply because she believed he owed her something? But she had to try. The risk of accepting his offer was high, but the cost of not taking it was even higher.

Things had been much easier in the salad days immediately after the plague (and the fact she was calling the days after humanity's near-extinction the salad days really drove home how bad things had become). Food, medicine, and weapons were everywhere, like a benevolent deity had cracked open a giant piñata of survival supplies. Why hadn't she socked more away? Hidden it away for a rainy day? She hadn't taken the long view; she had looked at the world through blinders. That had been the first domino. God, there were no easy decisions anymore, not a one. The only way to calculate the wisdom of a decision was to still be alive after acting on it.

Oh, a bad choice?

Do Not Pass Go, Do Not Collect $200, You're Dead.

The sound of footsteps broke her out of her trance, and she instinctively pulled Will against her. A trio of men approached them; she focused on the one in the middle, a tall, thin man wearing jeans and a black leather jacket. He was middle-aged, perhaps a few years older than she was. His hair was shorn close to his head, but a thick salt-and-pepper beard masked the lower half of his face. His eyes were big, uncomfortably so, like they had been installed on the wrong face.

He stared at Rachel for a few moments, long enough that it became uncomfortable before she broke the stare and glanced down at Will. When she looked back up, he had turned his attention to Alec.

"Welcome home, buddy," Gravy said, giving the man a big hug.

He stepped back but kept his hands on Alec's shoulders. The concern on his face was evident.

"Thought we'd lost you," he said.

"Believe me, I thought the same thing."

"Who are your friends?"

Alec stared at Rachel for a bit, and it occurred to her Alec didn't know her name.

"I'm sorry," he said.

"Rachel. This is Will."

He turned back to Gravy.

"They helped me out of a very bad situation," Alec said. His face darkened and he took a deep breath. "Very bad."

Rachel's stomach flipped.

"Thank you for bringing our boy home," Gravy said. "Not many will stick their necks out like that anymore."

"Well, here we are."

"Indeed."

Everyone stood quietly, the silence quickly becoming awkward.

Alec was the one to break it.

"I think we owe these people a good meal, a roof over their heads tonight."

Gravy ignored him, keeping a wary eye on his guests. Long enough to make Rachel shift her weight from foot to foot, cough nervously in her hand, glance around at the others.

"Gravy?"

He blinked and turned to Alec.

"Dinner? A place to stay?"

He smiled.

"Of course. Where are my manners? I hope you'll consider staying here a couple of days. We are rationing our supplies, but the day I don't open my home to folks in need... well, that's a day I don't want to see."

Will's stomach rumbled, loud enough for everyone to hear.

She couldn't decline the offer now.

"I'm sorry we can't offer you more than a brief respite."

"It's OK," Rachel said. "We'd be happy to stay for a bit. We could use some time off the road."

He clapped his hands together, a smile digging its way out of his beard.

"Wonderful!"

"Chung, please show our guests to Tuttle. It's nice and quiet."

"Thank you."

"We'll have some food and water brought over. Again, I'm sorry it's not much."

"We're grateful for anything you can spare."

Gravy clasped his hands together, quickly bowed his head in reply. This little meet-and-greet was in its death throes now, everyone running out of things to say.

As Rachel and Will followed Chung, she was reminded of boring cocktail parties at Caltech, when she'd find herself trapped in an interminable conversation with a socially awkward professor.

He led them to a dormitory near the center of campus. It looked Jeffersonian, white columns against brick that resembled a skull of a mysterious desert creature. The name *Tuttle* was carved into the stone header above the portico. They went inside.

It was dank and cold in the foyer, the air musty and sharp in her nostrils. A bulletin board was mounted on the wall next to the stairwell, still bearing the flyers and notes from before the plague. The pages had yellowed with age, the corners curled around the rusty thumbtacks holding them in place. One flyer for a math tutor SEE JUSTIN TUTTLE 143. Another for club soccer tryouts starting August 17.

August 17.

A Tuesday.

Her mother had died that very day, August 17, as the sun set, the thin high clouds above the dying city of San Diego turning fiery red. Nina Kershaw had been the first to come down with it, early that morning. The three of them, Rachel, her mom, Jerry, had stayed up late into the night, glued to the television, watching coverage of the outbreak. They sat three wide on the sofa, under a blanket, the table covered with vitamins and antiviral pills Jerry had ordered online. They alternated between CNN and MSNBC and Fox News on the new seventy-inch television her mom had bought Jerry for his birthday in May.

Thinking back on it now, it had been horrible to watch the news on that monstrous screen, the colors and sounds of this riot in Denver, of that plane crash in Norfolk, of this burning hospital in Albuquerque, so bright and alive it felt like they were right there.

Rachel had nodded off around four. An hour later, the heat radiating from her mother's feverish body woke her up, the left side of her body drenched. As she swam to the surface of wakefulness, she couldn't figure out why she was so hot.

"Mom," she'd whispered, as if waking her up gently would help her escape the disease's clutches. No response.

"Mom!" she was yelling now, waking up Jerry.

Nina had come around, barely, her fever spiking, you could feel her baking, how could someone be so hot? Rachel collected all the kitchen towels, soaking them under the faucet, plastering them to her mom's broiling arms and legs and forehead. She didn't bother taking her temperature; you didn't need a weather forecast to know it was raining.

"Bring in the parakeet!" her mother had said, delirium setting in.

Jerry came absolutely unglued.

"Jerry, the fucking parakeet!"

They rushed her upstairs to the bedroom, tucked her into bed, closed the door. Jerry insisted on quarantining her, even taking a "decontamination shower," as he called it, even though she didn't know how it differed from a regular shower. Jerry barred Rachel from the room, which to be honest, she hadn't objected to that much – she was reluctantly conscious of the fact that deep down, her primal urge to survive was firing up.

First was the pointless call to 911, which had stopped taking calls days earlier. But Jerry insisted, and they spent thirty minutes listening to the hold music, a bizarre instrumental version of a Taylor Swift song.

"Please bring me the parakeet!" she called out.

And then she wailed.

"Jerry, they're not answering," Rachel had said, pushing her mother's plaintive cries out of her head. She was trying to remain calm because she figured someone needed to, but truth be told, the fear inside her had been gargantuan, hot and choking, as she waited to start baking with fever.

He looked at her, began nodding his head, and then uncorked his iPhone into the wall; it blew apart into a hundred pieces. She supposed the remains of the phone still lay on the floor of their tony living room in that fancy San Diego subdivision.

Second came Jerry's ill-advised decision to try and make it to the hospital, despite the ticker on the bottom of the screen announcing that San Diego-area hospitals were no longer taking any new patients. They made it two blocks before encountering a massive traffic jam on Spotswood Avenue, the cars abandoned, no way through.

It was over. They had lost, and sometime in the next few hours, she would heat up like a brick oven and die at the age of nineteen before she had done anything in her life.

As they drove home, Rachel in the backseat with her mother, she caught a glimpse of Jerry in the rearview mirror. He was crying. She never forgot that. Tears streaming silently down his face, his eyes wide open. Back at the house, Jerry carried Nina to the front porch; he sat with his wife of four years on the swinging bench and rocked back and forth, whispering to her. Rachel stood on the porch and watched, glad Jerry was taking the lead here.

Nina died thirty minutes later.

They sat there on the porch together.

"You'll be in the south wing," Chung said, breaking her out of her daydream. "We don't really maintain the other sections of the dorm."

"You get a lot of visitors?"

"Every now and again," he said. "Gravy won't turn his back on anyone in need."

He said it with a tone of exasperation.

"That's rare in this world."

"Among other things."

She didn't press the issue.

He unlocked the door and they followed him down the hallway to the first room on the left, which faced east across the campus. It was a standard dorm room, two twin beds. More nostalgia on the walls, but Rachel paid it little mind. She didn't need another walk down memory lane, seeing as the previous one was still playing out the string.

Jerry went downhill quickly that night, sitting on the porch with Nina's body in his arms. He sat there as he started coughing, as the nosebleeds began, as his internal furnace really started cranking. His consciousness faded like a dying campfire, but he wouldn't let her go. Rachel waited on the porch with them; she was afraid that when he finally winked out for the last time, her mom's body would tumble to the porch like a dropped coin.

Jerry didn't last long; he died eight hours after he started showing symptoms, but to his credit, he did not let go of Nina. In death, his arms stiffened around his beloved bride's corpse, and Rachel sat cross-legged on the porch, that hard unforgiving wooden porch, all night with them, the skies thick with the tang of smoke, the chatter of automatic weapons, the whisper of helicopters buzzing overhead, until the sun rose. Their cat Hobbes sat in the window behind the bench, decidedly uninterested in the fall of man.

Rachel stayed at the house for another few days, waiting to die, waiting to live, waiting for someone to come help. She buried her mom and stepfather in the backyard in the middle of that gigantic, choking, suffocating quiet. She called her father several times, but the lines were down, and she'd only been able to leave a single voicemail message. She did not know what happened to the cat.

She left San Diego on the morning of August 23, first making her way to Lake Tahoe, where Jerry and Nina had a condo, before turning east, planning to cross the country to find her father.

"Ma'am?"

Chung again.

"You all have a good night."

"Thank you."

He left them alone.

"You OK, bud?"

Will sat on the edge of a bed, fiddling with a fingernail on his pinkie. His head was down, his chin almost touching his chest. Preteen boys were chameleons, she decided right then and there. Look one way and you saw the man he was growing into. Turn your head just so, a change in the light, the opaqueness of a shadow cast and there was the little boy he had been not very long ago.

"They were eating people," he mumbled.

He looked up.

"Right?"

She looked at him, tapping her clenched fists together, unsure of what to say. The room was deathly quiet but for the patter of raindrops on the windows and rooftop.

"Yes."

His chin dropped back down.

"Why would they do that?"

"A lot of people have forgotten how to be nice."

He guffawed, almost derisively, as if annoyed by his mother's attempt to sugarcoat the horrors of their world.

"That's a long way from being nice."

"You're right, sweetie," she said.

She turned his question over in her mind for a bit, wanting to give him a better answer. It wouldn't be a good answer because she doubted there was one.

"The truth is, some people have forgotten they're human. They're no better than animals, wild animals who will do anything to stay alive."

"Would you ever do that to stay alive?"

She was shaking her head even before he finished the question.

"No. Absolutely not."

He looked back up at her, his jaw set, his eyes wet and bright.

"I would rather die."

GRAVY CAME to see her later in the evening.

Will was asleep, and she sat under the portico in the cool night air, looking up at the stars. It was a clear night, one of the clearest she could remember, and she wondered if this was a hint their perpetual autumn might be coming to an end. The enduring nature of the cool clammy weather had been wildly frustrating. It couldn't last forever, they kept telling each other, but one way or another, it had. Maybe the nuclear exchanges alone hadn't been responsible for the climate. Maybe it had been that and humanity's mass die-off. Maybe they had pushed the planet beyond the point of no return, and this was the way things were going to be.

Still, she didn't want to believe this was mankind's epilogue. A disjointed, confused mess where they bounced around like free radicals extinguishing each other until there were none of them left. She ran her hands through her hair; a thin clump came free. The cord was thin and dry and brittle. That had been happening more and more often lately, an unwelcome byproduct of nutritional deficit. What was next? Scurvy? Was she a pirate?

The sweet smell of pipe tobacco harkened Gravy's arrival.

"Good evening," he said, emerging from the darkness.

He had a clear, soothing voice, one made for public radio.

She nodded.

"Mind if I join you?"

She gestured to the empty seat next to her on the porch. He sat next to her with a contented sigh.

"Nothing like a good sit, wouldn't you agree?"

She glanced at him but didn't reply.

"Thank you for bringing Alec home."

She nodded.

"He didn't want to talk about it."

"No," she said. She said it declaratively, to make it clear she wasn't going to discuss the subject either. If Alec wanted to share what had happened to him, that would be up to him. It wasn't her story to tell.

This cloaked the discussion with a shade of tension.

"Your accommodations are acceptable, I hope?"

"Yes, they're fine, thank you."

"How's your son?"

"He's fine," she said, without any real knowledge if that were true.

"He's very young," Gravy said.

"He's small for his age."

"Is he your biological son?"

"No."

"I'm a patient man," he said, "but I don't like being lied to."

Her shoulders sagged. What was the point in lying about it anymore?

"Yes, he is my son."

"And he was born after the plague."

Rachel didn't reply.

"Remarkable," he said. "You're a very lucky woman."

Rachel took a deep breath and let it out slowly.

"Sometimes I'm not so sure."

He lifted a single eyebrow.

"Yes, I suppose it must be quite a challenge."

"You were the headmaster here?"

"Yes," he said. "This was a school for kids with behavioral problems."

"Really?"

"Yes."

"But..."

"Everyone is so nice?"

"Yeah."

"When it all went down, these boys were so scared. So scared. A few boys ran off during the outbreak, and, I presume, got sick. We never saw them again. The rest fell in line pretty quickly. That first year was rough, but we managed. Weird what the end of the world can do to a person."

"Indeed.

Another pause.

"I have to ask," she said. "What kind of name is Gravy?"

He laughed.

"My real name is Gary. Gary Fanwood. When I was a kid, my little brother had a hard time saying my name, and it came out as Gravy. The nickname stuck."

"You were very lucky to not get sick."

"I believe a higher power was looking out for us."

She bit down the urge to ask about the seven billion people who hadn't warranted such protection. But their survival made sense at some level. Medusa was a virus, subject to the laws of virology. The outbreak had ended because the pathogen had found no more hosts to infect. And although the virus might be still swimming in her bloodstream, the fact Alec hadn't gotten sick probably meant immune survivors couldn't transmit the virus to others. It had only been two days, but Medusa had been nothing if not speedy. More importantly, if there were women out there who had never been exposed to Medusa...

"Are there any women here?"

"No."

Rachel's mind was racing.

"I know what you're thinking," he said. "I made a list of all-girls' boarding schools, women's prisons, hell, I even went to a convent. We must have gone to fifty different facilities. I didn't find a single survivor."

That didn't mean there weren't non-immune survivors somewhere, but then she remembered that would simply mean more mouths to feed.

"I'm sorry."

She laughed.

"I think we're way past the point of apologizing to each other."

"I hope not," he said. "There's something civilized about apologizing to your fellow man. To express sadness or remorse, to empathize, I believe that is what makes us human."

They sat in silence for a few minutes, Rachel watching the stars, Gravy fiddling with his pipe.

"How long can we stay?" Rachel asked. No point in beating around the bush. She was going to take as much as she could for as long as she could.

"Two nights," he said, pausing to exhale a cloud of sweet-smelling smoke. "We can't offer much in the way of food, but we can give you one good meal before you go. Tomorrow night, a banquet, to thank you for rescuing Alec, and then the following morning, we'll send you on your way."

Part of her wanted to wake Will up and hit the road now, tonight, under the cover of darkness. Safety there, and she preferred anonymity to the unknown risks associated with casting your lot with others. She simply wasn't there yet, as friendly as these people seemed. Actual freedom was better than the promise of freedom. But the specter of starvation hung over them, that eternal cloud darkening their daily existence. You ate when you could eat. You didn't push a plate away. It was the cardinal rule.

"We would love to join you for dinner."

27

She woke with a start, forgetting where she was, almost forgetting who she was. Was she dreaming now or had she been dreaming before? Because it wasn't possible she was a gypsy traipsing across a post-apocalyptic wasteland, was it? She took a deep breath and let it out as she regained her bearings.

The room was clouded with the gloom of the early dawn. Will was still asleep, hard, the kind of rest that could only be built on a foundation of security and safety. Her body felt rested, if not a bit stiff. Amazing the restorative powers of sleep, amazing how good it felt when you had been deprived it for so long. Another week of it and she might start cutting into her deficit. She might start feeling human again. Knowing Will was safe, that he'd been cared for, that he had some food in his belly had been the equivalent of a sleeping pill. Every meal they could get inside their stomachs reminded her of the arcade games of her youth. If you could make it to the next checkpoint, the words EXTENDED PLAY would flash on the screen, getting you more bang for your video game buck.

She stepped out into the hallway, still dark at this early hour. Her foot brushed against something; she looked down and saw a small box by the door. She knelt and opened it to find four bars wrapped in foil and two bottles containing a purple-colored liquid.

A note reading DRINK ME was affixed to each bottle.

She smiled.

She took her breakfast under the portico. The beverage wasn't particularly tasty, but it wasn't bad, sort of like homemade Gatorade, and it washed down the chewy protein bars. She threw caution to the wind and ate both of hers as she watched the day brighten around her. In the distance, the sounds of the campus coming to life for the day.

Will was sitting up in bed when she got back to the room, blinking the sleep out of his eyes.

"Morning."

He acknowledged her with a yawn.

"How'd you sleep?"

A single thumb up in reply.

"Breakfast," she said, tossing the box on the bed.

He dug in, inhaling both bars in a handful of bites.

"Are we leaving now?"

"Tomorrow," she said.

"Why not now?"

"One more good meal, one more night's sleep. You know the rules."

"How much farther to Colorado?"

He drained the last of his drink.

"I don't know," she said. "Not as fast as we'd like, I'm guessing."

"We should go now," he said, yawning.

His face was gaunt, his eyes puffy.

No, they should stay. He needed to rest. Another full day of rest would do wonders for them and they would hit the road refreshed. It was the smart play.

~

Will didn't put up much of a fight. In fact, he had fallen back asleep shortly after breakfast. Rachel spent much of the day in bed herself, reveling in the quiet, in the solitude, in the knowledge that at least for today, they wouldn't have to fight to stay alive, they wouldn't have to be on high alert.

She wandered the hallways of the first floor, peeking into each room along the way. The rooms were sterile, having long been stripped of anything useful. It was a routine now, habit, she supposed, a muscle developed over the last decade, an instinct to check in every nook and every cranny of every new place for something of use.

A noise in the hallway startled her, freezing her in place. Like a computer program, she reached for her HK, even though it was back in her room. She turned back and saw Gravy near the door to her room, his palms out.

"I didn't mean to scare you."

"It's OK."

"Everyone ready for dinner?"

His voice sounded a bit high, reedy, more than she remembered from their earlier discussions.

"I think Will is still asleep," she said. "Let me check."

A quick check of the room confirmed her suspicion and she rejoined Gravy back in the hallway.

"Did you all get some rest?" he asked.

"Yes. Kid is still zonked out. I'd like to let him sleep a bit longer."

"Of course," he said. "We have time, I think."

He lingered in the doorway, and Rachel became aware of an awkwardness between them. It was his school, his building, but she got the sense he was waiting for an invitation.

"Would you like to wait with me?" she asked. "He'll be up soon."

"Thank you."

"Why don't we move to the next room?"

He nodded.

They each took a bed, sitting across from one another. Rachel placed the lantern on the end table between the two beds and closed the door. A plastic potted plant was perched on the end table next to her. The carpet was threadbare, worn to the concrete in some spots.

Gravy sat on the edge of the bed, his elbows on his knees, tapping his fingertips together.

"Thank you again for your hospitality," she said. "I can't tell you how much I appreciate your sharing your supplies with us."

"It's not a big deal," he said.

"It is a big deal. Very few people would do what you've done. Most would put a bullet in our heads. More efficient."

He took a deep breath and let it out slowly.

"Well then. You're very welcome."

They sat in silence for another few moments. Gravy continued to tap his fingertips together. Rachel was content to sit in silence; she had never been one to make small talk for the sake of filling a void of silence. He was handsome, she saw, stealing glances at his profile. A weariness about him she found warm, almost inviting. Someone who had seen darkness but hadn't let it drag him down into its depths.

"I have a confession to make," he said.

Fingertips tapping.

"Oh?"

"You're the first woman I've spoken to in a long time. Since it happened, in fact."

She did not reply.

"I have to admit, it's made me very nervous. I feel like I'm doing everything wrong. Like this thing I'm doing with my hands, I don't even know why I'm doing it. I don't know if I've ever done it before."

He stopped tapping his fingers together and looked at his hands like they had just sprouted from his wrists.

"Did you have a family? Before?"

"No. Divorced when I was twenty-five. Never remarried. Worked here six years before the plague hit."

"You're probably better off," she said.

"How so?"

"No entanglements. Less to worry about. Less to mess with your head. Everyone's fucked up now. The things we've seen. The things we've had to do to stay alive. I doubt anyone has been immune from that."

"I suppose you're right."

She got up and sat next to him on the bed. Her body was turned toward her host, her right leg folded underneath her. What was she doing?

Her eyes caught his in the dim light; his cheeks colored, and he looked away.

"Where are you headed? You and your son?"

"Nowhere in particular," she said. "Meat for the pot, roof over our heads. Keep plugging away. Like everyone else."

She waited as he processed that, wondering if he would dig any deeper.

"I hope you find a place to call home," he said.

"We'll see."

There was another silence.

"How do you all pass the time? Keep the crazies away."

"Every few months we produce a Shakespeare play."

"Really?"

"This surprises you?"

"Just unexpected."

"The men look forward to it," he said. "It's a little reminder of what we were once capable of. A reminder of something beautiful."

"When's the next show?"

"I'm afraid it's several weeks off still."

"Which one?"

"*Twelfth Night*."

"And is there an audience?"

"No," he said. "We do it for us."

Rachel looked down at her hands, trying to picture a stage production at this lonely outpost, these men living and breathing the art of a world long dead. This was what they had forgotten to do at Evergreen. They had become so obsessed with staying alive that they had forgotten to live.

"I wish I could see that."

He laughed.

"I'm not sure how the men would react to that," he said gently.

"After a decade of playing to an empty house, I think they'd freeze on stage."

"It's a nice thing," she said. "Just knowing about it makes me feel better."

"Do you believe in God?" he asked.

Miles Chadwick had been the last man to ask her that question, in those last days before her father and Sarah had rescued them from his clutches. Chadwick's God had passed a harsh judgment on them, had punished them, had used Chadwick himself to deliver that punishment.

"Not anymore. You?"

"More than ever. God is calling us all home, you see. He sent the plague to teach us a lesson. That all this shit we'd been wasting our time on had been just that. A waste. Texting and gourmet olive oils and red-eye flights to Vegas. This world we were left in, that's what He wanted us to see. The quiet. The beauty. That's our responsibility. To see the world the way He meant for us to see it."

This was not terribly dissimilar from what Chadwick had told her thirteen years earlier, but it felt different. A more benevolent viewpoint. Maybe Gravy was right; perhaps God had taken everyone home, the Christians, the Jews, the Muslims, the atheists, the Satanists, the Buddhists, all in one fell swoop. The ledger cleared. Everyone square with the house.

He held a fist to his lips; a river of tears slid down each of his cheeks.

The distance between them had been cut by half; she did not know how that had happened. She was close enough to smell his aftershave, close enough to reach up and wipe away the tears from his right cheekbone. She tried to remember if she had ever seen Eddie cry, and she could not.

Then she was swinging a leg over his lap, taking his face into her hands, pressing her lips to his. He kissed her back, timidly at first, and then wrapped his arms around her back and joined her in the crest of it. She kissed him hard, almost violently, needing the touch of someone who wasn't Eddie, who weren't the men who'd purchased her at Millicent's like she was an object, this embrace washing away the disappointment of her years with Eddie, remind her there were men who had not been Eddie Callahan, who had been better than Eddie.

She worked his jeans and briefs off while he did the same with her pants. She pulled her panties to the side and straddled him, sighing as he entered her. She didn't think about what she was doing or why she was doing it; for this moment, she simply enjoyed the sensation of being close to another human being. She closed her eyes and thought about their Shakespeare play, about sitting in the audience alone, watching these men live and breathe the art of a dead world. Gravy shuddered as she rocked back and forth above him, pressing his face against her chest. He didn't last long, barely a minute before he finished.

She leaned in and kissed him gently.

"I'm sorry about that," he said.

"Don't be," she said. "That was very nice."

"Yes."

She dismounted his lap, feeling a little bit dirty for taking advantage of him as she got dressed. That's what it had been, really. A little bit yes. As she re-adjusted her clothes, he traced a finger across his lips, perhaps to ensure the taste of her mouth against his was really there.

"Right."

"Do you think your God will forgive us?" Rachel asked.

"For what?" he asked.

"For doing what we had to do."

He looked at her with eyes that were bright and full and wet.

"I hope so."

Will was still asleep when she went to check on him a few minutes later.

"Ready, Spoon?" she whispered, shaking him gently by the shoulder.

She repeated the inquiry twice more before she got a response. He yawned loudly and rubbed his eyes.

"Hungry."

"Well, let's go take care of that, shall we?"

He nodded, and they stepped outside to join Gravy, who was waiting in the sickly yellow glow of an incandescent lantern. The light threw a rippling shadow against the wall behind him.

"Follow me," he said, avoiding eye contact with her. She started to regret their dalliance, which served only to depress her even further. It almost made her give up hope, right then as they walked to dinner, that their ability to make new connections had been permanently severed, that their new default setting was a state of war.

There was little chit-chat as they crossed the campus. She expected a guided tour, *Oh, this is the Science Building, that's the Performing Arts Center*, but Gravy didn't say a word. Maybe it was because she had just rocked his world. She felt like an asshole for thinking it.

Pride goeth before the fall, sweetie, remember that one.

She felt bad for thinking it because when you got right down to it, he had been a gentleman, and that was a category of men in woefully short supply these days. This man could have done anything to her and Will. Instead, she had found a group of people clinging to their civility in a world absent it.

There was enough light left in the sky to take in the campus, which was quite lovely. Gravy's people had maintained the grounds over the years, although certain buildings did look a bit ragged. To their west was the athletic complex, including a football field and an outdoor track-and-field facility. A bit farther north was a larger cluster of buildings, more dormitories and classroom buildings.

"How many students went here?" she asked, breaking a long silence.

"About five hundred," Gravy replied.

They continued in silence, entering the main quad a few

moments later. A bit of a breeze had picked up in the throughway between the buildings, chilling her. She felt naked without her HK, the reassuring weight of it hanging from her shoulder.

"We're here," he said, pausing before an old Victorian-style brick building. He seemed distracted again.

"It's a lovely building," Rachel said, glancing upward toward the gables.

They climbed the steps slowly. Rachel was looking forward to being indoors; the wind had picked up and the evening had broken chilly, the sky limned with bleak, gray clouds. Gravy held the door open for them, waiting as Rachel and Will entered the foyer before him.

The foyer was dimly lit, the shadows flickering against the wall. The murmur of voices in an unseen room tickled Rachel's ears. It had a ghostly timbre about it; she felt Will pressing up against her.

"I know, this is a bit of a creepy room," he said, sensing their discomfort. "It's the best building for storing food, so we made this our dining room."

He pointed toward a door to their left.

"It's through there."

Gravy led them inside, where Rachel got her first look at the community in full. As the presence of Will and Rachel became apparent, the vigorous chit-chat died from one table to the next, like power grids failing across a stricken city. There were six long wooden tables in the rectangular-shaped room, three on each side, lined up in two rows. The tables were crowded with men, most of them about her age, but a few older ones. Portraits of men long dead lined the walls. There was a door in the center of each wall, but it wasn't clear where those led. A series of oil lanterns bathed the room in a warm, inviting glow.

"Brothers," Gravy said after the room fell silent. "These are our special guests."

He placed a hand on Rachel's shoulder.

"This is Sister Rachel."

"Greetings, Sister Rachel," said the men, almost in unison.

"This is her son. Brother William."

"Greetings, Brother William," came the reply.

Gravy led them to three open seats, one at the head of the table nearest them, the two others next to the head. Will sat on the end seat, in between Rachel and Gravy. To Rachel's right was a thin man with a narrow face and a scraggly beard. She spotted Alec two tables away; she nodded at him, and he returned the gesture. In front of each person was a bowl full of a thick stew. Steam was still curling from the surface of the bowls. It smelled delicious, made her mouth water. Will dug in without waiting.

She smacked his hand.

"Wait," she hissed at him.

No one else seemed to notice Will's breach of etiquette, each man bowing his head.

Gravy's voice filled the chamber.

"Thank you, Lord, for this bounty," he said.

"Thank you, Lord, for this bounty," echoed the men.

"We do not ask why You have cast this judgment on the world."

We do not ask why You have cast this judgment on the world.

"It is not our place to know."

It is not our place to know.

"We see the beauty in the world, as You intended."

We see the beauty in the world, as You intended.

"Amen."

Amen.

The prayer concluded, the men dug into their bowls, the room silent but for the clink of ceramic against silverware, the silver against teeth.

Rachel took a bite of the hot stew. She didn't know what was in it, a mixture of meat and potatoes. It was salty, very salty, but it was delicious. Perhaps the best thing she'd eaten in years. She kept a wary eye on her Will, who was lost in his meal. The world had slipped away, just a boy and his supper.

"I can't tell you how much I appreciate this," she said to Gravy, who was focused on his bowl, stirring the stew with his spoon. She had thanked him over and over, but for some reason, it didn't seem like it was enough.

"I'm sorry."

"For what?" she replied. "For making us leave? You can't be sorry about that."

"It's just that we're running low on food."

"I understand," she said.

"No," he replied. "I don't think you do."

He glanced up and looked around the room. The other men were engaged in chatter and seemed oblivious to the sudden chill at the head of the table. Gravy's mood was beginning to frighten her.

"What's wrong?" she asked, reaching out and wrapping her fingers around the palm of his hand.

He looked at her, his eyes wide and blank. He looked very far away.

"You have to understand."

"Understand what?" she asked, pulling her hand away from his.

"I'm sorry. I had no choice."

The four doors opened simultaneously, and a hush swept across the room. Rachel leaped from her seat, accidentally flipping over the bowl of stew in the process. A dozen heavily armed men and women, dressed in black pants and heavy barn jackets, poured into the room, surrounding all of them.

"Hands on your heads."

One of the men sitting at a table close to the back door made a move inside his jacket, but a deafening burst from one of the guns blew him off his seat. He landed in a heap on his back, his left leg wrenched under the lip of the table. A ribbon of blood laced the wall behind him.

"Hands on your heads."

As they complied with the request, Rachel stole a glance at Gravy. There was a resigned look on his face, one that said he wasn't surprised at all. He stared blankly at their captors, his eyes wide and unblinking.

"You sold us out," she whispered.

"Quiet," barked one of the gunmen.

A burst of commotion near the doorway caught Rachel's attention. She turned her head toward the sound, where she saw a sight that chilled her to her core.

One last person had entered the room. It was a face Rachel had only seen once before, but it was one she remembered easily.

The woman who had wanted to take Will.

Priya.

28

Rachel's body turned to stone. Her eyes darted around the room, looking for some answer, some solution, some way out of this mess. Her mouth went dry.

There was no way out of here.

"The woman and the boy," said Priya.

The two gunmen closest to Rachel approached her and Will and motioned toward Priya with the muzzles of their guns. Rachel took Will's hand and together they followed the men toward Priya. As they neared the door, Priya motioned them to continue.

Rachel and Priya locked eyes. As Rachel exited the dining room, she could hear the woman's words to one of her men, as clearly as if she had whispered them into her own ear.

"Kill the rest."

Rachel held Will close as they followed their captors down a long corridor, trying to cover his ears with her right arm as the room behind her erupted into apocalyptic gunfire. Behind her was Priya, flanked by two women. Over the staccato bursts of the dozen automatic weapons, she could hear screaming, but it was brief. And then it was over.

Will had started to cry, his body heaving and hitching against her, but she kept him moving, unsure if the slightest deviation from Priya's direction would result in their execution. Then they were outside again, trailed closely by the group that had remained behind to follow Priya's extermination order. Their work done.

Just like that.

As casually as asking someone for the time, she had ordered the execution of more than thirty people. Her head swam, and she began to salivate. It felt like she was floating, the ground underneath her unmoored. She was sweating and she felt lightheaded.

It was the Citadel all over again.

The ledger had been balanced.

All those women.

All these men.

All dead.

She let go of Will and struggled to keep her balance. Bent over, hands on her knees, the ground swaying. Then her stew came up all at once, a furious rush, and she was pissed at herself because that was good food she was puking, you stupid woman, that's good food you're leaving here on the not-so-manicured grounds of the Deephaven School for Boys.

Gravy was dead. This kind and decent man who had betrayed her was dead and fuck him, it was his fault he was dead. He might as well have shot himself in the head. And she had let herself believe he wanted to help them.

You see, Eddie? Do you see? See what would have happened?

She buckled to the ground, her legs crossed underneath her. The ground was slightly damp, the dew staining her knees, sending a chill through her, but she didn't care. Around her, activity. A nondescript SUV pulled up nearby. The familiar beep-beep-beep signifying the hatch opening.

Several of Priya's confederates re-entered the building with dollies. Scavenging what remained. She wondered what promises Priya had made to Gravy. Two years' worth of food! A trip to Hawaii!

Everyone wanted to believe they were merely one step away, one deal away from salvation. This trade, that sellout. This close to happily-ever-after. Like the get-rich-quick real estate seminars from the old days. Did hope have no mercy on humanity? Couldn't it just let them be? Hope preyed on humanity through its lies, through its false promises, tricking the world into thinking that sunnier days were right around the corner. Problem was, you never made it to that corner because there was no corner. It was a mirage, an illusion. There was no hope. They were already dead, trapped in these mortal coils, swirling to the bottom of the hourglass.

She became aware of a presence behind her. It was Priya. She was smoking a cigarette. Like the first time they had met, she was dressed impeccably, her hair perfectly coiffed. This made Rachel hate her almost more than anything else.

"So," Rachel said. "Here we are."

"Here we are."

"How did you know we were here?"

"My search for your son is no secret," she replied. "We've been operating up in this area for several years. I made it clear there would be a hefty reward for your capture."

Rachel's skin crawled. While she was playing kissyface with Gravy, Priya had been close by, hidden in the seams of his hospitality. Betrayal layered upon betrayal. She had made the mistake of trusting someone; it was an error in judgment she would not repeat, although that was probably because she would be dead soon. Hell, even her son had known better, his insistence they leave that morning looming large in her mind.

"Way to live up to your end of the bargain."

Priya's eyes briefly flashed with anger, but the moment passed.

"Sometimes we have to do things that are not easy."

"I'm coming with you," Rachel said. "If you want him to cooperate, you will need me there."

"I'm afraid not, my dear."

"I'm not letting you take him without me."

"What choice do you have?" Her eyes narrowed, and Rachel got a brief taste, like a swish of wine in her mouth, of the evil inside this woman. In some ways, she frightened Rachel even more than Miles Chadwick had.

Priya left Rachel sitting on the ground and turned her attention toward winding down their activities at Deephaven. This morning, this had been a home, a place to live, a place to survive. Now it was just another dead place. Another point of light extinguished. She imagined an aerial map of the place, a fresh red X superimposed over the image of the campus. Like the one over Evergreen, over the world. There would be a lot of red X's on the map these days.

Priya was right. She had no choice.

No choice but one.

"Wait."

Priya paused.

"What if I could offer you something better?"

Priya turned slowly to face Rachel, who did her very best to keep her jaw set, her eyes on her captor.

"I'm listening."

RACHEL TOLD PRIYA EVERYTHING.

She made Rachel repeat the tale to her chief lieutenant, a man named Kovalewich. He was a squat man with a thick gray beard. He listened carefully as Rachel told the story a second time, beginning with her capture by Chadwick's goons all those Septembers ago and ending with the discovery of the tattoo on the man back in Lincoln.

"That's a pretty amazing story," he said.

"It's the truth."

"A mother's love," Priya said.

"What's that supposed to mean?"

"You expect us to believe that not only are you mysteriously connected to the conspiracy behind the plague, but that you managed to get caught by these conspirators and that your father managed to rescue you? I'd have a hard time believing any one of those stories, let alone all three."

Rachel took a deep breath and let it out slowly. She had to convince these people yet, it all sounded as ridiculous as Priya suggested. Rachel wasn't sure she would believe the story if their roles were reversed.

"Is it any less believable than what we've all been through?"

"Meaning?"

"This world we're in." She turned to Kovalewich. "Did you ever think you'd grow up to be a lieutenant to a post-apocalyptic warlord?"

He ran a thumbnail against his lip. He glanced at Priya.

"What did you do?" Rachel asked, nodding her head to signify the Before.

"Director of HR for a small hospital chain." He sounded small when he said it, as though it was the first time he had thought about who he'd been in a very long time.

"And now look at you."

He looked at Priya again, but her face gave no quarter, showed no emotion.

"We'll have a chat about this," she said. "Wait here."

Priya and Kovalewich climbed into their vehicle to palaver. Will was still under the guard of one of Priya's henchmen, whom she approached as she waited for the referendum on her life to end. Will was in the front seat of the truck, his face pressed to the window. She waved at him, but it earned her nothing more than a barely perceptible nod of the head. Jesus God. This could be it. This really could be the last time she ever saw Will. There was nothing to stop them from simply leaving her here, from disappearing into the gloomy evening.

"Get back," the man hissed, raising his gun at her. The exchange of words drew the attention of another, who sauntered over to join his comrade.

"I can't say hi to my son?"

She stared at his round little face in the window, the panic rising in her.

A little more post-traumatic stress disorder for you, my sweet boy? After all, it has been almost two whole days since the last horrific thing I've put you through.

She watched Priya's contingent shuffling to and fro, preparing for their departure, and she wanted to curse them. All these fools, mourning the fact they hadn't been able to have kids. Did they not know how lucky they were? Did they have any inkling of the burden she carried? No. What did they plan on feeding these kids? Hopes and dreams didn't do much for empty tummies. The more of them there were, the faster they could all starve to death.

And even if she found this place in Colorado, what then? The odds were excellent they were starving too. Probably hadn't counted on mankind's itchy nuclear trigger finger to wreck its cupboard, although looking back, she couldn't imagine why that wouldn't have crossed their minds.

She couldn't save the world, she was no Vin Diesel, may he rest in peace, coming to save the day, finding the canister of Medusa virus and firing it into space seconds before it had been unleashed against humanity. The world was already dead. That's what these people didn't understand. They were already dead. They were all dead.

She was dead. Priya was dead. Will was dead.

All she could do was try to stretch it out a little bit longer. Will deserved better than a brief coda to his existence at Evergreen. He deserved to be happy and warm and comfortable, if only for a little bit. She would die to get that for him. If she had to hop in bed with this mass murderer, then she would. It didn't matter. Because they were already dead.

"Hey!"

She was shaken loose from her daydream, looking up to see the guard pointing back toward Priya's vehicle. She was motioning for her to join them; Rachel blew Will a kiss then turned to head back toward Priya without waiting to see if he reciprocated. If she didn't see his response, then she wouldn't have to know he hadn't blown one back to her. That seemed too awful to contemplate.

The man was lighting a cigar as Rachel rejoined them.

"Good news," Priya said. "We're going to take a flyer on you."

She let out a deep breath, one she'd been holding in since they retreated to consider her tale.

"Thank you."

"It would be shortsighted not to explore this angle," Priya said. "Despite the unlikeliness of it all, here you are. Your son was born after the plague. The very fact of Will is a huge thing, you see. He exists in a world where he should not. That gives me hope that all is not lost. That life will prevail. That we will prevail."

Rachel considered this, juxtaposing it with the situational assessment she had just conducted. Priya, she of the mass execution order, she was the hopeful one. Rachel, trying to keep her son alive, was the pessimist. That was a crazy thing to wrap her head around.

"Let us be clear about one thing," Priya said. "We're going to find out why the babies are dying. And if we can find out, then all the better for you and Will.

"But if this goes sideways, there will be hell to pay."

29

By the time the group finished strip-mining Deephaven, it was full dark. Priya made the call to make camp and shove off in the morning. To ensure Rachel didn't try anything stupid, Priya split her and Will up for the night. Rachel didn't know where Will was sleeping, but she was back in the same dorm room. Priya placed a guard outside her room and left her with two cans of food – corn and black beans. Rachel ate them slowly by the light of the lantern, savoring each bite. When each can was half-full, she mixed the remaining portions together. Black-bean-and-corn salsa. A full belly, a clear head. Nothing extraordinary. That was natural, that was the way things were supposed to be.

She found herself wondering about the others they had left behind in Evergreen. What had become of them? Had they gone their separate ways, the bonds tying them together having finally dissolved? Maybe Priya had gone back to kill them after discovering Will was gone. Her train of thought continued motoring along the track to the future, as unknowable as the fate of those in her past.

The quest had shifted. Before, it had been a matter of idle curiosity, something to pass the time while they foraged for food. But now the tables had turned. For as long as she could remember, food had been her primary mission. Protecting the warehouse at all costs. It had consumed all of them, her, her dad, Harry and the others. And it had broken them all; they had lost something along the way. It was as if they lived to support the warehouse rather than looking at it as something to support them. And not just her group. Even these monsters, these cannibals that fed on weary strangers were no different.

But for now, food was no longer the issue. This group was well-equipped, well-armed. Her very life now depended on this quest. Will's life. To save Will, she would have to save them all.

She slept fitfully, waking up every little bit, cold, sore, her eyes gummed with goop. She dreamed about Schrodinger's cat, both alive and dead at the same time until you opened the box and the world would collapse to one choice or another and the cat would be either alive or dead. There were no other options. Terror gripped her tightly. What if there were nothing there? What if they made it to Colorado only to find her family had been nothing but the random byproduct of an experiment gone terribly wrong?

The dim light of dawn filtering through the window shades put an end to her sleep for the night, and the morning rolled into being. Game pieces moving into place, small moves that would begin to snowball into bigger moves, into big decisions that would determine how this all turned out.

Calm. She needed to be calm. A bit of yoga loosened her stiff muscles, cleared the lactic acid that had built up. Vinyasa. Downward dog. Warrior One. Warrior Two. She did the moves until her muscles began to burn, until they began to ache. The exercises helped her clear her head, wash away the dregs of fatigue still lodged in her body.

A knock at her door. She waited, assuming correctly that whoever was on the other side of it would open it without being invited. Kovalewich stood in the doorjamb, looking fresh and rested. Just another day at the office for this guy. All he needed was a cup of Starbucks, his name misspelled on the side of it, steam curling skyward. Headed to the morning budget meeting.

"Ready to hit the road?" he asked congenially.

For a man who had helped execute thirty people the evening before, he seemed remarkably at peace. How was that possible? It was supposed to matter, killing someone. It was supposed to be a hard thing to do. Not that it could never be done, sometimes it had to be done, but good God damn. What had the years done to these people? Had she missed that much in her little cocoon? Was this how it really was? Had the last ten years of her life been nothing more than a carefully constructed illusion?

"Let's go," she replied, strongly desiring to shut down this conversation before it got started.

She followed him outside, where the group was busy breaking down the camp, loading the trucks. Four black Suburbans idled in the access road that swirled toward the front door of the administration building. A woman emerged from that doorway, carrying a banker's box under her arm.

She looked anxiously for Will, her rational mind knowing he was fine but panicking nonetheless.

There.

He was sitting in the front seat of the first van, his legs dangling over the side. Priya was with him, playing a game of some kind. Rock-paper-scissors, from the looks of it.

Will shot Paper.

Priya shot Rock.

A big smile opened up his normally dour face as he covered her dark-olive fist with his hand. She couldn't see Priya's face, but she seemed at ease, her shoulders rounded, her movements lithe and soft.

They shot again.

Will, Paper again.

Priya, Paper.

A woman approached her, drew her attention. Priya tousled his hair and went back to work. Immediately, her body went rigid again, her shoulders stiff and square.

It hit Rachel like a truck.

This was what they were looking for.

Will's inherent innocence and spunk. Childhood. The spark of life that had been missing for so long. When you were around it all the time, you forgot what it was like when it wasn't there. After all, it wasn't only the fact that Will was born after the plague. It was that he was so much younger than everyone else. The plague's brutal aftershocks had been unkind to its very youngest survivors. Sometimes late at night, her thoughts turned toward the immune babies and toddlers that had died simply because there had been no one around to take care of them. For every ten small children immune to Medusa, Rachel bet that eight had died in the ensuing weeks, simply unable to care for themselves.

"It's time," a voice behind her said.

It was Kovalewich. Rachel had not heard him come up behind her.

One by one, they loaded into the caravan. Will was in the third vehicle, Rachel in the fourth. They were a fearsome sight together, this many people, vehicles, weapons. It exuded an aura of control, of power. All these years, they had been on the defensive. Reacting instead of acting. Look where that had gotten them.

The caravan began to move, chugging away slowly from the Deephaven Administration building. The day was cloudy but bright, the sense that blue skies were right around the corner, even though they weren't. Every now and again, a thicket of clouds would break, revealing a swatch of blue behind it, but then it would seal up just as quickly, like it had remembered its place in the world.

They ran west for the balance of the day, averaging about twenty-five to thirty miles per hour. Compared to the snail's pace she had become used to, it felt like she was aboard a rocket ship. With each passing mile the caravan chewed up and swallowed, they cut deeper into a world totally unknown to Rachel. Until this trip, she hadn't ventured farther than a ten-mile radius of the compound since they had moved there. Around her, the world was returning to nature. The road they were currently traversing, Interstate 44, had devolved into a weed-choked nightmare. What would Dwight Eisenhower say about his beloved Interstate System now?

It had never seemed this menacing when they were on foot or bicycles, but from inside a moving vehicle, the highway felt haunted. The familiar thrum of tires on concrete had been replaced with a mild susurration. In some spots, especially along the shoulders, where the weeds had really thrived and contributed to a thick layer of humus, small bushes had begun to grow. A burgeoning forest on the edge of the roadway. A few more years and these roads would be impassable by car.

Moss-coated billboards advertising truck stops and tobacco outlets and the *WORLD'S CHEAPEST FURNITURE MADE IN AMERICA* were a reminder of the world gone by. There weren't many cars out here, a few, but they were more part of the scenery than anything. They stopped at each one because you never knew where you might find a can of food, but that first day, there was nothing for the effort.

Exit ramps.

Exit 143B.

Towns called Coalfell and Norwich.

Faded highway signs.

Taco Bell 1.3 miles

Kayleigh's Diner 0.5 miles

These exit ramps led to dead places now.

It made her sad.

They drove for ten hours, covering about four hundred miles. One stop about midway to refuel. Rachel was fascinated by the group's fuel supply, all of which was stored in the trail car. Fuel had been like a unicorn for her community. They had tried to make their own a few times, but all they got for their efforts were a few blown engines and one explosion that killed Debbie Coleman, an Evergreen resident. A woman who had played guitar and sometimes ate up the quiet and the lonely with her beautiful, mournful music.

As dusk fell, the lead car took the exit for Clearmill. Rachel caught a glimpse of a motel marquee as they sledded down the ramp.

They made a quick right, then another, which put them in the parking lot of a Holiday Inn Express. Like locusts, they descended upon the long-forgotten motel, and, with the precision of a special-forces unit, quickly took over the building. Around them, a dark Hardee's and a gas station, probably still sitting atop a lake of thousands of gallons of inert gasoline. How much easier their lives could have been if the gasoline had lasted even a couple of years before going stale.

Priya and two others stayed behind with Will and Rachel while the rest made quick work of the three-floor establishment. Rachel was alone in her vehicle with the driver, who smoked a foul-smelling homemade cigarette. The smoke burned her eyes and made them water.

"You mind if I wait outside?"

"Go ahead," he said, his voice rough like sandpaper. It was the first time the man had spoken all day.

She alighted from the vehicle, relishing the thick cold air she pulled into her lungs. As she wiped the smoke-induced tears from her eyes, the passenger door of the lead vehicle creaked open, Priya climbing out.

"The cigarettes," Rachel said.

"Ah, yes," said Priya. "He's very proud of those."

A moment of silence.

"How was the ride?"

"My back hurts. It's been years since I've been in a car that long."

"Like the old days."

"Other than the skeletons in rusted-out vehicles and bushes growing in the middle of the interstate, it is exactly like the old days."

Priya laughed, an honest-to-goodness laugh. The sound was almost alien to her. It felt good to make someone laugh, even Priya. Pride, man. That's why it was one of the deadly sins. Pride goeth before the fall.

"You're going to honor our deal, right?"

"Of course," Priya said. "Why wouldn't I?"

"Not much honor these days. Thieves or otherwise."

"This isn't personal, my dear. Like I said, I'd be a fool not to explore all options, all contingencies."

Silence.

"I had a son," Priya said, her voice suddenly small and far away. "He was eleven. We lived near Philadelphia. The virus hit there early on. He died that first week, before anyone really knew how bad it was going to get. It was still just a bad flu then, an early start to flu season. Remember how hot it was?"

"I was in San Diego. Weather never really changed there."

"Oh," she replied.

"So he died, and the doctors told me it had gotten into his lungs, and that's why he had died. Bad luck. I was a single mother. My husband died in a car accident when Raj was two. Just the two of us. And then it was just me. And then it was *really* just me. I watched everyone around me die. Every single person I knew died."

She paused and smiled.

"Isn't it funny?" Priya asked.

"What?"

"We tell our stories of surviving the plague like they're unique. As though my story is extra special or somehow more horrible than yours. It's all rather self-important, isn't it? We all want to be the best, the most unusual, the standout."

She paused.

"Why do you think that is?" Priya asked.

"Same as anything else," Rachel replied. "People want to think they're special. Even when we're not."

"Do you think we are special? People, I mean?"

"We evolved. Evolutionary luck."

"You're a scientist," Priya said. "Perhaps an engineer. Or you were, once upon a time."

"How did you know?"

"Scientists have a certain humility about them. Of their place in the world. You understand it was just as possible that we didn't evolve. And really wouldn't have cared."

"It's true. Any one of a million things breaks differently, and some other species would have dominated the earth."

"One with better sense than us."

"Probably."

"People were wretched."

Hello, pot? Kettle is on line two. Would like to discuss colors with you.

Rachel's left eyebrow arced upward, just enough for Priya to notice.

"You're wondering why I killed the people at the school."

"It had crossed my mind."

"Will is too important."

"What does Will have to do with it?"

"Until we know what's special about him, it would be a grievous error to have his existence become common knowledge."

"But you said people knew about him."

"Rumors, really. Conjecture. A myth. A legend. I don't think anyone really believed he existed."

Rachel didn't reply.

"You really don't know how desperate people have become, do you?"

"I guess not."

"People have gone off the deep end. The loneliness. The sadness. The idea that all this is for nothing. All the suffering was for nothing."

"And if it got out he really existed?"

"I believe there would be a religious component to it."

"Meaning what?"

"You agree that the vast majority of people alive before the plague believed in God?"

"Yes, of course."

"Didn't that strike you as odd? That literally billions of people devoted their entire lives to a supreme all-powerful being they had never, ever seen? A deity who had never once in recorded history provided irrefutable proof of his existence?"

"You don't believe in God."

"You'll forgive me if I don't put much stock in that fairy tale. I'm supposed to accept as fact that a man rose from the dead from a story told over and over again, massaged, spun, re-massaged and re-spun?

"I guess I never thought of it that way."

"Either way, I think it's highly probable people would view Will as a gift from God. Or God Himself. The Second Coming and all that."

A chill tickled Rachel's spine.

"Do you mind if I ask who Will's father was?"

"He doesn't have one."

For the briefest of moments, Priya's dark olive skin paled, almost to ash.

Then Rachel began to laugh.

"His father's an asshole. At least he was. He's dead."

"I see."

"Besides, what do I care what people think about him?"

"My dear, after that, all bets would be off. We would be in uncharted waters. For the sake of humanity, we have to find out what's special about him. We will find out. I promise you that. I am sorry if there is collateral damage. But we have to find out."

Rachel felt a buzzing on the bridge of her nose, that sensation that things were getting away from her, that things were beyond her control and there was nothing she could do about it.

"What were you? Before?"

"Police officer."

Rachel's eyebrows elevated slightly.

"Don't fit the bill, do I? Not too many Indian women working as officers."

It didn't fit the bill, no, but that wasn't the point. The point was that they'd all forgotten who they were. Humanity had forgotten itself. All the things they'd been, all the things they'd done, all the things they were capable of had been swept under the rug.

She let the comment slide behind them in the wake of the moment. A stitch of commotion from the second floor drew their attention. Rachel glanced up and saw Priya's comrades escorting two people downstairs, their footfalls heavy and clanging on the metal steps.

They were brought before Priya, two bedraggled middle-aged men. One had long hair tied back in a ponytail. His beard was speckled with gray, but it was mostly just dirty. The second man was heavier set and balding. He wore a blue New York Giants sweatshirt that had seen better days. Both were a bit wild-eyed.

"What have we here?" Priya asked. There was something unnerving about her accent, something precise and frightening. Charming and cultured once upon a time. No longer.

"Found these two upstairs." It was one of the guys from Rachel's vehicle. "It's bad."

"Show me," Priya said. "Rachel, come along. You need to see what I'm talking about."

Rachel paused, glancing over her shoulder toward the vehicle carrying Will.

"Relax," she said. "He will be fine."

Rachel's gaze lingered on the boy a bit longer before she turned and followed Priya. The stairs felt rickety, the years of weather and wind and rain taking their toll on the metal bolts and screws. It was nearly full dark; the beams from their flashlights hitched and bounced as they scaled the steps, navigated the breezeway, past the shattered remains of a vending machine.

Rachel's heart was beating so hard she could feel it in her ears. She didn't know why she was so nervous. Obviously, Priya wanted to prove her point, to justify the way she handled things. Truthfully, Rachel didn't care. People did what they wanted, and they had let it be that way. The S.S. *Morality* had long since set sail.

A half-moon hung in an unusually clear sky; its silver light shimmered against the windows of the rooms they passed along the balcony. The group had paused at the doorway at the end of the concourse, the men and women huddled around the entrance, shifting to get a good look at the interior but hesitant to go in.

A thick, rich smell hung in the air. Metallic. Meaty. It was different than the smell of sickness and death she remembered from the heady days of the plague, mostly gone now, but occasionally, she would catch a whiff of something, and it would all come back, all the way down to the color socks her stepfather was wearing on the day he died.

The crowd parted as she and Priya approached the doorway. Somebody handed Priya a flashlight, and she stepped into the room without a moment's hesitation. A woman motioned for Rachel to follow her into the room, the stench growing as she drew closer. Rachel paused for a second at the threshold and then stepped inside.

It was a standard hotel room, two queen-sized beds, a small round table, a chest of drawers, a cheesy art print hanging on the wall. Rachel followed the beam of light from Priya's flashlight around the room. A puddle of blood on the carpet by the dresser. A larger one in the space between the beds. Still another. Knives and other sharp instruments on the table. Then the flashlight settled on the bed closest to the door.

She moved the light a bit higher up on the bed. At first, Rachel didn't know what she was looking at. Then her head processed the thing her eyes were seeing. It was a woman. At least, it had once been a woman. Now it was ... desecrated, that was the best word Rachel could think of. Desecration. She looked away because there was no need to look.

"You see?" Priya asked.

"OK. It's not the first time I've seen it. What's your point?"

"The world is full of terrible things. And terrible people. This is what happens when you lose all hope. You become a monster. You become the thing you fear. For all I know these guys were middle school principals or medical supply salesmen and now this."

Rachel had heard enough of Priya's oral dissertation on the current state of the human condition. She went back outside and leaned against the railing, looking out on the dead town spread out before her.

She became aware of a presence behind her.

"Like I said, who knows what happens if people find out about your boy."

They went back downstairs to the parking lot, where the two men were down on their knees, their hands laced together above their respective heads. The light from the lanterns illuminated them in a small sphere of light. They said nothing, made no sound.

Someone handed Priya a gun.

She pressed the barrel to the nape of the first man's neck and pulled the trigger. Rachel started at the sound of the shot; gunfire never lost its visceral punch, even if she had lost a chunk of her hearing during the gunplay of the last decade. Before the dead man's body had finished crumpled to the ground, she repeated the action with the second man, the two gunshots coming so close together they seemed to amplify one another. The report echoed, bouncing across buildings.

They slept.

At three a.m., Rachel got up and went to the room where the dead woman lay. She pulled the cheap blanket, bearing a pattern that could best be described as a kaleidoscopic nightmare, from the second bed and covered her remains.

She sat with the dead woman and cried.

30

They drove for three days, churning west through the plains, the upper peaks of the Rockies coming into sharper relief on the horizon. The schedule was rote. On the road by seven a.m., lunch at noon, stopping at dark. Powered by the biofuel, the vehicles only managed a top speed of about thirty miles per hour, and they only managed that on a few stretches of road. The pace was maddening to Rachel, some long-dead part of her still remembering how fast cars used to travel, and then she would remind herself she could be walking. Will rode in the lead car, Rachel in the trail vehicle. Priya alternated between them, probably to compare their stories. That was one thing she didn't have to worry about. She was telling the truth; she had no idea if Priya was, but she wasn't in any position to second-guess her at this point.

The first night, they took shelter in a sturdily built farmhouse. The paint had peeled, and moss carpeted the exterior like a bad rash, but the structure was sound. Priya kept a guard on Rachel all night, but she was too worn out and her back was too sore to even contemplate an escape. The events of the previous night had drained the group's energy, and they had all turned in early. Rachel slept at the end of the hall in a musty-smelling bedroom with a sentry outside her door. She didn't know where Will had slept.

They camped outside the second night, the surrounding terrain not giving up any shelter worth hunkering down in. Again, Priya kept them separated, except at dinner, when they were allowed to sit across from one another.

"I'm not the monster you think I am," Priya had said as they ate their beans.

Rachel didn't reply.

Then someone had broken out a guitar, and they sang some Rolling Stones, some Beatles, even some Avett Brothers, an alt-rock-folk-bluegrass-hipster band popular right before the end. The last tune was called *Murder in the City*, a quiet little number about the importance of family and that one had made Rachel tear up a little, or maybe it had been from the smoke of the campfire. If Will had seen her cry, if he asked her about it, she would say it was from the smoke.

Music was a rare thing these days, and when they heard it, it sounded particularly special, almost forbidden. What business did music have in this world? Harmony and song were anathema to this world in discord. And that made it sound all the sweeter.

The third day on the road dawned wet and chilly, the rain thrumming against the polyester tents they had pitched. They were a hundred miles from Denver, which would put them there around midday, assuming they didn't hit any obstacles. Rachel hadn't slept well, tossing and turning all night, even briefly debating an escape attempt because she was pretty sure Will was three tents over and she could take the guard outside her tent, and they could make it to one of the vehicles in the ensuing chaos. But she was only pretty sure that's where he was, and so she had lain in her tent, dozing more than sleeping. Shivering in the cold.

When she emerged from her tent at dawn, she felt thick and slow, her eyes sticky with sleep, her head hurting. The unknown of today added another layer of stress. Perhaps there would be answers; maybe there would only be more questions. But as she crouched, relieving herself in the bushes, she understood today was different, its outcome murky.

The group, fourteen of them in all, was buzzing, a current running through them as they ate and addressed their morning constitutionals. They all wanted to know what was out there. It wasn't just her quest anymore.

Will woke up a few minutes later. He popped out of his tent, tufts of wild hair poking out in every direction. As he made a beeline for the chow, she noticed that little attention was being paid to him.

Now, Rachel. Now.

She finished her business and pulled up her pants. As she fastened the last button, she charted a course that would intersect with Will's, a straight line that would bring them together near a large rock on the edge of the camp. Twenty yards. Fifteen. Ten. They made eye contact moments before she hooked her arm around his waist and pulled him past the rock, toward a copse of trees that guarded the camp's northwest flank.

"Run," she said. "Now."

They bolted.

Behind her, she heard a burst of shouting, Priya's normally reserved voice limned with anger.

"Hurry."

The idiocy of this maneuver dawned on her as they negotiated the uneven terrain of the forest. The ground, caked with dead leaves, cascaded gently, forcing them to regulate their speed. Heavy rustling behind them as Priya's group gave chase.

Where would they go?

What would they eat?

She didn't even know where the hell they were.

She hazarded a look over her shoulder, a decision she immediately regretted. Her injured ankle began to throb as she negotiated the uneven terrain, a relief map of exposed roots and rocky ground. White hot pain surged up through her leg, making her stomach flip. Eventually, her leg buckled and she stumbled to the ground in a heap. Will, who had been off her right hip, tripped over his mother's leg and landed headfirst into a mound of dirt and leaves.

"Mommy!" he barked, rolling to his side and sitting up.

Knowing the game was up, she took her time, rolling to a sitting position, facing back in the direction of the camp. A group of four came up on them and quickly surrounded them.

"Can't blame a girl for trying, right?"

They walked back to the camp as rain began to fall; Rachel made the trip under her own power, but every step was painful, her ankle tender and fiery. She didn't know why she had tried something so foolish, so exquisitely stupid. She could not abide being Priya's puppet, playing to her agenda. That meant compromising who she was, what kind of mother she was. On her own, she could think, she could analyze, and if necessary she could abort. But under Priya's thumb, she would have to go all the way, *damn the torpedoes, full speed ahead*, with a woman who represented all that was evil and wrong and twisted in the world.

Priya did not look happy when they got back. Her jaw was clenched tight, the muscles under her cheekbone rippling. Her hands closed and unfurled again, closed and opened. She was a cornered animal, looking for a way out.

"Was it worth it?" she asked in a measured voice.

Rachel couldn't look at her. It wasn't worth it, but she didn't want to admit that to her.

Priya drew in close to Rachel, her lips nearly touching Rachel's ear.

"I'm sorry," Priya said. "But there are always consequences."

With the speed of a cobra, Priya grabbed Rachel's left hand and snapped her pinky finger like she was breaking a pencil. The crackle of the bone breaking was as bad if not worse than the stab of pain she felt. Her eyes watered and a grunt escaped her lips, but she refused to scream.

Priya let her go, and Rachel cradled her injured her hand against her chest. Steam curled from her overheated skin, even in the chilly rain. They stared at each other, the world around them falling away from her periphery until there was nothing but Priya. Her eyes were stone dead, the visage of a woman who had plucked the wings from a housefly, who had used a magnifying glass to scorch a trail of ants. Rachel vowed she would find the answer Priya was looking for, she most certainly would, and then she would kill her.

"Bring me some medical tape," she said.

No one moved.

"I said bring me some goddamned medical tape!"

This galvanized her troops and suddenly there were half a dozen people looking for medical tape, digging through packs and first-aid kits until someone brought her a roll of it from their medical kit. Priya tore off two long sections and affixed them to her sleeve.

"Give me your hand," she said.

Rachel extended her hand to the woman; her finger trembled from the trauma Priya had inflicted upon it. Priya gently straightened the finger and splinted it against Rachel's ring finger, binding them together with the lengths of tape.

"Are we done with the silliness now?"

Rachel nodded.

"Don't you see?" Priya asked. "We need each other. You never would have made it without me. I can't save us without you. Without Will. The fate of the human race may depend on our alliance. I'm not saying you have to like me. But understand that your success depends on mine.

"Are you ready to see this to the end now?"

Rachel's finger throbbed.

"Yes."

THEY HIT the Denver city limits shortly before noon, the skyline coming into view as they rounded a curve along Interstate 56. As they rounded a curve, Rachel could make out the shadowy outline of the Rockies in the distance, veiled by the mist and the low-hanging clouds. She'd been to Denver only once before, when she was in ninth grade and she and her mother and Jerry had flown here for a cousin's wedding. A boy had tried to kiss her at that wedding, and she had turned her cheek at the last moment, giving him nothing but a mouthful of her hair. She tried recalling his name but she could not.

It was the biggest city Rachel had seen in years; she had forgotten how massive the buildings were. From a distance, Denver looked none worse for the wear, about what you'd expect on a quiet day in the big city. Dead traffic still choked the eastbound lanes headed out of the city, but nature was doing its best to win back the territory. Hearty weeds had overwhelmed the rusted and deteriorating hulks of metal, as though the cars had invaded a nature preserve and not the other way around.

There were a few stalled vehicles in the westbound lanes toward the city, but clearly, running for the hills had been man's final play as Medusa had pulled civilization down to its knees. Near an exit ramp, the blackened remains of an Abrams tank bisected the column of traffic, perhaps positioned to stop the exodus from the city. Rachel couldn't figure out why the tank was there, but relatively little from those last days made any sense. The caravan decelerated as they approached a thicket of stalled cars ahead of them. Priya, currently riding shotgun, turned toward Rachel.

"Well, my dear," she said. "We are at your mercy now. Time to deliver on your promise."

"We need to find out more about Penumbra."

"Well then, we need to find ourselves a good old-fashioned phonebook, don't we?"

It seemed silly, so ridiculous that Rachel began to laugh. Their fate might rest in a decade-old copy of the goddamn Yellow Pages.

"I say something funny?"

"Nope," Rachel said. "You're right. Let's find a phone book."

They descended the next exit ramp, which put them on a once-busy thoroughfare in the eastern outskirts of the city. There was a small subdivision north of the artery, connected by a narrow two-lane road. A crumbling sign announced they were entering Wellesley, *a Pippert Neighborhood*!

The caravan rumbled through the ritzy neighborhood, home to dozens of sprawling McMansions, once-pure green lawns and, in December, dazzling Christmas light arrays, but white lights, Rachel bet, because white lights seemed classier somehow. They pulled into the first driveway, a stone-paved semicircle, and curled around toward the front entrance.

"Let's go."

Rachel alighted from the car, with Priya and two of her guys right behind her. There was no thought of escape, not anymore. That had been dumb, a decision built on fantasy, on white-hat thinking, on a belief that because she was in the right, she would find salvation.

The foursome scaled the brick steps and someone kicked in the door. It flew open easily, the door and the jamb both weakened by years of water damage. The tang of mildew and mustiness tickled Rachel's nose as they breached the threshold.

"Check the kitchen," Priya said to Kovalewich as they inspected the foyer.

The house was still tidy. Somewhere, a steady drip. There was a small sideboard standing against the wall, a stack of phone books perched on top. Rachel flipped open the slimmest of the three volumes and paged her way over to the *P's*. She spent a few moments scanning the tiny print before she found it. There it was. Penumbra Laboratories. 720 18th Street Northwest.

"Here it is," she said.

"Good. Let's roll."

The kitchen scout returned empty-handed.

"Nothing. Place was cleaned out."

"You mind if I check something?" Rachel asked.

"Be my guest."

Rachel stepped gingerly down the corridor toward the galley kitchen. It was magnificent, equipped with top-of-the-line appliances, Viking all the way. But there was something specific she wanted to see. She crept toward the sink, simultaneously hoping to see and not see what she was looking for.

It was there.

A pot. A handful of utensils, two spoons, two forks. A butter knife.

One of the last moments of normalcy from the world that was now behind them, frozen in time here. When this person had set these down in the sink, was the trouble already brewing, already at their doorstep? Did she have an ear toward the news, hearing the empty promises that *the outbreak was under control, that the death tolls were being wildly exaggerated, that no, ma'am, there is no plan to quarantine the city of Denver because there is no need for a quarantine in the city of Denver.*

She didn't know why she did this to herself. There was nothing she could do about it, and yet sometimes she found herself longing for the past, for those last few idyllic moments before it had all changed. The tacos at the beach. And what made it worse was that Will had never experienced the good things in the world she'd come from. He'd never had the tacos or gone to a Padres game or flown on an airplane or been to the movies, sat in the dark, his fingers slick with popcorn butter. He'd never been to a sleepover, never had a best friend. He'd never woken up on Christmas morning, run downstairs in footie pajamas to see what was waiting for him under the tree. No baseball games, sitting in the stands, feet dangling over the edge of the seat, the ground caked with empty peanut shells and sticky with old soda.

"Something on your mind?"

She turned and saw Priya standing at the long granite counter that did a marvelous job finishing off the kitchen.

"No. We have what we need."

They were underway a minute later. Back out of the driveway. Back out of the subdivision, along the windy road running by a manmade lake, a playground with equipment so high-tech it still looked brand new. Complete with that extra-safe, extra springy fake mulch that absorbed the impact of little bodies better than the real thing.

The neighborhoods were the worst. Where the children had played outside and the summer air was redolent with the aroma of grilling meat and the throaty growl of lawnmower engines and the electronic chimes of the ice cream truck on warm afternoons. A chapter closed forever, before Will had ever had a chance to do those things.

THEY PICKED up a map of the city at a gas station about a mile west of the neighborhood. It was brittle and yellowed and, despite her care, the sections came apart in her hand when she tried to unfold it in the cargo area of her Suburban. Carefully, she pieced them back together and studied the best route to Penumbra, using the map index to locate the streets on the grid.

"We're here," she said, tapping their location on the map with her index finger.

"And the lab?"

"Here." She traced a finger diagonally to the upper-left corner of the map, the northwest part of the city, and double-tapped their destination.

"Good," Priya said, a softness in her tone Rachel hadn't detected before. It was almost hopeful.

"How are we on fuel?" Rachel asked.

"We're fine."

She patted Rachel on the shoulder and gave it a squeeze. She found the friendly touch revolting. This woman was a killer. This woman had her own agenda. The fact their interests were currently aligned meant nothing. Just because she wanted the same thing as Rachel did not make them the same. She would still be a mass murderer, someone who had crossed a line you could not uncross. The enemy of your enemy was not necessarily your friend. At some point, their paths would diverge, and after that, all bets would be off.

"I'm going to make it count," she said. "Am I going to have your help? I don't have any idea what I'm going to find out there. You know everything I know."

"You'll have my help."

"Do you know much about Denver?"

Priya pointed to the northeast part of the city.

"The airport is here," she said. "I've heard that's dangerous."

"Anything else?"

"Some areas in the west and south can be dicey."

"So we steer clear of those areas."

She pointed back down at the map and traced a route from their current location to the northwest corner of the city.

"This is how we'll do it."

Priya nodded.

It felt good to take charge. If they were going to do this, then might as well do it her way. No regrets. If it all went to hell, at least she wouldn't have to sit back and wonder if her way would have been better.

"Are your people going to be ready?" Rachel asked. "I need to know Will is going to be safe. Anything happens to him, and we're done."

"My people are very skilled."

"They better be," Rachel said, sighing.

Priya drove, Rachel riding shotgun. Priya had agreed to let Will ride in their vehicle. They ran west along East 38th Street, a major collector road carrying them deeper and deeper into the city. The first ten minutes took them through older neighborhoods. The streets were quiet, but there were obvious signs of life around here. Smoldering fires burning in old oil drums. The lingering smell of food being cooked. The sense of being watched.

"Does anyone else know about Will?" Rachel asked.

Priya and the driver exchanged a glance.

"I need to know," Rachel said.

"Maybe," Priya replied.

"Here in Denver?"

"Possibly."

They turned north at Quebec Street, more industrial. Past a metalworks building, a cardboard recycling facility and a nondescript warehouse. The buildings were a bit taller and bigger here, a sense of claustrophobia slipping around her like a blanket. As Priya drove,

Rachel's eyes were locked on the rooftops, looking for any movement, anything out of the ordinary. They rolled on. She checked her map; the lab was still a good six miles away.

When the attack came, it came fast.

A whistling sound filled the air.

Then the Suburban behind them exploded.

31

Priya turned the wheel hard, sending them skittering out of control. The truck bounced up and over the median before landing hard in the southbound lanes. She spun the wheel in the opposite direction, tipping the heavy vehicle up on two tires. Rachel's heart froze as she waited for the centrifugal forces to finish the job, to flip them over and leave them wounded prey for their unseen attackers.

But the SUV bounced back down on all fours, giving Priya a chance to retain control. Rachel turned awkwardly in her seat, wrenching her back to check on Will. He looked fine, still upright and buckled in; he too had turned his body, his eye on the conflagration behind them. The second vehicle in the caravan had forked off the roadway and up into a building, where it was burning like holy hell, engulfed in flames. The third and fourth vehicles had stopped, seemingly unsure of their next move. The street was nondescript, nothing remarkable about it. A handful of broken-down vehicles lined the north side of the street. At the end of the block, a large Dumpster, brown with rust, big holes eaten away in it.

Kovalewich was the first in their vehicle to act. He shot out the rear window and sprayed the street with a hail of bullets. They didn't hit anyone, but the very act of reacting made Rachel feel better. Priya mashed her foot against the gas, throwing everyone back in their seats as she accelerated them out of the killing zone.

A flicker of light in the corner of Rachel's eye, this one from the right. Another bloom of fire as the trail vehicle, the one carrying their fuel reserves, ate a shoulder-launched missile and exploded, illuminating the gloomy street in an orange-red glow. This was all the invitation the third vehicle needed; it punched forward from its dormancy, so quickly it nearly rear-ended Rachel's rig. A rifle muzzle emerged from its passenger-side window, firing haphazardly.

Ahead of them, a large brown box truck had burst through from the cross street, blocking the road. It was an old UPS truck, the famous logo badly faded on its rusted exterior. A quartet of shooters poured out from the cargo area, armed with heavy weaponry. They immediately began firing, the guns' massive bullets pinging hard against the Suburban's front grill.

"We've got company," Priya hissed as she turned the wheel hard again, fishtailing to a stop in the middle of the street.

"Got'em."

He flung open the rear passenger door and took cover behind it, readying a shoulder-mounted rocket-propelled grenade launcher. He fired once, the projectile screaming through the air before it pierced the cargo truck's engine block. It exploded in a fireball, the rapidly expanding bloom of fire engulfing three of the shooters. The surviving shooter ran for cover at the curb, taking refuge behind a burned-out sedan.

Priya hitched forward, and the surviving vehicles continued down the block. Rachel held her breath, waiting for the shockwave of fire and heat that would mean the end for them, for her, for Will. Every second stretched like putty into an eternity. A third launch flew wide, striking the road behind them and splintering the roadway into a shower of hot chunks of asphalt. Bits of broken roadway pinged the vehicle.

More gunfire, but she couldn't tell from where.

Rachel's head turned from side to side as she looked for their attackers. Were they ahead of them? Behind them?

"Hang on," Priya said.

She made a hard left, the Suburban's back end fishtailing wide before she spun the wheel the other way to tame the beast. Rachel watched the other vehicle follow suit, still unscathed. Thirty seconds went by without another attack, then another thirty seconds. They were running east now, in an undeveloped area of east Denver.

"How much farther?" Priya asked.

Her hands trembling, Rachel stretched out the map across her lap and tried to focus, but she was having a hard time wrangling her wits to the ground. The map was a swirl of unformed shapes and colors that made no sense. How had she read this not even an hour ago?

"Give me a second."

"Now, Rachel, I need to know now."

"Give me a goddamn second!"

She inhaled a deep breath and let it out slowly.

Time slowed around her. The sound of the tires thrumming over the road. The heavy breathing of the other occupants of the car. The engine revving. These calmed her. The map began to make sense. She pressed her thumb against the key to measure the distance then made a rough guess of the remaining distance to Penumbra.

"Three miles. Give or take. We're going to run west to Martin Luther King Boulevard and then head north. The lab is in an industrial corridor."

"Everyone keep your eyes open," Priya said

They rode in silence for a bit, Rachel trying to process what had happened. Once again, circumstances had dictated strange bedfellows. She tried to feel bad about the people who had died in the other vehicles, but she couldn't. They were coldblooded killers. She didn't care that they were dead.

A burst of static from the CB radio. Priya keyed the mic.

"Yes?"

"Everyone OK?" came a shell-shocked voice.

"All OK. You?"

"Michele took a bit of shrapnel in the arm. Bleeding, but should be OK. Should we go back for the others?"

"Wish we could. Too dangerous."

A bit of static before the CB clicked off.

"Roger that."

Regular people checking on each other. Regular people, like herself and her dad and Harry, trying to do the best they could, play the cards they were dealt. No one was innocent. They all had blood on their hands.

"You know who they are?"

Priya didn't reply.

"Who were they?"

"Religious group," she said. "They believe in Will's divinity."

"Jesus H. Christ."

"Kind of."

"You knew, and you took us right through there."

"I wanted to flush them out," Priya said. "They're known to be a bit rash."

Rachel wanted to strangle the woman, but she counted to ten, keeping her eyes on the prize. This was not the hill to die on. If they could figure out why Will had survived, what it would take for the babies to live, then maybe they could figure out their other problems. Maybe a big old injection of hope would fire up humanity's engine, make the problems they had seem a little more manageable. Make no mistake, the problems were not insignificant. But they were not impossible. They could solve the food problem. Hell, hadn't Priya had her hands on those seeds? Life would find a way, as long as they kept fighting. Then they could all let go of the past together, absolved of their sins, baptized in the blood of new life.

The sound of new life. Perhaps someday, the sound of children again.

She glanced back at Will, who sat with his arms crossed. A quick thumbs up. He returned the gesture. It would have to do for now.

Sure, one could argue they were better off without children, because what were they going to feed them anyway? But maybe they hadn't come up with a solution to the food shortage because they weren't properly motivated. If you had nothing to live for, then what was the point of trying to keep living? In some very real way, they had all given up. Maybe if the babies lived, they would think of things they hadn't yet. Their minds would be open to new ideas, to new connections, new approaches they hadn't yet considered.

The idea that the answers to all their questions might be tucked away in her own body, in the body of her little boy was a bit hard to deal with. Even now, with the evidence laid out before her, she didn't want to believe something about her, about her family, had cast a long and terrible shadow over the world.

What if it didn't work?

So what if it didn't work? The trying was the important thing. Not sitting around and waiting to die. That's all they were doing really. Killing each other while waiting to die. Hell had come to earth.

She was going to find the truth if it killed her.

THEY RAN UNMOLESTED for another half hour, Rachel navigating, Priya following the route but frequently doubling back to ensure they weren't being followed. They stayed out in the open, away from tall buildings, away from spaces that closed up around them. Rachel pressed her hand to the window; it was cold, the coldest it had been yet this season. It was early spring, probably April, best as Rachel could guess. Much of the winter snow had melted, but there was still plenty lying about. They didn't use the heat in the truck, as it was too much of a drag on their fuel efficiency, which was bad enough as it was.

Eventually, they made it to 18th Street, a long and winding road cutting through alternating tracts of commercial development and undeveloped real estate that would bear nothing but unrealized potential.

"This is it," Rachel said. "Up on the left."

There was a sign at the corner of the intersection reading

PenLabs. Underneath that, the following inscription: *A Proud Subsidiary of the Penumbra Corporation!* A thin range of trees flanked either side of the access road. Priya pulled to the side of the main road without turning; the second vehicle lay in behind them.

"Got any binoculars?" she asked.

Priya snapped her fingers and someone handed her a pair of field glasses. She held them to her face. A large brick structure lay about a half-mile distant. The sizable parking lot in front of it was empty.

"What's your plan?" Priya asked.

"Well, I was thinking of going up and knocking on the door."

"Are you kidding me?"

"Look," she said, "I'm not a spy or a soldier. I don't know anything about cloak-and-dagger shit. The one thing I have going for me is this tattoo. That will buy me some tokens."

Priya's eyes narrowed as she considered this.

"They might kill you."

"They might. Do you have a better idea?"

Priya shrugged.

"It's your funeral if you're wrong."

"There's only one way to find out," she said. "Will, let's go."

"Oh, I don't think so. He stays with me."

"Like hell he does," Rachel said, bristling with anger, her hackles up. "Will, out of the car."

Priya nodded to Kovalewich, who took Will by the arm.

"You let him go."

"Rachel, let's dispense with this nonsense. Will stays here. End of story. You know he's my insurance policy. You insult my intelligence when you act in a way contrary to that. It will just anger me, and that is not something you can afford right now."

"Fine," Rachel said, a hint of defeat in her voice. "Can I have a few minutes with him?"

"Take all the time you need."

Priya and the others got out of the car and left Rachel alone with her son.

"You really have to do this?" he asked.

"I do, buddy. It's important."

"Can I come?"

"No, you need to stay here."

"But I can be brave."

"You have been so brave. You're the bravest kid I've ever known. You saved Mommy's life."

One devious benefit of raising Will in a world without other kids was that he'd never learned to shorten her honorific to Mom. She could be Mommy for as long as she wanted to be. And he had been brave. No kid should have to go through what he'd been through.

"When will you be back?"

Her stomach flipped.

"Buddy, I don't know. As soon as I can."

He let out a sharp breath, squared off his shoulders.

"OK," he said, and in a flash, she saw his future in his face. It passed in the flicker of a second, like a bolt of lightning, but for just a second, the little boy that he still was fell away, like a skin being shed, leaving behind a man hardened by the world in which he'd grown up, but maybe properly equipped to handle it. She could only hope she had done enough because she had no idea if she would ever see him again.

She leaned in to hug him, but he drew back from her a hair, as if he was preparing himself for a life without her. The gap between them was only a few inches, but it felt interstellar. A spike of sadness ripped through her. A boy rejecting a hug from his own mother. She stood up and tousled his hair. It felt cheap and phony, but it was all she would get from him today.

And then it hit her.

He was saying goodbye.

Priya was waiting for her at the front bumper when she was done.

"I remember how difficult that age could be," Priya said, her voice empty and far away.

Knives of guilt ran deep into Rachel's soul. There was nothing she could say. She had her son, and Priya's lay dead somewhere, probably in some hospital morgue, a pile of bones. Bones of the children, bones of the world.

"I'm going to go on then," Rachel said. "How long will you wait?"

"Three days. You need to be back by then or we go."

Rachel's heart fluttered. Three days to finish this or she would never see Will again. She went to the back and strapped on the heavy backpack, already loaded with supplies. Priya had agreed to give her a gun, but it was unloaded, a small supply of ammunition in a separate compartment, lest she try something foolish.

"Remember that your ammo is limited. You need to make it count."

She nodded.

"If this goes south on me..." Rachel started to say, before her voice caught in her throat.

"He will be fine."

Rachel nodded.

"See you soon," Priya said.

32

Rachel crossed 18th Street, even pausing to look both ways, and headed up the access road. She hugged the tree line, not hidden necessarily but not anxious to advertise her presence.

The walk was quiet, peaceful. It was a chilly afternoon but the sky was reasonably clear. The air was redolent with pine. Her journey reminded her of another incursion, one made by her father many years earlier. Once upon a time, he had done a great thing. It had started like this for him, she supposed, alone and terrified. Certain that death was close by, that those he cared for would be lost forever.

And he had made it.

She had to finish what he had started, even if he would never know how deep the rabbit hole went. She would solve the mystery he never could, unlock the secret that had kept all of them alive when so many had died.

After a quarter mile, the trees thinned out, and she came up to a security booth and gate, which was fixed in the upward position. She withdrew her pistol and made sure it was loaded. The parking lot was wide and open, pockmarked with potholes. Thick weeds and hard-scrabble bushes grew from the fissures in the asphalt.

First, she checked the booth, which was empty. There was an old binder sitting on the built-in desk; the faded lettering read *Visitors' Log* decorating the cover. The pages inside had long since fused together into a thick brittle clump. A check for any forgotten supplies came up empty.

The window in the booth gave her a clear line of sight to the front of the building. There was no movement, no sign of life, and her heart sank. The compound appeared as desolate as everything else in the world.

What if this were it? What if there were no answers to be found?

Pushing those thoughts away, she emerged from the booth and crept across the parking lot. The gun was up, her finger on the trigger, her head rotating from side to side, ahead and behind her. Nothing.

Another minute brought her to the front of the building. The doors were intact, tinted, revealing nothing of the building's interior. Her heart pounding, she tugged on the door pull and was relieved to find it unlocked.

She opened it and stepped inside.

To her great surprise, the lights inside were on. Her ears picked up the faint buzz of power coursing through the building. Electricity. Her first taste of it in thirteen years. She stared at the lights, blinking at their brightness, forgetting how harsh and invasive artificial lighting could be. Still, for a moment, this modern-day comfort they'd taken for granted whisked her back through time and she could still feel, deep inside her soul, a different version of herself, one who had never seen the plague come to pass.

Hell, maybe they could just live here!

She was standing in a square-shaped foyer, unremarkable, minimalist in design. No reception desk, no waiting area. There were doors to her left and to her right. Alphanumeric keypads mounted on the wall next to each door, both with indicator lights shining red. The hacker in her awoke, a long-mothballed version of herself that had once wreaked havoc on any computer network that drew her attention.

The problem with password protection was that it had only been as strong as the person's willingness to create a strong password. And when you got right down to it, most people had been fundamentally lazy about passwords. Many years earlier, Rachel had read a research paper positing that three different codes could open ninety-five percent of four-digit password-controlled systems.

She tried the first.

0000

A beep, followed by a click. The light shined red.

Her breath caught.

1234

A beep, followed by a click. The light shined red.

Her heart skipped a beat.

One last guess. It was commonly used in laboratories, as accidents were common and often called for a fire/EMS response. She took a deep breath and let it out slowly. If this didn't work, the odds of successfully hacking the door would plummet.

0911

A beep, the *thunk* of the lock disengaging. The light shined green.

A laugh sprang free from her throat.

Achievement unlocked, stealing a phrase from the video game lexicon once popular with her generation.

After wiping her hands dry, she readied her gun and slipped through the door. Bright fluorescent bulbs shining down from the ceiling left her feeling naked, exposed. The corridor immediately doglegged right, opening up on a long hallway. On either side of the hall were several small laboratories. As she edged down the hallway, a splash of *déjà vu* washed over her, her memories from the Citadel as strong as they had been in years. The massacre of the captured women during the Citadel's unraveling. Seeing her father. Shooting Miles Chadwick in the stomach as they had struggled to escape. Her skin crawled.

A much larger laboratory sat at the end of the hallway.

A sign reading CLEAN ROOM was posted above the double doors

There was something different about these labs than the ones at the Citadel.

No biosafety cases.

Not as clinical.

Something industrial.

She pushed on a door, but it refused to budge. Then she wedged her fingers in between them and leaned her weight into separating them. Slowly, the doors began to slide on their tracks, squealing in protest. It had been a while since these doors had been opened. Her arms began to burn but finally, there was a gap wide enough for her to slip through. Before entering, she waited a good two minutes to make sure the doors wouldn't automatically slide shut behind her. She didn't want to be inside the lab and find out the doors were shatterproof.

When she was satisfied she'd be able to get back out, she stepped inside. She gave the lab a quick once-over. There were six computer workstations, three on each side of the room. A bookcase stuffed full of thick three-ring binders on the back wall. Above the bookcase was a large LED screen. In the center of the room, a seventh computer, this one a desktop, sat on a rectangular table.

Her head swam with confusion.

What was she looking for?

She didn't know.

She ambled over to the desktop and pressed the spacebar. A fan whirred and the screen blinked to life to reveal a login screen. Two fields, calling for a user name and password. She passed on trying to hack that for the time being. She turned her attention to the binders on the bookcase. After checking back down the hallway to make sure she was still alone, she grabbed a binder and set it down on the desk.

The words stamped on the cover of the binder chilled her to the bone.

Pb-815: Human Trials

AIRBORNE AEROSOL EXPOSURE
ITERATION EIGHT
FAILURE

The date November 11, not quite four years before the outbreak, was stamped underneath. She'd seen the PB-815 moniker before, many years ago, when she was at the Citadel. It was the official name Chadwick's group had assigned to the Medusa virus.

Her heart pounding, she flipped open the binder to the first page.

She found it difficult to focus, her brain processing only bits and pieces of the terrible crime memorialized in these pages.

Twenty-three-year-old Caucasian female

Sioux Falls, South Dakota

Exposure ... 3.6 seconds ... Subject Zero

Symptomatic ... Bleeding from Ocular Cavity ... 18.3 hours

Remained conscious

Seizures

Time of death: 0715

Infectious Waste Protocol

She flipped the page.

Forty-six-year-old Latino male

Subject terminated.

And again.

Fifty-eight-year-old African-American female

And then one more.

Six-year-old Asian male

...

Subject 17

...

Recovered from infection

...

Subject terminated

She slammed the binder closed, her breath coming in big, sloppy, ragged gasps. Hell inside these pages. Pure hell. Her head hurt. Her legs buckled, and she sank to the ground in a heap, bawling. She could not wrap her head around the evil at work here. A peek behind the curtain of the preparations that went into all this. She flipped the binder back open to the last entry she had read and traced down the page to the line that had caught her attention.

Recovered from infection. Subject terminated.

Recovered from infection. Subject terminated.

A little boy had survived infection with an older version of the virus, *and they had killed him anyway.* Her stomach heaved, and she vomited on the floor. Her whole body hitched, and it took all her strength to stay up on and her hands and knees.

She rolled back into a sitting position, crossing her legs and holding her head in her hands. Being at the Citadel, that had been bad enough, and she thought it would have prepared her for all this. But it was worse, much worse, seeing this place, seeing the binder, seeing the description of this little boy, nothing more than a science experiment to these people, disposed of like a broken piece of lab equipment. A shattered beaker.

But she had to keep pressing. She still hadn't learned anything she didn't know. This binder, horrific as it was, simply added detail work to a nightmarish landscape, one with which she was already intimately familiar. There was another picture she needed to see in full, one of which she had only seen the barest outline. Still no clue how she was connected to this.

After wiping her mouth with the back of her hand, she struggled back to her feet, using the edge of the desk to support her shaky legs. A few cleansing breaths, her sea legs returning, blood again warming her clammy face. She turned her attention to the computer screen in front of her, dark again after having returned to sleep. The screen blinked back to life after a quick touch of the mouse.

Two fields awaited her.

User Name

Password

The first step was to search the workstation for sticky notes, index cards, old notebooks, anywhere this computer's primary users may have scribbled down his log-in information. No matter how many times system admins told people to never do that, without fail, they did. Not that she could blame them.

Your password requires a capital letter, a lower-case letter, an Arabic numeral, a bottle of unicorn tears, the menstrual blood of a virgin, and your favorite lasagna recipe.

She checked every square inch of the lab, even flipping through every page of the binders on the shelf. But she came up empty.

She sighed, reaching back into mothballed files for her hacking skills, long since packed away. Some folks had a gift for it, an intuition about how to break into closed computer systems, but it had never been like that for Rachel. There had been few systems she was unable to hack, but it always took her a long time and a brute force approach. And now, more than a decade later, she would try to call on those cobwebbed skills again.

Well, no time like the present.

The longest journey and all that.

She started with most likely suspects, *Admin* for the user name and *1234* for the password. Holding her breath, she tapped the Return key.

A new window splashed onto the screen.

The user name and/or password is incorrect

(1) Failed Attempt

Nope, it wasn't going to be that easy this time around.

She focused on the second line of the message. Most systems allowed as many as three attempts before locking out a user, but she suspected this one wouldn't be so forgiving. If she blew it this time, she might create all sorts of problems for herself.

Her focus shifted to this hack, the world falling away from her as she debated the best approach. It had been a closed system, no link to the outside world. The only thing she had going for her was that she was standing at the terminal itself. Hacking this place from the outside would have been a monumental challenge.

Think, Rachel, think.

But no solution would reveal itself. It had been too long, the finer skills required for this kind of hack long since atrophied. She was useless. All her accomplishments, all her education, now worthless in a world like the one she'd spent the last decade in. And when she needed it most, the arrow was no longer in the quiver.

A sound startled her.

Her face was still tilted downward toward the screen; she glanced up over the top of the monitor, giving her a clear look at six armed men coming down the hallway. It was hard to tell if they had seen her through the glass doors, if they could see her standing at the monitor. If she fired now, she might be able to cut them down before they knew what had happened. She sighted one of her visitors, hesitated. If she fired, she'd take one out, maybe two if she were lucky. They would cut her into ribbons and Will would be alone. She needed to be smarter than that. Long range thinking now. Two and three steps ahead. If they had wanted her dead, she would be dead.

Slowly, she raised her hands and stepped around the monitor. Six of them in all she saw now, in two columns of three. Very heavily armed. Flak jackets, bulky. Probably bulletproof vests protecting them from any bad decisions she might choose to make.

When they saw her, the group stopped its advance, the muzzles of their rifles zeroed in on her. She didn't know if the glass was bulletproof, but she wasn't particularly keen on finding out. One stepped clear of the others and motioned for her to step out of the lab. Keeping her hands up, she complied with his request and joined the group in the corridor.

"Search her."

A second gunman patted her down, not bothering to spare her dignity. His hands were rough and hard up and down her legs, across her abdomen, her breasts, around her back, even in her buttocks. There wasn't anything lurid about it, that was what struck her. This was a man doing his job thoroughly.

"She's clean."

The leader activated a walkie-talkie hanging from his hip.

"Base, Markham," he said.

"Go ahead."

"Target has been acquired. Adult Caucasian female. Found her in the nanotech lab."

Nanotech?

"Kill her."

The one who had searched her clipped the back of her legs with his gun and Rachel buckled to the ground.

"Roger that. Markham out."

"No, wait!"

The open line of the walkie-talkie hissed.

"Will await confirmation of subject's termination."

The hissing clicked off.

The gunman hooked the communicator back to his belt.

"We'll do this outside," the leader said. "Less mess to clean up."

They took each of her arms and began escorting her back up the corridor whence she had come. Rachel's heart was a frightened horse that had gotten spooked. Her legs were jelly, her brain frozen. She could not form a single thought in her head.

Think, think, think.

Her feet began to drag behind her, slowing their progress. The bright lights buzzing down from above gave her a headache.

A way out, there had to be a way out.

But she said nothing. She would not beg for her life.

They went back through the access door she'd been so proud of bypassing less than an hour ago, back into the entry foyer, and then outside. It was drizzling again, the rain her clothing, the water seeping through the fabric, chilling her. A pair of pickup trucks idled in front of the building.

"Down on your knees."

"No."

The gunman struck her in the face with the butt of his weapon, staggering her. Her cheek had split open and blood trickled along the jawbone to her mouth.

Will's face, bright and hopeful and naïve, filled her field of vision.

Will.

Will.

Will.

"Get your boss back on the line."

"Get her up on her knees."

Rough hands grabbed at her arms and torso, pulling her up on her knees.

"Listen to me."

"I don't have to listen to anyone except the man on the other end of this line," he said, tapping the walkie-talkie's plastic housing,

"Yeah?"

"That's right."

"Well, you get him on the line and tell him my name is Rachel Fisher."

"What?"

"Just do it."

He looked at her with a puzzled look on her face, the way a dog might look at you when you sing to it. It had been a weird thing for her to say, and that by itself made it stand out. It was the green M&M in a universe of brown ones. The others stood idly by, shifting their weight from one to another, engaging in nervous tics, adjusting vests, shifting strap placement.

If it didn't work, she'd have to show them the tattoo, but then they would know she was at the Citadel, and that was a card she wanted to keep close to the vest for now. "It can't hurt to call it in, right?" she asked.

Silence.

"If you kill me, and you're wrong, there's going to be hell to pay."

Silence.

The man nervously clicked his tongue against his teeth. The sound writ large in the stillness of the Colorado afternoon. She could see him working it out in his head. He didn't want to call the boss back and incur his wrath if it turned out she was lying; she could only hope he wanted to find out she'd been telling the truth after he killed her even less.

His hand dropped to his hip, inches away from the walkie-talkie.

It hung there for what seemed like an eternity.

"God help you if you're wrong."

He unhooked it and pushed the Talk button.

"Base, Markham."

They waited in the shadow of the open line's hiss.

"Is she dead?"

"Negative."

"Why the hell not?"

"Sir, this woman says her name is Rachel Fisher. Does that mean anything to you?"

The line hung open.

Then a mutter, barely audible, but enough for her to make it out.

"My God."

A crackle of static.

"Bring her back."

Relief flooded through her veins and she let out a shaky breath.

They boarded the vehicles, Rachel sitting shotgun in the lead truck. Before she'd had a chance to process what was happening, they were off. They followed the same access road back out to the highway, where Priya had dropped her off. She looked anxiously for them as they turned north, but they were gone.

33

They drove west-northwest for an hour, up into the foothills of the Rockies. The sun had begun to set, its weak rays gilding the snow-capped mountaintops like dull gold paint. Rachel sat enveloped in darkness, wearing a ski mask over her head, the eyeholes stitched closed.

As they climbed the switchbacks, carving their way up the mountain, she became uncomfortably aware of the growing distance between herself and Will. This was the farthest she had ever been away from him, and the chance of a successful reunion grew more remote as the gap between them widened. Priya's three-day clock loomed large over her head. As the moon rose, they turned onto an old logging road, narrow and rutted. Their headlights carved twin cylinders through the darkness.

She thought they would pepper her with questions, but no one said a word.

"How did you find me so quickly?" she asked.

No one replied.

She gave up and leaned back against the headrest. She dozed. Her eyes were heavy and she felt sleep pulling her down into its embrace. Sleep would be good now. She needed to rest when she could. The vehicle's big shock absorbers kept the jarring to a minimum, the bouncing soft and lulling her into dreamland.

She slept.

Thirty minutes later, the vehicle lumbered to a stop.

"We're here," said the leader, shaking her by the shoulder and peeling off her mask.

Rachel yawned. Her neck was kinked from an awkward sleeping position, but her head was clear, her body relaxed.

The driver spoke into an intercom mounted on a brick pillar attached to an iron gate. A moment later, the gate whirred open, and they drove through. The well-maintained road curled around a copse of pine and sequoia before straightening out. A huge structure loomed ahead, the glow of electric lights burning in the distance. The road broke to the north, climbing a bit more into the mountain before tapering to a narrow sliver of asphalt. They passed the edge of a huge building that reminded her of a ski chalet.

The caravan came to a stop at the main entrance of the complex. Someone opened her door for her and she climbed out, careful to maintain her balance, a tricky prospect with her hands bound together. She stretched her back and took in the scene. The gigantic chalet stood before her, all gray stone and sloped roofs. Lights burned in the windows, and the chilly air was redolent with good cooking smells. Garlic, maybe, or onion, she couldn't quite pinpoint it. Around her, patches of snow shimmered in the yellow light of the moon. An ornate fountain adorned the large entrance plaza.

"Where are we?" she asked.

"Welcome to Olympus."

She rolled her eyes so hard she was thankful it was dark; if they had seen her do it, they probably would have shot her. Olympus. Of course it had to have some fancy nickname, maybe something that made it easier for these psychopaths to swallow what they had done.

They passed underneath a suspended covered walkway connecting two wings of the chalet. The leader used a keycard to access a door on the building's western wing, which brought them inside a large foyer. It was toasty warm inside, the kind of warmth she hadn't felt in many years. It felt so good, so natural, the memories of thousands of dark and cold nights slipping away in the blink of an eye. They made their way toward a stairwell catty-corner from the entrance.

As she mounted the first step, she heard something that froze her in place. A sweet, tinny sound she hadn't heard in a long time. It had come from this floor, a bit farther down the corridor. She was hearing things. She had to be. A weird whistle of the wind, an unseen door squealing closed. Then she heard it again.

There was no question now.

She broke free of her captor's grip and sprinted down the corridor toward the sound.

"Hey!"

Laughter now, it was laughter she was hearing. There was no doubt in her mind.

Footfalls of the men chasing her down. They needn't have worried; she wasn't planning to go anywhere. She had to see.

More laughter and shouting and giggling.

But not just any laughter, not just any giggling.

She found the room that was the source of the commotion. There was a small porthole in the door; she cupped her hands around her face and peered through the glass. It was a large activity room, about thirty-by-thirty square, populated with arcade games and foosball tables and old-school pinball machines.

She got only a few seconds to see what was inside the room before they pulled her away, back to the staircase. She went quietly, her mind a blank notebook. Her whole world had been reset. The last dozen years blown away in the blink of an eye.

The room had been full of children.

34

Even as they pulled her away, the sounds of the children echoing in her ears, she wasn't entirely sure she hadn't hallucinated the entire thing. There were no other children. It was a fairy tale, a myth, maybe like the one people had told about Will. That was the world they lived in, after all, one trafficking in rumor and conjecture and speculation, hope's distant cousins.

"This way," the leader said, leading Rachel down the hallway as the faces of the children loomed large in her mind. She kept glancing over her shoulder, back toward the room, that beautiful, magical, unbelievable room. More, she wanted more time to look at their faces, to hear their voices, to smell them, to hug them and love on them, not for them, but for herself. Her greedy little self.

They climbed four flights of stairs, the ascent leaving her winded in the thinner air of the Rockies. The stairwell opened on a small foyer, all wood paneling and thick carpet. It was warm and cozy and made her sleepy. Her escort knocked on the heavy oak door across from the stairwell. As they waited, she considered the ramifications of what she had seen. Children. Born after the plague. The human race wasn't going extinct after all. The answer lay here.

A moment later, the door swung open; a tall, thin silhouette stood before her. When he stepped into the light, her breath caught in her throat, the memories of the children going dark like someone had pulled a plug in her mind.

She had never seen this man before, not in person, but she knew exactly who he was. Many years ago, at the Citadel, she had seen his portrait hanging on a wall, right before Sarah Wells had blown the place to hell. The same lifeless eyes. The beak nose. The narrow face. The wild springy hair. It was as if the portrait had come to life and this man had stepped out from it. Today he wore the most pedestrian of outfits – a pair of khaki pants and a blue oxford shirt. The ordinariness of his clothing only seemed to amplify his terrifying nature.

Leon Gruber.

He took another step toward her, folding his arms, rubbing his chin, like he was inspecting a piece in an antique store, trying to figure out if it was worth what they were asking for it.

"You wait out here," he said gently. "Ms. Fisher and I have some things to discuss."

Her stomach muscles clenched tightly at the sound of her name.

"You know who I am, don't you?" she asked. Her voice sounded small, felt small, like she was a little girl who'd peed on the carpet.

"Yes, I do," he said, his face bright and terrible and happy.

"How?"

"My dear," the man said. "You look just like him."

"Who?"

"Your grandfather."

RACHEL FOLLOWED Gruber inside his office on a pair of wobbly legs, staggered by his revelation. She crumpled into a wingback chair by a fireplace, not bothering to wait for an invitation. Gruber went to the bar near the window.

"You look like you could use a drink," he said, plinking ice cubes into a pair of glass tumblers. She turned toward him but was unable to formulate a response. Her mouth was dry, her lips stuck together. It was as if she had forgotten how to speak.

"Hearing no objection," he said, continuing his preparations of the cocktails.

As he fixed their drinks, she took in the room around her. It was a study, wood-paneled like everything else she'd seen so far. Sporting a lot of wood here, the joke broke free out of subconscious, and she giggled, clapping a hand over her mouth because laughing didn't seem to fit here, not now, not tonight, maybe not ever again. Everything around her felt different. Like the world had been wearing a mask all along and it had now been ripped off. And underneath, it was the same but not the same.

"Something funny?"

"I don't know," she said, and that was the literal truth.

He joined her by the fireplace, handing her the drink before taking his seat next to her. They sat quietly, watching the fire crackle and ripple. It felt good. As Rachel sat there, stealing glances at this man who had ruined so much, who had found the loose thread in the fabric of humanity and pulled it until it had unraveled, until it had all come undone.

"My name is Leon Gruber," he said. "I'm the director of this facility."

She took a sip of her drink; it burned going down, but not in an unpleasant way. It had been years since she'd had a drink and immediately it made her head swim. From the corner of her eye, she could see him staring at her. There seemed to be a real sense of surprise there.

"My goodness," he said. His voice was high-pitched, a bit flinty. It was devoid of any accent she could identify. "You look just like Jack."

Her skin crawled at the familiarity of it all. Old buds, Gruber and her dear old Gramps. She had no recollection of Jack Fisher; she had never even met him. There weren't many branches on her father's family tree, and after her mother had taken her to San Diego, she'd had very little contact with that side of the family. Jack Fisher had died when she was fifteen, lost at sea when an unexpected squall had overturned his sailboat during a fishing trip.

She had flown back to Virginia for the funeral, the first time she had traveled alone. She'd felt so grownup, walking down the jetway by herself, tucking her bag in the overhead compartment, ordering a lemonade from the flight attendant on her Delta flight from San Diego to Richmond, perhaps flying right over this very mountain as she crisscrossed the country. They had the funeral at an old church in Culpeper, Virginia, a rural stretch of horse country near the foothills of the Shenandoah. They had both been uncomfortable negotiating the small service, the reception following at the home of the minister, held there because there had been no other relatives. She sat in a hard, uncomfortable chair next to the buffet spread, near the cold cuts and cheeses and the stale cookies and the punch, watching as people loaded their plates and not care about her grandfather one whit or whittle.

She was finding it hard to breathe, the rage crashing through her like a flash flood. A strange unpleasant scraping sound filled her ear canal; it was her teeth grinding together.

"I can't believe you're here," Gruber said.

She didn't reply.

The metallic nature of his voice ate away at her, eroding her ability to think rationally. She looked for her own voice, but the words would not come. How did you speak to the Devil himself, to evil in human form? Once she had considered Miles Chadwick to be an evil man, but he had been nothing. He had been a tool, a piece of equipment wielded by this man, by this monster standing before her.

It took every bit of willpower for her not to tackle the man and choke the life out of him and there was no doubt in her mind she would succeed, that she would kill him before they could pull her off him.

But that was reckless thinking, simple fantasy. She had work to do, and a lot of it.

"I wondered if I would ever meet you," he said.

"There are children here," she said, her voice small and cracking. "How?"

"I'll explain everything. But first, I have to know something. How on earth did you find us?"

She had been preparing for this moment since they had captured her, considering her answer carefully. If she told the truth, he would know she had been at the Citadel. Was that a piece of intelligence worth concealing? She sorted through the permutations and decided it was in her best interest to keep that close to the vest for now.

"On my eighteenth birthday," she lied, "I received a call from a lawyer in San Diego. Said he had something for me. I went down there, and they gave me this letter. It was very short."

"What did it say?"

"It said someday I might have very strange questions about my family, and if that day ever came, I was to find Penumbra Labs in Denver."

And now for the kicker.

She laughed softly, more of a snicker than anything.

"I'll be honest with you, Mr. Gruber. I really thought it was a prank. I didn't know who the letter was from. The lawyer said he wasn't authorized to disclose the identity of the person who wrote it."

"Did you tell anyone?"

"I may have shown it to my roommate," she said. "Before I threw it away."

"You never asked your father?"

She shrugged. The rank perspiration of deception slicked her body.

"I didn't think about the letter for years," she said. "Even after the plague. I was living in this community..."

She almost said *Nebraska*, where the Citadel had been, but that would be asking for trouble.

"Anyway, one night, this guy got really drunk and was hassling me and my father – you know he survived too, right?"

She didn't wait for an answer.

"He was killed a few months ago – and this guy says, I'll never forget it – '*what makes your family so goddamned special*?'

"And all of a sudden, I remembered the letter," she said. "It scared me to death, tell you the truth. I couldn't remember all the details in it, but I remembered Penumbra and Denver. After our community fell apart, I figured I had nothing else to lose."

"My goodness," Gruber replied. His eyes were shiny with tears.

"Who wrote the letter?" Rachel asked. "How did they know I might someday have questions about my family being special?"

This was a bit of a risk, but one worth taking. It was only natural she would have questions, particularly now that she was having this discussion validated the contents of this nonexistent letter.

Gruber took a sip of his drink, undoubtedly trying to decide how much of her story was bullshit.

"You had a child after the epidemic, didn't you?"

"I did," she said. "Yes. He was born two years after the plague."

"Where is he now?"

"He died."

A look of puzzlement crossed Gruber's face.

"How, if you don't mind me asking?"

"He, uh, was killed in an accident when he was five."

"I'm very sorry to hear that."

Gruber raised his glass, which shimmered in the light of the fire.

"To your son."

"Thank you."

"Do you know why you're still alive? Why your father survived? Why your son survived?"

She felt like she had been shoved onstage, into the world's saddest story, in front of the countless billions who had perished, in front of all the generations that would never be, the faceless, the nameless, the born and the unborn, who were looking at her and asking why.

Another one of those moments where you knew what the answer was, but you didn't want to admit it.

Occam's razor.

The simplest explanation was usually the correct one.

"We were vaccinated."

"Precisely," he said.

If she were honest with herself, she had suspected this to be the case for years. It was the only thing that made any logical sense. One day many years ago, she had sat down and tried to calculate the probability that three generations of her family had been naturally immune to the virus, based on their best guess as to its mortality rate. If it had just been her and her father who'd been immune, she could have written it off to dumb luck. But Will. Will's immunity changed the game. The odds were so infinitesimally small as to be no better than zero.

But when would she have received a vaccine? She had grown up in San Diego, living her wonderfully geeky life, never even having met her grandfather. She scoured her memory banks for any one-offs, any medical visits or procedures that stuck out for one reason for another. Nothing. Bits and pieces of memory floated through her subconscious, but she could not pull them together into a coherent picture. And now she was confronted with this place, full of little ones who shared Will's stout defense to the Medusa virus. It was their mothers Rachel was most like.

"Before the plague," he continued, "I owned the Penumbra Corporation. To the extent anyone could own a publicly traded company back then, I guess. Ever hear of it?"

"No."

"It was a big company. More than a hundred thousand employees worldwide. One of its subsidiaries was a company called PenLabs," he said. "The name speaks for itself, I would imagine. PenLabs had several defense contracts, including one for the development and production of bioweapons."

"I thought America didn't produce biological weapons. Didn't we sign a treaty?"

"Please don't be naïve," he said. "These were black ops, the blackest of black ops. Technically, they didn't exist."

"Are you saying Penumbra created the Medusa virus? That you did this?"

"No, that's not what I'm saying. Not exactly. We did develop the Medusa virus as a bioweapon, a last-resort weapon, if you will."

"Jesus Christ, why?"

"About ten years before the outbreak, the U.S. military came to us and asked us to build it," he replied. "And we were better equipped than anyone in the world to do it."

"Just because you could do it didn't mean you should have."

"That's where I disagree," he replied. "If we didn't, someone else would. I hired the best virologists and genetic engineers. And the best nanotechnology team ever assembled. Our security protocols were second to none."

"Obviously, seeing how everyone is dead."

"Well," he said, looking away, toward the fire. "That's on me a little bit. This virologist I had, Miles Chadwick, he turned out to be an anarchist. By the time we got wind of what he was doing, it was too late. We were able to vaccinate the folks here. But that was it."

But she played along, watched him ruminate about how it had come to this.

"If you don't mind me saying, you don't seem terribly broken up over it."

"Ms. Fisher, I've had thirteen years to try and make my peace with what that man did. I never will fully do that. I have all these people to look after."

"How did my grandfather fit into all this? How did you even know him?"

He smiled a wistful smile. The good old days.

"I met your grandfather when we were freshmen at Princeton. We lived across the hall from each other."

Rachel's stomach flipped as she struggled to keep a straight face. The fate of the world had turned on the decision of a Princeton housing official decades ago. Good Lord if that didn't twist your noodle.

"We were like brothers. Eventually, he came to work for me at

Penumbra, and I put him in charge of our nanotechnology division. Jack was an extraordinarily brilliant man."

"What does nanotechnology have to do with all this?"

"We built the vaccine with nanotechnology. Or more specifically, your grandfather was one of the primary architects behind it. The nanovaccine was specifically designed to target and destroy the virus upon exposure. "Our nanotech was going to change everything. I mean everything. He was a genius, truly."

"And I was given this vaccine."

"Correct."

"My son never received the vaccine."

"The nanoparticles that make up the vaccine are self-replicating."

"And they transfer to the fetus?"

"Exactly."

"I guess I should thank you."

"Your grandfather is the one who deserves your thanks. You're alive because of him."

"What are you talking about?"

"Jack hated the Medusa project. It drove him like nothing I'd ever seen. He didn't believe the government would use it as a weapon of last resort. It's like Chekov's gun. You see a gun in the first act, it had better go off by the third one. He believed the virus would one day get out and he wanted a way to fight it."

"If he hated the project so much, why did he keep working here?"

He chuckled softly.

"Leaving the project was not an option."

"I'm not sure I understand."

"The Pentagon had a way of being very convincing."

She tilted her head in confusion.

"These men, they wanted their bioweapon, you see. They left us no choice."

"Everyone has a choice," she said.

"Not one your grandfather was willing to make."

"Then my grandfather was a coward," she said, her skin prickly and hot.

Gruber looked down at his drink.

"You think he was afraid of what they would do to him?" he asked, his eyes focused on the liquor swirling in the glass.

"Everyone has a choice," she repeated.

Gruber got out of his chair and stoked the fire with the black poker. A large log in the center, weakened by fire, split in the middle with a satisfying *pfft*, sending a plume of flame high into the flue. Immediately, a burst of warmth washed over her.

"Jack didn't care what happened to him," he said, his back to her as he worked the fire. "And they knew it. One day, this man from the Pentagon comes here for a progress visit. By then, the bigwigs knew Jack was pushing back hard, that the project was too dangerous to continue, and to be honest, I was starting to agree with him. I was ready to pull the plug, destroy all the remaining samples of the virus. We weren't even at the final iteration of the virus, and that was terrifying enough. That was No. 6, which had a mortality rate of eighty-two percent.

"We're in the conference room with this guy from the Pentagon," he said. "Mr. Cunningham was his name. And Jack is raising holy hell, and I mean it, he was apoplectic. When he got angry, this vein on his neck would bulge out, and it was rippling that day."

Rachel felt a chill. She'd seen the same vein on her neck bulge when she got good and lathered.

"Then Cunningham opens an envelope and slides an eight-by-ten photograph right under Jack's nose.

"Jack looks down, and the blood drained out of his face. He went white as a sheet."

Rachel felt cold.

"What was the picture of?" she asked, knowing what the answer would be.

Gruber looked up from his glass.

"It was of you."

Her shoulders slumped down.

"And this Mr. Cunningham said, 'finish the job, or there won't be enough left of her to identify the body.'"

"No," she said.

"The outbreak began a year later."

Her stomach lurched and it took all her willpower to keep what little food in her stomach down. She stood up from her chair, took in a deep breath, let it out, took in another. Inhale, exhale. Inhale. Exhale. It wasn't possible. It was impossible. The world had died so she could live.

"No," she said again, as if she could undo all that had happened by simply denying what Gruber was telling her.

Because as it stood, she wasn't sure she could hold onto rational thought much longer. Like a balloon breaking free of its anchors, she felt her mind begin to drift away from reality because reality was no place she wanted to be right now. How did you process what Gruber had told her, that the fate of humanity had passed through her without her even knowing it? One day, maybe when she'd been in high school or perhaps even middle school, perhaps in fourth-period biology, maybe eating lunch in the cafeteria, hunched over her laptop, evil men had started an engine of destruction, evil men had negotiated mankind's extinction.

It was a lot for a girl to take in.

She crumpled back into her seat, her mind blank, her body cold and rigid. It was as if she had finally died, Medusa finally infecting her like it had infected no other, attaching itself to her soul, to her essence, braiding itself to her until there was no difference between one and the other.

Rachel was Medusa.

Medusa was Rachel.

Gruber polished off his drink and set it on the table. Just two friends enjoying an after-work cocktail. He got up, smoothed his pants, placed a hand on her shoulder.

"There's much more I'd like to tell you," he said, standing up. "Perhaps in time."

"What happens to me now?" she asked.

Somewhere in the back of her mind, Will. A tiny flicker of light, a whisper of hope.

"I'll need to think very carefully about that. I have a community to run here. And we're approaching one of our most important events of the year."

She briefly considered inquiring further but decided against it. If he wanted her to know more, he would tell her. Besides, most of the tale he was telling was probably bullshit anyway. The idea Chadwick had gone rogue was simply too much to believe. Not to mention that she had her own agenda.

"How many people live here?"

"Over a thousand."

This perplexed her most of all. That there had been so many people willing to snuff out humanity, to bring about this harsh cataclysm. Like they had been building a bridge or raising a house. Was that really who they had been?

"I must say, I'm quite surprised," he said.

"By what?"

"You've taken all this quite well."

"The world is what it is. I guess I'm glad to be alive."

"We'll talk again soon. Until then, your movements will be restricted, but you'll be comfortable. You'll have food, water, shelter."

He left.

35

She didn't sleep all night.

They had put her in this small room on an upper floor. It was spartan, a twin bed, a desk, a chest of drawers, the walls bare. She was curled up on the bed, her mind working a million miles a minute. She did some breathing exercises, trying to rein in her runaway imagination.

Her thoughts kept drifting back to the playroom, to the children. There must have been at least twenty of them, many of them clearly much younger than Will, some as young as two. As she lay in the dark, she painted the scene as best as she could in her mind's eye, trying to remember every detail, every face of every child she had seen in those precious few seconds. A girl of about three with a long ponytail hunched over a coloring book, her chubby little fingers wrapped around a crayon. A boy, maybe five or six, smiling a big toothless grin at something that had caught his fancy, out of Rachel's view. Her eye swept to the corner of the room, where two little girls were dancing on an electronic mat in sync with the dance video game on the large television screen. One had strawberry hair and freckles, beautiful freckles, more than the stars in the night sky.

It was like having an out-of-reach itch scratched. The room was electric with life, with hope, with joy, more than she had seen since before Erin Thompson's baby had died. In fact, part of her was glad they had hustled her away from the room; it was almost too much to process, that sudden, dizzying rush of sugar that hit your brain from a bite of delicious chocolate pie.

She got out of bed and went to the window facing the Rockies. In the light of the moon shimmered across the snow-capped peaks to the west. Focusing on the vista beyond helped calm her. She hadn't had this kind of view at the Citadel, that was for sure.

The Citadel.

The walled compound in the hinterlands of Nebraska. Home to fifty men and fifty women who had dedicated their lives to wiping out the human race and starting anew. But something had gone wrong with their monstrous plot, something that had left every woman there infertile.

And so they had set out to find out what had gone wrong with their plan. That led to Rachel's capture on a highway not far from here, now that she thought about it, while she'd been traveling to Virginia to find her father, back when she hadn't even known if he'd survived the outbreak. She and the other women, more than thirty in all, poked and prodded and tested until Chadwick had figured out that yes, indeed, it had been their own vaccine that had sterilized the women.

The place had come undone because of it.

It had led to a failed uprising.

But what Chadwick had died not knowing was that the babies of those surviving women, the ones they had impregnated at the Citadel, would die too.

But Rachel's baby had not.

One of these things was not like the other.

It could not have been a coincidence that the one baby who had survived had been born to the woman whose grandfather had had his fingers in this apocalyptic pie. Like winning the SuperBall lottery before stepping onto an airliner that crashed in the ocean.

It proved Leon Gruber was a lying sack of shit, it was proof he had been in it from the beginning, that Chadwick was never supposed to succeed in rebuilding society. Chadwick and the others at the Citadel had had one job, to wipe the slate clean and then when he had done that, Gruber had cut him loose.

Planned obsolescence.

No. Not just Gruber.

Her knees buckled under her.

That meant her grandfather had been in on it as well.

Dear God in heaven.

A flash of memory.

During her time at the Citadel, Chadwick's chief lieutenant, Dr. James Rogers, had tried recruiting her into a coup against Chadwick. He and a handful of the others had regretted what they had done, way too late for it to make any difference for the world, but regret nonetheless. And just before Chadwick had sniffed him out, he had started to confess something to Rachel. They'd convened a surreptitious meeting, huddled together around lanterns in a little warehouse office on the edges of Beatrice, Nebraska. What was it he had said? That there was more to the story? Something like that. In the end, it really didn't matter what he had started to say; moments later, Chadwick's stormtroopers had burst in, rounded them all up and an hour later, the traitors had all been executed.

Maybe he was about to tell her about this place. Maybe he was about to tell her she had been vaccinated. If she'd been vaccinated against Medusa, and her baby had survived where the others hadn't, it could only mean one thing.

There were two vaccines.

It made sense. It was how Gruber would ensure his people, and his people alone would populate this new world. At some point during her pregnancy, these tiny microscopic machines had wound their way into unborn Will, where they had protected him from that moment forward.

And although the naturally immune women weren't infertile, they were infecting their babies with the Medusa antibodies flowing through their veins. That's why the babies died. If she could get her hands on the vaccine, she could reboot humanity's hard drive. If she could do that, then anything was possible. Her body buzzed with excitement. A future. Thinking about the future with something resembling hope had been a rare act indeed.

She needed two things.

First, for the vaccine to still exist.

That was what worried her the most. If there were no more vaccine, if they had used it all, or worse, if Gruber had destroyed the remaining supplies, then that was game, set and match.

The second thing she needed was to find it.

THE NEXT DAY, a woman came to see Rachel bearing a simple but tasteful black dress. It reminded Rachel of that last terrible dinner at the Citadel, when Chadwick had executed dozens of his purported supporters as the place unraveled. Hell, maybe she would get lucky a second time. The woman was a sweet wisp of a thing, fair-skinned, her face fresh and young. But crow's feet around her eyes belied a much older woman, probably older than Rachel was. A large birthmark colored the top of her forehead near her hairline.

"My name is Jody."

"Rachel."

"I know. Everyone is talking about you."

"What are they saying?"

"Is it true?"

"Is what true?"

"That your grandfather designed the vaccine?"

"It would appear so."

"Wow."

"Yeah. So what's the dress for?" Rachel asked, desperate to change the subject.

"For you to wear tonight."

"What's tonight?"

"The Lottery."

"What's that?"

"The population here is strictly controlled. Once a year, six women under the age of forty are given permission to have a baby."

This must've been the important event Gruber had mentioned.

Jody's eyes cut to the ground.

"This is my last chance," she said with an odd smile and a strange inflection in her voice; she held up her hands with fingers crossed.

"Oh," Rachel said, not really knowing what to say.

There was a wistfulness about this woman, a yearning, a sense that this Lottery meant far more to Jody than she was letting on. It was peculiar, but Rachel couldn't quite put her finger on why that was. On some level, the Lottery made a certain kind of business sense. Gruber had to make sure their resources could support their population.

"I'll be back to get you this evening."

WHEN RACHEL STEPPED inside the auditorium a few minutes before the appointed hour, Jody by her side, a hush fell over the crowd. Hundreds of people craned their necks to get a look at her, this prodigal daughter returned. Rachel could only imagine what people had been saying about her, how much of it had been truth peppered with a rumor, or perhaps it had been the other way around.

They were in the chalet's main ballroom, which had been retrofitted with enough stadium seating to fit Olympus' entire population. The sight of this many people in one place was dizzying; she hadn't seen such a large crowd since the plague. Not even the Market had been so crowded. A profound sense of loneliness washed over her; all these years, they'd been so alone.

"This way," said Jody, extending her arm down the aisle.

In an aisle seat in the front row, there was a placard with her name on it. She removed the card and sat down next to an older woman; she felt the flush heat of embarrassment creep up her chest as hundreds of sets of eyes bore in on her. Rachel glanced quickly at the woman next to her. She wore a pantsuit and was frightfully thin. She wore no makeup. The woman made no move to engage her; Rachel sat quietly with her hands folded in her lap.

The buzz in the crowd died down quickly. Eventually, people got restless as they waited for things to get started. She glanced around the utilitarian space they were in. Nothing adorned the walls. Function over form all the way.

A few minutes later, Gruber emerged from the wings, striding purposefully across the stage to the podium. Under his arm was a leather portfolio, which he opened before him. He tapped the microphone once, a burst of static, and he began to speak.

"Good evening. Welcome to the Annual Lottery."

He opened the portfolio. The old leather creaked in the silence that had come down on the room like an anvil. A thousand people and not a soul breathed. She glanced around the room and caught a glimpse of Jody. The woman was on the edge of her seat, her eyes wide, her face frozen in a blank stare. Her hands, clenched in prayer, tapped metronomically against her lips.

"Before we start," Gruber was saying, "there's someone I'd like you all to meet. As you all know, it was James Rogers' and Jack Fisher's brilliant vaccine that allowed us to survive the epidemic all those years ago. I only wish we'd been able to make more before it was too late. That said, I know Jack would be thrilled that we soldier on, thanks in large part to him, that because of the vaccine flowing through the veins of every one of us, the human race will live on."

"To Jack!" someone called out.

Laughter, followed by a crash of applause that swept across the room like a wave. Then everyone was on their feet, cheering, whistling, hooting and hollering. As Rachel looked around the room at these men and women, young and old, white and black, Asian and Indian and so many other ethnicities, a thought took root and began to grow. Some wept, others crossed themselves, still others hugged one another.

"To Jack, indeed," said Gruber. "And today, I have a very special gift for all of you."

Gruber caught Rachel's eye and motioned for her to stand up. She rose to her feet sheepishly. Hundreds of pairs of eyes locked on her like heat-seeking missiles. She raised her right hand to acknowledge their warm welcome.

"This is Rachel Fisher," he said. "Rachel is Jack's granddaughter."

A murmur through the crowd.

"She's been out there for a dozen years, clawing and scratching to stay alive," he went on. "It should come as no surprise to anyone that the Medusa virus was no match for Jack Fisher's granddaughter."

He laughed at his own joke; she noticed he didn't mention whether she had also been vaccinated.

"I hope you will welcome Rachel to our little community. I hope Rachel will accept our offer to stay with us."

Someone began to clap, and quickly it spread, the applause rippling out to all corners of the audience. Within seconds, the crowd was on its feet again, the ovation deafening. The woman to her left embraced her in a hug, unseen hands patting her on the shoulder, caressing her cheek. It was as surreal a moment as she had ever experienced.

Gruber beamed from the podium, looking down at his co-conspirator's progeny.

The celebration began dying down and everyone returned to their seats.

"Thanks, everyone," he said. "Moving on, I know you're anxious to hear what else we have on the agenda. So I will cut right to the chase. The winners of this year's Lottery are as follows."

He then read off six names.

"Shannon Freeman.

"Amy Munn.

"Elizabeth Parker.

"Hala Abouassi.

"Jennifer Newsom.

"Michele Stehle."

A gasp or giggle or burst of subdued applause followed the announcement of each name. Rachel stole another glance at Jody, whose chin had dropped to her chest. Tears fell silently onto her blouse, darkening the fabric where they landed. She was fumbling with her hands.

Gruber closed his portfolio and looked out over the crowd.

"This concludes the Lottery," he said. He exited stage left, back into the wings.

Just like that, it was over. The crowd burst into chatter; the room was awash in tears, laughter and even a little argument.

An escort took Rachel back to her room, where she tried to process what had happened.

Why did she care?

So what if sad little Jody didn't get to have kids? She had helped make this happen.

Reap what you sow, bitch.

36

As evening descended on Olympus, Jody delivered Rachel's dinner. The woman's face hung in the same sad rictus that Rachel had seen in the auditorium. Redness rimmed her puffy eyes; it was clear she had been crying. Jody set the tray of food down on Rachel's bed, paused, pressed a finger and a thumb to either side of her forehead. Despite herself, Rachel's heart went out to the woman.

Gruber's endgame remained a mystery to her. It was as if he didn't know what to do with her now. He could kill her, but there seemed to be little value in exchange for that. He didn't know about Will; that was another bit of intel he wouldn't be able to use against her. The vaccine flowed through her veins; her having a son wouldn't exactly be earth-shattering news, especially here, where he wasn't unique, where he was one of many.

"Are you OK?" Rachel asked. The words were out of her mouth before she realized it.

"I'm fine."

"You sure."

Jody ignored her, drifted toward the door, stopped.

"That was my last chance."

"I'm sorry."

She stood at the doorway, scratching at the jamb with a single fingernail.

"Why is forty the cut-off age?" Rachel asked.

"One of their rules."

"What happens if you break the rule?"

"The pregnancy is terminated. It's a capital offense."

Rachel's heart hardened to stone.

"You made the bed," Rachel said. "Now you can lie in it."

Jody lifted her downcast chin, glanced back over her shoulder.

"What do you mean?"

"You were part of this."

"Part of what?"

"The way things are."

"Sure, I guess."

"Pretty nonchalant about being a mass murderer."

"What are you talking about?"

Now she had turned around to face Rachel.

"Don't try to rationalize," Rachel said, even as a sliver of doubt crept inside her and began burrowing.

"Rationalize what?"

The conversation was becoming more and more tangled, like recalcitrant headphone cords.

"I mean, I guess I was lucky," Jody said.

Rachel didn't say anything, hoping the woman would let the discussion unspool without her interference. Jody's chin had dropped back to her chest.

"Never thought it would turn out like this."

She lifted her chin up.

"You ever think about it anymore?" Jody asked. "The outbreak, I mean?"

"I try not to."

"We'd been here two weeks when it started," Jody said. "We were here for a corporate retreat. I worked for NorthStar, that was one of Penumbra's subsidiaries. Pretty sweet, huh? A month in this place? Then we started seeing the news reports about the outbreak."

She paused and smiled an embarrassed smile.

"I was always a bit of a germophobe. I think I was paying attention before anyone else."

Like the virus that had brought her here to this place, the doubt began replicating wildly inside Rachel. Jody was telling the story of a random survivor, not of an apocalyptic conspirator. Either she was an exceptional liar or...

She didn't know. She didn't know. She didn't know.

"I remember being so excited to get sent on this trip," she said. "I'd never been away from my kids that long," she said, her voice cracking, "but it was such a big honor, I couldn't turn it down."

"I worked in the Seattle office," she said. "Then they grounded the airplanes. Then Mr. Gruber wouldn't let us leave. Said it was too dangerous. By then, I didn't have any place to go. Then they told us about the vaccine."

"What did they say?"

"They told us it was an airborne strain of Ebola. Said PenLabs had been working on a vaccine for Ebola, but they weren't sure if it would work.

"It was terrifying," she said, her eyes closing. "All of us lined up to get the vaccine. The slightest sniffle or cough and people would flip out."

She was rambling now.

"I remember the last time I talked to my kids. They were all sick by then. It was on FaceTime, you remember FaceTime?"

Rachel nodded, a lump in her throat.

"I was hysterical. There was no way to get to them. Can you imagine that? Having to watch your kids die on an iPad?"

"I'm sorry."

"Did you have kids?"

"I was in college then," Rachel said, carefully wording her response so as not to lie to her. For some reason, she did not want to lie to this woman.

"Oh."

"Anyway, Michael – Michael is my husband now – Michael and I wanted to have a baby. I wanted to have a family. To be a mother again. You know? And now that's all over."

"I'm sorry."

"It's OK. Well, it's not OK. It's how it is. Amazing what you get used to, you know. I mean, I get up every day and get on with my life. That's something, right? I have a safe place to live. I want for nothing. Everyone pitches in."

Rachel took Jody into her arms and held her tightly. Something inside the woman disintegrated, and out flowed the tears, an explosion of a dozen years of anxiety and worry and grief that had been building up. She'd reached her breaking point was all. Rachel held her until the crying subsided to subdued weeping and sniffles, the last remnants of a terrible emotional hurricane sweeping through.

Jody broke the embrace first. Her eyes were shiny and wet, but her face looked calm.

"I don't know what came over me," she said. "I'm sorry."

"Don't be."

Jody left.

FALLOUT from the Lottery spread swiftly across the chalet. By the time Jody left Rachel's room, the place had fallen dead silent. People had retreated to their rooms to celebrate or mourn, depending on the news they'd received.

After waiting several hours, Rachel jimmied the lock open and exited her room, which was at the end of a long corridor on an upper floor of this wing. The plush red carpet swallowed up her footsteps as she made her way down the brightly lit hallway. The silence was eerie in the brightness of the corridor.

The stifled cries of despair greeted her as she passed by one doorway. Pity. She felt pity for these people, here with their warm beds and hot meals. She couldn't even fault them for staying here because where would they go? How would they survive out there by themselves, let alone with a baby? No, Leon Gruber had them by the pubes. He had trapped them here to execute his vision, punishing them with life. There was no doubt in her mind that Jody would much rather have died with her children back in Seattle than live here.

But pity did not solve her very pressing problem.

She was running out of time to find the vaccine.

Using her left arm as a canvas, she sketched out a very rough map of the chalet with a pen from her room. The upper floor appeared to be exclusively residential. At the far end of the corridor were the stairs. She entered the stairwell and slipped down to the third floor. It was cooler down here, almost chilly. Quiet but for the hum of electricity. More closed doors. Panic began tickling her insides like a rat loose inside a wall. The place was too big. Did she think she was going to stumble across a bag marked FREE VACCINES?

Her breathing was becoming a bit ragged; she stopped and set her hand against the wall. Calm yourself, girl. Calm yourself. This was a Hail Mary pass anyway. She had nothing to lose. If she failed, Will would be lost to her forever. But maybe that was for the best. She wouldn't be able to take care of him or keep him safe.

Perhaps there was a medical clinic somewhere, a separate building deeper on the grounds of the compound. On the move again, back into the stairwell, down to the main level, outside. It was snowing lightly and she was cold. She edged her way along the building's façade, the dusting of snow crunching under her shoes.

At the corner, she turned right and continued up a slight incline. She felt small here, alone. This was what her father had done for her. Alone. Afraid. Cold. Her father, dead now, her father who had died with his daughter hating him. She was sorry for what she had said at his funeral. That should have been between them. Instead, she had embarrassed his memory in front of so many to whom he had meant so much.

All those years and she hadn't said a word to him. She had chosen to be afraid, to take the easy way out. And now it was too late. The only thing she could do now was finish this. Find the answers he never could. Save his grandson, save all of them. She could do that for him. After all, it was only because of him there even was a Will.

Will.

The easy way out. She had done the same with Will, hiding him from the way the world was. Look where that had gotten them. A young man woefully unprepared for the world in which he lived. Unprepared because she had been too afraid to do what needed to be done. All these years, she'd lived her life in fear.

She shut off her *If-Then* machine. That thing could wreak untold devastation if you let it. The past was past and could not be unwritten. The future was still open, at least for the next little while.

A deep breath, and she was on the move again, around to the back of the chalet. The pathway cut up into the hillside toward another building, also bearing that Bavarian motif, but far smaller than the main chalet. She followed the path, caution fully tossed into the wind swirling around the mountain tonight. At the entrance, she paused, glancing around, feeling like a teenager sneaking out for a night of revelry.

As she opened the door, a bright light filled her field of vision, the pop and hiss of sulfur filling the air. It rendered her temporarily blind as wide-open pupils absorbed the blast of white light. She held up a hand and sought darkness, anything that would help her regain her bearings.

"Awful late for a stroll, isn't it, Rachel?"

Despite the cold icing her skin, Leon Gruber's metallic voice chilled her soul at a depth she couldn't have previously imagined. With that one statement, her whole world went up in a mushroom cloud around her. Her vision was still impaired, but she could just make out some activity around her, shapes and blurs. Then a crack, a sharp shooting pain to the head, and the world went dark around her.

~

Concrete.

Sleep.

She dreamed.

She'd been having the same dream for years.

She dreamed about Will playing in an elementary school recorder concert, standing in the front row, making sweet and terrible music. They sat in the school gymnasium, in metal folding chairs that ruined spines, crowded together like sheep, watching their children make terrible music through smartphone screens, making videos they would never watch.

Then afterward, she and the other moms would take the kids for ice cream, and the boys would ditch their little clip-on ties and blazers and run around the shop's patio, annoying the other customers, chasing each other, dribbling little trails of melted ice cream behind them. It was springtime and the evening air glittered with the light of fireflies, a world where the plague had never happened. She always woke up when she started to yell at him.

It was so routine that she knew she was dreaming, but it always ended the same way, getting up to yell at Will, drawing the side-eye of her fellow moms who were content to leave well enough alone.

A shower.

She woke up, but her eyes remained closed.

Another shower.

Her head was pounding where she'd taken the wallop.

Ice-cold water slithered up her nose and she began coughing, as it raked her airway, big, hacking coughs that served only to make her headache worse. The coughs vibrated in her skull, amplifying the pain exponentially. Another shower, a chilly spray of water blasting her face, making her cough and sneeze, spraying mucus everywhere. Her head bobbled from one side to another until she focused all her efforts on stabilizing it.

"She's awake."

"Just kill me and be done with it," she muttered. Her words came out in a sticky, clumped mess, owing largely to her terribly dry throat.

"So brave."

She opened her eyes slowly. It seemed to take an unusual amount of effort to complete such a simple task. One managed to come to half-mast, but the other remained closed, puffy and gummed shut with goopy crust and dried blood.

A drab, empty room, damp and cold. Square, gray walls, gray concrete flooring. Her head resting against a cold wall. She was in a metal folding chair (*poetic, really fucking poetic*). Her hands were bound together with a pair of zip ties. She was dressed in pants and a short-sleeve t-shirt. She shivered.

There was an empty chair set immediately opposite her. While she waited for someone to fill it, she sighed, the totality of her failure laid out before her. Her insides ached, a scar on her soul, knowing she had fallen short, that Will was gone now, forever, that she would die here and he would never know what happened to her.

Footsteps.

She looked up with her one good eye to see Leon Gruber taking a seat before her. He wore a heavy parka and snow pants. Just seeing him dressed warmly made her feel even colder.

"A letter from an attorney, huh?"

She shrugged.

"Not a bad story, to tell you the truth," Gruber said. "And I was sitting there, wracking my brain, trying to figure out where the hell you had come from. I mean, it was such an impossibility that you would ever find us. And I almost went for it. Can you believe that? You almost had me fooled. But since you were here, it was as plausible an explanation as any."

"What gave me away?" she croaked. Her throat was dry and the words came out harsh and sticky.

He grabbed her arm and flipped her wrist over.

The tattoo. The phoenix rising from the ashes.

"You were at the Citadel."

She nodded. There was no point in obfuscating. It was time to lay it on all the table.

"Is Chadwick dead?" he asked.

"Yes."

"Some years ago, I took a trip there, saw the ruins. Did you see the explosion?"

"Yes," she said. "Why did I get the vaccine?"

"Your grandfather. It was part of the deal."

She shivered.

"What deal?"

He leaned to the side of his chair and held up a silver metal briefcase.

"Do you know what this is?"

He unfastened the latches and set the open case on her lap. It was padded, a deep velvety red, divided into dozens of smaller compartments. He withdrew a small vial and handed it to her.

She studied the affixed label carefully.

PB-815, LOT 522, HUMAN VACCINE

12-DOSE VIAL 2.0 mL

070894

The Medusa vaccine.

She gently rolled the small vial between her fingers. This was it. The future of the human race was in her hands. Erin Thompson. All the women who had lost their babies.

"Your grandfather wanted you to survive the plague."

"No."

"You don't want to believe he was involved," he said. "I can understand that. But without him, none of this would have been possible. Oh, he had his doubts, of course. And he made me promise to vaccinate you."

"When was I vaccinated?"

"About three years before the outbreak. We bribed a nurse at your pediatrician's office to slip in an extra shot during a school physical."

Guilt ripped through her. Like an arrow in flight, her life had been soaring toward the plague since the day she was born, toward the end of all things. Everyone she had ever met, ever become friends with, from the first boy she kissed to her high school biology teacher to the guy who delivered her Chinese food her freshman year at Caltech, had been a walking corpse, ghost in the flesh, already dead.

The world was dying, a hidden tumor tucked away, as her survival had been planned and bargained for. It made her feel dirty, used, a pawn in some grand game that she wasn't even aware was being played.

"Jesus Christ," she whispered.

"You shouldn't judge your grandfather," he said. "He did this partly for you."

Her stomach roiled at this.

"He wanted a better world for you. For your children."

"I never asked for this," she said. "The world was doing fine before you deleted it."

"That's such naïve thinking. This idea we were all equal, that we were all in it together, it was so destructive. What's that old joke?"

"What joke?"

"Half the people in the world are below average? I couldn't have that. We needed to evolve from our troglodyte existence. Mankind was stuck in first gear, the one percent held back by the rest."

"So you killed everyone."

"I simply added a catalyst to the system. I let natural selection take it from there."

"I don't get it," she said. "You're no different than Chadwick. I had this exact conversation with him thirteen years ago. *Kill everyone, and you too can live in this utopia! Hooray!*"

He shook his head, but she went on.

"Besides, what's the point of living in a world like this? Do you know what it's like out there? It's all-out war. People are starving to death. Every day."

He smiled.

"You're thinking about this all wrong," he said. "There's much more."

"What else is there? The food is running out. You'll all be dead soon. I wish Chadwick was still alive just so he could see how badly you all screwed up."

He dropped his chin and shook his head, *tsking* her for her short-sightedness.

"I'm disappointed in you. What's the point of going to all this trouble if I'm going to be dead in a few years? If I didn't make contingency plans for our survival?"

"I don't know."

"Do you know why we have the Lottery?"

"No."

"I believe in chaos theory. In entropy. The idea that left to their own devices, systems will act unpredictably, usually to their own detriment. Usually to the point of collapse. We prepared for every eventuality. Do you know why the crops stopped growing?"

"The nukes, probably."

"Very good. We ran an algorithm that predicted a ninety-eight percent chance of a nuclear exchange within twenty-four days of the initial outbreak. A ninety-four percent chance of the global temps dropping by eight degrees Fahrenheit. We had to be prepared. We developed hybrid crop strains that would thrive in a world where the temperature dropped twenty degrees.

"But we had to make all this worth the effort. That we would be the stewards of this new world for a lot longer than one might think possible."

Her head was starting to ache, and she was having a hard time following his line of thinking. He was telling her something important, something vital, but her brain wasn't putting it together. Bits and pieces of a larger picture.

"There were two vaccines," she said. "Two."

"That's right."

"Why?"

"Chadwick's responsibility was to develop and produce the virus," he said. "He was a brilliant doctor, brilliant. But he was a bit unhinged. I never really trusted him. I didn't know what he would do. I knew I would never be able to control what he did in Nebraska. And so your grandfather worked with Dr. Rogers to create the second vaccine. We knew the Citadel would come undone after they discovered their vaccine had sterilized the women."

"Aren't you breaking the bad-guy code?" she asked, smiling, a little punch drunk.

"What do you mean?"

"Telling me your whole plan?"

His face darkened as he leaned in close, his lips at her ear. His warm breath tickled her skin.

"I wanted you to know. I wanted you to know that you owe whatever life you've led for the past thirteen years to me. I wanted you to know your grandfather paid for your life with the human race."

Her stomach clenched as he spoke, his words like dark clouds raining blood and death on the ground of her soul. In that moment, she was glad her father was dead, that he would never have to know this terrible truth about his own father, about their family. Death would be better than having to walk around with this knowledge in her head. This was worse than survivor's guilt, a feeling that this was somehow her fault, that the dead world around her was her fault.

"Anyway, back to the Lottery," he said. "We carefully control the number of births because the babies born here are going to live a very long time."

"What?"

"The nanovaccine does more than protect you from PB-815."

"I'm not following."

He smiled strangely at her.

"Rachel, have you been sick even once in the last fifteen years?"

Her brow furrowed as she considered the question.

"I, uh. Yeah, sure."

"When?"

She scoured her memory banks, thinking back to the last time she'd been under the weather, fighting off a cold or stomach bug.

"Think back to the last few years before the plague. Did you miss a single day of high school because you were sick?"

No.

She had not.

At her graduation, the principal had handed her a certificate for never having missed a day of high school. It was the only time, Principal Greyson had said, the school had ever awarded that certificate. Her freshman year in college, less than a year before the outbreak, a stomach bug had ravaged her dorm, but she had remained healthy. Every single person on her floor had come down with it except her. She escaped outbreaks of mononucleosis, influenza, even ringworm.

"No."

"And after the epidemic, did you ever get sick, even once?"

Cold and flu had still circulated during their years at the warehouse; there seemed to be enough human contact to keep the bugs moving, especially in the absence of annual flu shots. And they had dealt with other illnesses, cholera, even an outbreak of typhoid fever. But again, she had never gotten sick, not once.

Her three months with Millicent unspooled like a home movie. She'd had sex with dozens of men, and she had never come down with so much as a urinary tract infection. Every one of the girls had contracted at least one sexually transmitted disease – but not Rachel. Not once.

And Will had never been sick in his life. Never once. No ear infections. No croup. No sniffles. Not one runny nose. He had never thrown up, had never even run a fever. How had she never noticed that before?

"No," she said through gritted teeth. She didn't want the answer to be no, she didn't want to believe what Gruber was telling her.

"You've received the ultimate gift," he said. "The gift of life. A hundred years from now, I'll still be here. Five hundred years from now. All these people, you've met, they'll still be here. That's why I don't care about this bleak world you're so despondent about. All those people will die. In time, even the skies will clear, and we will have this beautiful, pure world to call our own."

Rachel simply stared at him, her mouth hanging open.

"What are you doing here?" he asked. "Why did you come?"

"I wanted to know the truth."

"And now that you know it, was it worth it?"

"Yes."

"You could've lived the rest of your very long life in peace."

Her head was spinning. She was dead; Gruber was going to kill her, probably in the next few minutes. But Will. Her heart broke for him. Bad enough he'd grown up in this world. Worse was knowing he might be wandering the earth out there alone for God knew how long.

Should she try to cut a deal?

Bring him in?

Tell Gruber about him?

If these people didn't know the truth about the plague, then maybe Will could live with them in beautiful, blessed, blissful ignorance. His conscience would be rightfully clear. He could be around other kids for the first time in his life. He could be happy. Maybe Gruber would spare her too. Will would have his mother. They could have a life.

And she would carry this secret about the plague to her grave. And when she died, if there was a Maker to meet, if there were debts to be paid, they could settle this matter then.

Throwing her lot in with Leon Gruber.

That was a tough pill to swallow.

But she could someday try to make it right. To make things better. There were women out there right now who could become mothers again. That valise with the vials of vaccine, she could take it one day, take it out into the world and vaccinate women so they could have kids again. If Gruber was right, they could wait for the climate to stabilize again and maybe the crops would grow again.

But would he even want to cut a deal?

He might kill Will just to spite her.

She sat there, mulling it over, this terrible choice. Will. It had to be about Will. Since the day he'd been born, every choice was for him, to make his life better, to fill his toolbox as best as she could so when the day came, he could take care of himself, protect himself, perhaps extract some joy from this mine of misery in which they lived.

But she couldn't do it; she couldn't bring herself to say the words to Gruber. She didn't even want him to know Will existed. He didn't deserve to know about Will. She was afraid it would bring him joy to see her grandfather's wish granted at yet another level.

"What now?" she asked.

He rubbed his chin.

"Seems like I have three choices. One, I let you go. You don't know where we are. You live your life. I feel like I might owe that to your grandfather."

He studied her carefully, like he was trying to decide between two entrees on a dinner menu.

"But you're a bright girl. You might someday find your way back here. After all, you're going to have the time to look. I don't want to spend my life looking over my shoulder.

"Two, I let you stay here. The others would accept you. But I sense you're a crusader. That you'll undo everything here out of some misguided sense of justice or duty."

"What's the third option?"

"I kill you."

Her skin turned to ice.

"Put yourself in my shoes," he said. "I've made it. I succeeded. The game is over. The people here are going to outlive everyone out there."

He made a dismissive motion with his hand, as though she and all the other survivors were nothing more than roaches scurrying about.

"Give me the vaccine, and you'll never see me again."

"I personally vetted the Penumbra employees I brought here before the plague. They were chosen for their intellect, for their psychological mettle, for their physical health. And they've done beautifully."

"Don't you see the flaw in your own thinking?"

"What flaw?"

"Complex systems are unpredictable. They want to collapse, they trend toward failure. Why is this any different? By extending everyone's lifespan, you've simply increased the chance of that happening."

His face darkened for a split second then brightened just as quickly.

"You are indeed Jack's granddaughter. But you're wrong, Ms. Fisher. No theory is infallible. And if chaos theory is not infallible, that means it can be proven wrong. And that is exactly what I intend to do."

"You can't design your way around human nature. We are who we are. These people, their little psychological quirks will pop on you sooner or later. You're a fool. Just like Miles Chadwick was."

He reared back and smacked her across the face, the pop of flesh echoing in the empty room. Blood rushed to her cheek and it felt warm, but she made no move to cradle it with her hand.

"See?"

Another smack, harder this time, so hard it toppled the chair over. Her shoulder hit the concrete floor first and a bolt of pain shot through it. As her shoulder throbbed, Gruber knelt next to her, grabbed her ear, pulled her head off the ground.

"Thank you, Rachel. You've made my decision very easy."

37

The night crawled by, Priya's deadline looming ever larger in her head. Exhaustion enveloped her, but she couldn't sleep, a combination of the cold and the fear. She didn't know what the air temperature was, but she didn't need to know. The misty puffs she expelled with each breath told her all she needed to know. It wasn't cold enough for her to freeze to death, although she was starting to wish it were.

Tell him about Will, a tiny voice cried out.

Will was all the insurance either of them would ever need. Gruber's guarantee of his safety would be more than enough to buy her silence. In her mind, the next decade, things that had yet to pass played out. Over and over, she saw Will playing with kids his own age, Will growing up.

But she hadn't been able to say the words.

She sat there on the cold floor, her elbows propped on her knees, her head in her hands. The words hadn't come out when she had the chance. Because she would know. She would know Will's future would have come at a terrible price. She was his mother. Her job was to do what was best for him. That was it. The problem was that it wasn't as easy as it looked on the surface.

Doing what was best didn't mean only finding food and a safe place to lay his head. It was more than that. If she gave him up to Gruber, the truth would eat at her like lye, dissolving her insides. In some way, she would be endorsing what he had done, what Chadwick had done to those women. Fruit of the poisonous tree.

And if that meant no happy ending for her, for her sweet Will, then that's how it would be. She would die on her feet. She would die with her soul intact. She didn't want to die, no more than anyone, but thanks to this *la-dee-dah* vaccine running through her veins, it sounded like she'd have to be able to feed herself for a good while to come. And who knew when the skies would clear, when the crops would grow again.

In the end, she would know she had done her job as a mother.

As she sat there, acceptance of her fate curing like concrete, the door screeched open. When she looked up, she was surprised to see Jody standing in the doorway. She wore jeans and a heavy gray fleece.

"What did you do?" she whispered. Her words, even muted, echoed across the empty chamber.

"What are you talking about?"

"I'm on kitchen duty," she said. "I'm supposed to ask you what you want. For your last meal. It's for tonight. What did you do?"

"I guess I've overstayed my welcome."

"I don't understand."

"There's a lot you don't understand."

"I don't have a lot of time," she said. "Please tell me."

Rachel climbed to her feet.

"The lab. Do you know where it is?"

"Yes."

"Can you take me there?"

Her shoulders sagged.

"I'm not sure I should."

A long silence as Rachel considered an alternative. She couldn't afford to wait for Jody to make peace with her decision.

"It was him, right? Gruber?" she asked suddenly. "The outbreak?"

"Yes. He was behind it."

Her jaw clenched, her lips tightening.

"Deep down, I've always known," she said. "I think most people do. No one wants to be the one to say it. There's always been a shadow over this place. It seemed too perfect, too clean. You know that feeling when you know something and you don't want to admit it?"

"I do."

"I would push it away, tell myself I was just imagining it."

Her eyes were shiny with tears now.

"Why do you stay?"

"We have nowhere to go," she said. "He's telling the truth about that, right?"

She nodded.

"Few years back, there was an unauthorized pregnancy," Jody said. "They took her outside, right in the square behind the chalet. Put a blindfold on her. Shot her in the head. We all had to watch."

"I'm sorry."

"It never happened again."

Another pause.

"We have to go now," Rachel said. "I don't have a lot of time to explain. But he showed me a metal valise. It had hundreds of doses of the vaccine inside. If we can get these out, back to where I came from, it will give people hope. Maybe we can figure out the food problem."

She was talking crazy now, but she didn't care. It was worth the risk. It was worth dying for.

"The seeds," she said. "He mentioned hybrid seeds that grow in this climate."

"Those are kept in a safe too."

"Dammit."

There had to be a way.

"Take me to the lab," she said.

"Can't. The guard is outside the door."

Rachel held up a single finger and closed her eyes, taking a moment to get her bearings. She couldn't do it all at once. It had to be like one of her coding sessions.

One thing at a time.

"I've got an idea," Rachel said.

She moved to the back of the room, away from the door and began running in place as hard as she could. After a minute, her legs began to ache and a deep burn settled into her chest. Her legs pistoned quickly beneath her, a muscle car revving its engine. A necklace of sweat formed at the hollow of her neck as her body began to cool itself. She pushed herself even harder, the sweat dripping off her now, even in the chill of the room.

When her muscles began to fail, she nodded toward Jody. She lay down on the cold hard floor and began twitching as violently as she could. Her legs flopped, her eyes rolled back in her head, and she left her mouth partly open, a bit of drool snaking to the floor underneath her. She was completely winded, her mouth hanging open, sucking in huge gobs of air. The altitude had taken its toll on her; if she kept this pace up, it wouldn't be an act much longer.

"Help!" Jody called out, banging on the door. "Something's wrong!"

The guard rushed into the room, his rifle up.

"She's having a seizure," Jody yelled, her voice breaking with worry.

"What the hell is wrong with her?"

"I don't know," Jody said breathlessly. "She said she wasn't feeling well, and then she collapsed."

"She's fakin'!" the man said. "She knows what's coming."

Rachel went still, her eyes closed as Jody pleaded with the guard.

"Look at her, she's beet red," Jody said.

"Check her forehead," the guard said.

Rachel felt Jody's warm hand against her forehead.

"Jesus, she's burning up."

"Let me see."

The guard's bigger, rougher hand replaced Jody's and pulled back just as quickly.

"Shit. Is she breathing?"

"I think so," Jody said, her voice appropriately spiced with panic. "Look, her chest is moving. What do you think's wrong with her?"

"Fuck all if I know," he said. "But I ain't taking any chances."

"You think it's Medusa?"

"Jesus Christ, now I do!" he said, stepping back and wiping his hands on his shirt. "The hell with this, I'm getting out of here."

"I'll tell Gruber."

The man grunted in frustration.

"Remember, we're vaccinated."

"Right," the man said, his breath ragged. "OK, I'll get her to the clinic. You get word to Gruber."

Rachel went as limp as she could as the guard yoked her into his arms. Through half-lidded eyes, she could see how big the man was. He outweighed her by at least a hundred pounds and carrying her would not be much of an issue. Jody led the way, the guard trailing behind.

The pair hustled out the door and into a small anteroom that was bracketed with a stone staircase at its opposite end. Up the stairs. Rachel lay limp, feeling helpless now. A bottle bobbing along the surface of the ocean, its fate still in doubt. Maybe it would wash up on the shore, or perhaps it would be dashed along the rocks.

The stairs brought them to a short corridor that led outside. He was focused on getting her to the lab, which afforded her the chance to steal a few glances of their route. They were behind the main chalet, headed for the same building where Gruber had caught her earlier. It was still daylight, the weak sun at its peak. There were people out and about, getting on with their day, doing their jobs, living their lives. Maybe it could have been like that for them. Maybe not.

Then inside again; the warmth felt good against her chilling skin. Her body temperature was returning to normal, so that part of the ruse would be lost. Too bad. Nothing worried people more than a high fever. Shades of Medusa. He navigated a long corridor before making a sharp left at a T-intersection.

A noisy commotion erupted around her.

"What the hell is this?"

"She's sick," the guard barked. "She spiked a fever and then started having seizures."

"Get her into Exam 2."

Now she was on an examination table, the crinkle of sterile paper under her body as her weight settled onto it.

"Get the zip ties off her."

The room exploded into a cacophony of panicked medical jargon. An oxygen mask was strapped to her face. The squeeze of a blood pressure cuff on her arm. Someone slid a pulse oximeter onto her fingertip. A sharp point into her arm as blood was drawn.

BP one-sixty over one-twenty.

O2 sat is normal.

Pulse is one-forty-five.

Check her for signs of trauma.

Need a Chem-7, full workup. I want those results ASAP.

She lay perfectly still, wondering how long she could maintain the charade, how long she would have to keep up the charade, hoping the numerical value assigned to the former outweighed the latter. Eventually, the activity began to subside as the condition of the patient stabilized. Increasingly confident their most precious patient wasn't going to die on them, their voices returned to normal.

"What do you think happened?" a woman asked.

"Hard to say," said a second woman. "Maybe altitude sickness. Stress could have triggered an autoimmune response. We'll have to see what the blood work says."

The last two care providers exited the room, leaving her by herself. It gave her a chance to explore her environs for the first time. Nothing spectacular. A standard examination room. A long counter with a series of cabinets mounted underneath.

Don't suppose the secret vaccine briefcase would be in here, huh?

As she waited in the room, she repeated the workout, driving her heart rate and body temperature upward. When the doorknob jiggled, she quickly lay down on the exam table. The door swung open, and Leon Gruber stood before her, his arm wrapped around

Jody's neck, a large knife to her throat. Her eyes were wide with horror, tears spilling down her cheeks. Dangling from his right hand, the one holding the knife, was the silver valise.

Then he slashed Jody's throat open.

Rachel screamed, scurrying toward the back corner of the bed as Jody's lifeless body crumpled to the ground. If Rachel hadn't been sedated, she might have had that heart attack after all.

"Quite the performance," Gruber said. "Very impressive."

Rachel could not take her eyes off Jody's body, which had been nearly separated from her head. A pool of blood was spreading across the floor, shading the floor in a deep crimson red. The glug of blood cascading onto the linoleum floor reminded her of an upturned cup of coffee.

"You came for this," he said, lifting the briefcase.

A glint of silver flashed under the fluorescent light, pulling Rachel's gaze from Jody's body. After setting the briefcase down on the counter, he unhitched the latches and flipped open the lid. Then he plucked a vial out and held it out for her to see. Rolled it between his fingers. Tossed it in the air, making Rachel gasp, saving it from its gravity-defined fate at the last second.

"This is all the vaccine we have left," he said. "This little bottle. This is enough for twelve people. You could give this to twelve women, kill the antibodies to the virus, and they would have beautiful, bouncing, healthy babies. Babies who would grow up."

He tossed the vial into the middle of the room. It arced, end over end, before striking the floor and shattering into a thousand pieces. He repeated the act six more times with six more vials, the floor now slick with a thin mixture of Jody's blood and vaccine solution.

Rachel looked for something to say, but the well was dry. What was there to say in the face of such evil, of such darkness? Maybe Eddie had been right. Maybe they should have made the deal with Priya. Maybe Priya would have found the answer where she and her father had failed. Maybe there was method in her madness; maybe the end justified the means. Instead, she was here, watching Leon Gruber extinguish humanity's fire, perhaps forever. There would be no way to undo what he was doing, no way to turn back the clock to a place where they still had a future.

As she watched the clear liquid of the vaccine swirl together with Jody's blood, an empty finality settled deep inside her. Not sadness, not regret. Not even a sense that she'd come so close to seeing it all the way through. A giant void. Perhaps it was better this way. Perhaps humanity was capable of nothing better than destroying itself.

A memory of San Diego flickered, a rocky outcrop overlooking the beach she'd found in high school. It wasn't far from their house, a ten-minute walk up Dunlap Avenue. Sometimes she would stop for tacos and eat while watching the waves gently caress the shoreline, the way a new mother might kiss her baby at night. Her view pulled out suddenly, like an overhead satellite view, retracting from the tiny you-are-here of the little rock and then she could see all of it, the entire country, the strange cartographic shape of the country, which had always reminded her of a terrifyingly obese turkey, the big belly of Texas scraping the ground, the proud plumage in the northeast. Then the sky-blue of the oceans, she wondered about the oceans; how had marine life done in the years since the plague? Had the changes in the climate wreaked their havoc on them?

An empty planet.

A faint boom reached her ears. At first, she thought she was hallucinating, a side effect of the sedative they'd given her. Then a second one; Gruber's head tilted toward the door as he reacted to the sound as well. Something was happening.

"Get up," he barked. "Now."

He moved fluidly across the room, his heavy boots crunching the bits of glass underneath. His aged countenance concealed his vim and vigor, and he was on her, yanking her off the bed with the coiled strength of a man half his age.

"We're moving," he said. "Try anything and I snap your little neck. We clear?"

She nodded.

"Say it."

"Clear."

Gruber dragged her back outside, where they walked into a maelstrom of panic. The far end of the chalet was ablaze. Thick black smoke curled into the late afternoon sky, catching the wind like a child's balloon and drifting east.

What the hell?

Small arms fire peppered the afternoon air.

A whistling sound, followed by another boom as the chalet took another hit.

Briefly, she entertained the fantasy that Jody had somehow spread the truth about Gruber to the others, that they were rising up against him, casting off the shackles of lies that he'd used to keep them here. But that fantasy died as quickly as it had been born. Wishful, naïve thinking. Jody had been right. These people knew the score. They wouldn't bite the hand that fed them, no matter how dirty the hand.

One of Gruber's men flagged him down.

"What the hell is going on?" he snapped.

"An attack."

One chance. While he was distracted. She cocked an elbow and drove it backward into Gruber's flank; he grunted and his grip loosened just enough for her to slip free. She bolted for the building housing the clinic, where Gruber had left the metal briefcase.

"Kill her!"

She took a zig-zag route as she sprinted across the clearing; the bullets chewed up ground behind and around her, but she remained a clean sheet for her would-be killer. The gunfire ramped up sharply as the battle below her intensified. It was chaos around her, and her thoughts went to the children who lived here. Where were they? Would they live? Would they die?

Once inside the clinic, she retraced the route back to her examination room, where the briefcase sat perched on the counter, right where Gruber had left it. Jody's body lay where it had fallen. Rachel grabbed the briefcase. She had it. It was in her hands. In the chaos outside, she could slip away. She had no dog in this fight. Back down to Priya. She would hide some of the vaccine. She could do it.

The sounds of battle had drawn closer to the front of the clinic, so she retreated deeper into the building, looking for another exit. Her heart was racing, racing, her mind locked on the children of this place. She paused again along a rear corridor, small Exit signs marking the way.

She was fooling herself if she thought there was a decision to make. The decision was made. It had been made long before she arrived here, probably long before she had even had Will. She couldn't leave the kids here to die. There was no plan beyond that, but simply leaving them here was not an option. Save as many kids as she could.

She peeked outside. Bodies littered the ground in the plaza; the fighting continued unabated as Gruber's troops had begun to shake off the surprise and mount a counter-offensive. The air was thick with the pungent tang of smoke, of gunpowder. Rachel scanned the woods surrounding the chalet, wondering if she could get out that way. This building backed up to the rear of the narrow valley in which the chalet compound was nestled. Beyond that, the mountain climbed sharply, disappearing into a thick scarf of fog.

If nothing else, it would be a good place to stash some of the vaccine. Not all of it. Some of it. An insurance policy. She edged her way around the building, toward the tree closest to the corner. She stepped around to the tree's backside and dropped to her knees, digging out a hole in the snow between a pair of crossed roots. She dug until her fingers were numb. Then she flipped open the valise, revealing four rows of twelve vials each. Hundreds of doses, nestled in red velvet compartments. A starter kit for humanity. But she couldn't keep all of them; she needed to give most of them to Priya. Four vials. That's how many she would keep. The vials were factory sealed and would probably survive a few hours buried in the snow here. One by one, the small bottles disappeared into the pockets she'd carved out. This method of vaccine storage probably wouldn't pass muster with the FDA, but hey what did they know anyway? When she was done, thirty-eight vials remained. She could only hope Priya would believe her.

She clapped her hands clear of the snow and climbed back to her feet. Now she had a clear line toward the woods. Keeping her eye on the melee, she sprinted across an open patch of ground. This brought her to the rear of the main chalet, where she hugged the wall, staying in shadows growing longer as the afternoon wore on. Shouts and screams filled the air as people battled the blaze still burning in the corner. It appeared to be under control, or at least, it wasn't spreading.

About fifty yards north of her, a door swung open, and a mass of humanity poured out. A heavy stream of folks, mostly children, a few adults, escaping the fire. Many were crying, some of them uncontrollably. Rachel counted three women and two men shepherding the kids.

"This way, kids," the younger woman snapped, guiding them toward the mountain. "Right now."

A huge explosion rocked the valley, the world knocked off its axis before snapping back into place. Rachel turned in time to see a bloom of fire erupt from the opposite end of the chalet, chunks of concrete and glass spraying the ground. The first column of smoke now had an eager twin.

They had to get away from the building.

She sprinted toward the group, gesturing toward the woods as she drew closer.

"That way!" she yelled. "Into the tree line."

The woman stopped and turned to face, sizing her up.

"You're the granddaughter."

"Rachel."

"We tried putting out the fire, but the smoke got too thick."

"What happened?"

"Not sure. We were in the classroom. Lot of dead back there. I don't know where all the parents are."

"Are these all the kids?"

"Most of them. I can't be sure."

The chatter of gunfire interrupted them.

"We need to move."

Like a swarm of fish, they flowed along the edge of the building *en* masse. At the end, in groups of three and four, they raced up the hill-side and into the woods, the snowpack thick around the base of the trees.

They came to a clearing, where Rachel stopped the group.

"What's your name?" Rachel asked one of the women at the front.

"Iris."

She was young, probably in her early twenties, rail thin, her skin as black as onyx, contrasting sharply against the white snow.

"Iris, can you get us a vehicle?"

The girl pressed the heels of her hands against her forehead, her jaw clenched.

"I'm not sure," she said. "We don't have that many."

Rachel felt panic rising in her. She still had to get back to Will with the briefcase, and she was God knew how many miles away from the rally point. These people were in the biggest trouble of their lives and Rachel did not know what to do for them. She looked down at the faces of the children, standing in the cold, some of them not even wearing jackets.

Farther down the mountain was nothing but trouble. Cold, cold death.

Up top, there were supplies, weapons, vehicles.

The vaccine she'd hidden away.

If she were careful, if she were stealthy, she could exploit the gaps created by this sudden skirmish to her advantage. She swept her gaze over her the faces in this crowd, looking longingly up at her, feeling very much their tutelary. She had to trust they would do what she said. That she could leave them for a little while and not worry herself sick over two dozen small children.

"Wait here. Don't go anywhere. Don't wander off. I'll be back soon."

"Where are you going?"

"Get us a ride."

38

Rachel followed her footsteps through the snow, the powder crunching under feet. Back at the tree line, she paused and spied on the battlefield. From here, removed from the core of battle, it looked like a video game, tiny characters moving back and forth on a pixelated backdrop. The gunfire continued, but it had a far-away quality to it.

She moved up a bit higher through the trees, which gave her a panoramic view of the huge compound. The main gate was smashed, the metal folded in over itself like some great being had punched it in the stomach. Two bodies lay prone in the snow, surrounded by reddish snow cones. Her gaze moved farther up toward the chalet. Parts of it were on fire, the blaze taking its time but moving steadily. Soon, the entire structure would be engulfed.

The firefight continued in earnest below. One group of attackers had taken cover behind the black SUVs, firing machine guns. Another paced their impromptu perimeter with rocket-propelled grenade launchers. Still more prowled the grounds.

A whistling sound. She looked up in time to see another explosion, this one in the heart of the chalet building. This strike must have hit something load-bearing; the roof collapsed like a failed soufflé. Smoke and debris poured from the gash in the building as a section of the outer wall crumbled.

Just another day in the good ole U.S. of A.

She turned her sights on the area around and behind the chalet, where she saw more similarly dressed attackers combing the grounds. Dozens of bodies littered the grounds. These people had no chance. They were reaping what Gruber had sown. No matter now. She needed to get to one of those trucks and get her raggedy group of refugees down the mountain. She needed to get back to Will.

She pushed a bit farther up the mountain, her feet sinking into the snow. A large tree at the edge of the trail gave her decent cover, let her review her options. A straight line to the trucks wouldn't work; she'd be too exposed, there were too many attackers. Her best bet would be to go back around the burning chalet, stay as close to the building as possible. The body of an attacker lay in the snow about midway from her current spot and the corner of the building; the muzzle of his gun was pinned under his body. A weapon.

It would take her a good thirty seconds to cover the distance, during which she would be completely exposed. At this point, there was nothing she could do but hope for the best. Maybe pray a little. She wondered where Gruber was, whether he was even still alive. A little part of her had expected a final showdown with him, because that's how these things were supposed to go, right? She, her dad and Sarah had had one with Miles Chadwick and it had been a doozy. But that's not the way life played out. Life was messy and twisty and not all the plot threads tied together. And so was death.

It scared her a little. Not that she might die. She'd long ago made her peace with that. But that she would die and Will would never know what happened to her. Her body would lie here in the snow, slowly decomposing until there was nothing left but the bones. Whenever she saw human remains, and man alive, had she seen a lot of them in the past thirteen years, it always made her sad to think that that had been it, that whatever that person had been had stopped forever.

She took a deep breath and bolted before she could change her mind. She flew across the snow like an arrow, her feet churning, kicking up clouds of in her wake. A few feet shy of the body, she slid low, coming to rest abreast of the dead woman's body. The woman was on her stomach, her left arm reaching out over her head, her legs forever origamied into a runner's pose. When Rachel saw the woman's face, she gasped.

One of Priya's.

Priya was here.

But how?

And where had Priya gotten all these people? When she'd left them, there were only about ten of them.

Did it matter? They were here.

Had she brought Will with them? Was he down there right now?

Sweetie, wait in the car, we gotta go kill everyone.

Quickly she searched the dead woman's go-bag. Binoculars. Ammo. A grenade. After taking a moment to ensure she was still alone, she pressed the field glasses to her face and zeroed in on the main caravan of vehicles, four in all. Two more vehicles than she'd left behind at the lab. Where had they come from? The windows were lightly tinted, which partially obscured her view of the interior. Maybe a silhouette of a small figure in the back seat, maybe a trick of light and shadow. She zoomed out her view, focused now on finding Priya.

A slower sweep this time, moving from one vehicle to the next. Nothing. The attack was concentrated on the main chalet now, as they seemed hell-bent on turning the building into rubble. Despite being outnumbered, the group was still riding the element of surprise like a wave. But the tide appeared to be turning; perhaps Priya's group had bitten off more than it could chew.

She stuffed the binoculars back in the bag and tucked the submachine gun under her arm before continuing down the hill to the cover of the building. As she did so, she considered her best option to save Will. It was simple when you thought about it. She had to help Gruber's people fight off this attack.

In the cover of the building, she paused to study her new weapon. It was an M4, not unlike the one her father had given her, passed on from Sarah Wells. Knowing she had the same weapon Sarah carried on her final mission made her feel better. Rachel had only spent a few minutes with the woman, right there at the end of her life, right before she had sacrificed herself for Adam and Rachel. Her father had loved her deeply, that much she could tell. And she had loved her father back. At a time when you saw what people were made of, what people were really made of, Sarah Wells had chosen to die for them.

A round of gunfire chipped away at the wall around the corner, breaking her out of her daydream, showering her face with bits of concrete dust. She steadied the gun and returned fire, hitting nothing, but tamping down the attack. The gunfire resumed, countered with another burst from her weapon. A flicker of movement to her left caught her eye. Two more shooters were approaching from the left, but she couldn't tell if they'd spotted her. She fired again, missed again.

As she moved, she fired off a couple more bursts, painfully aware of her limited ammunition. There were two more clips she had taken from the bag, but that was it. And her problems were multiplying; the two new players drew closer. In the fog and smoke, she couldn't make out if they were Gruber's or Priya's.

She fired.

The pair dropped to the ground and returned fire, pushing her back around the corner. A way out was what she needed, trouble closing in quickly around her. Both sides would be out to kill her. There was a door a few yards ahead of her, hanging slightly open. She flung the door open and ducked in.

Smoke curled along the baseboards, but it was still cool down here. She took a moment to soak her shirt in the snowmelt at the threshold before continuing down the hallway, trying to keep her bearings. Her destination would be the other side of the building; all she needed to do was keep a steady course.

The corridor here was wide, a bit smokier now. She pressed the wet shirt to her nose, the icy fabric a glorious relief from the smoke, and kept moving. Fifty yards deeper in, she came to an intersection, took in one branch, took in the other. She went left because it seemed too obvious to go right. Panic began stirring inside her; maybe not fully awake yet, but blinking the sleep out of its eyes.

The place was deserted, the fire pushing everyone outside. On her left was a control room, equipped with computer workstations, the wall adorned with maps of the surrounding area. She paused at the door, trying to think if there would be anything worth scavenging here. Her mind came up empty; she pressed onward.

Supply closets and storage rooms awaited her in this part of the chalet, but she passed those by as well. The smoke had thickened, but there were no signs of fire yet. Up next was a large kitchen, which did warrant a stop. She made a quick run, grabbing whatever food she could. Bread ends, a box of crackers, and a box of beef jerky went in her pack. She ate a piece of jerky as she made her way back out to the corridor and headed deeper into the chalet.

Smokier now, blacker and denser, rolling, twisting, almost alive, another entity in here with her now. She tied the wet shirt around the lower half her face. Memories of fire safety drills from elementary school came back to her, reminding her to stay low, so she got on her hands and knees.

This made for slow going, but it was worth it - the air was clearer down by the floor. Her skin grew warmer with every inch, sweat slicking her body in the rising warmth. She made another right turn, back toward the middle, hoping beyond hope the ceiling had not caved in.

A few more minutes of crawling brought her first taste of fire. The flames were inside the walls here, starting to push their way out like angry apparitions, licking at the ceiling, popping, cracking. In some places, the walls had disintegrated, replaced by ramparts of fire. There were a few bodies here. This was bad, this was very bad, but she kept on. It couldn't be much farther to the main entrance.

The coughing started in earnest here, her makeshift breathing mask starting to fail under these deteriorating conditions. The first spasm was bad, her lungs straining, her eyes watering. She took a quick break to clear the irritants from her lungs, but a quick one because the air quality was only going to get worse.

After a few more yards, the corridor opened up onto a large reception area. A pile of rubble from the partially collapsed ceiling lay in the middle of the foyer, bisecting it into two equal sections. Above her, the sounds of cracking and warping as the guts of the building began to feel the burn.

Ahead of her was the main entrance. And ahead of her was her biggest problem. A curtain of fire ringed the doorway like a beaded curtain in a college freshman's dorm room. It was lightly burning now, but there was no way to get through without exposing herself to the flames. Behind her, there was a huge crack and splintering as another part of the ceiling caved in. Immediately, the temperature jumped ten degrees, the heat searing her back now.

She draped the still damp shirt over her head and face and, without another thought in her head, bolted for the exit. She hit the door at full speed as the flames seemingly reached out to grab her, kissing and licking at her arms, the terrible heat eating away at her coat. Screaming, she fell through the doorway and into the outside, angling her body toward one of the large fake plants guarding the entryway.

As she crouched behind the heavy pot, which was almost as tall as she was, she winced in pain, careful not to cry out. She took in a couple deep breaths, the cold damp air soothing on her battered lungs. She used handfuls of snow to extinguish any hotspots on her clothing. While she caught her breath, she conducted a quick surveillance.

A long circular drive connected the main access road to the chalet's entrance plaza, putting the caravan a good fifty yards away from her position. Priya no longer appeared to be focused on the chalet itself, given the extensive damage they had already inflicted.

Running a mobile strike team in an operation this large, she would be concerned about supplies and ammunition.

Another sweep of the caravan with the binoculars. Once more, she focused on the second vehicle. Keeping her hands steady, she looked for any clue of the vehicle's occupants. Perhaps a shimmer of movement. Maybe not. She was going to have to get closer.

The front lines of the battle had shifted to her right, Priya's troops hunkered down behind the vehicles and a small outbuilding. Gruber's army had the higher ground, using the fountains and a ski rental shop as its base of operations. There was about a hundred yards of open ground between them, a no man's land laced with crossfire.

Staying low, she scurried across the driveway toward a support post and took cover again. Still a long way to go. The good news was that she didn't have to worry about being too quiet. The gunbattle was deafening, a veritable shooting gallery, the report of dozens of automatic weapons echoing in the valley, bouncing off the mountains.

Another scan of her surroundings, checking in front and behind her, side to side. The chalet was really burning now, rapidly approaching a point of no return if it hadn't hit it already. The next chunk of the route would be the most dangerous; she would be totally exposed to Gruber's people, who would shoot her first and not bother asking any questions if they saw her. But the angle of her planned route gave her a bit of hope. To see her, they would have to turn their heads more than ninety degrees, and in their current situation, that would be unlikely.

She switched out the magazine for a fresh one, slamming it home as she ran. Her burned arms throbbed with pain as she ran, making it uncomfortable to even hold the weapon. Still, she held it fast as she neared the rear vehicle.

She came in at the right rear bumper of the trail vehicle, staying low, creeping along the edge of the car. Priya's team had shifted a bit farther north, away from her. But they had concentrated the bulk of their force at the lead and second vehicles, which would make approaching it very risky.

Now she was inching along, certain each step would be her last. The cacophony of the gunfire grew steadily as she moved, a terrible wave of sound crashing down on her until she could barely think. Her target was the rear passenger door of that second vehicle. What she would do when she got there remained a bit of mystery.

Improvisation! A programmer's best friend!

Then she was there.

She crept along, passing the rear of the still-running vehicle, passing through a cloud of exhaust, a single whiff of which made her head a bit swimmy. She paused at the rear passenger door, contorting her body to peek through the window. Two of Priya's soldiers were about twenty feet away from her, the driver-side doors open to give them cover and shield. Again, her position left her exposed, virtually a sitting duck for Gruber's shooters.

Then an idea came to her.

Thinking back to her game with Will, she tapped rhythmically five times against the door and waited.

Tap, tap, tap-tap, tap

She steadied her gun, her finger snug on the trigger, ready to unload on any non-Will individuals who emerged from the car. Nothing.

She repeated the knock.

After an eternity, she got her answer.

Tap, TAP.

Will.

Gently, the latch released and the door swung open slowly. Her entire body froze, the moment stretching out forever, the laws of space and time no longer applicable here. Then a little hand wrapped around the doorframe, pulling its owner toward the opening. Then he was there, his face shaded by the edge of the door, the shadow of the front passenger seat.

They locked eyes, and she motioned for him to join her. He nodded his head, his eyes wide, his lips pulled tight. She smiled her biggest smile, trying to defuse his fears, hoping they covered the terror in her eyes. He extended a skinny leg and started to climb out before freezing in place.

Rachel sensed movement behind her, and her stomach flipped. The feel of cold metal at the base of her skull. She glanced behind her.

Leon Gruber.

39

"Get up," said Gruber. "I see that machine gun, so do it slow."

Rachel considered her options. If she made a scene, she might draw the attention of Priya's people. She stood up slowly, keeping the gun close to her body.

"You have a son."

"I do."

"Get inside the car," he said. "Leave the gun on the seat. Son, stay where you are."

She climbed over Will, giving his arm a quick squeeze as she went by, and crouched in the second row of the car, by the passenger window. The Suburban was spacious and gave her room to draw back from Gruber, keep some distance from the man.

"The gun now."

She set it down on the first row.

A flicker of movement drew her attention.

"No one move," Priya said, stepping up behind Gruber and pressing a gun to his head. Gruber froze, his face tightening into a grimace.

Rachel eyed her carefully as she struggled to take control of Gruber. Quickly, she reclaimed her gun from the seat and trained it on them. Priya kept Gruber between Rachel and herself as a human shield. She pushed them inside the vehicle and pulled the door closed behind them.

"Mommy!"

"Quiet," Priya snapped.

Then Gruber drove an elbow into Priya's midsection and dove to the floorboard, bringing his gun up toward Priya. Rachel swung her gun back toward Gruber, painfully aware of Will's presence in a potential crossfire between these three. Priya recovered quickly and retrained her gun at Rachel's head.

"Don't you see?" he asked, cutting his eyes toward Rachel but keeping his gun trained on Priya.

"See what?"

"It's almost poetic, this predicament."

She ran the permutations through her analytical head. A stalemate. Any move right now would almost certainly prove fatal. But there had to be a way out. It was a proof to be solved, a math problem, game theory. The best solution was for everyone to walk away. If these two simply thought it through, they would come to the same conclusion.

"What do you want?" Gruber asked, directing his query to Priya. "Why did you come here?"

"To burn it all down," she said.

Rachel turned slightly toward Priya, keeping her eyes squarely on Gruber.

"What?"

"Humanity had its chance, my dear," Priya said coldly. "I'm here to finish the job."

"But you said-"

"You were right not to trust me."

"You could've killed us."

"And I'm glad I didn't. Because then I would never have found out about this place, and my work will have been for nothing. This is the holy grail. Humanity's last gasp. Once we finish here, there will be no more second chances, no more Hail Marys. This is where it ends. I'm in no hurry to die, but it matters little whether I survive this or not."

The briefcase.

That was the key.

That it live on beyond today.

Gruber may have had his moment in the lab with her, playing God, torturing her with his power over her, over life itself. Priya, destroying it all. Two sides of the same coin of evil here in the car with her.

"Wow," she said, the word slipping free like a puff of wind.

It was growing steadily warmer in the car, which was becoming pungent with the gamey smell of fear and stress. Faces were flushed, breathing heavy. There was no way out of here, she saw that now. They would all die. Game theory assumed the players would act rationally.

But, Rachel reminded herself, Priya wasn't acting in her best interest; she was playing toward an irrational end game. She was the wild card. She was the threat. Whatever had brought her to this point was irrelevant. Whether Rachel liked it or not, Gruber's people were the solution, always had been. She had to dispatch Priya first.

But the thing was, the thing she couldn't get out of her head - maybe she wasn't acting in her own best interest either. She was acting in Will's best interest. And Will's life currently sat in the hands of a very irrational actor.

Her shoulder began to ache, and her singed arms stung; the others were fatiguing as well, hitching their shoulders, their arms trembling. They were reaching the endgame here. And if she didn't come up with a solution quickly, she would be left to the mercy of fate.

And then it hit her.

"I want to show you something."

Keeping her gun up and her eyes on her adversaries, she reached down into her pack and rooted around until she found it. Then she held up the grenade for everyone to see.

"Anyone moves, we all die."

"What the hell are you doing?" Priya asked softly.

"We're all gonna die here today," Rachel said. "I see that now. This way, I get to pick when we go out. And I want you to know that you didn't control shit. You have until the count of three to let my son go. Or we all die."

"You're bluffing," Priya said.

"Three."

"You didn't have time to remove the pin."

"Two."

"You're both fucking crazy," said Gruber.

"One."

Rachel lobbed the grenade like a softball, taking the moment to kick up the gun and slide her finger into the trigger well. Priya's grip on her son softened, her eyes tracking the grenade as it arced end over end and began its downward trajectory. It clattered harmlessly to the ground, and a moment later, it became clear the grenade was still secured, the pin still in place.

It would have to be enough.

"Will, get down!"

The boy pushed free of his captor just as Rachel kicked up the gun, sliding her finger in the trigger well as he dove to the floorboards. Her timing would have to be perfect. Mindful of her son's presence near Priya, she turned and fired a burst into Gruber's chest. She swung back to take out Priya, but it was too late. She had pulled Will close to her, the gun pressed squarely against his head.

"No!"

Behind her, Gruber grunted, the sound of his gurgling huge, the coppery smell of his blood and gunpowder hanging in the air. Her arms ached, her body ached, her head hurt.

There was only one card left to play. And she was going to play it. At the end of the day, she was Will's mother, and she was going to pick Will's life over the life of all the babies yet to be born. How could she not? She was his mother. History could judge her, fate could judge her, God Himself could judge her. She would pick her son every day of the week and twice on Sunday. If God or fate or karma had wanted a different outcome, these would not have been the stakes.

"If I give you what you want, will you let us go?"

"What is it you think I want?"

"I hid a suitcase full of vaccine in the woods," she said, her heart breaking as she gave in. "Hundreds of doses. It lets women give birth to Medusa-immune babies. If you get that, it doesn't matter what happened here."

Rachel watched her work it out in her head.

A fighter came up to Priya. He was injured, bleeding from a wound in his shoulder.

"We can't hold them off much longer," he said, struggling for breath in the thinner altitude.

"Look," Rachel said, "if I'm lying you can kill us both."

Priya looked to her soldier, glanced out the windshield toward the battlefield, where it was becoming clear her gambit had failed. Much of the compound was destroyed, but it had come at a terrible price. And now there was nothing to stop her from cutting her losses, simply killing her and Will right here in this Suburban.

"Let's go."

They alighted from the car into a chilling quiet that had descended on the chalet. The battle appeared to be over. This was it. In a few minutes, Rachel would surrender virtually all of humanity's last hopes to this woman.

"Give me two guys. We're taking a little stroll into the woods."

"Yes, ma'am."

They waited a few minutes until her two charges joined them. After explaining what they were doing, she shoved Rachel in the back and they started anew, following the cut of the driveway, around the ruined chalet, and then to the tree line. The mishmash of footprints pointed the way to the edge of the property and into the woods.

"Keep moving," she said. "If you don't do exactly what I say, I'll splatter his brains all over the snow. How do you think that would look?"

She ignored her, watching her footing, studying the terrain, looking for the tiniest opening that would let her save Will. They dropped into the woods, their pace slowing a bit now. Ahead, she could hear her flock, chattering nervously. The barren trees were thick here. Heavy roots crisscrossed the ground, more akin to a relief map. Clouds of fine snow wafted about in the steady breeze that had picked up.

"There are others," Rachel said. "They escaped with me."

"Make it clear to them. If I sense any trouble, the boy dies."

She paused and turned to face her son. He looked scared but alert.

"You OK, buddy?"

He nodded.

"It's almost over. Can you hold it together for Miss Priya a little bit longer?"

"Yeah," he said it, almost sighing the word.

They covered the last fifty yards in silence, concentrating on negotiating what little trail there was here. Here the trees were so numerous there was barely enough room to slip through them. It made for slow going and all but eliminated any possibility of escape. After about a hundred yards, the trees began to thin out and the trail opened up on a large clearing, where the group was waiting for Rachel. She could hear them before they saw them.

"Stop," Priya said

Rachel and Will froze.

"What's that sound?"

The children. Priya could hear the children. She didn't know about them yet.

"I said there were others."

Priya was visibly shaken now, her eyes wide, her hand tightly gripping the barrel of her weapon. They continued through the trees, Rachel's mind on overdrive now. Surprise. The element of surprise was on her side now. She knew what lay ahead. She'd seen them. After a few minutes, the trees thinned, giving her her first glance at the group, now seated in a circle, talking quietly. There was a narrow trailhead here, allowing them to walk single file.

"Buddy," she whispered, "slide ahead of me."

Will did as he was told.

Behind her, the crunch of the trio's footsteps in the snow grew louder as they hurried to catch up. As she neared the clearing, she slowed down, narrowing the gap between herself and Priya. She hazarded a glance back toward the woman; her head swiveled from side to side, anxious, on alert. Her gun was up, aimed squarely at Rachel's back. Her escorts had lagged back a bit.

Twenty yards now from the clearing.

A giggle.

"What is that?" Priya asked, her voice suddenly cloaked with fear. It was a strange sound, Rachel now knew, when you hadn't heard it in a decade.

The sound of a child laughing.

Ten yards.

"What the hell is going on?" she asked.

Rachel played it off.

"We're almost there," she said.

Five yards.

Rachel cleared the trees and stepped to the side of the clearing, just enough to give Priya room to come through.

A few more seconds.

Priya stepped into the clearing and saw the children.

"Dear God," Priya said.

Rachel glanced back at the woman, who stared at the children with her jaw hanging open. There it was. Their future, right here. The future Priya was desperate to stop was already underway.

Now, Rachel. Now.

She lowered her shoulder and drove into Priya's midsection like a linebacker. The shock of seeing the children must have frozen her because she put up virtually no defense at all. Her gun flew out of her hand, banging against a tree at the edge of the clearing and dropping down into the snow.

She reared back and delivered a jab to Priya's chin. The woman turned slightly at the last second, reducing the punch to a glancing blow. But she was still recovering from the hit Rachel had laid on her, gasping, clawing for air. Rachel lunged for the gun, reminding herself this was now a one-on-three battle. She flipped over to her seat and slithered up against the tree as Priya rolled over onto all fours.

Adrenaline flowed through Rachel's veins as she struggled to get a bead on her target, even as the two escorts closed in on the scene. Then they were in the clearing as well, and they too were stunned into still life by what they saw.

Rachel swung the gun toward them and fired twice. At such close range, they were easy pickings. Each took a round in the torso, dropping them to the snow. That threat was now neutralized. But it had given Priya time to recover; she leaped onto Rachel and grasped wildly for the gun, which proved tough to hang onto with cold fingers.

They were face-to-face now, inches apart, Priya's forearm sliding up Rachel's neck toward her throat. Rachel pushed the gun up, near her clavicle, pointed toward Priya's face. But she couldn't fire, she couldn't get her finger inside the trigger well. And Priya's forearm was now pressing against her throat, cutting off her full intake of oxygen. Priya had the upper hand here, the leverage; in a few more seconds, she wouldn't be able to breathe at all.

"Mommy!"

Will's voice was everywhere in the clearing.

Fight, goddammit, fight!

They locked eyes, Priya's round brown eyes, filled with hate, filled with rage, filled with sadness, staring at her. The sadness of the world lost, the sadness of the babies lost, of the babies that had never been born.

From the corner of her eye, she detected movement. A blur of movement coming toward them. Will.

"Mommy!"

No. No, sweet Will, stay away.

He jumped on Priya's back and tried to pull her free, but the woman was too strong; she had locked herself to Rachel's body. She reared back and grabbed Will by the collar, swinging him clear and back into the snow. But her weight shifted, just a hair, just a smidgen, giving Rachel clearance to get her finger around the trigger.

She fired.

The boom echoed through the clearing and up the mountain, the vibrations rattling free the beards of snow clinging to trees, showering the area around them with fluffs of white.

Priya's body went slack, her forearm easing up on Rachel's throat as the bullet tore through her, but her eyes remained open. They went blank, totally blank, as though someone had pulled the plug on her. Rachel shoved Priya's body off her and pushed up onto her hands and knees. She vomited in the snow.

"Mommy!" Will called out, sliding next to her, throwing his little arm around her back.

"You OK, Spoon?" she croaked.

"Yeah," he said. "Is it over?"

She wept.

"It's over."

She washed her mouth out with a handful of snow; then she pulled her son close, hugging him tightly, breathing him in. He had saved her. He had turned the tide. Around them, the crowd stood mute, watching the bizarre scene unfold before them. She kissed him on the cheek and then stood up.

"Love you, bud."

He nodded.

Nearly twenty people in her charge now, nearly all of them children. There would be many more back at the ruins of Olympus, wondering what to do now.

They had little food. Their shelter was in ruins.

But they were free. These women were no longer bound by the stricture of their oppressive Lottery. These children would have a future, that much she would see to. They were in her charge now. And most important of all, they had the vaccine.

She passed out the little bit of food remaining in her pack, told the group to share it. They ate in silence. Their faces were long and dirty and sad. Will sat quietly in a group of kids for the first time in his life, his eyes bouncing from child to child. He had never spent time with other kids. Ever. The enormity of that burden made her tear up as she sat there. It hadn't been fair. Not fair at all.

A little girl, maybe seven, approached her. She wore a heavy jacket and ski pants. Her face was small and round and Rachel wanted to scoop her up and read her stories and drink hot chocolate with her.

"I want my mommy."

"We'll go back and look for her."

"Is she dead?"

"I don't know. We'll try to find out."

"OK."

She tottered away, chewing on her jerky.

They would find out, Rachel decided. They would wait. They would scavenge for supplies. They would find the hybrid seeds Gruber had mentioned. They would do the best they could, and they would press on. If Gruber's wild claim was to be believed, they all had many decades ahead of them.

They would start again.

She thought about her father.

I hope you can rest now, Dad. I forgive you.

Whatever debt he had built up to her, he had paid off in spades. He had done the best he could with the equipment he had. She liked to think she had done the best she could with Will. No beating around the bush. It was a terrible world out there. If the last few months had taught her anything, it was that every day, every minute could be their last. Maybe there would be no happy ending for all of them, for any of them. Maybe they would have to be satisfied with a happy present. A happy moment. Here and there. Putting those moments together like a puzzle until it resembled a picture worth looking at.

She saw Will smile at something one of the kids said.

Then he laughed.

~

~

~

ABOUT THE AUTHOR

David lives in Richmond, Virginia, where he works as a novelist and attorney. His first novel, *The Jackpot*, was a No. 1 Legal Thriller on Amazon in 2012 and was later published in Bulgaria. His second book, *The Immune*, was published in 2015 in serial format and made it to the top of Amazon's bestseller list for post-apocalyptic novels.

He is the writer and creator of a series of popular animated films, including *So You Want to Go to Law School*, which were featured in the *Washington Post*, the *Wall Street Journal*, and on CNN. They have been viewed nearly 3 million times and are always available on YouTube.

Email him at dwkazzie@gmail.com